Primrose
and the
DREADFUL
DUKE

GARLAND COUSINS #1

EMILY
LARKIN

www.emilylarkin.com

Publisher's Note: This is a work of fiction.
Names, characters, places, and incidents are a product of the author's imagination. Locales and public names are sometimes used for atmospheric purposes. Any resemblance to actual people, living or dead, or to businesses, companies, events, institutions, or locales is completely coincidental.

Primrose and the Dreadful Duke / Emily Larkin. – 1st ed.

ISBN 978-0-9951396-0-2

Cover Design: JD Smith Design

A Baleful Godmother

Novel

It is a truth universally acknowledged,
that Faerie godmothers do not exist.

CHAPTER 1

Primrose Garland liked books. All kinds of books, but especially books written many centuries ago, and most especially books that were the *real* thoughts of *real* people. Pliny's letters, for example. Catullus's love-sick poems. Marcus Aurelius's philosophical musings.

That morning, she was reading Aurelius again, experiencing the same delight and wonder that she always felt. Aurelius had been an emperor in Rome, she was a spinster in London—and yet here she was, reading his private notes to himself, his musings on life. It was extremely intimate, this insight into a man's thoughts. Sometimes it felt as if he were talking directly to her, that if she turned her head, there he would be: Marcus Aurelius, Emperor of Rome, seated at the writing table, and he'd look up from his notes and say to her, "Dwell on the beauty of life. Watch the stars, and see yourself running with them."

That was one of her favorite quotes. It had made her cry the first time she'd read it. Two sentences that a stranger had written more than sixteen hundred years ago, and they'd made her cry.

Which was why she loved Aurelius so much.

So when she looked for the second volume of his *Meditations* and realized that she'd left it in Staffordshire, Primrose was a little annoyed. But only a little, because it wouldn't take more than a few minutes to fetch it.

She went upstairs to her bedchamber and locked the door, so that no servant could walk in and discover the Garland family secret, then she clasped her hands together, took a deep breath, and pictured the library at Manifold Park, and in particular, the shadows behind the black-and-gold lacquered screen in the corner.

Primrose wished herself there.

In the next instant, she was.

There was a familiar moment of vertigo—the library seemed to spin around her—and then everything steadied into place.

Primrose held her breath and listened intently. The library *sounded* empty.

She peeked around the edge of the black-and-gold

screen. The library *was* empty. As it should be when the Garland family was in London.

Primrose crossed quickly to where Aurelius was shelved, selected the volume she wanted, and wished herself back in her bedchamber in London.

In the blink of an eye, she was.

The vertigo hit again, as if she'd spun around a thousand times. Primrose waited until it passed, then glanced at herself in the mirror. She always expected her hair to be disheveled and her clothes to be a windswept tangle after translocating, but they never were. She looked as neat and well-groomed as one would expect of a duke's daughter.

Primrose unlocked her bedroom door and went down to the morning room. A housemaid was clearing away the tea tray. "Would you like another pot of tea, Lady Primrose?"

"Yes, thank you, Elsie."

Primrose crossed to the sofa, thinking how shocked the maid would be if she told her she'd just traveled to Staffordshire and back.

But of course she didn't tell the housemaid. She couldn't tell a soul. It was far too great a secret. And even if she *did* tell Elsie, the girl wouldn't believe it.

No one would.

Primrose curled up on the sofa and returned to her reading.

CHAPTER 2

An evening in early June, London

Oliver had enjoyed being a soldier. Not the killing, of course, but the camaraderie, the sense of purpose, the challenges, the fun. When the letter had arrived informing him that he'd inherited his Uncle Reginald's dukedom his first emotion had been astonishment. His second had been chagrin. He'd planned to be a colonel by the time he was forty; instead, at twenty-nine, he was a duke. Not that being a duke wasn't without its challenges or its sense of purpose. Or its fun, for that matter.

Oliver glanced around the ballroom. His gaze passed over shimmering silks and spangled gauzes, glossy hair and rosy lips—and the bright eyes of young ladies searching for husbands.

He'd enjoyed balls when he'd been a cavalry

captain in India. They'd been rare events, something to look forward to—the dancing, the flirting, the snatched kisses in shadowy corners.

Balls as a duke in London were quite a different matter. In fact, when a duke had so many caps set at him as Oliver did, he had to exercise caution else he'd get caught in the parson's mousetrap. A prudent duke didn't snatch kisses from respectable young ladies—not unless he wanted to end up with a wife. A prudent duke didn't even flirt while he danced.

A prudent duke could get mightily bored if he wasn't careful . . . but Oliver had a strategy for that.

He made his way across the ballroom, replying to the murmured greetings of *Your Grace,* and *Duke,* and *Westfell,* before coming to a halt in front of Miss Elliott and her mother.

"Lady Elliott." He inclined his head in a coolly ducal nod. "Miss Elliott."

"Your Grace." Miss Elliott curtsied and glanced up at him through her eyelashes. She was only nineteen, but she had mastered the trick of tucking her shoulders back slightly to bring her bosom into more prominence. Lush breasts tilted up at him, snug in a nest of ribbons and silk.

Miss Elliott—like most unmarried young ladies—was on the hunt for a husband, but even if Oliver had to be prudent, it didn't mean that he couldn't enjoy her efforts to snare him. He awarded Miss Elliott one point for the upwards glance and two points for that enticingly displayed bosom, then he gave her his most charming smile and led her onto the dance floor.

Miss Elliott started the cotillion with three points. She increased this to six points rather rapidly—by sending him three more of those glances—and then she exercised a masterful ploy: she bit her lower lip briefly and moistened it, a move that looked bashful but most definitely wasn't, not with the glimpse of her tongue she'd given him.

That was five points, right there, and they'd been dancing less than a minute.

Oliver gave her his most charming smile again. "Do you like horses, Miss Elliott? I must tell you about my mount, Verdun."

He described Verdun in detail, from his ears to his hooves, while Miss Elliott tilted her enticing bosom at him. "I'm certain you're a magnificent horseman, Your Grace," she said, when he'd finished describing the precise length and color of Verdun's tail.

The compliment sounded genuine. Oliver added another two points to her tally and launched into a description of the horses of every officer he'd ever served with in India. He was rather enjoying himself. This was a game: Miss Elliott's bosom versus his ridiculous monologue.

The cotillion lasted twenty minutes, and Miss Elliott made very good use of them. When Oliver returned her to her mother, she had accrued one hundred and forty-three points.

His next partner was Lady Primrose Garland, the sister of his oldest friend, Rhodes Garland—and the only unmarried young lady in the room whom he knew *didn't* want to marry him.

"Lady Prim," he said, bowing over her hand with a flourish. "You're a jewel that outshines all others."

Primrose was too well-bred to roll her eyes in public, but her eyelids twitched ever so slightly, which told him she wanted to. "Still afflicted by hyperbole, I see."

"You use such long words, Prim," he said admiringly.

"And you use such foolish ones."

Oliver tutted at her. "That's not very polite, Prim."

Primrose ignored this comment. She placed her hand on his sleeve. Together they walked onto the dance floor and took their places.

"Did I ever tell you about my uniform, Prim? The coat was dark blue, and the facing—"

"I don't wish to hear about your uniform."

"Manners, Prim. Manners."

Primrose came very close to smiling. She caught herself just in time. "Shall we discuss books while we dance? Have you read Wolf's *Prolegomena ad Homerum*?"

"Of course I haven't," Oliver said. "Dash it, Prim, I'm not an intellectual."

The musicians played the opening bars. Primrose curtsied, Oliver bowed. "I really *must* tell you about my uniform. The coat was dark blue—"

Primrose ignored him. "Wolf proposes that *The Iliad*—"

"With a red sash at the waist—"

"And *The Odyssey* were in fact—"

"And silver lace at the cuffs—"

"The work of more than one poet."

"And a crested Tarleton helmet," Oliver finished triumphantly.

They eyed each other as they went through the steps of the dance. Oliver could tell from the glint in her eyes and the way her lips were tucked in at the corners that Primrose was trying not to laugh. He was trying not to laugh, too.

"You're a fiddle-faddle fellow," Primrose told him severely.

"Alliteration," Oliver said. "Well done, Prim."

Primrose's lips tucked in even more tightly at the corners. If they'd been anywhere but a ballroom he was certain she'd have stamped her foot, something she'd done frequently when they were children.

"Heaven only knows why I agreed to dance with you," she told him tartly.

"Because it increases your consequence to be seen with me. I *am* a duke, you know." He puffed out his chest and danced the next few steps with a strut.

"Stop that," she hissed under her breath.

"Stop what?" Oliver said innocently, still strutting his steps.

"Honestly, Daisy, you're impossible."

Oliver stopped strutting. "No one's called me that in years."

"Impossible? I find that hard to believe." Her voice was dry.

"Daisy." It had been Primrose's childhood nickname for him, in retaliation for him calling her Lady Prim-and-Proper.

Oliver had been back in England for nearly a month now, and that month had been filled with moments of recognition, some tiny flickers—his brain acknowledging something as familiar and

9

then moving on—others strong visceral reactions. He experienced one of those latter moments now. It took him by the throat and wouldn't let him speak for several seconds.

Because Primrose had called him Daisy.

Oliver cleared his throat. "Tell me about that book, Prim. What's it called? Prolapse ad nauseam?"

"*Prolegomena ad Homerum.*"

Oliver pulled a face. "Sounds very dull. Me, I much prefer a good novel. Especially if there's a ghost in it, or a headless horseman."

And they were off again, arguing amiably about books, the moment of emotion safely in the past. Primrose knew a lot about books. In fact, Oliver suspected that she preferred books to people—which would be why she was still unmarried at twenty-seven. Primrose was a duke's daughter *and* she was pretty—that ash-blonde hair, those cool blue eyes. If she wanted to be married, she would be.

Therefore, he deduced that she didn't want to marry. Which made her unique in a ballroom filled with young ladies on the hunt for husbands.

"Do you know Miss Ogilvie?" he asked her.

"Vaguely. She seems quite nice."

"Nice? She's a dashed harpy, is what she is."

"You can't call her a harpy," Primrose objected. "A siren, perhaps, but harpies have claws and—"

"Miss Ogilvie is a harpy," Oliver said firmly. "Beneath the evening gloves, she has claws."

"Now *that* is hyperbole."

"It's metaphor," Oliver corrected her. "She's a *metaphorical* harpy. She wants to feast on my carcass." And *carcass* was a metaphor, too; it wasn't his body Miss Ogilvie wanted to devour, it was the title and fortune that he'd so unexpectedly inherited.

Primrose uttered a small sound that his ears barely caught.

"Did you just snort, Prim? That's not very ladylike."

"You're the most idiotic person I've ever met," she told him severely.

Oliver opened his eyes wide. "Ever? In your whole life?"

"Ever."

"High praise, Prim. Very high praise. You quite unman me."

This time Primrose *did* roll her eyes, even though they were in the middle of a ballroom.

Oliver grinned at her. He could tell she was struggling not to grin back.

At that moment, the dance ended. Oliver escorted Primrose from the dance floor. He could see Miss Ogilvie out of the corner of his eye: the glossy ringlets, the ripe bosom, the dainty evening gloves that hid her metaphorical claws.

"Marry me, Prim," he joked. "Save me from Miss Ogilvie."

"I'd sooner marry a crossing-sweeper. You're even more of a fribble than that cousin of yours."

"I'm wounded." Oliver placed his hand over his heart, tottered a few steps, and sank down on a gilded chair. "*Mortally* wounded. I may expire here, right in front of your eyes."

"You can't expire now," Primrose told him. "Miss Ogilvie is waiting to dance with you."

Oliver pulled a face. "Maybe I *should* become a crossing-sweeper."

"Addle-pate," Primrose said.

Oliver laughed, and climbed to his feet. "Thank you for the dance, Prim."

Primrose demurely curtsied, as all his other partners tonight had done. "It was a pleasure, Your Grace."

"Don't, Prim," Oliver said, and this time his tone was serious.

Primrose's glance at him was swift and shrewd. She didn't ask what he meant; instead, she said, "Away with you, Daisy," and made a brisk shooing gesture. "Miss Ogilvie fancies herself as a duchess."

"Not *my* duchess," Oliver muttered. "Not if I have any say in the matter."

Miss Ogilvie had alabaster skin, a delightfully full lower lip, and a bosom to rival Miss Elliott's. Like Miss Elliott, she had mastered the trick of displaying her bosom to full advantage.

Oliver didn't like her at all.

His antipathy had been instantaneous and instinctive. Miss Ogilvie was pretty, charming, vivacious—and ruthless. Oliver wasn't certain exactly how he knew she was ruthless. Something in her eyes? In that light, musical laugh? All he knew was that he had seen people like Miss Ogilvie before, not in ballrooms but in the aftermath of battle, looting the wounded of their belongings.

But the fact that he disliked Miss Ogilvie didn't mean that he disliked dancing with her. On the contrary, dancing with her was often the highlight of his evening. He had a special voice for her—a monotonous drone—and a special topic—Trésaguet's method for paving roads—and he always managed to stand on her toes and fall out of time with the music.

Primrose Garland would have given him the sharp edge of her tongue if he'd tried such tactics with her; Miss Ogilvie gave him smiling glances and flaunted her breasts and at the end of the dance she said in a soft, sweet, admiring voice, "You're so knowledgeable, Westfell."

Oliver could imagine the expression on Primrose's face if she'd been close enough to hear those words. He puffed out his chest and said, "I fancy I know a lot about a lot of things." Then he escorted Miss Ogilvie back to her aunt.

Her score: one hundred and sixty-one.

The ballroom had become rather warm. Faces were shiny and shirt-points wilting. Oliver found himself craving fresh, cool air. He was bespoken for two more dances, but after that he'd slip away, and that was something he'd never done as a soldier: leave a ball early. Lord, he'd danced until dawn more than once—

"Oliver," a cheerful voice said at his elbow.

Oliver turned. "Uncle Algy." He shook his uncle's hand heartily. "How are you, sir?"

"Very well, my boy. Very well indeed."

Lord Algernon Dasenby was one of Oliver's two surviving relatives. He was a burly fellow with graying hair and merry eyes and a booming laugh. It was Uncle Algy who'd dealt with the paperwork while Oliver had undertaken the six-month-long journey back from India, Uncle Algy who'd gathered the documents required by the House of Lords—proof of his parents' marriage, proof of his birth—so that by the time Oliver had finally set foot on English soil there were only a few legal hoops to jump through and it was done: he was the ninth Duke of Westfell.

Ironic, that. He trod in the footsteps of the seventh and eighth dukes every day, drank from the same glasses they'd drunk from, slept in the same great four-poster bed, even pissed in the same chamber pot, and yet he'd never met them when they'd been alive.

Not that he repined.

Oliver didn't need to have met his grandfather to know he'd been a coldhearted bastard—how else could you describe a man who cut off a son for daring to refuse an arranged marriage? And Uncle Reginald had been a coldhearted bastard, too, for obeying the parental injunction to sever ties with his brother.

Uncle Algy hadn't obeyed the parental injunction. Oliver had childhood memories of his uncle's brief, secretive visits—the rumble of voices in the parlor, the laughter, the pipe smoke, his uncle winking at him when he arrived and slipping him a guinea when he left.

Strange to think that Uncle Algy was now Oliver's heir.

He would have stayed talking to his uncle if he

could, but the musicians were picking up their instruments again and the next aspiring duchess awaited him. Regretfully, Oliver bade his uncle goodbye. A dozen more steps and he hove to in front of Miss Buxton.

Miss Buxton's main ploy for hunting dukes was a simper. Oliver didn't like simpers. Every time Miss Buxton simpered, he deducted one point. Her score rapidly sank below zero. By the time the musicians played the final notes, she had reached minus eighty. Tonight's lowest score.

One more dance to go and he could call it a night.

It was while he was heading towards his final partner that Oliver encountered the second of his two surviving relatives: Uncle Algernon's son.

"Ninian." Oliver looked his cousin up and down. "You look very, uh . . ." *Pretty* was the word that sprang to mind.

Their Uncle Reginald, the eighth duke, had been in his grave for more than a year. The time for mourning was long past, but Ninian was lingering in shades of lilac and lavender.

Lilac and lavender were colors Oliver would never willingly wear, but there was no denying that they suited Ninian's golden hair and blue eyes. He looked beautiful. But Ninian always looked beautiful.

"Do you like it?" Ninian said. His gaze was bright

and hopeful, and he might be a fribble and a fop, but he was also Uncle Algy's son and Oliver's only cousin.

Oliver strove for a compliment. "Very pretty coat. What color do you call it?"

"Periwinkle," Ninian said, beaming.

"Suits you," Oliver said, and then, "Excuse me, Ninian; I'm claimed for the next dance."

His last partner for the night achieved a respectable one hundred and twenty-eight points, not because of her bosom, but because she had a very pretty pair of dimples. Oliver liked dimples, and in another time and place he might have tried to coax a kiss from Miss Norton. But he was no longer a devil-may-care dragoon captain, he was a prudent duke, and so he escorted Miss Norton back to her mother, unkissed.

Oliver was aware of young ladies hopefully eyeing him. He made for the door, not pausing long enough for anyone to catch him.

A flight of stairs beckoned him downwards. He breathed a sigh of relief and descended to the vestibule. A footman fetched his hat for him. Oliver stepped outside. It wasn't completely dark under the portico—flambeaux burned, keeping the night at bay—but it was blessedly cool and quiet after the ballroom.

A dozen marble steps led down to the street, gleaming in the light from the flaming torches. Oliver stood for a moment on the topmost step. Funny that one could feel lonely in a city as large as London, but he did feel lonely at this moment, had in fact felt lonely rather often in the month he'd been back on English soil.

If this were India, he'd have Ned Lovelock at one shoulder and Tubby Hedgecomb at the other, and they'd be laughing together, enjoying being young and alive.

But this wasn't India.

Oliver put his hat on, tilted the brim until it sat just right, and promised himself that he'd call on Rhodes Garland tomorrow. A few hours in Rhodes's company would make him feel less alone.

His ears caught the faint scuff of a shoe behind him—and then someone shoved him violently between the shoulder blades.

Chapter 3

*O*liver tumbled down the sharp, pale marble steps to the street. If he hadn't had so much practice falling off horses, he might have broken his neck. But he'd spent eight years in the cavalry and he'd come off horses more times than he could remember, so he managed not to break any bones. It did hurt, though.

He lay sprawled on the paving stones for a moment, his own cry of alarm ringing in his ears, while the night spun jerkily around him—shadows and torchlight—and then he caught his breath and cautiously pushed up to sitting. *Ouch.*

"Sir?" someone called out. "Are you all right, sir?"

Footsteps pattered down the marble stairs. Someone crouched alongside him. One of the footmen from the vestibule, his expression turning to horrified dismay when he recognized Oliver. "Your Grace! Are you all right?"

19

"Perfectly." He climbed to his feet, while the footman fluttered solicitously around him.

Oliver rolled his shoulders and rubbed the back of his neck. He looked up the steps to the portico. The flambeaux flared and the shadows writhed, but the portico appeared to be empty.

Oliver rubbed the back of his neck again. He distinctly remembered someone shoving him. "Did you see anyone under the portico with me?"

The footman picked up his hat and brushed it off. "With you, sir? No."

Had he imagined it? No. He could still feel the pressure of a hand between his shoulder blades. "Did anyone leave the ball immediately after I did?"

"No, sir." The footman handed Oliver his hat.

"Did anyone leave just before me?"

The man's brow wrinkled. "I don't think so, Your Grace. But people have been coming and going all night."

Yes, of course they had.

Oliver turned the hat over in his hands. Who on earth had pushed him down those stairs? A stranger? Someone he knew? And *why*?

Oliver glanced at the footman. The footman gazed anxiously back at him. Was he anxious because he'd pushed Oliver and didn't wish to be found out? Or anxious because a duke had almost died on his employer's doorstep?

"Would you like to come inside, sir? Perhaps sit down?"

"No," Oliver said.

"Shall I fetch a carriage for you, Your Grace?"

"No," Oliver said again, and then: "How did you know I'd fallen? Did you see it?"

"No, sir. I heard a cry."

He'd called out as he fell, he remembered that. And he remembered hearing the scuff of a shoe behind him. And he remembered a hand between his shoulder blades. It wasn't his imagination. Someone *had* pushed him. But most likely not the footman.

Oliver put on his hat. "Thank you," he told the man. "Good night."

"Are you certain I can't fetch you a carriage?" the footman said.

"I'm certain." Oliver fished in his pocket and pulled out a guinea. "Thank you for your help."

He walked down the street, not striding as briskly as he usually did; he was going to be sporting some bruises tomorrow. But he was used to bruises. Bruises didn't bother him, nor did broken bones. What *did* bother him was that someone had pushed him down those stairs.

At the corner, Oliver paused and glanced back at that tall townhouse, that portico, those stairs.

Who had shoved him? And why?

He went to sleep feeling rather perturbed, and woke eight hours later feeling much more the thing. No one had been trying to kill him. It had been a mean-spirited prank, that was all, perpetrated by someone who'd had too much to drink and was perhaps a little jealous of Oliver's good fortune. He'd been foolish to imagine it could be anything more than that.

He felt rather less cheerful when he climbed out of bed. Damn it, he hadn't had this many bruises for quite some time.

A warm bath helped with the stiffness, and a hearty breakfast and a ride in Hyde Park restored Oliver to good spirits. He spent several hours learning to be a duke, reading reports from his bailiffs that made little sense now, but would once he'd toured his estates—then strolled across town to visit Rhodes Garland.

Rhodes was staying at his father's townhouse on St. James's Square, as he always did when in London—although "townhouse" was a misnomer given that the building was the size of a mansion. Sevenash House was its name, because Rhodes's father was the Duke of Sevenash, and one day Rhodes would be Duke of Sevenash himself.

But hopefully not for a long time.

Rhodes's father wasn't the sort of duke Oliver's grandfather had been. Sevenash was cut from entirely different cloth. He'd stood by Oliver's father when he was cut off, and he'd stood by Oliver when his father had died, and stood by him again ten years later when his mother had died. It was Sevenash who'd paid for Oliver's education at Winchester and Cambridge, Sevenash who'd purchased his commission into the dragoons.

Oliver had been too young and too bewildered to protest about Winchester, but he'd protested about Cambridge, and about the dragoons, too, and Sevenash had merely smiled at him and said, "Nonsense. You're my godson. Of course I'm paying for it."

What Sevenash hadn't said—but that Oliver had known—was that Sevenash loved Oliver almost as much as he'd loved his own children. And what Oliver had never said—but hoped that Sevenash knew—was that he loved Sevenash almost as much as he'd loved his own father.

Sevenash had been there when Oliver had needed him, and Oliver had repaid Sevenash in the only way possible: by being the best student he could and the best soldier he could. In all honesty, he hadn't been a very good student—he'd had no aptitude for conjugating Latin and Greek verbs—but he'd been a damned good soldier. He was proud of how good a soldier he'd been, and he hoped Sevenash had been proud, too.

For a moment, standing there in St. James's Square, Oliver felt a pang of regret—he *had* wanted to make colonel by the time he was forty, damn it—and then he shook his head and laughed. He'd inherited a dukedom and a fortune and he was feeling sorry for himself? "Dasenby, you addle-pate, you don't know how lucky you are," he said under his breath, and then he ran up the marble steps to Sevenash House.

A footman opened the huge front door.

Oliver stepped into the entrance hall and handed over his hat and gloves. His most visceral wrench of recognition since returning to England had occurred right here in this entrance hall—a wrench so strong that it had actually brought tears to his eyes.

He didn't feel that wrench today, just a sense of coming home. Here was the vast black-white-and-gray marble floor where he and Rhodes had played their own version of hopscotch—the white squares boiling seas, the black squares bottomless pits, peril in every jump; there was the imposing double staircase with the banisters they'd slid down. In fact, the first time he'd broken his arm had been on this marble floor after sliding down those sleek banisters.

Sevenash House was enormous by anyone's standard. Usually it was brimming with bustle and noise, footsteps, voices, laughter, but the duke and his duchess had departed for Gloucestershire two days ago, taking Rhodes's three young children with them and a great many servants, and the house felt much emptier than Oliver was used to, even though it *wasn't* empty. Rhodes was still here, and his sisters.

The butler, Forbes—who'd been Edward the footman when Oliver was a boy—welcomed him with an un-butler-ish smile, calling him *Your Grace* in exactly the same tone in which he'd called him *Master Oliver* all those years ago.

"Afternoon, Forbes," Oliver said cheerfully. "Is his lordship at home?"

"Yes, sir."

Rhodes Garland, Marquis of Thayne and heir to the dukedom of Sevenash, was in the library reading the *Gazette*. Or rather pretending to. The newspaper was in his lap, and he was staring at it, but if he'd actually been reading it, Oliver would have eaten his neckcloth. Rhodes had a sad, faraway look on his face, a look that Oliver guessed he'd worn a lot since his wife, Evelyn's, death last year—not that Oliver knew that for certain, since he'd been in India when Evelyn had died, but he knew he'd seen that look on Rhodes's face quite a few times in the past four weeks.

"Hello, old fellow," he said.

The unhappy, distant look vanished. "Ollie." Rhodes put aside the *Gazette*. "What are you doing here?"

"Came to visit you." Oliver strolled across to the sofa and sat, stretching out his legs. Damn it, his knee hurt from tumbling down those stairs. "Didn't see you at the Cunninghams' ball last night."

"Balls," Rhodes said, in a tone that implied that he classed balls only slightly above going to the dentist to have a tooth drawn. Then he made what was obviously a determined effort to smile. "Would you like something to drink? Madeira? Sherry? Brandy?"

"Brandy," Oliver said.

Rhodes poured them both a glass and they sipped and talked, and talked and sipped, and finally Oliver got Rhodes to laugh. The first laugh was the hardest, but once he got Rhodes past that hurdle, each laugh came more easily, and by the time the clock on the mantelpiece struck half past four, Rhodes was slouching in his armchair, looking cheerful and relaxed. The door swung open and Primrose entered, dressed in a very handsome riding habit. "Rhodes, please say you'll come with us to Hyde

Park." And then she saw Oliver, and halted. She looked momentarily disconcerted. Color rose in her cheeks. "I beg your pardon. I didn't realize you were here." She bit her lip for a brief second, and then said brightly, "Would you like to come with us to Hyde Park, Oliver?"

"Us?"

"Aster, Violet, and me. We always ride in Hyde Park at this hour."

Oliver glanced at Rhodes. "Want to join the Grand Strut, old fellow?"

Rhodes hesitated, and Oliver could clearly see his reluctance. Primrose must have seen it, too, because she said, "Not if you don't want to."

"I'll come with you tomorrow," Rhodes said, and something in Primrose's expression made Oliver think that Rhodes had said the exact same thing yesterday.

"Of course." Primrose smiled again, much less brightly, nodded to Oliver, and left the library.

There was a moment of silence, then Rhodes said, "More brandy?"

"A little." He surrendered his glass and watched Rhodes pour. A bust of Cicero presided over the crystal decanters. "That's not the same Cicero whose nose we broke off, is it?"

"No."

Oliver accepted his glass back. "Lord, can you remember how panicked we were?"

"I remember that you tried to stick it back on with paste from the schoolroom. Your expression, when it fell off again . . ." Rhodes uttered a crack of laughter.

They talked and laughed and sipped their brandy, and it felt so much like old times that Oliver almost couldn't believe that he'd been away from England for eight years. But that was the mark of the very best friendships: that you could pick up where you'd left off, however long you'd been apart.

Come to think of it, he'd picked up with Primrose in much the same way.

At seven o'clock, Primrose poked her head into the library again. "Rhodes, are you coming to the Turvingtons' ball tonight?"

Rhodes seemed to tense slightly. "Do you need an escort?" he asked, in a very neutral tone.

Primrose hesitated. Oliver could tell that she was as aware of her brother's reluctance as he was. "No," she said. "Aunt Rosemary has said she'll take us."

Rhodes relaxed fractionally. "Then I shan't come."

Primrose bit her lip, and then said, "We're dining with our cousins first. Will you at least join us for that?"

"Not tonight," Rhodes said.

Primrose nodded, and glanced at Oliver. She seemed to be trying to impart a silent message.

Oliver wasn't entirely certain what that message might be, but he thought he could guess. Primrose was worried about her brother, worried that he didn't appear to want to leave the house. "I'm dining at my club tonight," he said. "Care to join me, Rhodes?"

"You're not going to the Turvingtons' ball?"

Not with his knee this sore. Oliver shook his head. "I don't feel like dancing tonight. Dinner and a bottle of good claret, maybe a game of cards. What do you say?"

Rhodes considered this invitation for a moment, turned his glass around in his hands, once, twice, a third time, and then said, "Well . . . all right."

⁓

At eight o'clock Rhodes went upstairs to put on a fresh neckcloth. Oliver strolled out to the entrance hall to wait for him. Primrose came down the staircase in a soft rustle of blue silk. She crossed to Oliver. "Thank you."

"For what?"

"For making him laugh. For making him go out." She looked down at the floor, traced a pattern on the marble with the toe of one dancing slipper, glanced back up at him. "He's been . . . not himself since the children left."

"Why didn't he go with them?"

"It's family tradition. Mother and Father take the children into the country in June and the rest of us stay in London. Evelyn and Rhodes used to call it their furlough month—when they could dance until dawn and be giddy and irresponsible." She looked down at the floor again, traced another pattern with her toe. "When Rhodes decided to stay in London, I thought maybe . . . but I was wrong. He doesn't want to dance. He doesn't even want to go outside."

"He's blue deviled," Oliver said.

"You think I don't realize that?" Primrose said tartly, and then she sighed and pressed both hands to her brow, as if her head ached. "I beg your pardon, Oliver."

Oliver shook his head. He didn't mind Primrose's tartness.

"He should have gone with the children," Primrose said, lowering her hands. "I *told* him that, but he won't listen to me."

"You want me to talk with him, persuade him to go?"

Primrose gave him a swift, hopeful glance. "Would you? *Could* you?"

"Count it as done," Oliver said. "He'll be heading for Gloucestershire before the week is up."

"Thank you." She smiled at him, relief shining as brightly as tears in her eyes, and he realized just how very worried she was. "If he says he has to remain in London because we need a chaperone, tell him that's nonsense! We can stay with Aunt Rosemary and Uncle Jerram."

"I won't let him play that card," he promised her.

"Thank you," Primrose said again. She stood on tiptoe and kissed his cheek lightly. He smelled her perfume, a faint hint of orange blossom. "I'm glad you're back in England, Oliver."

Oliver almost blushed, a reaction he didn't quite understand. To hide it, he said, "Even though I'm an addle-pate?"

Primrose tried to repress a smile, and failed. "Even though you're an addle-pate."

"Most magnanimous of you, Prim," he said. "You set me all a-twitter."

Her eyelids twitched in that not-quite eye roll.

Footsteps came on the marble staircase, and the sound of feminine voices. He looked up and saw Violet and Aster, dressed in their evening finery. At the same moment, a footman opened the huge front door. Cool evening air flowed in, bringing with it the smell of coalsmoke and the sound of hooves on cobblestones.

"The carriage is here, my lady."

Oliver escorted the three sisters out to the carriage and handed them up into it, bestowing extravagant compliments as he did so. He compared Aster to the goddess of the dawn, Violet to the most bewitching of sirens, and informed Primrose, the last to enter the carriage, that she outshone Helen of Troy herself.

"Hyperbole, Daisy," Primrose told him dryly.

Oliver grinned at her—and then caught her gloved hand, detaining her on the jump step for a moment. He leaned close, inhaling her orange blossom scent. "Don't worry about Rhodes," he whispered. "I've got this."

Her eyes met his. She squeezed his fingers briefly. "Thank you," she whispered back.

He took Rhodes to dinner at his club—Brooks's, on St. James's Street—and found Rhodes surprisingly resistant to the idea of going to Gloucestershire. It was obvious that Rhodes missed his children, but he appeared to be trying to prove something to himself. Oliver wasn't quite sure what. That he wasn't still heartbroken after the death of his wife? That he was capable of carrying on as usual?

Clearly, Rhodes *was* still heartbroken, he wasn't capable of carrying on as usual, and he missed his children and should be in Gloucestershire with them.

But Oliver knew when not to push, so he let the matter rest. Tomorrow was another day, and he would win this skirmish—even if Rhodes didn't realize yet that it was a skirmish.

"I've been invited to a house party in Oxfordshire next week," he said instead. "Lord and Lady Cheevers."

Rhodes looked up from his beef. "Ah, that explains it."

"Explains what?"

"I received an invitation, too. Couldn't figure out why. They move in an older set, the Cheevers. Great cronies of your Uncle Algernon. That'll be why you're invited—because he's going. And Prim and I have been invited so that you don't get too bored."

"Prim's been invited?"

Rhodes nodded, and then turned his attention back to his meal. "You going to go?"

He hadn't planned to, but Shipton-under-Wychwood was practically in Gloucestershire. "I'm thinking about it," Oliver said. "What about you?"

Rhodes hesitated.

"No need to make up your mind right now," Oliver said easily. "Like some more claret?"

He soon had Rhodes laughing again, and by the time they'd finished both their meal and the claret, Rhodes was leaning back in his chair, looking mellow and relaxed and not a little sleepy. The club was growing busy. Oliver saw his Uncle Algernon heading for the cardroom, where whist and hazard were played for high stakes. "Care for a game of cards?" he asked Rhodes.

Rhodes stifled a yawn and shook his head. "I'm for bed. But don't let me stop you."

Oliver was feeling sleepy himself. "Not tonight."

They had to wait in the vestibule while a footman fetched their hats and gloves. Oliver's cousin, Ninian, was waiting, too. He was dressed for dancing, lace spilling over his wrists, jewels twinkling in the folds of his neckcloth. His waistcoat was a confection of lilac and cream, with silver threads glinting in the embroidery, and his tailcoat was a handsome shade of lavender. He looked almost as pretty as the Garland girls had in their ballgowns.

"On your way to the Turvingtons' ball, are you?" Ninian said, pulling on his gloves. "So am I. Shall we go together?"

"We've decided to give it a miss," Oliver said.

"Oh." Ninian looked a little disappointed. "Well, enjoy your evening." He raised one hand in farewell and exited.

Oliver accepted his hat and gloves from the footman and donned them. He and Rhodes strolled outside. It was barely midnight, early by London standards. They paused on the pavement for a moment and inhaled the coalsmoke-tainted air. "Want to ride out to Richmond tomorrow?" he asked Rhodes. "Get some fresh air?"

For once, Rhodes didn't hesitate. "Yes."

They parted ways, Rhodes heading back to Sevenash House, Oliver bound for his own ducal mansion in Berkeley Square. He strolled along St. James's Street. There were quite a few pedestrians, not all of them sober. At Piccadilly, he waited for a hackney to pass and then a town carriage with a nobleman's crest on it.

A post-chaise swept into view, traveling slightly too fast, the four horses sweating, the postilions dusty and eager to reach their journey's end. Oliver waited for it to pass, too—and as he waited, someone shoved him violently between the shoulder blades.

CHAPTER 4

Oliver tumbled headfirst into the street, right in the path of the post-chaise. He fell heavily—rolled—one of the leaders stepped on him, and then the horses passed over him in a clatter of iron-shod hooves and loud jangle of harnesses, and the bulk of the carriage blotted everything out.

Oliver curled up into as small a ball as he could, aware of huge wheels scything past. Something brushed his wrist, plucking at his cuff—and then it was over.

He uncurled himself and scrambled for the pavement on hands and knees, dimly aware of shouts and cries of alarm.

Oliver didn't try to stand. He stayed on his hands and knees for a moment, gulping for breath. There was thunder in his ears. The thunder of hooves and carriage wheels, the thunder of his heartbeat.

Voices jabbered at him. It took a moment for the words to make sense. "Sir? Are you all right, sir?"

Oliver lurched upright, staggered, and caught his balance. "I'm fine," he said. "Fine." But he wasn't; he was shaking, and he couldn't quite seem to catch his breath.

He looked for the post-chaise. It had halted some yards ahead, the horses snorting and tossing their heads, the postilions white-faced, craning their necks to look back, probably fearing they'd killed him.

They very nearly *had* killed him.

Half a dozen people were clustered around him, wide-eyed and excited. He didn't recognize any of them. "Did you see who pushed me?" Oliver asked.

His audience gaped at him. "Push you?" said a man who looked like a lawyer's clerk. "Ain't no one 'as pushed you."

Oliver knew damned well that someone *had* pushed him. "Did you see anyone running away?"

The little crowd began to melt into the shadows, people stepping back, turning from him, moving off into the dark. Did they think he was going to accuse one of them of trying to kill him?

One man didn't turn away. A crossing-sweeper. He held out an object. "Your 'at, guv'nor."

Oliver's hat didn't look like a hat anymore. It had almost been cut in two by the carriage wheels.

He took it and turned it slowly over in his hands. It could have been his arm crushed this flat. It could have been his *neck.*

He looked around, scanning the street, scanning the shadows. His audience was gone. The post-chaise was gone. He saw nothing out of the ordinary. No one loitering. No one watching.

The crossing-sweeper was still waiting, no doubt hoping for a penny in exchange for the ruined hat.

"Did you see what happened?" Oliver asked. "Did you see the person who pushed me?"

"I din' see nothin', sir."

Oliver looked down at the hat again, and then at his cuff, where he'd felt the carriage wheels pluck at him. The buttons were gone, either crushed or shorn off.

If he'd fallen one inch closer to the wheels his hand would have shared that fate.

The skin between his shoulder blades tightened in a shiver. What had just happened had been no mean-spirited prank; it had been someone trying to kill him.

Oliver looked around again. Piccadilly stretched in either direction. Torches and lamps burned brightly—and shadows gathered in the spaces in between.

No one seemed to be watching him from those

shadows . . . but that didn't mean that his attacker wasn't still nearby.

Oliver's house on Berkeley Square was two minutes away, but he didn't feel like making that walk alone.

He dug a guinea from his pocket and held it out to the crossing-sweeper. "Will you walk with me to Berkeley Square? I'm feeling unsteady on my pins."

It wasn't a lie, he did feel unsteady, and worse than that, he felt a little afraid.

CHAPTER 5

Rhodes had told her that he was riding out to Richmond that morning, so when Primrose went into the library she expected to find it empty. Instead, she found her brother and Oliver Dasenby seated on the sofa, heads bent close together, talking in hushed voices.

They looked up abruptly and stopped talking, almost as if they were children caught plotting mischief—except that they looked serious. Deathly serious.

Primrose's fingers froze on the door handle. Her heart gave a great, frightened *thump*. "What's wrong?"

"Nothing," Rhodes said.

Primrose studied his face, studied Oliver's face, and shook her head. "Something's wrong."

Oliver grimaced faintly, and turned to Rhodes, said something in a low voice.

The two men held a brief, whispered argument, and then fell silent. They turned their heads and looked at her again, with that unnerving seriousness.

"What?" Primrose said, still clutching the door handle. She knew that whatever it was, it was bad.

This time it was Rhodes who grimaced. He made a gesture, an opening of his hand, yielding to Oliver.

"Primrose," Oliver said, and then paused, as if debating the wisdom of telling her whatever the dreadful news was.

Primrose closed the door, crossed to them, and sat. "What is it? What's happened?"

Rhodes and Oliver exchanged another glance, and then Rhodes said, "Someone tried to kill Ollie last night."

Primrose's mouth fell open. After a moment, she shut it. After another moment, she said, "What?"

"Someone pushed him under a post-chaise," Rhodes said. "And the night before last someone pushed him down the Cunninghams' stairs."

It sounded too absurd to be true, but it clearly *was* true: Rhodes and Oliver had identically grim expressions on their faces.

Primrose had never seen Oliver look grim before. Usually there was laughter lurking in his eyes. But not this morning.

She studied him more closely. There was a faint

bruise on his cheekbone. "Is that from last night?" she said, touching her own cheek so that he'd know what she meant. "Were you hurt?"

"Not much." He shrugged. "One of the horses stepped on me, that's all."

"*Stepped* on you!"

"I've been stepped on by horses before, Prim," he said, in the sort of tone that men reserved for ladies who were fussing needlessly.

"One can *die* if a horse steps on one's head."

"It didn't step on my head. And before you ask, nothing's broken. I'm perfectly all right."

Primrose looked at him sitting there on the sofa, big and brawny and grim-faced, and decided that if he thought he was all right then he probably was. "Are you certain you were pushed? Might it not have been an accident?"

Oliver's expression became grimmer. He shook his head. "It was deliberate. Both times. No mistaking it."

"But who would do such a thing?" she said. "And *why?*"

"That's what we're trying to determine," Rhodes said. "Why would anyone want Ollie dead?"

Under other circumstances Primrose would have made a joke of it, would have said, *Clearly it's because he's so annoying.* But this wasn't a time for jokes.

She considered the question seriously. "The most obvious reason is that someone hates him."

"But who?" Rhodes said. "He's only been back in England a month. He hasn't had any arguments with anyone."

"Perhaps it's someone who hated him before he went to India?"

Oliver considered this for a moment, and then shook his head. "I've never had an enemy."

"Perhaps someone owes you money and can't repay it?" Primrose said. "A gambling debt?"

Oliver shook his head again.

"What about your *chère-amie,* then?" Primrose said. "Perhaps someone feels that you've poached on his territory?"

"I don't have a *chère-amie* yet," Oliver said—and then he grinned. "And it's very improper of you to mention the *demimonde,* Prim. Not ladylike at all."

Primrose felt herself blush, because he was correct. "Do we know it was a man who pushed you? Could it have been a woman?"

Oliver's grin vanished. He frowned—and then shook his head. "Whoever it was is pretty tall. Got me right between the shoulder blades both times. And strong. Strong enough to knock me down. My instinct is . . . it's a man."

Primrose frowned, too, and considered motives.

What reasons did men kill for? Revenge, money, women, politics.

"The Duke of Westfell has traditionally voted Tory," she said. "Maybe someone doesn't like that you're a Whig?"

"Uncle Algy's a Whig, too, and he'll be duke after me," Oliver pointed out.

And that was the most obvious answer: Oliver's assailant was Lord Algernon Dasenby.

"Could it have been him?" Primrose posed the question hesitantly, fairly certain of the reaction she'd get. "Your uncle?"

She was correct: Oliver stiffened, and shook his head. "Of course not!"

"He *is* your heir."

"It's not Uncle Algy," he said, in a voice that brooked no argument. "From the moment I got back he's done everything he can to help me!"

"Whoever it is," Rhodes said, "they want it to look like an accident. Could have put a knife between your ribs last night and we wouldn't be having this conversation."

Primrose shivered.

"You realize that if you *do* die," Rhodes said, "you'll be the fourth Dasenby to kick the bucket in less than two years?"

Primrose glanced sharply at him. So did Oliver.

"They were accidents," Oliver said slowly—and then, in the tone of someone asking for assurance: "Weren't they?"

"Were they?" Rhodes asked.

There was a long moment of silence. Rhodes broke it: "In the space of five months, Reginald Dasenby's two sons died, and then *he* died. That's . . . extraordinarily bad luck."

Primrose stiffened in sudden realization. "There was another Dasenby who died in those five months."

Both men looked at her. She saw their astonishment.

"I'll be back in a moment," Primrose said. "I need to check the dates." She caught up her skirts and ran from the library, up the sweeping marble staircase, and along the corridor to her bedchamber. She crossed to the escritoire, opened it hastily, and pulled out her journal.

As journals went, hers was rather boring. No gossip, no secrets, just notes about the books she was reading.

Tucked in among the pages were two items cut from the *Gazette*. Primrose removed them and studied the dates jotted at the top of each snippet, then shoved the journal back in the escritoire and ran downstairs.

Rhodes and Oliver both stood as she reentered the library. "Who else died?" Rhodes asked.

Primrose didn't answer that question; instead, she asked one of her own: "When did the duke's sons die?"

"Basil died in . . . November, I think it was," Rhodes said. "Middle of the hunting season."

"And Percival?"

"Five or six weeks later. Beginning of January."

"And the duke?"

Oliver answered that question: "March."

Primrose crossed to the great oak desk, with its French marquetry and lion's-paw feet.

"Who else died?" Rhodes asked.

Primrose laid the clippings on the desk. "Oliver did. It was reported in the *Gazette* at the end of December."

"Good Lord!" Rhodes said. "That's right. We thought you were dead, Ollie."

Both men converged on the desk. They stood, one on either side of her, and looked at the two pieces of paper. One was an account of the storming of the forts at Airani, Ranebennur, and Bidnur—and a list of the casualties—and then, in March, the correction: Captain Oliver Daintree had perished, not Captain Oliver Dasenby.

Oliver reached out and touched the first clipping

briefly. "Took my CO three months to realize he'd made a mistake. Lord, he was mortified. Kept apologizing to me."

He should have apologized to us, Primrose thought, remembering how stricken Rhodes had been, then she gave herself a mental shake. Oliver's commanding officer was unimportant; what *was* important were the consequences of his mistake.

"Basil fell off his horse and broke his neck in November," she said. "I'm going to call that an accident. Do you agree?"

Both men nodded.

"Percival died in a shooting accident in January. Was he alone when it happened? Were there any witnesses?"

"He was alone," Rhodes said.

"So . . . it might *not* have been an accident?"

After a hesitation, both men nodded.

"The duke died in March in a fire." She looked at her brother. "Did anyone else die in that fire, or was it just him?"

"It was just him," Rhodes said slowly.

"So that's possibly not an accident, either."

Another hesitation, another two nods.

"What I think happened . . ." Primrose moistened her lips, and chose her words carefully. "What I think is that the first death was an accident, and then *you* were reported dead, Oliver, and someone saw a . . . an *opportunity* that hadn't existed before, and so they took it."

"No." Oliver shook his head and turned away from the desk.

"It's not the only explanation for so many deaths in one family in such a short space of time, but it's the most logical one. And it explains why someone tried to kill you last night."

"It's not Uncle Algy!"

"Then it must be your cousin, Ninian."

He turned to look at her. "Ninian? That namby-pamby? He couldn't kill a fly!"

"He's tall," Primrose said. "And young and strong. And if you die his father becomes Duke of Westfell."

Oliver shook his head again.

"You think it's impossible?"

His gaze fell to the two newspaper clippings on the desk.

"It's possible," Rhodes said.

Oliver reached out and touched the second piece of paper, fingering the sentence that proclaimed him alive.

"Must have been one devil of a disappointment when the correction was published," Rhodes said.

Oliver pushed the clipping away, sending it skimming across the desk. "I've been in England for a month," he said, his tone almost angry. "Why wait so long to kill me? He could have done it that first week."

"Perhaps he likes you," Rhodes said. "Most people do."

Oliver pulled a face and pushed away from the desk. He strode to the nearest window and looked out.

Primrose had known Oliver her whole life. She'd seen him laughing and merry more times than she could count. On occasion she'd seen him quiet, tired, or thoughtful, and a couple of times she'd even seen him solemn, but she'd never seen him like this before. His arms were crossed, his jaw pugnacious. He looked dangerous—and nothing at all like the lighthearted and dreadfully annoying Daisy Dasenby.

"How flush in the pocket is your uncle?" she asked. "How flush is Ninian?"

"I don't know," Oliver said curtly.

"Your uncle's a gambler," Rhodes said. "Dips pretty deeply, from what I've heard."

Oliver scowled at him.

"Ninian's not a gambler," Rhodes said. "But he has some very expensive habits. Must spend a fortune on his wardrobe."

Oliver's scowl deepened, and then he burst out:

"I can't believe either of them would want money so badly that he'd *kill* for it."

"Maybe it's not the money," Rhodes said. "Maybe it's the title."

"I don't want the damned title! They can have it, for all I care!" His voice was fierce, a tone that she'd never heard Oliver use before.

Rhodes spoke the obvious: "That's not how it works, Ollie."

"I know, damn it!" Oliver still had his arms crossed over his chest, angry, defensive. "So what now?"

Now we try to find evidence that one of your relatives is trying to kill you, Primrose thought. Then she looked at Oliver's face and rephrased her words: "Let's try to find evidence that it wasn't them. If it's not, we should be able to prove it, correct?"

Oliver seemed to relax fractionally. "Correct."

"So let's find out where Lord Algernon and his son were when the last two deaths occurred."

"All right." Oliver uncrossed his arms and pushed away from the windowsill. "I take it there were inquests? Which were reported in the newspapers? Did you cut those out, too, Prim?"

"No," Primrose said. "I only cut out the items about you." And to her annoyance, she felt herself blush.

"The newspaper office will have them," Rhodes said. He looked from her to Oliver. "Shall we?"

They went by carriage. A horse might not have stepped on Oliver's head, but one had certainly stepped on his leg. He was limping. Primrose forbore to comment. She'd never thought of Oliver as prickly and short-tempered before, but today he was both.

Their findings at the *London Gazette* office didn't improve his mood. Several witnesses had given evidence at the inquest into Percival Dasenby's death on his father's estate in Leicestershire. Five other people had been in the woods that wintry afternoon, shooting pheasants. They'd all heard the fatal shot, although none of them claimed to have witnessed it. Both Lord Algernon and his son, Ninian, had given brief statements, as had Percival's bereaved father, and two gamekeepers.

Oliver's mood deteriorated further when they found the report of the inquest into the late duke's death two months later, on his Wiltshire estate. A fire had sprung up late one night in the duke's bedchamber. The coroner had concluded that it was the result of a candle tipping over. The only person who'd died had been the duke.

As before, a number of people had given statements. Servants and family members.

"Both of them were there that night," Rhodes said, stating the obvious.

"It's *not* Uncle Algy," Oliver said fiercely. "If it weren't for him I'd still be jumping through bureaucratic hoops."

"Then it must be Ninian," Primrose said. "He was at the Cunninghams' ball. He could have pushed you."

"He was at Brooks's last night, too," Rhodes said—and then, after a pause, he added: "So was Lord Algernon."

"Damn it, Rhodes—"

"Let's keep an open mind, shall we?" Rhodes said.

Oliver shut his mouth tightly.

Rhodes looked at her. "Was Lord Algernon at the Cunninghams' ball?"

Primrose nodded.

Oliver hissed between his teeth, but said nothing.

They went back to Sevenash House, where they sat down to a late luncheon. Oliver scowled while he ate. Rhodes didn't scowl, but he was frowning, a deep groove between his eyebrows. Primrose picked at her food. How could they discover if one of the Dasenbys had tried to kill Oliver?

Rhodes put down his knife and fork, pushed his plate to one side, and said, "It might be coincidence that three Dasenbys died in five months."

Both Oliver and Primrose looked at him.

"It might also be coincidence that Ollie was pushed under a post-chaise last night. Maybe someone's jealous of him, or maybe it's a friend of Lord Algernon's. Maybe it's someone who wants Algernon to inherit the dukedom, not Ollie."

Primrose put down her fork, dismayed. "Lord Algernon has *scores* of friends."

"I don't think it's one of Algernon's friends," Rhodes said. "I think it's most likely him or his son. Or perhaps the two of them together." He held up a hand to stop Oliver's protest. "But I know you don't think so, Ollie. So, let's start by proving it's *not* them."

Oliver's scowl deepened.

Rhodes was undaunted. "Let's give them both some rope and see if one or other of them hangs himself."

"How?" Primrose asked.

"The Cheevers's house party is next week. Lord Algernon will definitely be there, and I imagine Ninian will be, too." Rhodes leaned back in his chair. "What do you say, Ollie? Let's give your uncle and cousin some opportunities to kill you. See whether they take them or not."

"Opportunities to kill him!" Primrose said, alarmed.

"Opportunities that *we* choose," Rhodes said. "In circumstances *we* control. Ollie won't be in any danger. I'll be there." He tilted his head at Oliver. "What do you say, old fellow?" There was a hint of challenge in his smile.

"I say yes."

Rhodes looked pleased, and Primrose realized that he *did* believe that either Lord Algernon or Ninian—or both of them—was responsible for the attempts on Oliver's life.

"I'm coming, too," she declared.

Rhodes lost his smile. "No, you're not."

"I was invited to the Cheevers's, too," Primrose told him.

Rhodes's eyebrows drew together. "You are *not*—"

"You might find me useful," Primrose said. "Another pair of eyes and ears."

Rhodes closed his mouth. He knew as well as she did that she had an advantage no one else had, an advantage that went well beyond eyes and ears. But Oliver didn't know that—and it was *not* a subject to be discussed in front of him.

"We'll talk about it later," Rhodes said.

She and Rhodes did talk about it later, a discussion that almost degenerated into an argument. "I don't want you anywhere near the Cheevers's," Rhodes said. "It could be dangerous."

"You need me."

"No, we don't!"

"Can you translocate?" Primrose asked, her voice very reasonable.

Rhodes gritted his teeth.

"If there's any danger to Oliver, then both of us should be there. The more people who're looking out for him, the safer he'll be. In fact, if we want him to be the safest he can be, Vi and Aster should come, too."

"No," Rhodes said. "Absolutely not!"

Primrose understood his refusal. If there *was* danger, then she didn't want Aster or Violet anywhere near it, but equally, she wasn't going to let Rhodes and Oliver face danger alone.

"I'm coming," she said. "I was invited and I have as much right to be there as you do. And anyway . . ." She smiled. "You can't keep me away."

Rhodes gritted his teeth again. "All right," he said, with poor grace. "But Vi and Aster are *not* coming. I don't want you telling them anything about this. Your word on it!"

"I won't tell them," Primrose said, glad to have

won one battle. Although there was no denying that her sisters' gifts could have been useful, Aster's in particular.

And so, it was settled: she would go to Oxfordshire with Rhodes and Oliver.

A number of other things were settled that afternoon, too. The first one was that Oliver would stay at Sevenash House until they departed. It was a little eccentric, given that he had his own ducal mansion in London, but as Oliver was the only inhabitant of that mansion—not counting the servants—it seemed safer that he stay at Sevenash House. What Rhodes *didn't* say out loud was that both Algernon and Ninian Dasenby were more familiar with Oliver's mansion than he was, and if either one of them wanted to slip inside without the servants noticing, they probably could.

The second thing they decided was that Oliver wouldn't attend any more balls while in London—ostensibly because he'd sprained an ankle, but really to offer no more opportunities for assassination. He also wouldn't go to Brooks's club—or anywhere else—alone. He would only set foot outside Sevenash House in Rhodes's company.

The third thing was that when she, Rhodes, and Oliver went into Oxfordshire, Aster and Violet would go to stay with their aunt and uncle in Grosvenor Square.

These decisions made, Rhodes wrote to the Cheevers, confirming that he and Primrose would be delighted to attend the house party.

Oliver wrote to them, too, expressing his pleasure at the invitation and declaring that he was looking forward to a sojourn in Oxfordshire.

After that, there was very little to do. Oliver's valet relocated to Sevenash House, along with all of Oliver's clothes. Oliver's secretary didn't relocate, but Oliver gave him *carte blanche* to make decisions as he saw fit. "The man knows what he's doing. Kept things running before I arrived in England. And don't give me that look, Prim. I know I need to learn how to be a duke, but I can't make dukely decisions when I'm laid up with a sprained ankle, now can I?"

"*Dukely* isn't a word," Primrose told him.

"You mean I just made up a word?" His eyes opened wide. "How exciting!"

"God give me strength," Primrose muttered under her breath, and went upstairs to read Marcus Aurelius.

Oliver and Rhodes spent the rest of the week doing absolutely nothing constructive, as far as she could see. They were as lazy as it was possible for two strong, healthy young men to be—and it seemed to do them both good. Oliver was soon back to his usual self, walking with barely a limp, his prickliness gone, and Rhodes was in better spirits than he'd been since Evelyn's death sixteen months ago.

For Primrose the days passed in a parade of balls and soirées, and, as the date of departure drew closer, a lot of packing. Not that she had to pack—her maid, Fitchett, did it for her—but there were decisions to be made. Which gowns did she particularly wish to take with her? What footwear? How many books?

The very last thing that Primrose packed was her diary. She flicked slowly through its pages, finding first one newspaper clipping, and then the other.

She touched them with her fingertips.

When she'd read of Oliver's death in faraway India, the grief that she'd felt had astonished her. Laughing, annoying Daisy Dasenby was dead—and she had shed tears over it. Quite a few tears, over quite a few weeks. And when the correction had been printed in the newspapers, she had shed more tears in her relief that he lived.

Embarrassingly, she had almost cried, too, when Oliver had arrived back in London. Almost, but not quite, because he hadn't been exactly the Oliver Dasenby she remembered. His hair was still the same brown and his eyes the same hazel, but he'd seemed a lot bigger, taller and broader, and a great deal older, his face tanned by the Indian sun. He'd looked almost like a stranger . . . and then he'd made her an exaggeratedly florid bow and shaded his eyes with one hand and told her that her beauty quite dazzled him, and she'd realized that even if he looked different, he hadn't changed much in his years abroad.

That was when she'd almost cried—when she'd seen the laughter in his eyes, heard that teasing note in his voice, and realized that he was, truly, the Oliver of her childhood, even if he no longer quite looked like he was.

She had wanted to hug him tightly, then, and tell him how *glad* she was that he was alive. She hadn't, of course. Oliver would have wondered what was wrong with her if she'd done such a thing, so she had merely told him that his years in India hadn't cured him of his weakness for hyperbole, and given him a brief, sisterly peck on the cheek. But she had been glad to see him. Very, *very* glad.

CHAPTER 6

An afternoon in June, Oxfordshire

"Tell me about Basil and Percival," Oliver said, after they'd passed through Leafield. The chaise swayed gently as it bustled its way towards Shipton-under-Wychwood. "What were they like?"

He saw Primrose and Rhodes exchange a glance. They both hesitated, each giving the other the chance to speak first.

"You knew them better than I did," Primrose said finally.

Rhodes grimaced faintly. "Not really."

"You didn't like them?" Oliver asked, trying to interpret that grimace.

"I scarcely knew them," Rhodes said. "We moved in different circles for the most part, and when we were at the same events we generally avoided each other."

Oliver lifted his eyebrows. "You did?"

"Of course we did," Rhodes said. "*My* father sided with *your* father all those years ago. Westfell never spoke a word to Father after that."

Oliver digested this statement for a moment, then said, "Which Westfell? My grandfather or my uncle?"

"Both of them," Rhodes said. "And Basil and Percival carried on the family tradition by never speaking to *me* if they could possibly help it."

"Oh," Oliver said, disconcerted. "I didn't realize. I'm sorry."

Rhodes shrugged. "Not your fault, was it?"

No, perhaps it wasn't, but he couldn't help feeling uncomfortable, and perhaps Rhodes saw that, because he said, "It didn't bother Father, and it didn't bother me. As I said, we mostly moved in different circles, and even if our families *hadn't* been at odds, we'd never have been friends. Your uncle always behaved like a man with a stick up his, ah . . ." He cast a glance at Primrose. "That is to say that he was a very cold fish, and Basil was a cold fish, too."

"Was Percival a cold fish?"

"Percival was a *loose* fish," Rhodes said. "You know the sort. Up to every racket. Thought it was prime sport to box the watch."

The chaise slowed, then made a careful turn. Primrose peered out. "We've arrived."

61

Oliver looked out the window, too. He caught a glimpse of high gates, and then a long sweep of carriageway down an avenue of clipped yews.

"Now, Oliver . . ."

Oliver brought his attention back to Primrose. "Now, Primrose . . ." he teased.

She frowned sternly at him. "You *will* remember to be careful?"

Oliver's amusement evaporated. He had an abrupt memory of a hand shoving hard between his shoulder blades. He knew his assailant hadn't been Uncle Algy, and he doubted it had been Ninian, but even so . . . "I'll be careful."

Primrose drew breath as if to itemize all the ways in which he needed to be careful, but Oliver beat her to it: "I won't go near any staircases alone— inside *or* outside. I won't go walking alone. I won't go riding alone. I won't go shooting alone. I'll make certain I'm never alone with Uncle Algy or Ninian. In fact, the only thing I'll do alone is sleep—with my door locked and a chair jammed under the handle. Satisfied?"

Primrose eyed him for a moment, and then nodded.

When Oliver had inherited his uncle's dukedom, he'd inherited not only a title, a fortune, and a townhouse on Berkeley Square, but a ducal seat in Somerset, and estates in Cambridgeshire, Wiltshire, Shropshire, Leicestershire, and Kent. He hadn't visited any of those properties yet—his secretary was planning an extended tour of inspection that would take all of July, August, and September—so he had no idea whether he would actually *like* any of his new homes. Although "home" was probably the wrong word. Could a residence with several hundred rooms be called a home? Could it feel homelike?

Cheevers Court certainly didn't feel like a home. As mansions went it was large and square and gray, and it somehow managed to be both top-heavy and bottom-heavy at the same time. If the building had been a person, he—she?—would have had huge, beetling brows and heavy jowls and a lugubrious expression on his or her face.

Oliver stepped down from the chaise, glad to be able to stretch his legs. The carriage with their servants had arrived a few minutes before them, alerting the household to their imminent approach. Viscount Cheevers was hurrying towards them, his hand outstretched in welcome, a wide smile on his face.

It wasn't Cheevers's fault that he'd inherited such a gloomy beast of a mansion, and his greeting more than made up for all that dour gray marble. The viscount was beaming with joy, apparently delighted to welcome them to his country home, and his wife seemed equally delighted, nodding and smiling, and the two feathers in her turban nodded and smiled, too. Behind her was Uncle Algernon, beaming as widely as Cheevers, shaking Oliver's hand heartily, and behind him was Ninian. There was no way that Uncle Algy's joy was feigned, no way that the bright friendliness in Ninian's eyes could possibly be false—and in that moment, standing on the carriage sweep, with Primrose on one side of him and Rhodes on the other and the gray bulk of Cheevers Court looming over them all, Oliver knew that neither Uncle Algy nor Ninian had tried to kill him. And he also knew that he would prove it to Rhodes and Primrose while he was here. Prove it without a shred of doubt.

Oliver's bedchamber was a large room decorated in green and gold. It looked north, over parkland and a lake. Oliver's valet had already unpacked. A fresh change of clothes was laid out on the four-poster bed and a ewer of water sat on the washstand, steaming gently.

Oliver was used to the services of a manservant, but a duke's valet was far superior to an officer's bâtman. A duke's valet was able to shave Oliver more closely than he could shave himself, tie his neckcloth more skillfully than he could tie it himself, and choose his outfits more astutely than he could choose them himself. The man could probably wipe Oliver's bottom better than he could wipe it himself, if Oliver gave him the opportunity—which he wasn't going to do.

Oliver washed, shaved, and dressed in fresh clothes, while the sun sank lower in the sky, bathing everything in warm, golden light. Then he headed downstairs to meet the other guests—except that two steps down the long staircase he remembered that he'd promised not to descend any stairs alone.

Damn.

A promise was a promise, so Oliver gritted his teeth and climbed up those two steps and walked back along the corridor to Rhodes's bedroom, next to his own, and knocked.

"Ready, old fellow?" he asked, when Rhodes opened the door.

"Ready," Rhodes said, with a smile, and Oliver felt guilty for being annoyed.

They went downstairs together. The stairs were as steep as the Cunninghams' had been and there were a lot more of them. They were the sort of stairs that could break a man's neck if he was pushed down them—not that he was going to be pushed down them, because neither Uncle Algy nor Ninian was out to kill him—and the sooner he could prove that, the better.

Could he prove it tomorrow? *How* could he prove it?

Oliver was pondering these questions as they entered the drawing room. Quite a few people were gathered there.

Rhodes had said that the Cheevers's house parties catered to an older set, but it didn't look like it to Oliver. There were several young ladies present. He spied two whom he'd met in London—Miss Warrington and Miss Carteris—and two who were unknown to him.

Lord Cheevers made the introductions. Oliver said a polite, "How do you do?" to a middle-aged widow called Mrs. Middleton-Murray, and another "How do you do?" to her daughter. Miss Middleton-Murray was a lovely creature, with lustrous hair and flawless skin and a pair of dimples—but the moment Oliver met her eyes he made a discovery: Miss Middleton-Murray was a harpy.

He didn't know precisely *how* he knew, but he knew. Miss Middleton-Murray might have enchanting dimples, but a merciless and avaricious heart beat in her bosom.

One young lady yet remained to be introduced. Lord Cheevers led him across to her. "My daughter, Chloé," he said proudly.

Oliver had a moment of epiphany. *This* was why Cheevers was so delighted he'd accepted the invitation.

The Honorable Chloé Cheevers sank into a curtsy. She was a dainty little thing, dark-haired and slender.

Oliver inclined his head politely. "How do you do?" And then, because Cheevers was clearly waiting for more, "I don't recall seeing you in London."

Miss Cheevers blushed, and said something in an inaudible voice.

"I beg your pardon?"

"Measles," Lord Cheevers said. "Most unfortunate. But she's recovered now."

Oliver was unsurprised to find himself seated next to Miss Cheevers at dinner. Lord Cheevers wasn't an idiot. He had a captive duke and an unmarried daughter; of course he was going to seat them side by side.

Oliver embarked on his meal and prepared to score Chloé Cheevers on her efforts, but Miss Cheevers didn't appear to realize that this was her chance to catch a duke. She didn't tilt her bosom at him, she didn't send him admiring glances under her lashes, and she uttered not one single compliment.

In fact, it was impossible to give Chloé Cheevers a score because she wasn't playing the game.

Miss Warrington, seated on his other side, tilted her bosom at him fifteen times during the meal, earning herself thirty points. Miss Carteris, across the table from him, fluttered her lashes every time he looked in her direction, earning a respectable eighteen points. Miss Middleton-Murray was the clear winner, though. Her gown had a modest décolletage, revealing the merest hint of her cleavage, but the locket she wore nestled enticingly low. Every time Oliver glanced in her direction she touched her locket, a seemingly innocent gesture that drew his gaze to the ripe, shadowy promise of her breasts. By the time the dinner was over, she had accrued ninety points.

Oliver peered down the table at Primrose. He had a view of her between a silver cruet and a large *épergne*. She was talking with the man on her left, Lord Warrington.

Oliver studied her for a moment.

A casual observer might think that she looked rather like the Misses Warrington, Carteris, Middleton-Murray, and Cheevers. They were all young, all pretty, all wearing elegant gowns that exposed their pale shoulders and slender throats, all had jewelry gleaming at their earlobes and around their necks, all had smooth, soft skin and pink lips and shining hair. They almost looked interchangeable— but they weren't, because despite the multitude of similarities, Primrose wasn't like the others. She was *different*.

Primrose looked up at that moment and caught him staring at her. She didn't flutter her eyelashes like Miss Carteris or tilt her bosom like Miss Warrington; instead she cocked her head fractionally and lifted her eyebrows, a silent *What?*

Oliver crossed his eyes at her.

Primrose's eyelids twitched. He heard her voice in his ears as clearly as if she'd spoken aloud— *Idiot*—then she returned her attention to Lord Warrington.

Oliver bit back a laugh. He glanced at Miss Warrington. She tilted her bosom.

He glanced at Miss Carteris. She fluttered her eyelashes at him.

He glanced at Miss Middleton-Murray. She touched her locket.

Finally, he glanced at Miss Cheevers, sitting alongside him. She colored faintly and stared down at her place setting.

All of them painfully aware that he was a duke.

Except for Primrose, who didn't care.

The ladies withdrew, leaving the men in possession of the dining room. The port and brandy were passed around. Oliver leaned back in his chair, stretched out his legs, and listened idly to the conversation. He learned that Lady Warrington and Lady Cheevers were sisters, that Mrs. Carteris and Lord Cheevers were cousins, and that Miss Middleton-Murray was Lord Cheevers's goddaughter. He also learned that Uncle Algy and Lord Cheevers were quite as close friends as he and Rhodes were.

He glanced down the table at Rhodes.

Rhodes was leaning back in his chair, too, sipping his port and studying Ninian, his gaze narrow-eyed and thoughtful. As Oliver watched, Rhodes turned his head slightly and subjected Uncle Algy to an equally assessing stare.

Oliver found himself indignant on his relatives' behalves. If Rhodes had been nearer he would have given him a sharp nudge in the ribs. Uncle Algy wasn't a killer, and neither was Ninian.

In fact, the only killer in this room was himself: Captain Dasenby, slayer of insurgents and rebel soldiers.

Oliver grimaced into his port. For the first time since he'd received that astonishing letter from England eight months ago he found himself thinking that perhaps it *was* better to be a duke than a dragoon.

No more blood on his hands. No more madness of battle. No more strangers trying to skewer him with swords or blow holes in him with musket balls. No more kill-or-be-killed.

Except that someone *was* still trying to kill him.

CHAPTER 7

Primrose preferred to read in the evenings, but when one was a guest in someone else's house, one couldn't curl up in an armchair and bury one's nose in a book. One had to be polite, and sip tea, and converse with one's hostess.

Primrose did just that—sip tea and make polite conversation with Lady Cheevers. The viscountess had settled comfortably into matronhood. She talked fondly of her offspring—of whom Chloé was the eldest, told Primrose all about the family's recent bout of measles, and then fell into deep discussion with Lady Warrington about turbans, a fashion that both ladies favored.

Primrose had no interest in turbans. She removed herself to a sofa further from the fireplace and amused herself by watching the younger ladies prepare themselves for Oliver's arrival. Miss Carteris discreetly pinched her cheeks to give them more color, Miss Warrington shifted in her seat half a dozen times, finally settling on the position that was most flattering to her figure, and Miss Middleton-Murray nibbled on her lips until they were particularly full and rosy.

Even Miss Cheevers patted her hair.

At last, the door opened. The atmosphere in the drawing room altered in the blink of an eyelid. Spines straightened, bosoms swelled, and eyes became brighter. Miss Carteris tossed her ringlets. Miss Middleton-Murray bit her lips one more time.

Primrose watched the would-be duchesses as the men entered the room. The young ladies' eyes flicked rapidly from face to face, like gamblers assessing a hand of cards, deciding which ones to discard and which to keep.

Lords Cheevers and Warrington were quickly rejected. So, too, was Mr. Carteris.

Gazes lingered on Rhodes for a moment. He was handsome, wealthy, and heir to a dukedom, but he did also have three young children—so Primrose wasn't surprised when Miss Carteris, Miss Warrington, and Miss Middleton-Murray all settled on Oliver.

However, she *was* surprised when Miss Cheevers chose Ninian Dasenby.

That was interesting.

Even more interesting was that Ninian glanced around the room, clearly looking for one person in particular—and when his gaze lighted on Miss Cheevers he smiled involuntarily.

A romance, Primrose thought, watching the color rise in Miss Cheevers's cheeks, watching her shyly return Ninian's smile.

Equally interesting—but far more amusing—was the way in which Miss Warrington, Miss Carteris, and Miss Middleton-Murray were all sitting in their poses, trying to catch Oliver's eye without appearing as if that was what they were doing. Miss Carteris tossed her ringlets again and fluttered her eyelashes. Miss Middleton-Murray fingered her locket. Miss Warrington arched her back to bring her bosom into greater prominence.

Primrose watched Oliver, curious as to who he'd choose. His gaze flicked over one would-be duchess after another, and then found her. He smiled.

Primrose's heart gave a stupid thump in her chest.

Oliver took a step towards her—and halted, turning politely as Mrs. Carteris addressed him.

Mrs. Carteris said something that Primrose couldn't hear, but she recognized the tone: gay, laughing. Oliver listened for a moment, and then yielded to Mrs. Carteris's playful raillery, crossing to the sofa where Miss Carteris sat, desperately eager to be a duchess. Oliver seated himself alongside her—and glanced at Primrose briefly. He didn't grimace, but he did—for a fleeting second—cross his eyes.

Primrose bit her lip against inappropriate laughter, and looked away.

Someone loomed over her. Rhodes. He sat, making the sofa creak slightly. "Ollie's been captured by the Carterises."

"I saw." Primrose glanced around the room. Ninian and Miss Cheevers were seated side by side, heads bent together, talking in low voices. Lord Cheevers didn't look particularly pleased by this development, but Lady Cheevers was smiling upon the pair with benign goodwill.

Miss Middleton-Murray was eyeing Rhodes speculatively.

So, too, was Miss Warrington.

Primrose could have told them it was a vain hope. Rhodes wasn't ready to marry again. He probably never would be. If you'd had the perfect marriage with the perfect wife, how could you settle for anything less?

She glanced back at Oliver, trapped on a sofa with Miss Carteris on one side and Mrs. Carteris on the other. *Poor Oliver.* And then she looked more closely at him.

Oliver was pontificating, his chest slightly puffed out, a faint look of "cockerel" about him. He had a glint in his eyes that would have alarmed anyone who knew him well. When Oliver had that particular glint, he was up to mischief of some sort.

Primrose realized that it was Miss Carteris she should feel sorry for.

Miss Carteris didn't seem to feel sorry for herself, though. She was listening to Oliver with an expression of rapt and adoring attention.

Primrose shook her head, and turned her own attention to Rhodes. "What do you think of the Dasenbys?" she asked, very quietly. "Have you had a chance to observe them?"

Rhodes glanced at Lord Algernon, standing at the fireplace with their host, and then at Ninian, ensconced on a sofa with Chloé Cheevers. "I have."

"And?"

"I've seen nothing that indicates they wish Ollie harm."

"But you think one or the other of them does?"

Rhodes was silent for a moment, his gaze on Ninian Dasenby. "It's the most logical possibility."

Primrose didn't disagree.

She watched Ninian Dasenby for several minutes, and then transferred her attention to Lord Algernon—and like Rhodes, she saw nothing alarming.

Neither of them was gazing at Oliver with malevolence. In fact, neither of them was looking at him at all. Ninian was wholly focused on Chloé Cheevers, and Algernon was deep in conversation with Lord Cheevers. They both seemed utterly oblivious to Oliver.

But not so Miss Warrington and Miss Middleton-Murray, who were both trying to look as if they didn't mind *at all* that Oliver had been talking to Miss Carteris for nearly fifteen minutes—but whose tight smiles and darting glances in his direction clearly conveyed that they did, in fact, mind very much indeed.

Lady Warrington suggested that the young ladies play the pianoforte for everyone's entertainment. She volunteered Miss Carteris as the first performer.

Primrose spent the next forty minutes listening to the Misses Carteris, Warrington, Middleton-Murray, and Cheevers play the pianoforte. She had nothing against music—she rather liked music—but she wished she could have fetched her book and read it while she listened. Alas, that would have been rude, so she occupied herself by observing the others in the drawing room. Oliver was as bored as she was; she could tell by his smile, which was bland and courteous and very un-Oliver-like. Lord Algernon looked as if he was hugely enjoying himself, nodding his head in time to the music, and his son gazed at Miss Cheevers as if her performance was the most wonderful thing he'd ever witnessed.

He's besotted, Primrose thought. *Utterly besotted.*

She glanced at Rhodes. He wasn't listening to the music; he was thinking about Evelyn—she could tell by his face, by the way he was sitting—that sad, inward-looking expression, the stillness of his body.

She reached over and touched the back of his hand with light fingertips.

Rhodes jolted slightly, blinked, and looked at her, lifting his eyebrows in inquiry.

At that moment, Miss Cheevers's performance ended. Everyone clapped. Belatedly, Primrose did, too.

"Lady Primrose," Lord Cheevers said jovially. "Would you care to play for us?"

"Thank you, but I don't play the pianoforte."

"The harp, then, perhaps?" Lady Cheevers suggested. "We have a harp."

"Not that either," Primrose said. "I'm afraid I'm not musical at all."

She was aware of several ladies looking at her pityingly, and one—Miss Warrington—with something suspiciously like condescension.

Ten years ago, Primrose would have been embarrassed by the pity. Five years ago she would have been annoyed by it. But Marcus Aurelius was correct: One couldn't control the opinions of others, but one could choose *not* to be upset by them.

It was a concept that she still struggled with—but not tonight. Tonight she could look at that faintly superior expression on Miss Warrington's face and be amused rather than annoyed.

Lady Cheevers transferred her smile to her daughter. "Then perhaps you could play the harp for us, darling?"

Primrose thought of her book upstairs, and suppressed a sigh.

CHAPTER 8

The breakfast parlor at Cheevers Court was a large, sunny room decorated in pale green. When Primrose entered it, she found Lady Cheevers and the three Carterises seated at the long table—and Ninian Dasenby selecting his breakfast from the dishes lined up on the sideboard.

Primrose's pulse gave a little skip of excitement. Here was an opportunity to discover more about Oliver's cousin. She chose her food quickly, took a place several seats distant from the others, and cast a smiling glance at Dasenby. "Do say you'll join me, Mr. Dasenby."

Dasenby politely did, sitting opposite her.

Primrose spoke of commonplace nothings for several minutes, trying to find a topic that would set him talking. "I take it this isn't your first visit to Cheevers Court?"

"Father and I come here often," Dasenby said.

"Your families are great friends, then?"

"Yes."

"Then you must know Miss Cheevers very well."

Dasenby colored ever so faintly. "I do, yes."

Primrose waited for him to say more, but he didn't—which was frustrating. But she refused to give up. Instead, she applied logic to the problem. If she wanted to draw Dasenby out, she needed to talk about topics that interested him.

She spent a moment considering this. What did she know about him?

Dasenby was barely twenty-two. He was male. He was a fribble.

A fribble . . .

She examined his tailcoat. It was a color that she didn't recognize. A warm mid-blue, with a hint of lavender in it. "What color do you call your coat, Mr. Dasenby?"

"Periwinkle."

"It suits you."

"Thank you."

Primrose waited expectantly—and then realized that this, too, was a dead end.

"I like color," Dasenby said, almost blurting out the words, and then he blushed, hotly, and looked as if he wished he'd not spoken.

"What is it about color that you like?" Primrose asked encouragingly.

"I like how it can alter one's mood," Dasenby said, not quite looking at her, as if too embarrassed to meet her eyes. "And how it can change one's perception of a person or a place."

Primrose blinked, and then frowned faintly, not understanding. "Could you give me an example?"

He did meet her eyes then. "This room."

Primrose glanced around the breakfast parlor. The walls were a cool, pale shade of green.

"How does it make you feel, Lady Primrose?"

Primrose thought for a moment. "It's . . . calming. Restful."

"Now imagine how it would make you feel if it were painted yellow," Dasenby said. "Not lemon yellow, but a cadmium yellow. If you know what cadmium is?"

Primrose did. Cadmium was a rich yellow.

She tried to imagine it: the walls a warm golden color. With all those windows and that morning light streaming in . . . the breakfast parlor would be joyful and sunshiny. "It would make me feel happy," she said.

Dasenby smiled at her. "Precisely."

Primrose looked at him with a little more interest than she had before. "Which color would you choose for a breakfast parlor, Mr. Dasenby? This green or the yellow?"

"The yellow." He glanced around the room, his gaze lingering on the deeply set windows, the molded ceiling, the marble fireplace. "I like to imagine what rooms would look like if they were decorated differently. They can almost always be improved." He looked at her. "You've been inside my cousin's residence in London?"

Primrose nodded.

"The colors are wrong. It feels like a mausoleum. Cold."

Westfell House was magnificent, if also stately, formal, and rather forbidding. "You think Oliver should redecorate?"

"I would, if it were mine."

Primrose considered this statement. Did it mean that Dasenby had actively been thinking of putting himself in Oliver's shoes? That he wanted to be Duke of Westfell? Or did it merely mean that he didn't like the colors Westfell House was decorated in and thought that Oliver should change them?

She put this question aside to ponder later. "Do you look at people, too? Redecorate them?"

Dasenby blushed. That was answer enough. "Sometimes," he admitted.

"And do you think the colors a person wears can influence how they're perceived by others?"

"Yes." He hesitated, then took a deep breath and said: "I also think they can influence your perception of *yourself*. Some colors lift your mood when you wear them, make you feel good about yourself, and others don't." He raised one shoulder in a self-deprecating shrug as he said these words. It took Primrose a moment to understand exactly what that shrug meant: he was expecting her to laugh at him.

She didn't laugh at him. Instead, she looked at his clothes more carefully: the periwinkle of his long-tailed coat, the lavender and cream of his waistcoat.

The colors went together perfectly, complementing each other, and more than that, complementing him, with his wheat-gold hair and sky-blue eyes. The effect was harmonious, and rather beautiful. It was a pleasure to look at Ninian Dasenby.

"I think you may be correct," she said.

Dasenby looked slightly taken aback.

"How do those colors make you feel?" Primrose asked.

He looked down at himself, released his knife and smoothed his hand over the lavender-and-cream waistcoat. "They make me feel happy," he said. And then he blushed hotly.

Primrose pretended not to see the blush. "I don't pay much attention to my clothes, I'm afraid."

"Most people don't." Dasenby picked up his knife again. "Father calls me a tulip. And he's right, of course. It's foolish to pay so much attention to one's clothes." He said it with a laugh that was as self-deprecating as his shrug had been. Primrose could hear that he was expecting her to agree with his father, but she could also hear the words he didn't say: *But it makes me happier, and so therefore I do it.*

And what was the harm in it? Looked at dispassionately, it wasn't foolish of Ninian Dasenby to dress in a way that made him happy; it was *wise.* Such a simple thing to do, and such a profound effect.

"Whether it's foolish or not depends upon one's reason for doing it, I'd say." And Dasenby's reason, apparently, wasn't vanity. Or, not *only* vanity.

The door opened at that moment. Mrs. Middleton-Murray and her daughter entered.

Primrose assessed them in the light of her conversation with Dasenby, looking at the colors they wore. Mrs. Middleton-Murray was dressed in pale dove gray, while her daughter wore a pretty muslin gown trimmed with orange ribbon. The gray made Mrs. Middleton-Murray look like a respectable widow, which she was, and the orange ribbon made Miss Middleton-Murray look . . . bright and confident.

Primrose wondered what her own choice of gown said about her.

She glanced down at her lap. Her gown was a pale and rather cold blue. It was a shade that her dressmaker had told her went with her eyes, but it wasn't a shade that made Primrose feel particularly happy to look at. How did it make others feel about her? What impression did it give? That she was cool and aloof and standoffish?

She looked at Dasenby's tailcoat—and thought that she would prefer to be wearing periwinkle. It was a much warmer and more approachable color.

The door opened again. This time it admitted Oliver and Rhodes. Primrose looked at their clothes. Rhodes was wearing a quiet, sober brown, while Oliver's tailcoat was forest green. His waistcoat had green and cream stripes, with bright, glinting threads of gold, and he looked vibrant and alive, full of energy and good humor.

Yes, the color of one's clothes *did* influence how one was perceived . . . although perhaps her knowledge of Rhodes and Oliver was imbuing meaning into their attire? She knew that Rhodes was sad, just as she knew that Oliver was brimming with life and mischief.

And then she remembered that her task wasn't to think about colors or clothes; it was to observe

Ninian Dasenby. And in particular, to observe Dasenby interacting with Oliver.

Oliver and Rhodes filled their plates, and turned towards the table.

There was a moment that reminded Primrose of the drawing room the previous night, Miss Carteris and Miss Middleton-Murray trying to snare Oliver's attention with their smiles and their bosoms.

She caught Oliver's eye and gave a tiny jerk of her head at the empty seat beside her. He understood the message.

"Lady Primrose," he said cheerfully, and came to sit on her left. His plate was almost overflowing with sirloin and eggs. "How are you this fine morning?"

Rhodes took the seat to Primrose's right.

"I've been talking about colors with your cousin. Do tell him, Mr. Dasenby, how you would redecorate Westfell House."

Ninian Dasenby flushed. Despite his exquisite clothes he looked suddenly quite young, boyish and bashful.

Oliver glanced at Primrose, his gaze surprisingly shrewd, and then at Dasenby. "Let's hear it, Cousin."

Dasenby hesitated for a moment, and then plunged into exposition, hesitant at first, and then with growing confidence. Primrose didn't listen to his words so much as his tone. He sounded shy and eager. His expression was shy and eager, too, as was his posture, the angle of his head, the set of his shoulders.

He reminded her of something. It took her a moment to recognize what: a puppy seeking the attention and approval of its master.

Oliver dug into his food while Dasenby explained his vision for Westfell House. Primrose could tell from Oliver's bland, courteous expression that he wasn't really listening, but Dasenby didn't know Oliver well enough to realize that. He continued talking, leaning forward slightly in his enthusiasm, his face alight, diffident and passionate at the same time.

Primrose watched—and knew that Ninian Dasenby couldn't possibly be Oliver's assailant. Dasenby didn't want Oliver's dukedom; he wanted Oliver's friendship.

The door opened again. This time, Miss Cheevers entered.

Ninian Dasenby stopped talking in mid-sentence.

Behind Miss Cheevers came the Warringtons. The breakfast parlor was becoming quite crowded. Miss Warrington served herself quickly and took the vacant seat beside Oliver, looking smug. Miss Cheevers, after a moment's hesitation, chose the seat to Mr. Dasenby's right. She didn't look smug; she looked a little unnerved by her own boldness.

Ninian Dasenby bade her good morning.

Chloé Cheevers's cheeks colored shyly as she returned the greeting. Her gown was in the Grecian style, with little fluted sleeves. It was trimmed with a particularly felicitous shade of rose pink ribbon, and more rose pink ribbon held back her dark ringlets. She looked very youthful and very pretty.

Primrose watched as Chloé Cheevers stole a glance at Dasenby through her eyelashes. Not the sort of bold, playful glance that the Misses Carteris, Warrington, and Middleton-Murray threw at Oliver, but a glance that was timid and hopeful.

Ninian Dasenby glanced sideways at the same time. Primrose saw their eyes meet.

For a long moment Miss Cheevers and Mr. Dasenby stared at one another, their cutlery poised above their plates, then they both looked away, blushing. Primrose watched, amused, as they busied themselves with cutting their sausages—and then both glanced surreptitiously at each other again.

She looked at Oliver to see whether he'd noticed the romance playing out in front of him, but Miss Warrington had wholly engaged his attention.

Primrose busied herself with her own sausages. The day was off to a good start. She had learned three things.

First, that Ninian Dasenby wasn't nearly as much of a fribble as she'd thought.

Second, that he didn't want Oliver dead.

And third, that perhaps she ought to ask his advice on which colors to wear.

Primrose made no further observations during breakfast, but she felt that she'd made good progress. She had eliminated Ninian Dasenby as a suspect. Now, she just needed to observe Lord Algernon interacting with Oliver.

Her opportunity came a few hours later.

Cheevers Court possessed a large park, and in the middle of that park was a lake, and in the middle of the lake was a small, willow-fringed island that was perfect for picnics.

At one o'clock, the party set out across the lake in flat-bottomed punts, to take their luncheon on the island. It wasn't the entire party—Mrs. Middleton-Murray and Mrs. Carteris had elected to stay on dry ground—but everyone else had embraced the excursion eagerly. Including Lord Algernon. In fact, Lord Algernon was currently poling Primrose across the calm, sparkling waters of the lake.

Miss Carteris had won the battle for Oliver. She was gazing admiringly at him while he plied his pole.

Primrose wasn't gazing admiringly at Lord Algernon; she was attempting to interrogate him without being too obvious.

What questions could she ask in a five-minute boat ride that would give her insight into his character?

She knew very little about him. He was a duke's youngest son, accorded a courtesy title and nothing else. He was in his fifties. He was a widower. About his character, she knew nothing. Had he been resentful of his eldest brother? Or had he accepted his fate as third son with equanimity? Many younger sons had to work for a living. The army and navy and clergy were filled with second, third, fourth, fifth, and sixth sons. But Lord Algernon hadn't needed to resort to such a course; he'd married an heiress. Primrose was inclined to suspect that the marriage had been less of a love match and more of a deliberate strategy on his lordship's part—but perhaps she was maligning him? Perhaps he had loved his wealthy wife?

"You punt very well," she observed. "I collect you've done it before?"

Lord Algernon uttered his booming laugh. "Hundreds of times. Been punting since I was a boy."

"Did you ever punt with your wife?" Primrose asked, trailing her fingers in the cool water.

Lord Algernon laughed again. "Gad, no. Amabel was terrified of the water, bless her soul."

Primrose tried to evaluate this comment. Did the "bless her soul" indicate genuine fondness for his dead wife, or had it been tacked on to the sentence because it sounded good?

She decided there was no way of telling.

She glanced at Oliver. Somehow she needed to ascertain whether Lord Algernon felt that he deserved the dukedom more than Oliver—and whether he had the ruthlessness to kill for it.

"You must be relieved to have Oliver back in England."

"Relieved? Yes, you could say that."

Primrose observed his face from beneath the brim of her bonnet. "Especially after that report of his death. So terrible!"

"Yes. That was a shock. Quite a shock." Lord Algernon glanced across at Oliver's punt and his expression altered slightly, then he laughed again. "Doesn't know how to punt, that nephew of mine. He'll end up in the water if he's not careful." He looked away and plied his pole with careless ease, sending droplets of water spinning in the air like diamonds. "We'll be first across, mark my words, Lady Primrose."

Primrose wasn't at all certain how to interpret

the change of expression she'd glimpsed. It hadn't been inimical or resentful—but she didn't think it had been particularly happy, either.

She had no time to mull over it. Lord Algernon was correct: they were first across. Primrose climbed up onto the little jetty, disappointed with herself. She'd learned nothing during the brief voyage—other than that Lord Algernon was possessed of vigorous good health. Yes, his hair was graying, and yes, he was stout, but he was also tall and strong. Strong enough to push Oliver—or indeed anyone—under a post-chaise.

Whether he had the lack of compunction required for such an act was something she had yet to determine.

The island was tiny, but quite charming, with wildflowers growing profusely amid lush, green grass. Half a dozen servants had preceded them. Cushions lay heaped, shaded by large parasols, and a crisp, white linen tablecloth was spread on the grass. Upon it, a sumptuous luncheon had been laid out. "Oh!" Primrose said, involuntarily. "How pretty." And then she gave herself a mental kick. "Pretty" was a word she disliked. A *nothing* word. An unoriginal adjective used by people who lacked imagination. Far better to say how richly white the linen cloth looked against the luxuriant grass, or how deliciously the food had been arranged, or how enchanting the setting was. Any or all of those comments was better than *pretty*.

Miss Warrington came up alongside her. "Oh, how pretty!" she exclaimed, clapping her hands in delight and proving Primrose's point.

"Oh, how pretty!" said Miss Middleton-Murray, when she arrived.

And Miss Cheevers.

And Lady Warrington.

And Miss Carteris.

"Oh, how *pretty*," someone warbled in her ear.

Primrose recognized that voice: Oliver.

"It's not pretty," she informed him tartly. "It's charming and surprising and altogether quite delightful!"

"That's what I said," Oliver said. "Pretty." And then he laughed. "You should see your face, Prim."

"What's wrong with my face?"

He grinned at her, his eyes sparkling with good humor. "You were misnamed, you know. You should have been called Rose. Pretty, but prickly." He flicked her cheek with one finger, and then turned away, his attention on the food.

Primrose blushed hotly. Pretty? Had Oliver just called her *pretty*?

How different the word sounded when it was

applied to her. Not unoriginal at all, but rather . . . flattering.

He'd called her prickly, too, which was *not* a compliment. In fact, it stung slightly.

Primrose rubbed her cheek, and told herself that Oliver hadn't meant either the *pretty* or the *prickly*. He'd just been teasing her, the way he always had and always would. In fact, he'd probably moved on to teasing someone else now.

She looked for him, and sure enough, Oliver was standing amid a cluster of would-be duchesses, a slight swagger in his stance, pontificating.

Primrose watched for a moment, torn between amusement and disapproval.

"Ollie's at it again," someone said at her shoulder. Primrose didn't need to look around to know it was Rhodes.

"How can any woman want to marry him?" she asked. "He behaves like a conceited fool!"

Conceited fool or not, the Misses Warrington, Carteris, and Middleton-Murray were striving for Oliver's attention, giggling and tossing their ringlets and fluttering their eyelashes, each trying to outshine the others.

"He's a good catch," Rhodes said mildly.

Primrose suppressed a snort, but the truth was that Oliver was an excellent catch. He was a duke, he was wealthy, and despite that ridiculous swagger he was attractive. Very attractive—if one liked burly, sun-browned men with disgraceful senses of humor. "You were a good catch—you still are!—but no one ever behaves like that over you."

"I don't play up to it like Ollie. Do you think I should?" Rhodes thrust out his chest and struck a pose.

Primrose smacked his arm. "Don't you dare. One of you is more than enough."

CHAPTER 9

The picnic was surprisingly pleasant. Primrose leaned back on her cushions, feeling agreeably relaxed. The island had cast a spell over them all, an enchantment woven of dappled sunshine and a green-scented breeze, birdsong and the lazy hum of bees among the wildflowers. It took effort to concentrate on Algernon Dasenby, but concentrate she did. She nibbled a slice of ham, and watched him. Sipped a glass of lemonade, and watched him. Ate a grape, and watched him.

Lord Algernon smiled a lot and talked a lot and laughed a lot, but twice she caught him looking at Oliver, and both times a strange expression crossed his face.

She felt she ought to recognize that expression.

She'd seen it before, she was certain of it. But where? When?

Primrose frowned, and bit into a macaroon. It dissolved in her mouth, tasting of sugar and coconut.

That fleeting expression of Lord Algernon's was a serious one, a solemn one—but what did it *mean*?

Puzzle over it as she might, she couldn't decipher it. But she was convinced of one thing: whatever that expression meant, it was nothing inimical, nothing malevolent or dangerous. Lord Algernon didn't want his nephew dead.

Primrose finished the macaroon. She glanced at Rhodes. It didn't take great powers of perception to tell what he was thinking. His expression was pensive and his eyes and nose were suspiciously pink, as if he was trying not to cry.

Primrose wished Oliver were sitting alongside Rhodes, rather than amid a gaggle of young ladies. Oliver would make Rhodes laugh, if anyone could. Oliver had a gift for laughter. He was laughing now, as Miss Carteris picked wildflowers and wound them around the brim of her bonnet.

Primrose looked more closely at the flowers. Yellow, pink, blue—and white.

She glanced sharply at Rhodes, and caught him rubbing his eyes. They were even redder than they'd been before, swollen and a little bloodshot.

"Is that bishop's weed?" she asked Lady Cheevers, gesturing to the white blossoms that studded the grass.

Everyone looked at her, including Rhodes.

"Why, yes," Lady Cheevers said. "I believe that's what it's called."

Rhodes muttered what was probably a swearword and climbed to his feet. "Bishop's weed and I do not agree," he said. "If you'll excuse me, I'll return to the house."

Oliver and Primrose both stood at the same time, both spoke at the same time: "I'll take you back—I'll come with you."

"No," Rhodes said. "I don't need an escort. You stay here." He gave Primrose a significant look, which she had no difficulty interpreting: she was to keep watch over Oliver.

∽◦∾

A servant punted Rhodes back across the lake and everyone else resumed their picnic. Oliver's admirers decorated their bonnets with wildflowers and then Miss Carteris very prettily coaxed Oliver into accepting a few flowers for the buttonholes of his tailcoat. She placed the flowers herself, while the Misses Warrington and Middleton-Murray did their best not to look jealous.

Oliver glanced at Primrose briefly, over the top of Miss Carteris's head, and rolled his eyes.

Miss Warrington sprang to her feet. "Let's skip stones!" she cried. "I'm sure you're very good at it, Westfell."

"I am, rather," Oliver said, and winked at Primrose.

He and his three admirers went down to the shore and began hunting for small, flat stones. Primrose stayed where she was, watching Lord Algernon. From time to time he looked at Oliver, brief, amused glances that told her absolutely nothing—and then, when she was about to give up and hunt for wildflowers for her own bonnet, Lord Algernon finally did it: he gave Oliver that look, the strange, serious, solemn one.

Primrose stared at him.

What *was* the man thinking when he looked like that?

She saw Lord Algernon's lips press together, not angrily at all, but rather . . .

All of a sudden she recognized that expression. It was regret.

Primrose frowned, and tried to puzzle out why looking at Oliver should make Lord Algernon feel regretful. It took her a moment—and then it was blindingly obvious.

"Is Oliver much like his father?" she asked, when Lord Algernon reached for more grapes.

"The spitting image," Algernon said. "Got the

same laugh, too. Reminds me of Tristan every time I hear it."

Primrose nodded, and looked across to where Oliver and the young ladies were now competing at skipping stones. Miss Carteris was shockingly bad at it. She begged Oliver for a lesson. Oliver puffed out his chest and obliged, stepping close and taking Miss Carteris's hand for a moment, showing her the correct angle, the correct flick of the wrist.

Miss Carteris gazed up at him, her expression a pretty combination of shyness and adoration. She listened raptly, nodded several times, and then attempted to skip her stone. It sank with a loud *plop*, and she turned back to Oliver with dismay on her face.

Primrose repressed a laugh. She was certain that the *plop* had been deliberate.

This time Oliver spent considerably longer in his demonstration. He held Miss Carteris's hand for almost a full minute.

Primrose shook her head, admiring Miss Carteris's ploy. She glanced at the girl's rivals. They both had tight smiles on their faces.

This time Miss Carteris successfully skipped her stone. She gave a little skip herself and turned back to Oliver. Admiration glowed on her face. "Oh, thank you, Westfell. You're so *clever*."

Oliver's face twitched and Primrose realized that he was very close to laughing out loud. "I believe I have some skill as an instructor," he said pompously.

Primrose swallowed a laugh of her own. She looked at the Misses Warrington and Middleton-Murray, to see how they were taking their rival's machinations. Miss Warrington was still smiling tight-lipped, but Miss Middleton-Murray was giving Miss Carteris a startlingly venomous look.

Primrose lost the urge to laugh.

The look was gone in an instant. Miss Middleton-Murray smiled sweetly at Miss Carteris. "Well, done," she said, and then she clapped her hands together as if an idea had occurred to her. "Let's have a competition, the four of us. How about at the jetty?"

This idea was instantly taken up, and the foursome departed for the jetty. After a moment, Primrose climbed to her feet. The malice in Miss Middleton-Murray's gaze had been disturbing.

She followed Oliver and the would-be duchesses to the little jetty and stood in the shade of the willows, watching, while they chattered and laughed. Miss Middleton-Murray wanted to shove Miss Carteris into the water—Primrose could *see* it in every line of her body—but she had the wit not to do so; instead, she was everything that was sweet and lovely and charming. She commiserated with Miss Warrington on a poor throw, was effusive in her praise of a much better one, and when Miss Carteris threw a stone that skipped eight times, Miss Middleton-Murray clapped in delight. "Well done!" she cried—and slid her foot behind her rival's, so that when Miss Carteris stepped back, flushed with triumph, she stumbled and overbalanced.

It was very neatly done. If Primrose hadn't watched Miss Middleton-Murray spend the past two minutes maneuvering into position she would have thought it an accident.

But it wasn't an accident, and only Oliver's snatch prevented Miss Carteris from tumbling into the water.

"Goodness!" cried Miss Warrington. "Are you all right?"

Miss Carteris was undoubtedly all right, but she recognized a good opportunity when it presented itself. She clung to Oliver, exclaiming that he'd saved her from drowning, and when Oliver tried to disengage himself, she clutched him more tightly, protesting that she felt quite dizzy with shock.

Miss Warrington and Miss Middleton-Murray fluttered around her, each trying to outdo the other in solicitude.

"I know what she needs," Oliver proclaimed.

"She needs to sit in the shade and drink a glass of lemonade."

"Yes," Miss Carteris said in a faint voice, gazing up at him. "That's exactly what I need. Only . . . I'm not sure I can walk."

Primrose snorted under her breath.

Oliver knew his rôle. Gallantly, he swung Miss Carteris up into his arms.

Primrose glanced at Miss Middleton-Murray to see her reaction to this turn of events—and glimpsed an expression of such rage that she shivered involuntarily. She hugged her elbows, and stepped back into the shadows under the willows.

Oliver strode from the jetty, his fair burden in his arms. Primrose had a clear view of Miss Carteris's face. She was smiling triumphantly.

CHAPTER 10

The first thing Primrose did when she returned to the house was check on Rhodes. He was lying on his bed, dressed in shirt and breeches, a wet cloth laid over his eyes. His valet, Monsieur Benoît, was reading aloud to him.

The man broke off his reading, stood, and bowed to her. "Lady Primrose." He was a Frenchman, young and olive-skinned and dark-eyed, his English lightly accented.

"How is he?" she asked.

"Much better," Rhodes said, and the valet grimaced slightly, which Primrose took to mean, *Not really*.

She advanced into the room. "May I see?"

The valet put aside the book. He removed the cloth and placed it to soak in a bowl beside the bed.

Primrose understood immediately why the man had grimaced. Rhodes's eyes were swollen and bloodshot. "Do they still itch?" she asked.

"Like the devil." He looked past her and frowned. "Where's Ollie? You didn't leave him on his own, did you?"

"He's surrounded by Carterises right now," Primrose said. "What did Nurse use to ease the inflammation? Can you remember?"

"Of course I can't," Rhodes said. "It was bloody years ago!" And then he said, "Sorry, Prim. Didn't mean to swear."

Primrose waved aside the apology, and watched as Rhodes raised one hand to rub his eyes, caught himself, and lowered it to his side. His jaw clenched, and so did both his hands.

Primrose caught the valet's gaze and nodded at the bowl of water. The man carefully placed the cloth over Rhodes's eyes again.

Rhodes's hands clenched tighter, and then unclenched. He sighed. "Give the Cheevers my apologies, will you? I won't be at dinner tonight."

"Shall I send for an apothecary?" Primrose asked.

"No," Rhodes said. "Don't fuss, Prim. I'll be fine by tomorrow."

"Would you like me to stay with you?"

"No need. Benoît's been reading to me."

"I could dine up here with you," she suggested. "Keep you company."

"No need," Rhodes said again. "I'd rather you kept Ollie company."

Keep him safe, was what Rhodes meant. *Don't let anyone kill him.*

Primrose wanted to tell him that Oliver was quite safe, that she was convinced neither Lord Algernon nor Ninian Dasenby had tried to kill him, but she couldn't discuss that with Rhodes now, not while his valet stood beside the bed, alert and watchful.

❦

Back in her own bedchamber, Primrose locked the door. Rhodes's valet was extremely efficient, but he was also extremely young. He had no more idea how to treat Rhodes's eyes than she did. Therefore, she needed to talk with someone who *did* know what to do.

Primrose clasped her hands together, and pictured her mother's private parlor in Gloucestershire, with its Grecian sofa and rosewood worktable and the hand-painted screen in the corner.

The screen that had been placed there just for her.

She took a deep breath and wished herself there: in her mother's parlor, behind that screen.

An instant later, she was.

There was a dizzying moment of vertigo, when

she felt as if the world had tipped upside down and turned inside out, then everything steadied.

She cautiously peered around the edge of the screen.

The parlor was empty.

Primrose took a moment to refocus her thoughts. She built an image in her mind of her father's study: the shelves of books and ledgers, the desk, the armchair by the fire—and the screen in the darkest corner.

She wished herself there. When she peeked around the screen, she saw a man seated at the desk, head bent, writing swiftly. Frazier Garland, Duke of Sevenash.

◦◦◦

"Rose water," Primrose told Rhodes's valet twenty minutes later. "If you bathe his eyes with rose water, it will help. As will bathing them with cold milk. And you should set some chamomile leaves to steep in boiling water. Once the water's cool you can bathe his eyes with that, too."

"I shall do it at once," the valet said, heading for the door.

Before he reached it, someone knocked. It was Oliver. He posed in the doorway for a moment, chest out-thrust, hand on hip. "I'll have you know that you're looking at the most handsome, most courageous, and most fascinating man in all England."

Rhodes snorted loudly. The valet bit his lip, swallowing a smile.

"Who told you that?" Primrose said dryly. "Miss Carteris?"

"Naturally." He strutted into the chamber, thrusting his chest out even more. "I saved her life, you know."

Primrose waited until the valet had departed, then said, "You are such an idiot, Daisy."

Oliver looked affronted. "A hero," he corrected her. "I'm a *hero*."

Rhodes lifted the cloth covering his eyes. "What the devil are you talking about?"

Primrose told him in a few brief words, while Oliver crossed to the armchair by the fireplace and collapsed into it with a weary, theatrical sigh. "Marry me, Prim," he said. "Save me from Miss Carteris and her compliments."

"You're the hero," she reminded him tartly. "You can save yourself."

Oliver groaned. He tenderly felt his brow. "There are only so many compliments a man can take. I believe my head is ready to explode."

"You are the greatest addle-pate in England," Primrose told him.

"Ah," Oliver said, massaging his temples. "That helped a little. Another one, if you please, Prim."

"Goosecap," Primrose said, severely. "Nodcock. Jingle brains."

"Jingle brains!" Oliver lowered his hands. "Did you just call me a *jingle* brains?"

"What? You think you aren't one?" Despite her best intentions, she was grinning at him.

Oliver grinned back at her. "I know I am," he said, and then he gave a beatific sigh. "Thank you, Prim. I don't know what I'd do without you. I feel as good as new." He sprang up from the armchair, lifted her off her feet, and swung her around in a circle.

"Oliver!" she cried, clutching his shoulders. "Put me down, you great lummox."

"Lummox," he said, approvingly. "Well done, Prim." He lifted her even higher and twirled her around again.

Primrose discovered that she was laughing. No man had ever dared to pick her up before, let alone twirl her. Oliver swung her around again, and she felt—for a moment—as if she was no longer herself but someone much younger and more carefree.

She clutched Oliver's shoulders and looked down into his face, and all of a sudden it became difficult to breathe. Her heart beat faster, and it had nothing to do with the circles, but everything to do with Oliver's warm hands at her waist, his effortless strength, his playfulness, his grin, the laughter in his eyes. Woodland eyes. A little bit green, a little bit brown, with glinting flecks of gold.

It became even more difficult to breathe. Her laugh choked off.

Miss Carteris had been wrong; Oliver wasn't the most handsome man in England—but he was perhaps its most attractive.

"Unhand my sister, you great oaf," Rhodes said. He tossed a pillow at Oliver. It missed.

Oliver set Primrose on her feet and kissed her loudly on each cheek. "Thank you, Prim. You're the perfect antidote to Miss Carteris."

To her annoyance, Primrose felt herself blush. She smoothed her gown with hands that weren't quite steady. "You are abominable," she told him.

"I know," Oliver said cheerfully. He turned to Rhodes. "So, old fellow, are your eyeballs going to burst?" He picked up the pillow from the floor and hurled it at Rhodes with unerring aim.

Rhodes fended it off, snatched up another pillow, and threw it.

It struck Oliver in the chest. He gave a loud "Oof," and staggered back, flinging his arms out. His legs buckled. He collapsed dramatically to the floor.

Primrose considered telling them that they were

behaving like children, but she didn't, because Rhodes was laughing, and the more Rhodes laughed the better. Instead, she left them to it, letting herself out into the corridor. There, she stood for a moment. Her cheeks felt hot.

Oliver had kissed her.

Well, not *kissed* her kissed her, but those two kisses had definitely been more than the brotherly, cousinly, and fatherly pecks she was used to.

She touched first one cheek and then the other, storing the memory carefully away. It might be the only time Oliver ever kissed her.

That thought made something knot painfully in her chest. For the first time in her life she wanted *more*. More than she had. More than she could ever have.

It was a disturbing thought.

Now just wait one moment, Primrose told herself sternly. She was letting both her emotions and her imagination run away with her. She didn't want to *marry* Oliver.

Did she?

Primrose frowned and set off for her own bed-chamber, which was in quite another part of the house, the Cheevers having prudently separated their guests. The bachelors—Rhodes and Oliver, Lord Algernon and Ninian Dasenby—were in the

North wing; the unmarried ladies and their parents were in the South wing. Privately, Primrose had named the wings the low wing and the high wing, because the South wing was two feet higher than the North wing—and *why* had the architect done that? There was no logical reason for it.

She traversed a long gallery hung with paintings, and then a smaller, sunnier one that would be perfect for reading in—it even had deep wing-backed armchairs one could curl up in—and finally reached the South wing. The high wing. There was a short staircase up to it—four steps—which she climbed. At the top, a corridor stretched in both directions. She turned left—and almost bumped into Miss Middleton-Murray.

"Oh," she said, with a start.

"Lady Primrose." Miss Middleton-Murray recoiled slightly, and then caught herself and dipped a demure little curtsy.

"Miss Middleton-Murray," Primrose said coolly, remembering what she'd seen take place on the jetty. She gave a nod of acknowledgment and moved around her.

At the door to her bedchamber, she glanced back. Miss Middleton-Murray was still standing at the top of the stairs. Was she waiting for someone? Miss Carteris?

Primrose remembered the jetty again, and felt a shiver of unease. And then she scolded herself. Miss Middleton-Murray was hardly going to push her rival down the stairs. For one thing, she wasn't stupid. And for another, it wouldn't kill someone to fall down four steps.

⚮

In the privacy of her bedchamber, her reaction to Oliver's kisses seemed quite ridiculous. Two pecks on the cheek and she'd become totty-headed! "Oliver's not the addle-pate," Primrose said aloud. "*I* am."

She crossed to the window and looked down at the rose garden, with its winding paths and dancing fountains, sunny nooks and shady bowers.

And its lovers.

Primrose watched Mr. Dasenby and Miss Cheevers stroll together among the flower beds for a minute and decided that she'd been hasty with the word "lover." A decorous amount of space separated Dasenby and Miss Cheevers from each other. Primrose saw diffidence in the way Dasenby held himself as he spoke, shyness in the way Miss Cheevers replied.

Strange that she'd always thought Ninian Dasenby

was a fop: pretty, but without any substance. Today had taught her otherwise. He had substance. And he was unlike the other Dasenbys. All the Dasenbys she'd ever met had one thing in common: a great deal of self-assurance. Except for Ninian. He didn't have his father's bluff, expansive nature. He didn't have Oliver's lighthearted confidence. He didn't have his dead cousins' arrogance.

He was shy. Almost as shy as Chloé Cheevers. He just hid it better, behind exquisite clothes and an air of elegance.

Primrose watched them stroll, not touching, just talking, and knew that she wasn't witnessing a flirtation, she was witnessing the first tentative steps towards an understanding. Perhaps even a marriage.

She felt a strange painful sensation in her chest, and recognized it for what it was. "Envy," she whispered, her gaze on the two figures far below.

When she'd been Miss Cheevers's age she'd thought it possible she might marry. Now, she knew she probably never would, because she had ideals. Rather high ideals. Perhaps too high.

Her ideals weren't ideals of appearance or fortune or title; they were intellectual ideals. She wanted to marry a great thinker. Someone she could talk to about philosophy and history and science, about life and death and everything in between, about *ideas*.

Which was why her reaction to Oliver's kisses was so ridiculous.

Oliver was *not* a great thinker. No one would call him that, least of all Oliver himself.

Although he did possess a gift: laughter. The ability to be happy and to make those around him happy, and that was—arguably—as important to the world as great thinking was.

CHAPTER 11

*P*rimrose read for the rest of the afternoon. By dinnertime the memory of Oliver's kisses had faded and she was able to tidy it away in her mind as a trivial event. She felt exceedingly calm and rational as she dressed for dinner. When she chose her jewelry she didn't select the diamonds or the pearls, but instead the tiny golden pendant that she'd inherited from her great-great-grandmother, partly because she wasn't trying to outshine anyone or catch anyone's eye, but mostly because she preferred the pendant to anything else.

She looked in on Rhodes on the way down to dinner, and found the valet bathing his eyes with chamomile water. "Ollie already went downstairs," Rhodes said fretfully. Primrose heard his unspoken words—*by himself*—and realized that she hadn't yet had a chance to tell him that Oliver's relatives weren't trying to kill him.

It wasn't something she could discuss in front of the valet, so she merely said, "Then I shall see him down there."

Oliver was indeed in the drawing room. So were most of the other guests. The atmosphere was strangely subdued. Chloé Cheevers's eyes were reddened, as if she'd been crying.

"So dreadful!" Lady Cheevers said, twisting her hands in an agitated manner. She was wearing another turban, this one blue crêpe with pearl tassels.

Lady Warrington gave a melancholy shake of her head. "The poor girl. Such a terrible thing to happen. One should never run down stairs."

Primrose felt a chill of foreboding. "What is it? What's happened?"

"Poor Miss Carteris tripped on the stairs this afternoon."

Primrose's mouth felt suddenly dry with horror. "Is she *dead?*" She searched the drawing room for Miss Middleton-Murray. There she was, seated on the sofa looking solemn.

"Oh, no," Lady Cheevers said, hastily. "Nothing like that, Lady Primrose. But she broke her wrist, the poor dear. Her parents have taken her home."

A smothered look of glee swiftly crossed Miss Middleton-Murray's face—and was just as swiftly gone.

"Was she pushed?" Primrose blurted.

"Pushed?" Lady Cheevers repeated, a sharp note of shock in her voice. "Of course not. She tripped on her hem."

There were four fewer places set at the table, on account of Rhodes and the Carterises. The ladies still outnumbered the men, and Primrose found herself with Lady Warrington to her left.

Fortunately, Lady Warrington was a talker. By the end of the first course, Primrose had ascertained that the stairs Miss Carteris had fallen down were the very same ones Miss Middleton-Murray had been loitering alongside, that the accident had occurred not long after Primrose had seen her loitering, and that Miss Carteris had been alone when it happened.

By the end of the second course, she had learned that Miss Carteris had been on her way downstairs to practice a duet with Miss Middleton-Murray.

"They both have nice enough voices, but I fancy my Emma has the advantage. She has a truly superior talent." Lady Warrington spoke with a kind of smug conceit that made Primrose think of Oliver's posturing earlier. Lady Warrington had even puffed out her chest slightly.

"Emma had the best music tutors, of course. I made certain of that. No young lady can be called accomplished without proficiency in music. I think very poorly of parents who neglect their daughters' musical education. Very poorly, indeed." And then Lady Warrington must have recalled that Primrose wasn't musical, and that she was the daughter of a duke. She turned beetroot red.

Primrose almost disgraced herself by laughing out loud. She bit her lip and wished—quite desperately—that Oliver had heard that comment. *How* he would laugh.

That evening, instead of musical performances, they played card games. Lord and Lady Warrington sat down to silver loo with Lord and Lady Cheevers, and everyone else crowded around a table to play Speculation. Primrose was more interested in the participants than the game itself. She'd never realized it before, but one could tell a great deal about a person's character by observing how they played cards. The Speculation players fell into three distinct groups. There were those who erred on the side of caution, such as Ninian Dasenby; those like Oliver, who were reckless in their play and laughed whether they won or lost; and then there were the ambitious ones, who wanted only to win.

Lord Algernon and Miss Middleton-Murray fell into that latter category. Neither of them liked to lose. Lord Algernon's lips became thinner and Miss Middleton-Murray's laugh sharper.

Primrose excused herself after three games, saying that she wanted to check on Rhodes. Oliver pushed back his chair. "I'll come, too."

Primrose tried to tell him with a look that his relatives weren't trying to kill him and he could use the main staircase without fear of being pushed down it, but if Oliver saw her look, he failed to interpret it correctly.

There was a footman in the corridor. Primrose bit her tongue, holding words back until they reached the vestibule, which was empty except for shadows and candlelight. "Oliver—"

Oliver didn't give her a chance to finish speaking. He caught her elbow and said in a low, fierce voice: "Prim, you need to be careful."

Primrose blinked at him. "Me? Careful?"

He steered her to a shadowy corner and bent his head to whisper in her ear. "Miss Middleton-Murray tripped Miss Carteris on those stairs."

"You *saw* it? Why didn't you say something!"

He shook his head. "I didn't see it, but I'm certain

she did it. I knew she was a harpy the instant I met her."

"I didn't know she was one until this afternoon," Primrose said. "When Miss Carteris almost fell off the jetty . . . it wasn't an accident. Miss Middleton-Murray tripped her."

Oliver frowned. "What do you know about her, Prim? Miss Middleton-Murray?"

"She's Lord Cheevers's goddaughter. I'm guessing her circumstances are somewhat straitened, because the Cheevers were to have sponsored her début this Season. But the measles put an end to that."

"I don't follow."

"As I understand it, the nursery children caught the measles, and then Lady Cheevers and Chloé did, too, and since they couldn't go to London, Miss Middleton-Murray didn't go either. She has to wait until next year."

"Clearly she doesn't want to wait," Oliver said. "She wants to catch a husband now, and she's eliminating her competition."

"Yes." Primrose shivered, thinking of those stairs and Miss Carteris's broken wrist.

Oliver must have felt the shiver. His hand tightened reassuringly on her arm. "Then you'll be careful?"

"There's no need," Primrose said. "She knows I'm not a rival. I'm too old."

Oliver put up his eyebrows. "Old?"

"I'm twenty-seven, Oliver. An ape leader by anyone's reckoning."

He gave a loud snort. "Who's guilty of hyperbole now?"

Primrose ignored this comment. "Miss Middleton-Murray knows you'd never marry me. Everyone knows it."

"Do they?"

"Of course they do!"

"Well, I don't see how they can when *I* don't even know it myself."

Primrose's heart gave a funny little lurch in her chest. "Of course you know it."

"No, I don't." Oliver opened his mouth as if to say more, then shook his head. "That's by the by, Prim. Promise me you'll be careful." He tightened his grip on her elbow, and awareness suddenly blossomed inside her. Awareness of how strong his fingers were, awareness of how close they stood to one another, how alone they were at this moment, how *intimate* it was—the two of them in this shadowy corner of the vestibule, heads bent together, talking in low voices.

On the heels of awareness came a rush of heat. Primrose felt her cheeks grow warm.

Oliver gave her a little shake. "Promise me." His

voice was stern, even a little harsh, and for the first time since he'd returned to England, he sounded like a soldier.

"I promise to be careful," Primrose said. She didn't pull free from his grip, even though she knew she ought to.

They stood in silence for a moment, far too close, Oliver's hand on her arm. She could hear his breathing, smell his scent: sandalwood.

Her heartbeat accelerated. Her imagination took a foolish flight of fancy, telling her that Oliver might lean in to kiss her—

Oliver released her arm and stepped back. "I wish I knew where Miss Carteris fell. I'd like to have a look at those stairs."

"I know which ones they are," Primrose said. She rubbed her elbow. Her skin was warm from his hand.

They looked in on Rhodes, then Primrose showed Oliver the stairs down which Miss Carteris had fallen. Four steps only. An inconsequential number.

But enough to break a wrist.

At the top of the stairs, where Miss Middleton-Murray had loitered, they paused. The corridor was empty, lit by candles in sconces. "My room's that way." Primrose pointed left. "And so are the Carterises' and the Warringtons'. The Middleton-Murrays' rooms are that way." She pointed right, and as she pointed she noticed an alcove she hadn't seen before, meant for statuary but currently vacant. So much for her powers of observation.

"Stay where you are," she said, and walked to the alcove—three strides from the stairs—and stepped into it, tucking herself out of sight. "Can you see me?"

"No," Oliver said.

Primrose came out of the alcove and went back to the top of the stairs. "Miss Carteris tripped. Possibly on her hem, but most likely—"

"On a piece of string," Oliver said.

Primrose nodded, pleased that they had both reached the same conclusion. "If Miss Middleton-Murray was in that alcove holding one end of the string . . ."

"Then the other end must have been tied to this newel post." Oliver crouched and examined the post. It was quite ornate, with beading at the top and bottom. "That's where I'd tie it." He pointed. "Ankle height. And look . . . how convenient: there's a groove in exactly the right place."

Primrose crouched alongside him. They were

so close that their arms brushed. She heard his breathing again, felt his heat, smelled sandalwood. She examined the newel post carefully. Candlelight flickered and shadows wavered. "Is that a scratch?"

Oliver squinted. "Hard to tell in this light."

"It *is* a scratch," Primrose said. "I'd wager she cut the string off with scissors. She wouldn't have had time to untie a knot."

"No." Oliver stood. He stared down the steps, hands on hips. The angle of his jaw was grim.

Primrose stayed where she was, crouching, trying to imagine what had happened. "She tied the string to this post, and let it lie slack along the top step. It would have been practically invisible."

Oliver nodded.

"And then she waited in the alcove for Miss Carteris to come, and pulled it taut."

Oliver nodded again.

"And once Miss Carteris had fallen, she snipped the string off as fast as she could, and made herself scarce."

Oliver nodded a third time.

Primrose thought about it a little more. "You know, if I were to set such a trap . . . I'd do it in advance. Miss Carteris was only fetching some music—she'd have been in her room less than a minute."

Oliver glanced at her.

"I'd tie the string to the post beforehand and tuck the rest out of sight. No one would notice. Why would they? And then, when Miss Carteris went to her room, it would only take a moment to lay out the string and hide in the alcove."

Oliver considered this, his gaze flicking from the post to the alcove, and back. He nodded again.

"There's no proof, of course," Primrose said, standing.

"No. Supposition. But she did it. I can *feel* it. In my gut."

Primrose could feel it, too.

"Prim, you need to be careful. She could do it again. Promise me you'll—"

"I'll check the alcove before I go down the stairs. Every single time. I promise."

Oliver didn't look reassured. He eyed the spot where the string had most likely been tied.

"Don't worry about me," Primrose said. "You're in far more danger than I am. No one's tried to push *me* under a carriage."

Oliver's face twisted into a brief grimace.

"I don't think it was your uncle who pushed you," Primrose told him. "Or Ninian, either."

"Neither do I." He tilted his head and looked at her curiously. "What made you change your mind?"

"I'll tell you tomorrow. We can talk it over with Rhodes."

"All right." Oliver gave a nod. "Night, Prim. And for God's sake, be careful!"

"I will. Good night."

Primrose stood at the top of the short flight of stairs and watched him out of sight.

CHAPTER 12

*W*hen Oliver rapped on Rhodes's door the next morning, he found him wholly recovered. They went down to the breakfast parlor together. "We need to have a talk," Oliver said. "You and me and Prim. After breakfast."

But at breakfast, Cheevers proposed a morning ride for the gentlemen, and when they returned Primrose was nowhere to be found. None of the ladies were. "They're taking a tour of the house," one of the servants informed them, but in a building the size of Cheevers Court, that meant they could be in any one of two hundred rooms.

Therefore, when Ninian sidled up and shyly said he'd like to talk to Oliver and asked whether perhaps they could take a walk in the shrubbery, Oliver agreed. He wondered what Ninian wished to tell him. But Rhodes tagged along, and all Ninian spoke about for twenty minutes was Westfell House and the changes that Oliver could make to it now that he was duke.

Primrose was still absent when they returned from the shrubbery, so when Uncle Algy asked Oliver if he'd like to shoot rabbits, Oliver said yes.

"I'll come, too," Rhodes said.

"Best not to, Lord Thayne," Uncle Algy said. "Your eyes—"

"I'm perfectly recovered," Rhodes said, cheerfully. "And I'll take care to avoid bishop's weed." So come with them he did, sticking extremely close to Oliver, and while Oliver appreciated Rhodes's concern for his safety, it was rather trying. Plus, he had the feeling that Uncle Algy had wanted to talk to him privately.

By the time they had shot a rabbit apiece and given them to the gamekeeper to be delivered to the kitchen, the ladies had returned from their tour. "Where have you been all this time?" Oliver hissed at Primrose as they sat down to luncheon.

"Oh, everywhere! The widow's walk, the conservatory, the State apartments."

Oliver lowered his voice so that Miss Cheevers, seated on his other side, couldn't overhear. "Prim, we need to have that talk with Rhodes about you-know-what. As soon as possible. He's driving me insane."

"I'm going riding after luncheon. How about when I get back? Four o'clock?"

Well, that was annoying. "Who are you riding with?"

"The ladies."

"Can't you skip it?"

"No," Primrose said. "It was my idea. Sorry."

With that Oliver had to be content. Rhodes didn't let him out of his sight the entire afternoon. When Uncle Algy offered to show him the widow's walk, in what was clearly another attempt to speak to Oliver privately, Rhodes insisted on coming, too. The view was superb—out over the estate, the village, and what was left of the ancient forest of Wychwood—but the parapet was low and Rhodes stayed protectively close, not letting Uncle Algy within arm's reach of him. Oliver gritted his teeth and endured. And he endured all the different staircases on the way back down when Rhodes made certain to walk between him and Uncle Algy. It was a relief to reach the ground floor again. He checked his pocket watch. Quarter to three.

At ten to three, Ninian asked if Oliver would like to play a game of billiards, just the two of them. Rhodes tagged along. "To watch the action," he claimed.

Oliver gritted his teeth again. What did Rhodes

think Ninian was going to do? Stab him with the cue?

They were in the billiard room and Oliver was checking his pocket watch for the third time—twenty minutes past three—when the door opened. Uncle Algy poked his head in. "Ah, there you are, Oliver." He advanced into the room with a smile. "I wanted to give you this. Your father had one just like it, and when I saw it I couldn't resist buying it for you."

"This" turned out to be a small snuff box made of tortoiseshell and gold.

Oliver wasn't a snuff taker, but he knew how to be polite. "Thank you, Uncle. It's very handsome."

Uncle Algy beamed, and rocked on his heels. "Go on, try it. It's the sort your father preferred. A mix of Spanish Bran and Macouba."

Oliver was aware of Rhodes stiffening alongside him, and if they'd been alone he would have said, *Jesus Christ, Rhodes, the snuff's not poisoned.* But they weren't alone, so he couldn't.

"May I try it?" Rhodes asked, and Oliver *knew* that if he gave Rhodes the snuff box then Rhodes would somehow manage to empty its contents on the floor.

"And may I try it, too, Cousin?" Ninian asked diffidently, at Oliver's shoulder.

Oliver handed Ninian the snuff box first—which was merely delaying the inevitable. Ninian examined the exterior, then flicked the little catch, fumbling as he did so, managing to open the box *and* drop it at the same time.

Snuff went everywhere.

Oliver rolled his eyes at the ceiling, and then laughed, because really, what else could one do?

Ninian wasn't laughing; he was scarlet with mortification. Uncle Algy wasn't laughing either; he looked furious. Rhodes seemed pleased, though.

"I'm so sorry," Ninian said. "I have a jar of snuff. I'll fill it up for you." He snatched up the box and scurried from the billiard room.

Uncle Algy rang for a footman to sweep up the snuff. The poor man sneezed six times while he did so.

Ninian returned, and gave Oliver the snuff box. "I'm sorry," he said again, still pink with embarrassment. "I'll send to town for your father's mix."

"Don't worry about it," Oliver said. "I'm not a connoisseur. I wouldn't notice the difference."

Rhodes held out his hand. "May I try it?" he asked, and Oliver had a strong feeling of déjà vu.

He handed the snuff box to Rhodes and watched in resignation as Rhodes did exactly what Ninian had done: fumbling with the catch, dropping the snuff box on the floor.

Rhodes didn't go scarlet with mortification, although he made a good attempt of looking embarrassed. And he damned well *should* be embarrassed.

Ninian uttered a squawk of laughter, and then flushed scarlet again—no doubt because he'd just laughed at a marquis. "I'll refill it," he said, bending to pick up the snuff box.

"No, thank you," Oliver said. "I think we've all had enough snuff for one day." He plucked the empty box from Ninian's hand and thrust it into his pocket. "Thank you, Uncle. It's a very thoughtful gift. I shall treasure it." As punctuation to that final sentence, he sneezed.

A few seconds later Rhodes sneezed, too.

And then Ninian.

Uncle Algy didn't sneeze. He smiled tightly.

It was with relief that Oliver spied Primrose in the doorway. "You're back early."

"It's starting to rain." She stepped into the billiard room and wrinkled her nose. "What's that smell?"

"Snuff," Oliver told her. "Excuse us, Uncle, Cousin. Rhodes and I need to talk with Lady Primrose rather urgently."

He took Primrose by the elbow and hurried her from the room. Rhodes followed on their heels.

"If you weren't my best friend, I swear to God I'd murder you," Oliver said, when they finally found somewhere private to talk—which hadn't been easy. They'd tried the library first, but Lady Warrington was reading the latest edition of the *Ladies' Monthly Museum*. The housekeeper was arranging fresh vases of flowers in the drawing room, and footmen were laying the table in the dining room. Miss Warrington was practicing on the pianoforte in the music room. Lady Cheevers and her daughter were in the yellow salon, and Mrs. Middleton-Murray and *her* daughter were in the blue one. Lords Warrington and Cheevers were playing a hand of piquet in the cardroom. Even the breakfast parlor was occupied, by two housemaids polishing teaspoons.

At which point, Oliver had begun to feel rather harassed.

Primrose took charge, leading them across the vestibule (for the third time), past the library again, and the music room, and along a wide corridor. At its end, she threw open a door. "Here."

Oliver stepped into a room that was blessedly empty. He saw a black marble fireplace, walls hung with red damask, and furniture swathed in Holland cloths. His feet sank into deep, plush carpet. He glanced up at the ceiling and saw that it was gilded. "What's this room?" he heard Rhodes ask behind him.

"It's the State reception room."

The door snicked shut.

Privacy, at last.

Oliver swung to face Rhodes, put his hands on his hips, and said, "The snuff was *not* poisoned."

"It could have been."

"Only between the covers of a novel," Oliver said. "And this isn't a novel! It's real life, and in real life snuff is *not* poisoned."

"What on earth are you talking about?" Primrose asked.

"Uncle Algy gave me some snuff, and then Ninian did, too, and both times Rhodes thought it was poisoned!" Oliver flung his arms out on that last word, to give it emphasis.

"It could have been poisoned," Rhodes said stubbornly.

Oliver shook his head. "If you weren't my best friend, I swear to God I'd murder you." He cast himself down on a Holland-covered sofa and said to Primrose: "Tell him what you told me last night, Prim."

"Neither Lord Algernon nor Ninian Dasenby tried to kill Oliver," Primrose said. "I'm certain of it."

"So am I," Oliver said. "So as much as I appreciate you guarding me, Rhodes, you can stop."

Rhodes frowned. "What's your proof?" he asked his sister.

Primrose sat on what was possibly a lyre-backed chair. It was difficult to tell with the Holland cloth over it. "My proof is observation. I watched Ninian very closely yesterday. He hero-worships you, Oliver."

Oliver lifted his brows. "Hero-worships *me*?"

"Yes. So he's not going to murder you. And as for Lord Algernon, you remind him very strongly of your father. He feels a pang every time he looks at you. So he's not going to murder you, either."

Oliver lifted his brows even higher. "A *pang*? He told you that?"

"No. I read between the lines."

"That's all very well, Prim, but it's not proof," Rhodes said. "It's conjecture. And the whole point of coming here was to prove—beyond any doubt—that neither Lord Algernon nor his son wants Ollie dead."

"I'm convinced they don't," Primrose said.

"So am I," Oliver said.

"Well, I'm not," Rhodes said, a bulldog expression on his face. "We need to present them each with a chance to kill you."

"Fine," Oliver said, exasperated. "I'll stand at the top of the main staircase and pretend to be lost in thought and—"

"No," Rhodes said. "No stairs. And nothing with guns, either. It has to be *safe*, Ollie, or I won't have a bar of it."

Oliver considered telling Rhodes to sod off, and then he remembered that Rhodes's wife had died last year and that Rhodes was struggling to cope with that bereavement. And then he thought, *What will it do to him if I do die?* His annoyance evaporated. It suddenly seemed quite important to stay alive, not just for his own sake, but for Rhodes's sake, too.

"I have an idea," Primrose said.

Both he and Rhodes looked at her.

"We want something that could look like an accident, correct?"

"An accident, or a natural death," Rhodes said. "That seems to be the modus operandi."

"Then I suggest we give them the opportunity to drown Oliver in the lake."

"But Ollie can swim."

"He'll be drunk," Primrose said. "Or at least, they'll *think* he's drunk."

Rhodes frowned, and crossed to the sofa and sat beside Oliver. "Tell us your plan."

"My plan is that after dinner, Oliver invites one or the other of them for a stroll down to the lake—to talk privately or something—and he pretends to be extremely drunk and then wanders out to the end of the jetty, and if they *are* trying to kill him—"

"They'll push me in and watch me drown," Oliver finished for her.

"Yes." Primrose ticked off points on her fingers: "It'll be dark; there'd be no witnesses; a drowning would look like an accident; and it's not at all dangerous, because you *won't* be drunk and you *can* swim." She looked from him to Rhodes and back again. "What do you think?"

"I say, let's try it."

Rhodes nodded. "When shall we do it? Tomorrow night?"

"Tonight," Oliver said firmly. "Don't take this the wrong way, Rhodes—you're my closest friend and I love you dearly—but I can do without you sticking to me like a burr and rescuing me from snuff that *isn't* poisoned."

"It might have been poisoned," Rhodes said obstinately.

"We can't do it tonight," Primrose said. "It's raining, and you'd hardly suggest a stroll to the jetty in the rain, would you?"

Oliver reluctantly conceded this truth. "Tomorrow night, then."

CHAPTER 13

In the morning, it was still raining. Oliver stared at the rivulets coursing down his window and told himself that the rain would stop by nightfall—and then he took a deep breath and went next door to pick up his self-appointed protector before going down to breakfast.

But not only was Rhodes still in bed, he had a cloth over his eyes and a very worried-looking valet hovering at his bedside.

Oliver looked at the valet's face and felt a twinge of foreboding. "How bad is it?"

The valet grimaced. "Worse than before, Your Grace."

"But how can that be? He was perfectly all right when he went to bed."

The valet gave a very French shrug. "We do not know why, Your Grace."

Oliver crossed to the bed. "So, I guess you won't be coming down to breakfast, old fellow?" It should have been a relief—no Rhodes shadowing his every move today—but it wasn't.

"No," Rhodes said. His voice sounded a little husky.

Oliver sat carefully on the edge of the bed. "May I see?"

The valet lifted off the cloth.

Oliver stared, aghast. The man had been correct; it was worse than before. Rhodes's eyelids were swollen almost closed. His eyes—what little could be seen of them—were terribly bloodshot and his cheeks were flushed, as if he had a fever.

"Jesus, Rhodes . . ." he said helplessly. He looked at the valet, and saw his own anxiousness reflected in the man's face.

"Looks worse than it is," Rhodes said, with that worryingly husky edge to his voice, as if his throat was swollen, too. "I'll be fine by luncheon."

"I think you should leave here," Oliver said. "Today."

"Don't be ridiculous," Rhodes said. "Benoît, the cloth, please . . ."

The valet carefully laid the dripping cloth over Rhodes's eyes again. Rhodes seemed to breathe a sigh of relief. Oliver saw his shoulders relax slightly against the propped-up pillows.

"You need to see an apothecary."

"I have sent for one," the valet said.

"Well, then . . ." Oliver didn't know what else to do. He felt quite helpless, and it wasn't a sensation he liked. "I'll, um, I guess I'll go down to breakfast, then."

"Ollie . . ." Rhodes reached out blindly.

Oliver took his hand.

Rhodes gripped it tightly, almost painfully. "Promise me you'll be careful."

"I promise," Oliver said. "No guns, no snuff, no private talks with my uncle or cousin, and I'll look over my shoulder any time I'm near a staircase. I shall be as cautious as a fox is when the pack's let loose." And then he remembered the valet standing silently on the other side of the bed. He glanced at the man. The valet's face was perfectly blank. If he thought Oliver's words odd, he wasn't showing it.

After breakfast he went back upstairs with Primrose to check on Rhodes. The valet answered their knock, but didn't invite them in. "The apothecary is cupping his lordship. "

"Cupping?" Primrose tried to peer past him. "Is that necessary?"

"He believes it will help," the valet said.

"We'll come back later," Oliver said.

Primrose frowned. "But—"

Oliver took her elbow and drew her away. "Later, Prim. Give him some privacy."

They went back downstairs, where Oliver was almost immediately captured by the Misses Warrington and Middleton-Murray. "Do you sing, Westfell?" Miss Warrington asked, tilting her bosom at him, and Miss Middleton-Murray looked up at him through her eyelashes and said, "I'm certain you must, Westfell. You do everything so well!"

The opportunity was too tempting to resist. Oliver puffed out his chest. "I fancy I sing very well."

"Then let us practice some duets," Miss Warrington said, and Miss Middleton-Murray smiled at him, displaying her dimples, and together they whisked him off to the music room.

It was a trap, and he'd fallen right into it, but as traps went it wasn't too painful. Oliver rather enjoyed singing, and while Miss Middleton-Murray was merely a good singer, Miss Warrington was a superb one. His baritone and her contralto blended perfectly. Even Miss Middleton-Murray exclaimed over it. "Oh, how wonderful you sound together! You must sing another one. I'll play for you." And she sat at the pianoforte, smiling brightly, a dangerous glint in her eyes.

They swiftly gathered an audience. The older ladies were first: Cheevers, Warrington, and Middleton-Murray. Ninian slipped into the room with Miss Cheevers. Uncle Algy was next, and Lords Cheevers and Warrington. Even Primrose came to listen.

Miss Warrington enjoyed the attention. She blushed prettily and managed to stand closer to Oliver with every song that they sang. By the time they were on their third duet, her arm was brushing his. She didn't attempt to tilt her bosom at him as they sang. Her bosom wasn't the drawcard right now; her mouth was—those plump, supple lips, that deft pink tongue, those neat, white teeth. Oliver had never given it any thought before, but he realized now that singing exposed more of a woman's mouth than any other activity he could think of. Except perhaps sex.

"Bravo!" their audience cried, and, "Encore."

Miss Warrington suggested *Scarborough Fair.* Oliver braced himself for what he guessed was to come.

He wasn't wrong. Miss Warrington turned the ballad into something intimate between the two of them. "He shall be a true love of mine," she sang in her throbbing contralto, her eyes fixed adoringly on his face, her mouth shaping each word lovingly, the glimpses of her teeth and tongue full of promise.

"They sound as if they were made for one another," Lady Warrington exclaimed at the end of the song. "A perfect match!"

"Oh, Mother, don't," Miss Warrington said, blushing, and not quite managing to hide a smug smile.

Oliver couldn't roll his eyes, given that almost everyone in the room was looking at him, but he glanced at Primrose and to his astonishment, *she* rolled her eyes. He barked out a surprised laugh, and hastily turned the sound into a cough.

"Are you all right, Westfell?" Miss Warrington asked, laying her hand solicitously on his arm.

"Too much singing, I think," Oliver said, stepping back and politely freeing himself from her touch. He glanced at Miss Middleton-Murray, who'd been playing for them all this while. She was smiling, but he didn't like the cold glitter of her eyes. It made him think of Miss Carteris's not-so-accidental tumble down the stairs.

His urge to laugh was abruptly quenched. He crossed to the pianoforte and leaned one elbow on it, directing an appreciative smile at Miss Middleton-Murray. "Thank you for your accompaniment. We shouldn't have sounded half so good without you playing for us."

Miss Middleton-Murray accepted this compliment with a demur and a very pretty appearance of modesty, but the cold, angry glitter of her eyes didn't abate.

Oliver looked for Primrose again. He urgently needed to talk with her—and had indeed got two paces towards her when Lady Warrington detained him again, gushing praise at him as if she were a fountain that spouted words instead of water. Oliver nodded and smiled and tried to sidle away from her, aware that the music room was slowly emptying. He glanced at the pianoforte and discovered that Miss Middleton-Murray had abandoned her seat there. In fact, she was no longer in the room.

He turned his head, searching for Primrose. She was edging towards the door.

Oliver experienced a feeling close to panic. He almost opened his mouth and bellowed *Prim! Wait!* but fortunately Miss Cheevers said something to her, and Primrose paused to reply.

"Yes . . . well . . ." he said to Lady Warrington, inching sideways.

But Lady Warrington was in full spate. She inched with him, still talking, while Primrose finished speaking to Miss Cheevers, stepped towards the door, and gave a last glance over her shoulder.

Oliver caught her gaze and gave her the most significant look he was capable of, trying to shout with his eyes.

It worked. Primrose halted and raised her brows slightly in a silent *What?*

He couldn't mouth *I need to talk with you,* not while Lady Warrington was speaking to him. Instead, he lifted his hand and stroked his nose. It was a signal he and Rhodes had used at school when they had secrets to tell one another. He hoped Rhodes had shared the signal with Primrose. "Your daughter is very gifted," he told Lady Warrington at random. "If you'll excuse me . . ."

But the compliment set Lady Warrington gushing again. Now she was talking enough for two fountains. Oliver listened to her helplessly, while Primrose quirked her eyebrows at him. It appeared that Rhodes had *not* shared that signal with her.

He tried one more time, stroking his nose at Primrose—*I need to talk to you*—while simultaneously listening to Lady Warrington and edging towards the door.

Primrose frowned. After a moment, she rubbed her own nose with her fingers, as if trying to remove a smudge.

Oliver almost shook his head in frustration. He stroked his nose very deliberately again. Lady Warrington frowned at him. Primrose frowned at him, too. She pulled out her handkerchief and applied it to the end of her nose.

Oliver gave up trying to be polite. "Excuse me," he told Lady Warrington, cutting across what she was saying. "I really must speak with Lady Primrose."

He left Lady Warrington open-mouthed. It was unpardonably rude of him, but damn it, he was a duke now; he could be rude to a viscountess if the situation demanded, and this situation bloody well did. He crossed the music room in four strides, took Primrose by the elbow, and hurried her out the door.

"What's wrong with my nose?" Primrose demanded.

"Nothing. I need to speak with you. Privately. As soon as possible."

Her eyebrows lifted again. "Very well. Where?"

That was the question: where? He saw Lord Warrington disappear into the library, Mrs. Middleton-Murray into the yellow salon, and Lady Cheevers and Miss Cheevers into the blue one, followed a few seconds later by Ninian.

"The State apartments," he said. "In five minutes. *Don't* go upstairs first."

"All right," Primrose said, folding up her handkerchief and placing it in her pocket.

Oliver gave a curt, relieved nod, and watched her disappear down the corridor.

"Oliver," someone said at his elbow.

Oliver started, and looked around. His uncle stood there, smiling genially.

"Quite a voice you have. Reminds me of your father."

"Thank you," Oliver said.

"Would you like a game of piquet? Just the two of us?"

"I'm sorry, Uncle, but I can't right now. Perhaps later?"

Uncle Algy's smile fell, and Oliver felt a stab of guilt, but only a very little one. Talking to Primrose was more important than anything else right now, and besides, if he played piquet with Uncle Algy he'd be breaking his promise to Rhodes. "If you'll excuse me, Uncle?"

⁂

Two minutes later, Oliver stepped into the State reception room and closed the door quietly behind him. The room was empty except for its shrouded furniture. There was a faint smell of stale lavender, a scent he hadn't noticed the first time he'd been here, full of indignation at Rhodes's protectiveness.

Oliver paced, his feet sinking into the carpet. And paced. And paced. Doors stood open on either side of the room, leading to further chambers.

He peeked into the one on the left. It was a sitting room, with red damask on the walls and a black marble fireplace. It, too, had an open door, which led to a dressing room—also with red damask and black marble—and beyond that was the bedchamber. "Good God," Oliver said involuntarily. Not because of the four-poster bed beneath its Holland cloth, but because of the raised dais with the gilded columns upon which it stood.

Faintly, he heard a door open and close somewhere in the State apartments.

Oliver retraced his steps rapidly and found Primrose standing in the middle of the reception room. "Where have you *been*?" he said. "Tell me you didn't go upstairs."

"You said five minutes," Primrose said. "And it's been five minutes exactly. What is it? What's so important?"

"Miss Middleton-Murray," Oliver said. "I think she's—" He broke off and listened intently. Were those footsteps in the corridor?

Primrose turned her head towards the door. She'd heard it, too.

Oliver took Primrose's hand and dragged her into the next room, and then the next. They tiptoed hastily, the carpet hushing their steps. An enormous lacquered *chinoiserie* screen stood in one corner of the dressing room, red and black dragons cavorting across its panels. He drew Primrose hastily behind it.

They waited in silence while Oliver counted out a minute in his head. He heard no doors open or close, heard no footsteps. They were alone. When the minute was up, he realized he was still holding Primrose's hand. It felt so nice that he decided not to let go. Instead, he led her out from behind the screen and over to a Holland-covered sofa.

"What is it, Oliver?" Primrose asked, as they sat side by side.

"Miss Middleton-Murray."

"What about her?"

"I think she's going to try her trick with the string again. You need to be careful."

Primrose looked startled. "But what have I done to her?"

"Not you; Miss Warrington. But you use the same stairs and you could trip on a string just as easily as she could, and—"

Primrose winced. "Oliver, my hand."

Oliver relaxed his grip from crushing to firm. "Prim, you have to be careful. On any stairs. On *all* stairs. Promise me!"

"I promise," she said. "As long as you're careful, too."

"I'm always careful."

Primrose was silent for a moment, frowning. "If it *is* true . . . if she's going to do it again . . . she must be stopped."

"Yes."

"How could anyone think of such a thing, let alone *do* it? And not once, but twice!"

"If it's not right, don't do it," Oliver said, under his breath.

He didn't think he'd spoken loudly enough for Primrose to hear, but clearly she had, because she stared at him as if he'd sprouted a unicorn's horn in the middle of his forehead.

"What?" Oliver said.

"If it's not right, don't do it. If it's not true, don't say it."

"I agree," Oliver said.

"You read Marcus Aurelius?"

Oliver had a very well-thumbed copy of Aurelius, but he enjoyed teasing Primrose, so he said, "Who?"

"Marcus Aurelius. The Roman Emperor."

Oliver looked as blank as he could.

"You must have studied him at school," Primrose said, a note of exasperation entering her voice. "'If it's not right, don't do it. If it's not true, don't say it.' That's something he wrote."

"Aurelius?" Oliver wrinkled his brow. "Isn't he the fellow who wrote about vegetables?"

Primrose's brow wrinkled, too. "What?"

"'Is your cucumber bitter? Throw it away.' Always thought that was an odd thing to write down for posterity."

"It was a lesson in philosophy," Primrose told him, crossly. "He was illustrating a point."

Oliver grinned at her. "I know. Don't glare at me." He laughed at her expression.

"You are an idiot, Daisy," she said, trying to tug her hand free from his grip.

"A jingle brains," he agreed, not letting her hand go.

"Oliver," she said, tugging harder. "If someone should come in and see us—"

"You'd be ruined," Oliver told her cheerfully. "Utterly and absolutely ruined. Caught in an assignation with a duke! Why, we'd have to marry to save your reputation." He widened his eyes at her. "Now, that's a thought, Prim. Marry me. Save me from Lady Warrington and her warbling daughter."

"You are dreadful, Oliver! It would serve you right if I said yes."

He grinned at her. "I think what you meant to say was that it would suit me well if you said yes."

"Suit you? Of course not. It wouldn't suit either of us!"

"Wouldn't it?" Oliver pretended to consider this

statement for several seconds, and then shook his head. "I disagree. I think it might suit me."

Primrose blushed faintly. "Well, it wouldn't suit me!" She tried to tug her hand free again. "Do be serious, Oliver. I'm the last person you'd wish to marry."

"No, that would be Miss Middleton-Murray."

"The second to last, then," Primrose said, looking exasperated again.

"No, not that either." In fact, if he seriously considered the matter—which he hadn't until now—then Primrose Garland was probably at the top of the list of ladies he'd like to marry. Setting her physical attributes aside—which were manifold—he enjoyed her company more than any other female he knew. She was intelligent and interesting and fun to talk with—and most importantly of all, she treated him as Oliver Dasenby, not the Duke of Westfell.

He looked at her with fresh eyes. In fact, it felt as if this was the first time he'd ever looked at her properly. Not as Rhodes's sister, not as a childhood friend, but as a woman in her own right.

Her hand was warm in his, and they were seated so closely together that he caught the faint scent of orange blossom. For some reason that scent made his pulse speed up. Primrose really was *very* attractive. The soft lips, that slender waist, those plump breasts. The ash-blonde hair and cool blue eyes. That sharp brain and tart tongue.

He wondered what her mouth tasted like.

Primrose's eyes narrowed. "Why are you looking at me like that?"

Oliver had no idea what his expression was, but he knew what it meant: he wanted to kiss her. He, Oliver Dasenby, wanted to kiss prickly Primrose Garland.

He said that last bit out loud. "Prickly Primrose."

Primrose flushed again and looked away from him. She tugged her hand more sharply. "Do let go of me, Oliver."

"It wasn't an insult." He reached out with his free hand and touched her cheek softly. Her skin was as smooth and warm as he'd thought it would be. "I like your prickles."

Primrose batted his hand away. "Let *go* of me, Oliver. If anyone saw us like this . . ."

He released her. "So *prim*, Primrose," he chided.

"Sensible," she corrected him, standing hastily, smoothing her gown. "Honestly, Oliver, do you *want* us to have to get married?"

Have to get married? No. But marry? Possibly.

"*Do* come along. We need to check that staircase. And I want to look in on my brother."

His thoughts changed track abruptly. Good God,

how had he forgotten Miss Middleton-Murray? And Rhodes?

Oliver pushed to his feet and headed for the door. "Hurry up, Prim. Stop dawdling." He glanced back over his shoulder and grinned at her expression. "You really shouldn't pull faces. Not ladylike at all."

CHAPTER 14

They knocked on Rhodes's door. After a moment, the valet opened it. He didn't stand back to let them enter; instead he laid one finger to his lips.

"He's asleep?" Primrose whispered.

The man nodded, and stepped out into the corridor.

"What did the apothecary say?" Oliver asked in a low voice. "Did he have any idea what's causing it? How to stop it happening?"

"No, sir."

"Had he no suggestions?" Primrose asked. "Nothing at all?"

"Rosewater or milk, which we are already using." The valet gave a helpless shrug.

"There's one very simple solution," Oliver said. "Leave this place."

The valet met his eyes. "I agree, Your Grace. But his lordship refuses to consider it."

"If he's not better tomorrow, he won't have any choice in the matter," Oliver said.

The valet looked relieved. "Thank you, sir." He retreated back into the bedchamber and closed the door.

Oliver frowned at those blank wooden panels. He didn't like this. He didn't like it at all.

Beside him, Primrose gave a faint sigh.

Oliver knew her so well that his ears caught the tone of that exhalation: not exasperation, but worry. He looked at her, and saw that she was biting her lower lip.

"He'll be all right." Oliver put an arm around her shoulders and hugged her briefly.

She gave him a wan smile.

"If he's no better tomorrow, we'll take him to Gloucestershire. I promise. I'll tie him up in his bedsheets and sling him over my shoulder, like a villain making off with an heiress."

She gave a little choke of laughter. "I'd like to see you try."

Oliver grinned at her. "Be fun, wouldn't it?"

"Yes." And then she sobered. "Let's check those stairs."

They examined the stairs very carefully. No string had been knotted around the base of the newel post and carefully tucked out of sight, but that didn't allay Oliver's fears. There was a feeling in his belly—a clenching of his innards—that he'd only ever experienced in India: the natural apprehension one felt before a battle. No battle loomed in his future, but he was still afraid.

If Primrose tripped on these stairs . . .

Four steps was enough to break a bone—as Miss Carteris had proven.

Primrose wasn't afraid, though. "I'll check again after lunch," she said, as they headed back to the ground floor.

"*We'll* check," he said.

"Oliver, if you keep coming up here with me, people will start talking."

"I don't care." It wasn't quite the truth. While he didn't give a damn about his own reputation, he *did* care about Primrose's—but not enough to risk her falling down those stairs.

"I'm not helpless," she said, that familiar edge of exasperation in her voice. "Or incompetent. Or blind. I'll check the alcove every time I go downstairs, and if Miss Middleton-Murray is in there, I'll *see* her."

"I know," Oliver said. "But it worries me all the same." He put an arm around her shoulders for the second time that day and gave her a hug. "Promise me you won't come up here alone unless you absolutely have to, and that if you *are* alone you'll be very, *very* careful."

Primrose blew out her breath, and his ears told him that she wasn't as exasperated as she was pretending to be. "All right. But you need to be careful, too."

"I'm always careful." Oliver removed his arm, although he would have preferred not to. They descended another flight of stairs. As they reached the vestibule, he remembered something. "Oh, Prim, when I do this—" he stroked his nose, "—it means that I need to speak with you as soon as possible. In the State apartments."

Her eyebrows lifted and her chin tilted, so that she was looking down her nose at him even though she was shorter than him. "Or you could just *tell* me that you need to talk to me."

Oliver grinned at her. "That's a very governess look, Prim."

Primrose flushed and stopped looking down her nose at him. "*Or* you could just tell me," she said again, tartly.

"Secret signals are more fun."

Primrose rolled her eyes.

"What?" Oliver said, spreading his hands. "It's true!"

Oliver ate luncheon surrounded by young ladies. Miss Warrington very skillfully built on her success in the music room. She coupled their names together whenever she spoke—*when Westfell and I sang together*—*when Westfell and I chose our songs*—managing to imply that a bond had grown between the two of them. Then she reinforced this by sending him private, smiling glances, by speaking to him in a low voice just for the two of them, and, in what could only be an act of magic, by somehow managing to sit closer to him without moving either her place setting or her chair.

Oliver was fully aware of the appearance that he and Miss Warrington presented to everyone else at the table: familiarity, togetherness, intimacy.

Ordinarily, he would have awarded Miss Warrington high points for such tactics, but today he didn't. Today, he found himself watching Miss Middleton-Murray carefully, his foreboding growing as her dimples became more pronounced and her eyes sparkled more brightly.

Every time Miss Warrington said *Westfell and I*, he hid a wince. Every time she sent him one of those glances, he wanted to cringe. Every time she said something for his ears alone, he grimaced internally.

At the close of the meal Oliver caught Primrose's eye and stroked his nose imperatively, then he pushed back his chair and headed for the door.

Miss Warrington detained him with a hand on his arm. "Westfell," she said, gazing up at him through her lashes. "Have you seen the conservatory yet? It's quite magnificent."

"Perhaps later," Oliver said, disengaging his arm. He took two strides towards the door.

"I say, Oliver."

He stopped. "Yes, Uncle?"

"How about that hand of piquet? Not much else one can do in this rain."

"I'm sorry, Uncle, I can't right now."

He had almost reached the door when someone said at his elbow, "Cousin . . ."

He halted again. "What is it, Ninian?"

"Could I possibly have a word with you?"

Oliver looked more closely at his cousin. There were two anxious creases on Ninian's brow and his hands were performing a nervous little movement, as if he wanted to wring them but was restraining himself.

"I'm sorry, Ninian, I can't right now."

The creases on Ninian's brow multiplied.

Oliver reached out and gripped his cousin's shoulder and gave it a reassuring squeeze. "Later. I promise."

❦

Oliver let himself quietly into the State apartments. The red-and-black reception room was empty, as were the sitting room, the dressing room, and the bedchamber. Rain streamed down the windowpanes. Even though it was early afternoon, it was as dark as if it were twilight. Shadows were thick in the corners and if he'd had a timorous disposition he wouldn't have wished to be alone here, but he wasn't timorous; he was impatient.

He was checking his pocket watch for the fifth time when he finally heard a door open and close. A few moments later, Primrose joined him in the State dressing room.

"Ten minutes," Oliver told her, waving the pocket watch in front of her face. "*Where have you been?*"

Primrose did that trick of looking down her nose while looking up at him. "If you must know, I had to pluck a rose."

As euphemisms went, "pluck a rose" was one of

the most ridiculous Oliver had ever heard. Whoever the person was who'd first equated picking roses to using a chamber pot, he—or she—had to have been a complete idiot.

"Oh." Oliver jammed the watch back into his pocket—and then froze in mid-motion. "You didn't go up to your room, did you?"

Primrose stared at him for a moment, and then said, "Oliver, did no one teach you *any* manners?"

He felt himself flush—and ignored it. "Tell me you didn't go up to your room."

"Of course I went up to my room."

Oliver groaned out loud, and then swung away from her, clutching his hair with his hands.

"You should have been an actor," Primrose observed. "Such theatrics."

Oliver turned back to her and released his death grip on his hair. "It's not theatrics! Did you not *see* what happened at luncheon?"

"I saw several things at luncheon," Primrose said, seating herself on the Holland-covered sofa. "To which are you referring?"

"Miss Warrington, of course! Didn't you see what she did?"

"I saw her eat," Primrose said. "Two slices of ham, three tarts, and some grapes."

"She did a lot more than *eat*." Oliver paced to

the window and back again. "She made it look as if there's a bond between us."

Primrose opened her mouth.

He silenced her with a pointed finger. "And don't tell me I'm imagining it, because I'm *not.*"

"I wasn't intending to," Primrose said, mildly. "I was going to say that I thought she laid it on rather thickly."

Oliver snorted. "'Westfell and I,'" he mimicked.

Primrose laughed, and then abruptly sobered. "Miss Middleton-Murray wasn't pleased."

"No."

"Is that why you wished to talk to me?"

"Of course it is!" He crossed to the sofa and sat beside her. "I wanted to warn you. Good God, Prim, you have to be careful!"

"Thank you, but the warning is unnecessary."

"I'm going to check that staircase every hour," Oliver said grimly.

Primrose looked down at her lap, smoothed the muslin gown, and looked back at him. "Do you think we should tell someone?"

"Who? Lord and Lady Cheevers? They wouldn't believe it. No one would!"

"Then perhaps we should speak to Miss Middleton-Murray herself. Tell her we've guessed about the stairs, that we're watching her. Warn her off."

Oliver considered this for a long moment, and then said slowly, "My fear is that if we do that, she may try something else instead. Something we won't notice until it's too late."

"Or she might just give up."

"Possibly." Oliver conceded this with a shrug, and then admitted, "I want to catch her red-handed."

"Do you think that's possible?"

"I think we've got a good chance." He pushed to his feet. "I'm going to check those stairs again."

"I've just checked them," Primrose said. "There's nothing out of the ordinary. But if you don't trust my judgment . . ."

Oliver hesitated. He *did* trust Primrose's judgment. And her intelligence. He sat again. "We'll both check. As often as we can. We should have a signal for that. Something unobtrusive." He thought for a moment, and touched one corner of his eye with a fingertip. "This means I'm going to check the stairs."

Primrose nodded.

"And this means that I've checked them and they're safe." He gave her a thumbs up.

"That's a gladiatorial gesture," Primrose said.

"I know." He smiled at her. Tart, bookish Primrose Garland.

She didn't look bookish right now, seated alongside him on the sofa. In this shadowy room she looked otherworldly—her hair like spun silver, skin as pale as moonlight, eyes dark and luminous.

Otherworldly, and beautiful.

The impulse to kiss her was suddenly almost overwhelming.

Oliver stared at her, and listened to his heart beat out the seconds. What would Primrose do if he kissed her? Would she slap him? Kiss him back?

There was only one way to find out.

The Romans had a lot of quotes, and there was one for moments like this: *Fortuna audaces iuvat.* Fortune favors the bold.

Oliver reached for Primrose's chin, tipped it up, bent his head, and kissed her, a brief touch of his lips to hers.

Primrose stiffened. He heard her breath catch. She put one hand on his chest, but didn't push him away.

He waited a moment—two seconds, three seconds, four—and then kissed her again, letting his mouth linger this time, learning the contours of her lips, their smoothness, their taste, and it appeared that fortune *did* favor the bold, because instead of slapping him, Primrose parted her lips.

She'd never kissed anyone before, that much was obvious, but that was all right because Oliver had more than enough experience for the two of them.

He gathered her a little closer, cupping her nape with one hand, sliding his fingers into her silky hair, tilting her head just so, and set himself to the task of introducing Lady Primrose Garland to the art of kissing. He kept it teasing and light, letting her feel the gentle nip of his teeth on her lower lip, the tickling flicker of his tongue, and then, when she still didn't pull away, he deepened the kiss, daring to delve into her tart, sharp-tongued mouth, but her mouth wasn't tart at all, and her tongue was soft, not sharp.

Oliver stifled a low groan of pleasure. Heat flushed through him. He wanted to gather Primrose closer, to crush her to him, to plunder that sweet mouth.

Slow down, Dasenby, he told himself. *She's never kissed anyone before.*

But it was hard to remember that when Primrose was tentatively kissing him back and her mouth matched his perfectly and arousal was gathering in his blood.

Despite his best intentions, Oliver lost control of the kiss. He didn't notice the exact instant it happened; all he knew was that what had been slow and gentle had somehow become something much more urgent. Primrose was still the student and he still the master, but now *she* was in his mouth, now *she* was tasting him.

The State dressing room, with its Holland-covered sofa and rain-drenched windows, ceased to exist. His world narrowed to Primrose: her soft lips, her silky hair wrapped around his fingers, her hands clutching his lapels, her body pressing close. They kissed with single-minded focus. Hungry kisses. Intimate kisses. Kisses that didn't stop until they were both gasping for breath.

Oliver reluctantly dragged his mouth from hers. His heart was beating loud and fast and his head felt as if it was spinning. He stared down at Primrose. He'd known her his entire life, and yet in this moment she seemed like a stranger, someone passionate and intoxicating and full of secrets, someone exciting, someone he wanted to get to know better. A *lot* better.

Primrose disengaged herself and sat back. She touched her fingers to her mouth. She looked as confused as he felt. What the devil had just happened between them? Had he and Primrose really kissed like that? What did it mean?

"Why did you do that?" she asked, sounding breathless and dazed and not at all like herself.

Oliver's first instinct was to joke. It was usually his first instinct: to joke. But if he said something flippant—*It seemed like a good way to pass a rainy afternoon,* for example—he was afraid he'd offend

169

her, or worse, hurt her, and that was the last thing he wanted. It had been her first kiss, after all.

Primrose's first kiss.

All of a sudden what they'd just done seemed a *lot* more significant.

Was Primrose expecting him to propose?

Oliver felt a faint twinge of panic—and then he remembered what she'd told him this morning: *It wouldn't suit me!* Which meant that she didn't want to marry him, and if he did propose right now—which was what a gentleman ought to do after kissing an innocent and well-bred young lady—she would refuse him.

Why did that make him feel disappointed, not relieved?

"Why, Oliver?" she asked again.

Primrose had called him a jingle brains before, and right now that was exactly what he felt like. His thoughts were scrambled. He had absolutely no idea how to answer her question. With a joke? With the truth? What was the truth?

"Why did you kiss me?" she asked, and her voice had that familiar, tart edge to it this time. Hearing it steadied him.

"Because I wanted to," Oliver said, and then he said, cautiously, "Do you mind? Are you angry?"

Primrose looked away from him, towards the

lacquered screen looming in the corner. "No," she said. "I'm not angry."

His heart gave a leap of relief. "Then you won't mind if we do it again?" he said, and then hastily: "That was a joke, Prim." And then he said, less hastily, "Unless you don't want it to be a joke?"

Primrose looked at him, and Oliver found himself holding his breath.

"I don't mind," she said, after what seemed like a very long time.

"You don't mind if we do it again?" he said, just to make certain that they were both on the same page.

Despite the dim light, he saw a blush climb her cheeks. "I don't mind," Primrose said, her gaze avoiding his. "But not now." She rose. "If you'll excuse me, I want to see if Rhodes is awake."

"Of course."

Primrose walked briskly from the room. In fact, he thought she was trying not to run. After a moment, he heard the door in the reception room open and then close.

Oliver stayed where he was, on the sofa. He could taste Primrose in his mouth, could feel the impression of her lips on his. Arousal still throbbed in his blood.

He'd been right this morning when he'd thought they would suit one another.

CHAPTER 15

*O*liver did check the stairs again. Not because he didn't trust Primrose, but because he didn't trust Miss Middleton-Murray. Then he went to Rhodes's bedchamber, where he found Primrose.

For a moment it was awkward—he didn't know quite where to look, didn't know quite how to talk to her, and he could tell she felt the same way—and then the moment passed and everything was all right between them again—tart Primrose Garland and jingle-brained Oliver Dasenby—and when he teased her and she called him a fiddle-faddle fellow, Oliver laughed out loud in relief.

After ten minutes, Primrose excused herself. Oliver gave her a discreet thumbs up, telling her he'd checked the stairs, and she acknowledged this with an infinitesimal nod.

He spent the next half hour talking to Rhodes,

then went downstairs with an obligatory glance over his shoulder. No one lurked behind him waiting to push him to his death, but remembering that someone had tried to—twice—deflated his mood.

Someone, somewhere, wanted him dead.

Oliver descended the stairs slowly, meditatively.

It was still raining. Oliver found most of the ladies in the blue salon—and backed away from the door before they noticed him. The men had congregated in the library. It was a magnificent room, the ceiling fully thirty feet high, with a gallery giving access to the books on the upper level—a gallery that Oliver knew Rhodes would forbid him to set foot on, because it was perfect for accidental-but-fatal falls.

"There you are," Uncle Algy said, cheerfully. "I was about to send out a search party for you."

"I've been with Thayne."

"How is he?" Lord Cheevers asked, with a host's solicitousness.

Oliver grimaced. "Not good. He won't be joining us for dinner."

Uncle Algy's face folded into sympathetic lines. "How unfortunate," he said. Then he gave a sudden smile. "I say, would you all like some Madeira? I brought a special bottle with me."

There was a stir of interest, and Uncle Algy went to fetch his Madeira. "Ten minutes," he promised.

It was more like twenty minutes, not that anyone minded—what was there to do on a rainy day anyway? They gathered in the cardroom, a more masculine room than the library, with dark paneling and shield-back chairs and decanters lined up on the sideboard.

Uncle Algy had already poured Madeira into five crystal glasses. "Fifty-five years old," he said, showing them the bottle. "Same vintage as me. A good year." He gave his booming laugh.

"Let's have a game of cards while we drink," Lord Cheevers suggested. "Vingt-et-un, anyone?"

They took their places at the table. Ninian chose the seat to Oliver's right. He seemed rather nervous, shifting in his chair, fidgeting with his cuffs.

Cheevers produced a pack of cards and dealt, while Uncle Algy handed out the glasses of Madeira. He'd poured generously, and the most generous glass of all, filled almost to the brim, was Oliver's. "Duke gets the biggest glass," he said, with a wink.

Oliver gave an awkward laugh.

Ninian didn't laugh. He fiddled with his cuffs again, looking as agitated as a virgin in a whorehouse.

Uncle Algy lifted his own glass. "May a soldier's musket always be primed and ready for action," he said, with another wink at Oliver.

It was a toast Oliver had heard hundreds of

times—a toast he'd made himself, with just such a wink at his friends, because "musket" of course meant "cock"—so why did it make him feel uncomfortable to hear his own uncle speak those words?

Oliver gave another awkward laugh and raised his glass—and in that same instant, Ninian managed to fall off his chair and into Oliver's lap.

Oliver dropped his glass and only just avoided falling off his own chair. Madeira went everywhere.

Ninian scrambled to his feet, scarlet with embarrassment. "I'm so sorry." He pulled out his handkerchief and began mopping up the spilled liquid.

For a moment all was bustle—whisking the cards out of harm's way, wiping up the Madeira. Cheevers told Ninian he was a clodpole, in a tone halfway between laughter and scolding, and Lord Warrington teased him for already being in his cups, but Uncle Algy didn't say anything. His jaw was clenched. He was clearly mortified by his son's clumsiness.

Oliver didn't say anything, either. He was absolutely certain that Ninian's accident had been deliberate.

But why? Why on earth would Ninian do such a thing?

Ninian righted his chair and sat down again. He was still red-faced. "I'm so sorry, Cousin. Have my glass, please. I don't much like Madeira, anyway."

175

Ninian pushed his glass towards Oliver—and Oliver had the answer to his question. *This* was why Ninian had fallen off his chair: so that he could give his own Madeira to Oliver. The Madeira that had been sitting in front of Ninian while he fidgeted with his cuffs.

The hair lifted along the nape of Oliver's neck. He knew with absolute certainty that Ninian had slipped something into the glass.

He suddenly wished that Rhodes was sitting next to him.

"Thank you, Ninian," he said, and reached for the Madeira—and knocked the glass over with one fingertip.

Everyone leapt into action again, wielding handkerchiefs, scooping up the cards. Oliver said what was expected—apologies, a joke at his own expense—and accepted a new glass from Uncle Algy. A toast was made. They all drank. Cheevers and Warrington exclaimed over the Madeira, but Oliver barely noticed the flavor; most of his attention was occupied elsewhere.

Rhodes had been correct.

One of his relatives *was* trying to kill him.

CHAPTER 16

Primrose was in the blue salon, the better to keep an eye on Miss Middleton-Murray. She was listening to a discussion of the latest fashion in carriage dresses and thinking longingly of the yet-to-be explored library, when the door opened. Lords Cheevers and Warrington entered. Behind them was Oliver. Cheevers and Warrington were rosy-cheeked and merry. Oliver wasn't. In fact, he looked uncharacteristically grim. He glanced around the room, met her eyes, and stroked his nose, a brusque gesture. Then he retreated and closed the door.

After a moment, Primrose rose to her feet. "Excuse me. I'm going to check on my brother."

Lady Cheevers looked up, the plumes on her turban nodding. "*Do* let me know if there's anything he requires, Lady Primrose."

"I shall, ma'am."

She trod briskly across the vestibule and along the corridor, pausing to glance over her shoulder before opening the heavy, gilded door to the State apartments.

Oliver was waiting for her in the dressing room, pacing from one side to the other like a caged animal.

"What is it?" Primrose asked. "I checked the stairs less than an hour ago—"

"I think Rhodes is right," Oliver said, coming to a halt in the middle of the room. "I think Ninian's trying to kill me."

Primrose opened her mouth to say *What?* but no sound came out. She was too astonished.

"I'm almost certain he tried to poison me just now. With a glass of Madeira." Oliver frowned. "And he probably tried yesterday, too, with that damned snuff." He rubbed his brow, as if the frown hurt, and crossed to the window and stared out at the waterlogged gardens. "I want to do that thing with the lake. As soon as possible."

"But . . . Ninian hero-worships you, Oliver! He'd no more try to kill you than he'd—"

"He doesn't hero-worship me," Oliver said flatly, still staring out the rain-streaked window. "He wants me dead."

Primrose shook her head.

Oliver didn't see it, but perhaps he took her silence for dissent, for he said, "If you could have seen what he did, you wouldn't doubt it. It was so *fake,* so obviously a ploy to get me to drink from his glass instead of my own." The unfamiliar note in his voice wasn't anger but something else entirely, something bewildered and hurt.

Primrose crossed to where he stood. "Oliver . . ."

Oliver turned to face her. The twist of his lips was more grimace than smile. "We need to talk with Rhodes."

"Yes. But first tell me exactly what happened."

Oliver did. When he was finished, he said, "I know it sounds fantastical, Prim, but I didn't imagine it. On my word of honor!"

"Of course you didn't imagine it."

Oliver pressed the heels of his palms to his eyes for a moment, and then sighed and lowered his hands. Such a bleak sound, that sigh, and such a bleak expression on his face. So unlike Oliver.

She wanted to hug him, but didn't quite dare, so instead she placed her hand on his sleeve. "Oliver . . ."

Oliver had no qualms about hugging. He folded her in his arms. It wasn't a romantic embrace, though; it was the hug of a man who needed comfort.

Primrose hugged him back.

Oliver sighed again. "I wish this wretched rain would stop."

"It will. And as soon as it does, we'll set a trap for Ninian." Part of her still couldn't quite believe it. Not Ninian Dasenby. Not after she'd seen how much he admired Oliver. But Oliver believed it, and the tale he'd told was convincing.

Oliver sighed a third time, and released her. He gave that grimace-smile again. "Let's go tell Rhodes."

"He'll refuse to leave tomorrow, you realize. Regardless of his health."

Oliver was silent for a moment, and then he said, "I want him to stay. I want him here, with me."

"Then we'd better find a way to fix his eyes, hadn't we?" Primrose turned away from the window and headed for the door.

Oliver matched his stride to hers. The carpet hushed their steps as they crossed the State sitting room. In the reception room he took her hand and squeezed it. "I'm glad you came to Cheevers Court, Prim."

Primrose felt herself blush. "I'm glad I came, too."

"I'm lucky to have you and Rhodes as friends." Oliver dipped his head and placed a kiss on her cheek.

Primrose felt her blush grow hotter. Her heartbeat

sped up. She fumbled for something to say. "We're the lucky ones."

Oliver's mouth brushed her cheek again—and there was a pause in which the world seemed to hold its breath—and then the angle of his head shifted ever so slightly and his lips touched hers.

It wasn't a kiss like this morning's one—wild and unrestrained. This kiss was unexpectedly sweet, unexpectedly tender. Their lips clung together, and she tasted Madeira on his tongue, and then he lifted his head and gazed down at her. He didn't look bleak anymore. He looked . . . thoughtful.

For a long moment Oliver didn't say a word, just looked at her with his eyes slightly narrowed and the faintest of creases between his dark eyebrows, as if she was a question he was trying to answer.

Primrose's heart beat uncomfortably fast. She found herself holding her breath. Then Oliver's inward-looking expression fell away. He grinned at her, and flicked her cheek with one fingertip. "You're losing your prickles, Prim."

As far as Primrose could tell, the cupping hadn't helped Rhodes at all. His face was flushed, his voice husky, his eyelids swollen almost shut. She watched him while Oliver told his tale. Rhodes's expression grew grimmer and grimmer. When Oliver had finished, he said, "That does it. I'm not staying in this bedroom a moment longer," and he flung back the covers and climbed out of bed in his nightshirt.

"Easy, old fellow," Oliver said, grabbing Rhodes's shoulder and trying to push him back into the bed. "We don't need you yet. Have to wait for this dashed rain to stop—and for your eyes to get better."

Rhodes shrugged his hand off, swayed, caught his balance, and squinted around the room. "Where are my clothes?"

Oliver took Rhodes's shoulder more firmly. "Bed."

Rhodes was generally the most even-tempered of men. Primrose could count on one hand the number of times she'd seen him lose his temper. He wasn't even-tempered today. He scowled at Oliver. "If you think for *one* moment that I'm going to stay in bed while that little prick is trying to kill you, then you don't know me at all!"

Primrose opened her mouth to tell him that he really *ought* to be in bed, looked at his flushed, fierce face, and decided that Rhodes would like his younger sister telling him what to do even less than he liked Oliver telling him. She retreated to the window, instead.

The lake was visible from this angle, a gray blur

among the trees. Primrose stared at it, and thought about her plan to prove that Oliver's relatives weren't trying to kill him.

Except that one of them actually *was*.

She still couldn't quite believe it. Part of her wanted to cling to her own estimation of Ninian Dasenby—but there were three undeniable facts against him.

First, that he was in love with Miss Cheevers.

Second, that Lord Cheevers didn't want a mere Mister for his daughter; he wanted a duke.

And third, that if Oliver were to die, Dasenby wouldn't be a Mister anymore. He'd be heir to the Westfell dukedom.

Primrose stared at the distant lake, and listened to Rhodes and Oliver argue. She could still taste Oliver's kiss in her mouth and the smoky, caramel flavor of the Madeira he'd drunk.

She wished the rain would stop. She wished Rhodes's eyes would heal. She wished this was all over—the business with Ninian Dasenby, the business with Miss Middleton-Murray.

And she wished that Oliver would kiss her again.

She turned her head and looked at him, standing with his hands on his hips and his chin jutting stubbornly, arguing with Rhodes.

It seemed impossible that he'd kissed her only a

few minutes ago, impossible that he'd hugged her so close to him.

Oliver flung up his hands in exasperation and turned to her. "Prim, tell your brother he's being a damned fool."

Primrose looked from one scowling face to the other. Whoever she sided with was going to become even more frustrated and annoyed than he now was.

She considered this for a moment, gave an internal shrug, and said, "I think you should *both* stay here."

"What?" two voices said, identical in their indignation.

"You need to get back into bed," Primrose told her brother, pointing imperatively at the four-poster. "And put that wet cloth back on your eyes, and *you*—" she turned her finger in Oliver's direction, "—should stay here, out of Ninian's way."

Both men gaped at her.

A book lay on the windowsill, a ribbon marking the place. Primrose picked it up and poked Oliver in the chest with it. "Read to him."

Oliver took the book automatically. "But—"

"Dash it, Prim, I'm not an invalid," Rhodes said hotly.

"Bed," Primrose said, pointing. "Wet cloth. Now."

Rhodes muttered under his breath.

Primrose stepped around them both and headed for the door. "I'm going to check the stairs."

"Stairs?" Rhodes said. "Which stairs? Why?"

Primrose glanced back over her shoulder. "Oliver, why don't you tell him about Miss Middleton-Murray and her nasty little trick?"

"What?" Rhodes said.

"But only once he's in bed and has that cloth over his eyes." Primrose smiled sweetly at them both and let herself out the door.

In the corridor she almost collided with Monsieur Benoît. He was carrying several clean, folded cloths and a ewer of water. He must have come from the kitchen, up the servants' stairs.

Servants' stairs . . .

Primrose thought about servants' stairs while she made her way to the South wing. She climbed the four steps that Miss Carteris had fallen down, checked that no string was tied around the newel post, then went in search of the servants' stairs.

She found them almost opposite her own room, behind a discreet door.

The stairs were steep and narrow and uncarpeted, descending not just the four steps from the South wing to the main body of the house, but turning and plunging down towards the ground floor and the servants' domain: kitchen, scullery, cellars.

Primrose eyed the staircase thoughtfully. Miss Middleton-Murray was Lord Cheevers's god-daughter. She'd presumably visited Cheevers Court from time to time, knew the house well, was aware that these stairs existed.

She glanced back along the wide, carpeted corridor, towards the spot where Miss Carteris had tripped, and the shadowy alcove beyond where someone could have hidden—and then examined the narrow servants' stairs again. She'd wager all her books that Miss Middleton-Murray had gone down this staircase at least once. She could see it in her mind's eye: Miss Carteris falling; Miss Middleton-Murray swiftly cutting off the string and slinking down the servants' stairs, slipping into either the blue or the yellow salon, falling into conversation with the other ladies—and looking *so* surprised when someone brought news of Miss Carteris's accident.

Perhaps Miss Middleton-Murray had even come *up* these stairs to lay her trap?

Primrose nibbled on her lower lip. Really, it behooved her to explore these stairs.

She glanced along the corridor again, and then stepped into the stairwell and closed the door behind her. She tiptoed down one half-flight of stairs, then another. Above her, a door opened and closed. Footsteps began to descend briskly.

Primrose began to tiptoe faster, down another half-flight.

Below her, a door opened and closed. Someone started climbing the stairs.

Primrose froze.

Footsteps crossed the half-landing above her head.

Primrose felt a burst of panic. She squeezed her eyes shut and wished herself behind the lacquered screen in the State dressing room.

There was a moment of vertigo, when the world reeled around her—and then everything steadied.

She stood behind a screen in a cool, shadowy room. She heard rain against windowpanes, smelled stale lavender.

Primrose cautiously peeked out from behind the screen. Holland-covered furniture loomed like ghosts in the dim light.

She released the breath she was holding, and emerged from her hiding place. "Idiot," she told herself. It had been ridiculous to panic. The two people in the stairwell had merely been servants, not villains in a melodrama. They wouldn't have done anything to her, except stare.

Although, one of them *might* have been Miss Middleton-Murray's maid. Would she have told her mistress about it? The nosy duke's daughter found snooping on the servants' stairs.

Would Miss Middleton-Murray have realized *why* Primrose was in the stairwell?

Primrose turned this over in her head for a moment, and decided that she'd done the right thing, even though her motive had been wrong. Panic was never a good reason to do anything.

She let herself out of the State apartments and went back upstairs to Rhodes's bedroom. The valet let her in. Not only was Rhodes in bed with a wet cloth over his eyes, but Oliver was still there. They both turned their heads as she entered. "Well?" Rhodes demanded, lifting one corner of the cloth and looking at her with a bloodshot eye. "Has she rigged her trap on the stairs?"

Primrose glanced at the valet, and then back at Rhodes.

"Benoît's not going to tell anyone, are you, man?"

"Of course not, sir," the valet said. He went to the bedside table and dipped a fresh cloth in one of the bowls of water standing there.

Primrose watched him for a moment.

Benoît was young, but he was also intelligent. And discreet.

"No," she said. "She hasn't set up her trap yet. I'm going downstairs to keep an eye on her. Will you stay here, Oliver?"

Oliver hesitated, and then nodded.

Primrose stepped out into the corridor and closed the door. She went down to the blue salon again. Miss Middleton-Murray wasn't there. Nor was she in the yellow salon, or the library, or the music room.

Fiddlesticks.

Primrose blew out her breath, and climbed all the way back to the corridor in the South wing where she, Miss Warrington, and Miss Middleton-Murray had their rooms. Everything was just as she'd left it. No string tied around the newel post, no Miss Middleton-Murray lurking in the alcove.

Primrose retraced her steps to the blue salon. This time, Miss Middleton-Murray was there.

Primrose eyed her balefully, and picked up a copy of the *Ladies' Monthly Museum* and pretended to be absorbed in the fashion plates. She had only turned two pages before Miss Middleton-Murray slipped from the room.

When she hadn't returned after ten minutes, Primrose put down the magazine and went looking for her: yellow salon, library, music room, and then all the way up to the corridor in the South wing again.

Miss Middleton-Murray was nowhere to be seen.

Primrose wished the Cheevers had a smaller home. She wished there weren't quite so many stairs. She wished it wasn't going to take her ten minutes to get back to the blue salon.

She glanced over her shoulder. The corridor was utterly empty.

Primrose stepped into the alcove. She pictured the lacquered screen in the State dressing room. A second later, she was behind it.

She emerged cautiously, conscious of two conflicting emotions. One, relief that she'd avoided all those stairs again. The other, an emotion she hadn't felt since childhood: an uncomfortable feeling that she'd done something naughty and her parents would scold her if they knew.

She let herself out of the State apartments and headed back to the blue salon. Miss Middleton-Murray wasn't there. Nor was she in the yellow salon or the library or the music room.

Primrose gritted her teeth and prepared to climb up all those stairs again—or dare she translocate to her bedchamber?

No, not when her maid might be there.

"Fiddlesticks," she said, under her breath, and turned towards the vestibule and the main staircase—and then halted at the sound of feminine voices.

Miss Warrington and Miss Middleton-Murray came along the corridor, arm in arm.

"Where have you been?" Primrose asked, trying not to sound too peremptory.

"The conservatory. It's so *atmospheric* in this rain." Miss Warrington gave a theatrical shiver. "You really should take a look, Lady Primrose."

"Perhaps later," Primrose said.

Miss Warrington and Miss Middleton-Murray looked into the library, the blue salon, the yellow salon, and the music room. When they found Oliver in none of those places, they decided to settle in the blue salon, with Lady and Miss Cheevers. Soon they were deep in discussion over the latest fashions in bonnets. Primrose picked up the magazine she'd abandoned half an hour ago, and went back to pretending to read it. She was looking at a fashion plate of a lady wearing a turban rather like Lady Cheevers's when Miss Middleton-Murray rose to her feet. "Pray excuse me for a moment," she said.

Primrose watched over the top of the *Ladies' Monthly Museum* as Miss Middleton-Murray slipped from the room. Her heartbeat sped up. Was this it?

Primrose gave Miss Middleton-Murray a head start, and then climbed up to the South wing. Everything was exactly as it had been before: no string tied around the newel post at ankle height, no young ladies hidden in alcoves. She waited five

191

minutes, then ten, then fifteen—and then wished herself down to behind the screen in the State dressing room.

When she returned to the blue salon, she found the door slightly ajar. Laughter and animated voices issued from the room.

Primrose pushed the door slightly wider, and saw Miss Warrington toss her ringlets. Her cheeks were flushed, her eyes sparkling. Someone out of sight uttered a tinkling, musical laugh and said, "Oh, Westfell, you are so *droll.*"

Oliver had clearly decided to leave the safety of Rhodes's bedchamber. Primrose tutted under her breath. She hoped Oliver had looked behind himself before setting foot on the stairs.

She stepped into the salon and observed how one person could completely change the atmosphere of a room. A vivacious energy crackled in the air. Everything seemed brighter and more alive, as if Oliver had brought sunshine into the blue salon with him. Or perhaps lamplight was a better word, for Miss Warrington and Miss Middleton-Murray were fluttering around him like moths around a lantern.

Oliver glanced over the ladies' heads and met Primrose's gaze. His eyebrows lifted fractionally.

Primrose read the question there and answered

with a discreet thumbs up, telling him that the stairs were safe. She crossed to the seat she'd vacated and picked up the magazine again. She turned the pages, listening while Miss Warrington tried to coax Oliver into another duet and Miss Middleton-Murray tried to change the subject.

Despite the fact that Miss Middleton-Murray had almost certainly tripped Miss Carteris on the stairs and was quite possibly going to attempt the same trick with Miss Warrington, despite the fact that Ninian Dasenby had probably tried to poison Oliver that very afternoon, despite the fact that she was extremely worried about Rhodes's eyes, Primrose found a bubble of wholly inappropriate and slightly hysterical laughter growing in her chest. That overheard three-way conversation was like a comedy—Miss Warrington coaxing, Oliver stalling for all he was worth, Miss Middleton-Murray trying to change the subject.

The bubble of laughter grew bigger. Primrose bit her lip to hold it back and glanced over the top of the magazine.

Oliver caught her gaze, and idly stroked the bridge of his nose.

The laughter disappeared like a soap bubble popping. Oliver wanted to talk with her?

Primrose put down the magazine. She rose from

her chair. "Excuse me," she murmured, although no one but Oliver paid her any attention.

The route to the State apartments had become very familiar. Primrose thought that she could probably find her way blindfolded. She glanced around for servants, opened the door, and slipped into the reception room.

She walked through the sitting room and the dressing room, and peeked into the bedroom.

The sight of that wide bed on its dais sent her back to the dressing room. As she crossed to the window, she heard the door to the reception room quietly open and then close.

Primrose turned her head. Her heart gave an absurd little lurch when Oliver entered the dressing room. The taste of him was suddenly on her tongue again: Madeira. She felt stupidly nervous, stupidly shy. *Please don't let me blush.* But it was too late; her cheeks had grown warm.

"You wanted to talk to me?" she said briskly, turning away from the window, hoping that the shadows would hide her blush.

Oliver flung himself down on the Holland-covered sofa with a loud groan. "Save me, Prim."

"From what?"

"Females," he said, in the same tone that someone would say *the plague.*

"I'm a female," she reminded him. The heat was fading rapidly from her cheeks. Oliver hadn't wanted to speak to her; he'd merely wanted a reprieve from his admirers.

Why did that sting?

"Females who want to marry dukes," Oliver amended. He rested his head on the back of the sofa, gazed up at the ceiling, and gave a huge sigh.

Was she one of those, too? Did she want to marry Oliver?

When Oliver had walked into this room she'd felt as if she might—and then he'd opened his mouth and done what he did best: annoy her.

"It's your fault for leading them on," Primrose told him. "If you'd been standoffish from the start, they wouldn't be so zealous in their pursuit of you now."

Oliver rolled his head to look at her. "But where's the fun in that?"

"Not everything in life is a game," she said severely.

He grinned at her. "You really should have been a governess, Prim."

"And you should have been a clown!"

Oliver laughed. He made no move to stand, just stayed where he was, sprawled on the sofa, his head resting on its back.

"How you ever became a captain in the army is beyond comprehension."

"Oh, I never played the fool when I was on duty." He smiled up at her, his eyes gleaming softly in the shadowy room.

Primrose's heart gave a loud thump. She knew that men could be handsome, but she'd never realized that men could be beautiful. Oliver was at this moment, quite heart-stoppingly beautiful—those soft, dark eyes, that playful smile, the shadows painting hollows under his cheekbones. What had he just said? Oh, that he never played the fool on duty. "I find that very hard to believe!"

"I *do* know when to be serious, Prim. Just haven't had much reason to be lately. Feels like I'm on furlough, being back in England. But I'll be serious in performing my duties as Westfell, I promise—and I'll be *especially* serious when the House of Lords is sitting." Oliver spoiled this fine speech by grinning at her again.

Primrose sniffed.

"Come here, Prim." He held out one hand to her.

"Why?" She eyed his hand for a moment, and then reluctantly crossed to the sofa and placed her hand in his.

Oliver's fingers closed around hers, warm and strong. He pulled her down to sit alongside him. "Because you are the perfect antidote to Miss Warrington and Miss Middleton-Murray."

Primrose stiffened. "Because I'm prickly?"

"Because you're *real*," he said, putting one arm around her shoulders and drawing her closer. "You don't pretend to be something you're not."

The blush flared in her cheeks again. Her heart began to beat faster. Was Oliver going to kiss her? Primrose moistened her lips nervously, while shyness and anticipation chased one another in her chest. "You pretend. You pretend to be pompous and foolish and vain. Honestly, Oliver, do you not care what people think of you?"

"It's just a game, Prim. And I only play it with the ones who want to catch me. Not with anyone else."

Did he think that this was a game, too? Meeting in these secluded, unused rooms, sometimes putting his arm around her, sometimes kissing her?

The realization was cold and sudden: Of course he did. Of *course* this was a game to him.

If it weren't a game, he wouldn't be so relaxed right now. His muscles would be as taut as hers were, his heart racing just as fast as hers was. But instead, he was perfectly at ease, sprawled on the sofa with his head tipped back and his arm casually around her shoulders. This might be a different game from the one he was playing with the would-be duchesses, but it was a game nonetheless.

Mortification replaced the shyness and anticipation in her chest. How could she have been such a fool as to imagine there might be anything between them? That she might possibly be falling in love with Oliver? That he might possibly be falling in love with her?

"You shouldn't play so many games," Primrose told him, and she sounded just as prickly as he'd accused her of being.

"You disapprove?"

"Yes!" she said. "You flip-flop like a *fish*, Oliver. 'Settle on the type of person you want to be and stick to it, whether alone or in company.' Marcus Aurelius said that, and he was *right*."

Oliver tilted his head towards her. "He also said, 'Throw away your books.' Was he right about that, too?"

How could he grin at her like that? Couldn't he see that she was mortified and furious?

Primrose pulled away from him.

Oliver let her go. He stopped sprawling and sat up. Then he rested his forearm on the back of the sofa and leaned close. Very close. So close that his warm breath stirred her hair. "Prickly," he whispered, in her ear.

It didn't sound like an insult when he said it like that. It sounded like a compliment. Like a caress.

A shiver swept through her. Primrose's heart began to beat even faster. She tensed. "It's not nice to play with people, Oliver."

Oliver raised his head and looked at her.

Could he see how hurt she was right now? How angry she was with herself? With him?

Perhaps he could, because he said, "You think I'm playing with you, Prim?"

"Of course you are!"

He shook his head. "On my word of honor, I'm not."

She *wanted* him to be telling the truth. "Well, I don't see how you can expect me to know that," she said gruffly. "Not when you—"

"Flip-flop like a fish?" He grinned, his teeth flashing in the gloom. "You do have a way with words, Prim."

"I was going to say, when you *pretend* the whole time."

"Not all the time," Oliver said. "Not even half the time. And never with you."

Primrose remembered the Cunninghams' ball, when Oliver had puffed out his chest and strutted while they danced.

But he hadn't been pretending, then, had he? He'd been teasing her quite blatantly, and they'd both known it. There had been no attempt at pretense.

He had been purely—and annoyingly—Oliver Dasenby.

Oliver touched her cheek with a fingertip—and Primrose's thoughts froze in place. Her entire being focused on his finger. It slid slowly down her cheek, tracing a path that burned across her skin, then along her jaw to the very center of her chin, where it stopped.

Primrose found herself unable to breathe. She couldn't move, couldn't look away from Oliver. There was an expression on his face that she'd never seen before, a curious intentness.

Oliver tilted her chin up. His expression grew even more intent—and then he lowered his head and kissed her.

Primrose knew she ought to jerk her head away . . . but she didn't want to. Oliver's mouth was perfect, his finger on her chin was perfect, his kiss was perfect, *everything* was perfect, even the rain, even the musty lavender smell of the State rooms.

His tongue touched her lips, and then slipped into her mouth, and she lost the ability to think. She was no longer a rational creature but one ruled by instinct. Everything was action and reaction. Oliver's tongue sliding against hers; her breathless gasp. Her teeth nipping his lower lip; his answering growl of pleasure.

Oliver gathered her closer. Primrose gripped his waistcoat, fingers digging in without care for the delicate mother-of-pearl buttons or the fine embroidery.

When Oliver finally broke the kiss, they were both panting.

Oliver sat back slightly and took several breaths, then he laughed, a ragged, breathless sound. "To think I used to call you Lady Prim-and-Proper."

Lady Prim-and-Proper. How she'd hated that nickname. How she'd hated *him* when he'd called her that. It seemed impossible that Oliver had once been that boy, that she'd once been that girl.

"It seems so long ago," he said.

"Nearly twenty years." But it felt longer than that. It felt like a lifetime ago, someone else's lifetime, as if she and Oliver had never been those two children.

Oliver's smile faded. He reached out and rubbed his thumb gently along her lower lip, back and forth, back and forth. "If someone had told me back then that one day we'd kiss, I wouldn't have believed it."

"Neither would I," Primrose said. "Back then, what I most wanted to do was to wring your neck."

Oliver grinned. He puffed out his chest and preened slightly. "I do have that effect on people."

Primrose couldn't help laughing. "You are such an idiot, Daisy."

"I know," he said, still grinning. "But you like it."

And he was right. She did like it. A lot. She liked *him* a lot.

In fact, she liked him too much, because the truth of the matter was that she and Oliver Dasenby were never going to marry. He knew it. She knew it. And yet here she was, meeting with him alone, kissing him. It was shockingly disgraceful behavior. *Dangerous* behavior. If Rhodes ever found out . . . Worse, if her *parents* ever found out . . .

Primrose stood hastily. "I should check on Rhodes. Try to keep Miss Middleton-Murray occupied, Oliver. If she's busy trying to bewitch you, she won't have time to set traps on stairs."

He pulled a face. "Spoilsport."

Primrose ignored this comment, and marched briskly back to the reception room and let herself out the door. What she really wanted to do was stay on the sofa with Oliver, so she made herself climb the stairs to Rhodes's bedroom in the North wing. To her relief, her brother was in bed with a wet cloth over his eyes, listening to his valet read aloud.

Next, she went to the South wing, where she inspected both the newel post and the alcove, but found nothing. Primrose glanced right, glanced left, and listened intently for a moment. She heard no footsteps, no creak of floorboards, no voices.

Satisfied that no one was nearby, she stepped into the alcove and wished herself back down to the State dressing room.

The world spun for a brief moment—and when it steadied she was behind the red-and-black *chinoiserie* screen.

Primrose peeked around the edge of it, saw an empty sofa and shadows, and stepped out into the room—and collided with someone.

She recoiled with a small shriek. The other person uttered a choked, masculine scream and fell over backwards.

CHAPTER 17

Oliver started to scramble to his feet—and froze as recognition slapped him across the face.

The thing that had pounced on him from behind the screen—ghost, ghoul, whatever it was—was it . . . was it *Primrose*?

Primrose, whom he'd seen walk out of this room almost twenty minutes ago.

Oliver stared. And the longer he stared at that shadowy figure, that pale face, the more certain he became.

It *was* Primrose, her eyes wide and shocked, both hands pressed to her chest as if her heart was trying to burst free of her ribcage.

His own heart was certainly trying to burst free of *his* ribcage. His pulse thundered wildly in his ears.

And it wasn't only his heartbeat that he heard in his ears; his scream echoed there, too.

"Prim?" he said cautiously, still ready to fight or run, whichever seemed wisest, if the creature *wasn't* Primrose.

"You scared me," she said, in a voice that sounded faint and rather breathless.

Oliver climbed slowly and not quite steadily to his feet. *You scared me, too,* he almost said, although that was pretty damned obvious, given that he'd screamed and fallen over.

Screamed *and* fallen over.

He wasn't sure what bothered him most—that Primrose had heard him shriek and seen him go head over tail, or that he had absolutely no idea how she'd suddenly appeared behind that screen. He hadn't heard a damned thing, no doors opening, no footsteps, nothing.

"What the devil, Prim?" His voice sounded as breathless as hers, but much harsher.

"I'm sorry. I didn't think there'd be anyone here," she said, her hands still pressed to her chest.

Oliver stepped around her and looked behind the screen. The only things there were shadows. He examined the wall. There was no door that he could see.

He swung to face her. "How did you get behind this screen?"

Primrose stared at him for a long moment, then

her gaze flicked to the wall, as if she, too, was looking for a door.

"Well?"

She moistened her lips nervously, and didn't speak.

Oliver put his hands on his hips. "Prim . . . how did you get in here without me seeing *or* hearing?"

Her gaze turned to the wall again, as if hoping a door might have suddenly materialized.

"There's no door there, Prim."

She looked back at him, and gripped her hands together. "You won't believe me if I tell you."

"Won't I?"

She shook her head.

"*Tell* me, Prim."

Primrose stared at him for a long moment, and then turned on her heel. "Come with me."

"Where?" Oliver said, suspiciously.

"To talk with Rhodes."

"Rhodes?" He strode after Primrose. "Why?"

"Because I know you won't believe me, but maybe you'll believe him."

Oliver followed her through the State apartments and out into the corridor. They crossed the vestibule together. It was much brighter here, candles burning in the sconces. They climbed the stairs silently. Oliver went over the events of the past five minutes in his mind. Here, in the bright candlelight, everything seemed as unreal as a dream. He could almost believe it hadn't happened. Except that it *had* happened. Primrose hadn't been there one moment, and then the next, she had.

And he'd screamed. Like a girl. *And* fallen over.

They halted outside the door to Rhodes's bedchamber. Primrose raised her hand to knock, and then lowered it. "Are you sure you can't just forget it, Oliver?" There was entreaty in her voice, entreaty in her eyes.

Of course he couldn't forget it—whatever "it" was. But he could be a gentleman and cede to her request and pretend that whatever had happened *hadn't* happened.

Except that it would drive him mad, not knowing. And more than that, he *needed* to know, because he'd been kissing Primrose half an hour ago, and if they didn't talk this out he doubted they'd ever kiss again.

"I'm very certain," Oliver said.

Primrose accepted this with a wry twist of her lips. She knocked on the door. After a moment, Rhodes's valet opened it.

"Benoît, I'm sorry, but Westfell and I need to speak to my brother in private."

"Of course, Lady Primrose." The man stepped out into the corridor.

"If you could give us an hour?"

"Of course," he said again.

Primrose entered the bedchamber. Oliver followed on her heels and closed the door. Rhodes lifted the wet cloth half off, revealing one bloodshot eye. He squinted at them. "What's up? Is it Ninian? Did he try something?"

"No." Primrose clasped her hands together, took a deep breath, and said with the air of someone making a confession, "Oliver saw me translocate."

Rhodes seemed to understand this cryptic utterance. He grimaced. "Did he?"

"Yes. I'm sorry." She bit her lip, and then offered: "It was an accident."

"Of course it was an accident." Rhodes took the cloth off entirely, and placed it in one of the bowls of water on the bedside table. He looked at Oliver. It was difficult to decipher Rhodes's expression, with his eyelids swollen like that, but Oliver thought that he looked cautious, a little wary. "So . . . what do you think, Ollie?"

"I don't think anything because I don't *know* anything. What the devil is going on?"

Rhodes glanced at Primrose. "You haven't told him?"

"I thought he'd be more likely to believe you than me."

Rhodes snorted. "I doubt it."

"Should I fetch Mother?"

"Will the two of you stop being so cryptic and tell me what the *devil* is going on!"

Primrose and Rhodes looked at him, and then at each other. After a moment, Rhodes shrugged. "Primrose has a Faerie godmother."

Oliver laughed flatly.

"I'm serious," Rhodes said, and his voice *did* sound serious. "All the women in our family do. Mother, Prim, Vi, Aster. My aunts. My cousins."

Oliver laughed again. In fact, it probably couldn't even be called a laugh—too short, too flat.

"She grants them one wish each, when they turn twenty-three. Primrose chose translocation, which means that she can move from one place to another like that." Rhodes snapped his fingers.

Oliver shook his head. He didn't believe it. Couldn't believe it.

"Show him, Prim," Rhodes said.

Oliver glanced at her—and as he did so, she vanished, winking out as if she'd never existed.

"It's instantaneous," Primrose said from behind him.

He managed not to scream or fall over this time. He did give a colossal start, though. He jerked around to face her. Every hair on his body sprang upright.

209

"I wanted to be able to travel between both place *and* time, but Baletongue wouldn't let me. She said that time isn't for humans to meddle with. So I chose translocation."

Oliver wasn't sure which of those sentences to address first. It was all so enormous. *Too* enormous.

"Baletongue?" he said finally.

"My Faerie godmother."

Oliver uttered that short, flat, disbelieving laugh again. *I don't believe in Faeries,* he wanted to say. *Or Faerie godmothers. Or wishes or magic.* But how could he say that when he'd just witnessed Primrose vanish and then reappear?

Fuck. He rubbed one hand roughly through his hair. He wasn't drunk, was he? Did he have a fever? Was he hallucinating? Or was this perhaps a joke? A hugely sophisticated trick?

He looked at Primrose. Her expression was grave, anxious.

He turned his head and looked at Rhodes. His expression was grave, too.

This wasn't a hallucination.

It wasn't a joke or a trick.

It was real.

Oliver strode to the window and stared out at the rain-soaked landscape. He crossed his arms. He wasn't quite sure why he crossed his arms, whether he was angry or defensive or maybe whether it was to anchor himself, because the world had certainly tipped itself upside down.

Faeries?

Neither Rhodes nor Primrose said anything. Oliver listened to the rain pelt against the windowpanes. Finally he turned around. He didn't uncross his arms. "What does she look like, this Faerie?"

Primrose shivered. "Scary."

Oliver lifted his eyebrows. He uncrossed his arms. "Scary?"

"She has black eyes and sharp teeth like a cat."

Oliver leaned back against the windowsill. "How big is she?"

"About my size."

He glanced at Rhodes. "You've seen her?"

Rhodes shook his head. "She doesn't show herself to us."

"Us?"

"Men."

Oliver thought about this for a moment. "So, who else knows about her?"

"No one outside the family."

"Did Evelyn know?"

Rhodes shook his head. "And my children won't know, either. Best to keep it a secret."

"But your daughter—"

"Baletongue won't visit her."

Oliver frowned. "But you just said that she visits *all* the women in your family."

"Only those born into an unbroken female line," Primrose said. "The line continues with me and Vi and Aster, but breaks with Rhodes."

Oliver puzzled this through. "So, this . . . this legacy was passed from your grandmother to your mother, to you and Vi and Aster, and it will pass to your daughters if you have any, but not to Rhodes and his daughter?"

"Correct."

"And . . ." He narrowed his eyes. "Both your aunts had wishes. And Lily and Clem and Daph. And *their* daughters will have them—if they have daughters. But not Carlyle, or any daughters he might have?"

"Yes."

He glanced at Rhodes. "So how does that make you feel?"

Rhodes shrugged. "I'm going to be a duke. I feel pretty lucky."

Oliver laughed. This time it was a real laugh. Then he sobered. "So, if you're not going to tell your children about it, why did your parents tell you?"

"Because I'll be head of the family and it's safer if I know. For situations exactly like this." His gesture encompassed both Primrose and Oliver. "And maybe one day I'll tell my oldest son. It's a tough decision. Depends a lot on who my sisters marry. *If* they marry at all."

Oliver was reminded of the decision he'd been trying to make when Primrose had suddenly stepped out from behind that screen.

An enormous decision—which he wasn't ready to think about now, not while he was still reeling from this revelation.

He brought his attention firmly back to the matter at hand. Questions swarmed in his mind. He picked one at random.

"How come your family has a Faerie godmother?"

"One of our ancestors did something for Baletongue," Primrose said. "This is our reward."

"Reward? What on earth did this ancestor do?"

"We don't know," Rhodes said. "It was centuries ago. But whatever it was, it must have been big."

Big? It had to have been colossal.

"Do other families have Faerie godmothers?" Did half of the population of England have one, and he just didn't know?

Primrose shook her head. "We've always been told it's only us."

"So . . . what did Vi and Aster wish for? And your mother? Or is that a secret?"

"Mother can translocate, like me, and—"

An urgent knock sounded on the door.

Primrose closed her mouth. She crossed to the door and opened it. Rhodes's valet, Benoît, stood there, even though it hadn't been anywhere near an hour since he'd left. "Miss Warrington has had an accident on the stairs," he said.

"God *damn* it," Oliver said, pushing away from the windowsill. "Is she hurt?"

"It is possible that her nose is broken, Your Grace. The doctor has been sent for."

"Did anyone see it happen?"

"No, sir. She was alone."

"Which stairs?" Primrose asked. "Do you know, Benoît?"

"The same stairs that Miss Carteris fell down." The valet paused, and then gave an expressive Gallic shrug. "The housemaids are saying there is a ghost."

"No ghost," Oliver said grimly. "Just a goddamned harpy. Come on, Prim. Let's take a look."

CHAPTER 18

They walked briskly, along a corridor, across an echoing gallery, and then into a smaller one. The four steps up to the South Wing came into sight. A housemaid was on hands and knees at the bottom, scrubbing the carpet.

"Is this where Miss Warrington fell?" Oliver asked, when he and Primrose reached the girl.

"Yes, sir."

"Was there some blood?"

"Yes, sir."

Quite a bit of blood, Oliver guessed, looking at the size of the wet patch on the carpet. He hoped that Miss Warrington's nose was merely bruised, not broken.

The maid wiped her hands on her apron, her task finished. She picked up the pail and scrubbing brush and departed up the short flight of stairs, disappearing around the corner.

Oliver and Primrose waited until the sound of her footsteps had faded, then climbed the four steps themselves. The corridor stretched to the left and to the right, empty.

He really shouldn't be up here, with or without Primrose, but right now Oliver didn't care about propriety. He examined the alcove, but no telltale pieces of string lay abandoned there. Primrose was checking the newel post. She crouched and pointed. "Oliver, look."

Oliver looked, and saw nothing. He stepped closer.

Primrose was pointing to that exceedingly convenient groove at ankle height. It looked exactly the same as it had earlier. No, wait . . . was that a scrap of string tied around it?

His gaze leapt to hers.

"You see it?" Primrose said.

"I see it." Oliver turned his head, hearing voices approach from the long gallery.

"Oh, how perfectly dreadful!" He recognized that voice: it was Miss Middleton-Murray.

Primrose stood and grabbed his arm and pulled him down the corridor. They tiptoed hastily, almost running. Primrose opened a door, and shoved him into her bedroom—

Oliver halted and looked around.

This wasn't Primrose's bedroom. It wasn't anyone's bedroom. It was a servants' stairwell.

Primrose closed the door quietly. They stood on the small landing, listening intently, their heads tilted towards the door. Oliver heard nothing.

"We have proof now!" Primrose said, in an excited whisper. "We can tell the Cheevers!"

Oliver shook his head. "It's not enough proof," he whispered back. "Anyone could have tied that string. One of the servants, even."

"What? Of course a servant didn't do it!"

"I know, but we can't prove it, Prim."

"But—"

"The string doesn't tell us who set the trap, only that it was done."

Her brow wrinkled. "So . . . we shouldn't tell anyone?"

"I don't know." Oliver rubbed his forehead. "We need to think. But not here." He turned towards the stairs leading down. "Let's go."

"You go. I'll meet you in the State apartments in ten minutes."

Oliver nodded, took a step, and then halted and looked back at her. "Are you going to . . . you know?" He snapped his fingers like Rhodes had done.

Primrose hesitated. "Perhaps."

"Can you wait until I'm down there before you do it? I want to see it."

She shook her head. "It's too dangerous."

"Dangerous? How?"

"Think what would happen if I translocated to the exact same spot where you were standing."

Oliver did think about this for a moment. It made him shiver.

"That's why I used the screen, because I knew no one would be behind it. But you almost *were.*"

Oliver shook his head. "No, I wasn't."

"You were two feet from it!"

"And I'll stay two feet from it. I promise, Prim. I'd like to see it properly this time, that's all."

Primrose took her lower lip between her teeth. He could see her indecision.

"Please, Prim."

She released her lip. "All right. But *don't* stand behind the screen, Oliver."

"I won't. Word of honor."

Oliver was slightly out of breath by the time he reached the State apartments. He strode through the reception room, through the sitting room, and into the dressing room. They were the dreariest set of rooms he'd ever seen, the thin daylight barely penetrating the gloom, the dark red damask on the walls looking almost black, the shrouded furniture hovering eerily in the shadows.

Sepulchral. That was the word for these rooms: sepulchral.

He trod cautiously over to the red-and-black lacquered screen. "Prim?"

No one answered.

Oliver took two steps sideways, until his shoulder brushed the silk-covered wall and he had a perfect view of the space behind the screen.

He leaned against the wall, and waited. His heart was beating a little fast—and it wasn't entirely due to how hastily he'd come down the servants' stairs. An emotion prickled faintly across his skin. He wasn't quite certain what it was. Fear? Anticipation?

Don't scream this time, he told himself. *And do not fall over.* Because there really was no way for a man to recover his pride after he'd screamed and—

Primrose appeared behind the screen.

Even though he was expecting it, Oliver recoiled so hard that his head hit the wall. A sound came from his throat. A squeak this time, not a scream, but squeaks were almost as bad as screams.

And so, because it was simply impossible to re-cover one's manliness after screaming *or* squeaking, Oliver decided to play up to the moment like an actor in a bad melodrama. He clapped both his hands to his chest as if his heart had given out, staggered back a few paces, and collapsed to the floor with his arms outflung and his eyes closed.

After a moment, he heard quiet footsteps.

He opened his eyes.

Primrose stood looking down at him, her hands on her hips. "You really are an idiot, Daisy." Her face was in shadow, her features indistinguishable in the gloom, but he could hear that she was trying not to laugh.

"All the best dukes are," Oliver said, not lifting his head from the floor.

She might have rolled her eyes; it was a little too dark to know for certain. She sat down next to him, cross-legged like a Turk. "What are we going to do?"

Oliver reached for her hand and laced his fingers through hers. "About Miss Middleton-Murray?"

"Yes."

Oliver sighed, and pushed up to sit. "I don't know."

"We can't let her get away with it."

"No." Oliver scooted back on the carpet until his back was against the wall. He pulled Primrose towards him and tucked her close, one arm around her shoulders.

She leaned into him. "She probably won't do it again, you realize. She has no rivals here now."

"Doesn't she?" Oliver said, dipping his head to place a kiss on her soft hair. "I'm not so sure about that."

"You may not think I'm an ape leader, Oliver, but Miss Middleton-Murray does. She classes me with the spinsters and chaperones and old ladies."

"How very foolish of her," he said, kissing her hair again. It had the same scent as her skin: orange blossom.

"And as for Miss Cheevers, she's no rival either, because she's in love with your cousin."

Oliver lifted his head. "What?"

"Miss Cheevers is in love with Mr. Dasenby."

"The devil she is!"

Primrose gave an exasperated huff of breath. "How have you not noticed? She doesn't flirt with you at all."

"She's just a little shy."

"Very shy," Primrose said. "And head over heels in love with your cousin. And if you haven't noticed that, Miss Middleton-Murray *has*. Trust me."

"Miss Cheevers prefers that namby-pamby to me?" Oliver said, a little piqued.

"She does. Which is a good thing, because we don't have to worry about Miss Middleton-Murray setting traps for her."

Oliver grunted, no longer listening with his full

attention. He was thinking about Ninian. Ninian dropping the snuff box yesterday. Ninian knocking over the Madeira today.

He remembered the hand that had shoved him between his shoulder blades.

"But even if we can't catch Miss Middleton-Murray, we should be able to catch your cousin," Primrose said, as if her thoughts had followed the same path his had. "Just as soon as this rain stops."

"Yes," Oliver said, and even though it was only one word, his voice sounded harsh.

"Have you decided what you'll do with him?" Primrose asked, after a moment. "Will you prosecute him? Ship him to the colonies? Or merely warn him off?"

Oliver sighed. "I don't know. If he *did* kill Uncle Reginald or Percival—or both of them—then he deserves to hang. If he didn't . . . The colonies, I guess." He closed his eyes. "God, how am I going to tell Uncle Algy that Ninian tried to murder me?"

"Let's cross that bridge when we come to it," Primrose said. "One step at a time, Oliver—and the first step is catching him in the act."

"Yes." He sighed again, and opened his eyes. He wasn't used to feeling melancholy, but right now that's exactly how he felt: melancholy.

The rain probably had something to do with it.

And the gloom of the dressing room. And Rhodes's illness. Throw in Miss Middleton-Murray and Ninian, and it was no wonder his spirits were low.

But, he *was* a duke, and he *did* have his arm around Primrose Garland, so life wasn't completely terrible.

Oliver gave himself a mental shake. "'Do not say, 'I am unhappy, because this has happened to me. Say instead, 'I am happy, *although* this has happened to me.'"

He felt Primrose stiffen in surprise.

"That Aurelius fellow knew a thing or two," he told her.

She pulled away from his embrace, far enough that she could see his face. "I can't believe that you read him. That you like him enough to quote him. I thought you liked novels, preferably ones with headless horsemen or ghosts."

Oliver grinned at her. "I do. I read one once that had a madman, a secret passage, an oubliette, and *two* ghosts, one of them headless. Best book I've ever read."

He couldn't see her face clearly, but he was absolutely certain that Primrose rolled her eyes.

"Truthfully, Prim . . . I didn't think much of Aurelius at school." He gathered her close again, settling his arm around her shoulders. "But your father gave me a copy when I sailed for India, said Aurelius had been a good soldier and a good leader, and I should read him since I was going to be a soldier myself." He chuckled in memory. "I didn't want to read it; I won't deny it, Prim. In fact, I only read it out of obligation to your father. But the funny thing was that it made a lot more sense than it had at school. And I found myself going back to it, and every time I read it, it made even more sense."

"What's your favorite quote?" Primrose asked.

Oliver thought about this for a moment. "'The first rule is to keep an untroubled spirit,'" he said. "'The second rule is to look things in the face and know them for what they are.'"

"An untroubled spirit?" She uttered a faint, almost soundless, laugh. "Yes, that's you."

Her head rested on his shoulder, her hand rested on his chest. Her fingers idly twisted one of his coat buttons one way and then the other, not coquettishly, but absent-mindedly, as if she was thinking and didn't know she was doing it.

Quite likely, they were thinking the same thing.

Look them in the eye and know them for what they are.

Miss Middleton-Murray.

Ninian.

"'Think of the things which goad man into destroying man,'" he said quietly.

Primrose completed the quote: "'They are hope, envy, hatred, fear, and contempt.'" And then she said, "Miss Middleton-Murray *hopes* to be a duchess, and *fears* that she won't be."

"And Ninian envies me."

Primrose was silent for a moment. "No, I don't think so. I think he's afraid Lord Cheevers won't let him marry Miss Cheevers."

"What?"

"He's as much in love with her as she is with him. Hadn't you noticed?"

"No," Oliver said, feeling a little unsettled. Was he really that unobservant?

"But Lord Cheevers wants a duke for a son-in-law." Primrose twisted the coat button one way, then the other. "So . . ."

"I'm in Ninian's way."

She released the button and laid her hand on his chest. "I'm sorry, Oliver."

"So am I." He sighed, and then gave himself another mental shake. "'I am happy, *although* this has happened to me.'"

"It's easy to say," Primrose observed. "But not particularly easy to do. At least, *I* don't find it easy."

Oliver laughed. "No, I can't say I always do, either." He was feeling a lot less melancholy, though—and the reason for that wasn't Marcus Aurelius, but Primrose.

He rested his head against the wall and simply enjoyed the moment: sitting on the floor, his arm around Primrose Garland.

Unfortunately, the moment didn't last long. Primrose slipped out from under his arm, climbed to her feet, and dusted off her skirt. "Come on," she said, holding out her hand to him. "Rhodes will want to hear about that piece of string."

Oliver took her hand and stood, but he didn't release her. "There's something we need to do first."

"What?"

He drew her into an embrace. "Kiss."

"Oliver!" Primrose protested, but she didn't try to pull away. In fact, she tilted her face upwards, and when his mouth touched hers, her lips parted.

Oliver had kissed quite a few women in his time, and all of them had been more skilled at it than Primrose. But perhaps that was why kissing her was so special? Her innocent enthusiasm inflamed him in a way that practiced expertise never had. Or maybe it was because every other woman he'd kissed had been playing a game—the same game he'd been playing: flirtation, casual intimacy.

Primrose definitely wasn't playing a game—and for once, neither was he. And while that scared him a little, it also made his heart beat faster, made heat flush beneath his skin, made his blood pound in his head.

God, he couldn't get enough of her: that warm, welcoming mouth, the soft lips and smooth teeth and velvety tongue, the *taste* of her. And surely that was one of life's great conundrums? How someone with such a tart tongue could taste so sweet?

Oliver kissed Primrose until he ran out of breath, and then he raised his head and dragged air into his lungs. He was shaking ever so slightly, and he'd never done that after kissing a woman before. It was unprecedented. But then everything about kissing Primrose was unprecedented.

He held her tightly to him, while his breath slowly steadied and his pulse stopped galloping, and it was almost as good as the kissing had been: just standing here, their arms around each other, her cheek pressed to his chest, his cheek resting on her hair.

Even after his heartbeat had steadied and his breathing was even, Oliver was reluctant to let her go. Because this was the best moment of the whole day. The best moment of *any* day since he'd returned to England.

Such a simple emotion, happiness.

He felt it right now. Felt it in the marrow of his bones. And how ridiculous was that? His cousin was trying to kill him, and yet he was happy.

Because of Primrose.

Finally, unwillingly, Oliver released her.

Primrose stepped back, and smoothed her gown. "You are a very unexpected person."

"Me?" Oliver thought about tart tongues and sweet kisses, about young ladies appearing and disappearing in the blink of an eye, about Faerie godmothers and magical wishes. "So are you." He held out his hand to her. "Come on, let's go see your brother."

They held hands all the way to the reception room door, and Oliver was as reluctant to release Primrose's hand as he'd been to stop kissing her. Which was more than a little confusing.

Look things in the face and know them for what they are.

If he looked this in the face . . . it looked an awful lot like he was falling in love with Primrose Garland.

CHAPTER 19

By the time they'd brought Rhodes up to date, it was almost dinner time. Oliver went next door to change. His valet had a steaming pitcher of water ready, and a change of clothing laid out on the bed.

Oliver was tying his neckcloth when an urgent knock sounded on his door.

He paused, while his valet opened the door.

Monsieur Benoît stood in the corridor. He looked agitated. "I'm sorry to disturb you, Your Grace—"

"Is it Rhodes?"

"Yes, sir."

Oliver threw aside the neckcloth and strode out into the corridor, ignoring the fact that he was in stockinged feet and shirtsleeves. "What is it?"

Benoît ushered him hastily into Rhodes's bed-chamber and closed the door.

Rhodes was standing in the middle of the room

in his nightshirt. The bed was in a state of disarray, pillows tumbled on the floor.

"What's wrong?" Oliver asked.

"Your *fucking* cousin, is what's wrong," Rhodes said, his voice thick with rage.

"What?"

The valet picked up one of the tumbled pillows and brought it to Oliver. "Look," he said, peeling back the pillowcase.

Oliver looked. And then looked more closely. "Is that . . . ?"

"Bishop's weed," Rhodes said. His face was livid with fury, his fists clenched. "Your fucking cousin put bishop's weed in my pillows—and I am going to *kill* him—"

Oliver crossed to him quickly and caught him by one wrist. "Lower your voice, man. He's only two doors from here."

Rhodes paused on an inhalation, caught between rage and prudence.

"Benoît, how much of that stuff is in his bed?"

"I haven't searched properly yet," the valet said.

"Then let's do that now." He released Rhodes's wrist. "Stay here, away from the bed."

Rhodes hissed out a breath. He didn't say anything, just gave a curt nod.

Oliver and Benoît searched the bed. It took five

minutes, and in those five minutes they found bishop's weed not only in every single pillow, but also under the bottom sheet and beneath the mattress. There were even sprigs of bishop's weed tucked into the bedhangings.

Oliver's own rage grew while they searched. By the time they'd finished he was as angry as Rhodes. Perhaps angrier. He put his hands on his hips, took a deep breath, and tried to not be pushed into action by his rage but rather to *think*.

"All right," he said. "Here's what we're going to do." He turned to the valet. "Benoît, my cousin is trying to kill me."

The valet's eyes widened.

"He did this—" Oliver gestured to the disordered bed, "—to get Rhodes out of the way."

The valet looked from the bed to Rhodes, and then back to Oliver.

"I want to catch my cousin red-handed," Oliver said. "So, I think it's best if we pretend we haven't found the bishop's weed. Rhodes, you and I'll swap rooms. You sleep in my bed; I'll sleep here."

Rhodes gave a single nod.

"I want you to stay in my room all day tomorrow."

"But—"

"By evening you should be well enough to help me catch Ninian—but he won't know that. He'll think you're still laid up in bed."

Rhodes closed his mouth.

"Can you bear to wear my clothes tomorrow? I think it's best if you leave everything here."

"I agree," the valet said. "I want to check the linings and all the pockets before Thayne wears anything."

Oliver glanced at the clock on the mantelpiece. "Damn, I've got to go. Wait until everyone's at dinner before moving to my room. It's important that no one in this wing notices. My cousin *mustn't* hear of this."

"No one will see us," Benoît promised.

Oliver strode to the door. "I'll tell Primrose what's happened. And my valet. He'll be expecting you."

❧

By the time he had explained everything to his valet, Grimshaw, and hastily finished dressing, Oliver was late for dinner. He hurried downstairs, to find everyone in the drawing room—although "every-one" wasn't that many people now, what with the Carterises gone, and Miss Warrington and Rhodes confined to bed. Lady Warrington was absent, too—presumably with her daughter, upstairs.

"I beg your pardon," Oliver said. "I lost track of time." His gaze skimmed the faces, passing over his uncle, his cousin, and Miss Middleton-Murray, before coming to rest on Primrose. Damnation. He wished they had a signal for *I have to talk with you the instant dinner is over.* He tried to convey his message with a single glance, then let his gaze move on, to Lord Warrington. "How is your daughter, sir? I trust her injuries aren't too serious?"

"Broken her nose," Warrington said gruffly.

The temptation to look daggers at Miss Middleton-Murray was almost overwhelming. Oliver mastered the impulse. "I'm very sorry to hear it, sir."

At that moment, dinner was announced. Everyone rose. Oliver made a beeline for Primrose and offered her his arm. Private conversation was impossible, surrounded as they were by eight other people, but he lightly pinched the back of her hand and gave her a significant look, and then he knocked over a lyre-back chair and took a moment to pick it up again and set it on its feet.

"Honestly, Westfell," Primrose said, exasperation in her voice, while at the same time she bumped into a sofa table, knocking several ornaments askew. She paused to reposition them. By the time she was satisfied with their arrangement, they were the last people in the drawing room. Her eyes met his. "What is it?" she whispered.

"I need to speak to you. Immediately after dinner,"

233

he whispered back. And then he realized that the State apartments would be pitch black at that hour. "The library? I'll duck out before the port is served."

Primrose nodded, and they stepped into the corridor. A minute later, they were seated on opposite sides of the dining table.

Oliver unfolded his napkin. He had Miss Middleton-Murray to one side of him, and Miss Cheevers to the other. He suppressed a sigh, and wished that the meal was already over.

The first course was served. Oliver helped himself to chicken á la *reine,* asparagus, peas, and two beef olives. Then he turned to Miss Cheevers, ready to start polite conversation, but Miss Cheevers's attention was wholly occupied by the man to her right: Ninian.

Oliver observed her for a moment—the flush on her cheeks, the shy smile on her lips. Primrose had been correct: Miss Cheevers was in love with Ninian.

How the devil had he missed that?

With Miss Cheevers thus occupied, the only person Oliver could make conversation with was Miss Middleton-Murray. He brought out his favorite subject for harpies: Trésaguet's method for paving roads.

Miss Middleton-Murray was a very good actress;

whatever he thought of her, he had to give her that. She listened to his monologue with an appearance of rapt attention, and whenever he paused for breath she made no attempt to change the subject, but instead offered him compliments. "How fascinating, Westfell. Do tell me more," and "How *knowledgeable* you are, Westfell," and "I could listen to you talk for hours, Westfell; you make everything sound so interesting!"

During the second course, Miss Middleton-Murray changed her tactics, asking about the innovations he intended to make on his estates. "I'm sure a man of such intelligence and vision as yourself must have plans."

Intelligence and vision?

Oliver swallowed his wine the wrong way. It took all his willpower to avoid choking. Once he could breathe again, he glanced at Primrose. To his profound disappointment she hadn't heard Miss Middleton-Murray's words.

"Plans?" he said. "Why, yes, I do." And then he proceeded to describe in tedious and painstaking detail a great number of wholly fictitious alterations that he was going to make to the mansion on Berkeley Square—that being the only one of his properties he was familiar with so far. He talked about the roof tiles for a full ten minutes, then moved on to the wainscoting, then the skirting boards, then the banisters, then the window treatments. Thank God, at that point, the footmen came to clear the meal.

He was exhausted—and he had to wonder who'd suffered most during dinner: Miss Middleton-Murray, or himself?

The ladies withdrew. Primrose sent him a glance as she left the room, to which Oliver returned an infinitesimal nod.

The brandy and port were placed on the table.

Oliver pushed back his chair. "Excuse me for a few minutes."

He left the dining room, and stood in the corridor for a moment. All was silent. No ladies lingered outside the drawing room.

Oliver trod quickly and quietly to the library, opened the door, and slipped inside.

Candles were lit in the sconces and a fire burned in the grate, but the light barely penetrated the shadows. He couldn't see the high ceiling. Couldn't even see the gallery that gave access to the upper tier of shelves.

Two wing-backed armchairs were positioned in front of the fireplace. Oliver crossed to them to wait for Primrose.

As he reached them, a figure rose from the armchair he'd been intending to sit in.

Oliver was so startled that, for the second time that day, he squeaked. And then—because what else *could* one do when one had squeaked?—he flung out his arms and pretended to swoon on the floor.

"*Honestly*, Oliver," he heard Primrose say.

He opened one eye and peered up at her.

Primrose stood over him, her hands on her hips. "Was this why you wanted to see me? So that you could indulge in dramatics?"

"No." He opened his other eye, too, and grinned up at her. "You do knock a man off his feet, Prim."

She shook her head at this.

"You startled me," Oliver said, climbing to his feet. "I was about to sit in that chair." He was tempted to suggest that they *both* sit in it together, she on his lap, but this was the library after all, and anyone could walk in at any moment, so he gestured for her to sit again and took the neighboring armchair.

"What is it?" she asked.

"Your brother," Oliver said, sobering. He told her about the bishop's weed in Rhodes's bed, and about their secretly swapping rooms. "So you can't visit him anymore, because people would think you're visiting *me*." He glanced at the clock on the mantelpiece. "Dash it. I'd better get back to my port."

"And I to my tea." Primrose stood. "Oh—I almost forgot to tell you! The string's gone."

"String? You mean that scrap around the newel post?"

She nodded. "It was gone when I came down to dinner. Now the only evidence we have is two scratches."

"It's not enough," Oliver said.

"I know." Primrose pulled a face, and headed for the door.

Oliver followed.

They parted ways in the corridor, Primrose to her tea, he to his port.

CHAPTER 20

Oliver went to sleep to the sound of rain against the windowpanes—and woke in the morning to silence. He flung back Rhodes's bedcovers, strode to the window, and jerked the curtains open.

Sunshine flooded into the room.

Oliver felt a surge of grim exultation. *Today's the day.*

Someone knocked quietly on the door.

"Who is it?" he called.

"Monsieur Benoît."

Oliver unlocked the door and opened it.

Benoît brought a ewer of steaming water with him. "How's Thayne?" Oliver asked, as the valet set the ewer beside the washstand.

"He's much improved, Your Grace."

Oliver shaved and dressed hastily, then went next door to see for himself. He found Rhodes going through his wardrobe with Grimshaw.

"Your sleeves are an inch too short," Rhodes told him.

"Your arms are an inch too long," Oliver retorted. He stepped closer and examined his friend. "You look a hundred times better."

"I feel a hundred times better." The huskiness was gone from Rhodes's voice and his face was no longer flushed. His eyelids were slightly puffy and his eyes a little bloodshot, but compared to how he'd been yesterday it was nothing.

"Your eyes still itchy?"

"Tiny bit," Rhodes said. "I'll keep bathing them. Should be fine by tonight." He paused. "We *are* on for tonight, I take it?"

"We're definitely on," Oliver said.

Benoît departed to fetch a tray of breakfast for Rhodes, and Oliver went down to the parlor.

Four people were already at the long table: Uncle Algernon, Ninian, and Mrs. and Miss Middleton-Murray. They gave him four different smiles. If he was going to score those smiles, he would have awarded Miss Middleton-Murray full marks—ten out of ten for the pretty curve of her lips, the delightful dimples, and the warm admiration in her eyes—but he was no longer scoring Miss Middleton-Murray on anything.

Oliver piled a plate high with eggs and sirloin, and sat down next to her, the better to keep an eye on Ninian, who was seated opposite. Miss Middleton-Murray mistook his motive; she lowered her gaze to her plate, but not before he saw the triumph there.

He left the onus of conversation to his table companions, all of whom were close to finishing their meals. Miss Middleton-Murray was particularly cheerful that morning—on account of the sunshine, she said, which could have been true, but Oliver thought it was mostly on account of successfully eliminating her competitors.

Ninian wasn't cheerful. In fact, he seemed rather on edge. He kept darting looks at Oliver.

Oliver pretended not to notice. He chewed his food, and smiled, and nodded—and kept his thoughts to himself.

The door opened. Oliver looked up, hoping it was Primrose, but it was Miss Cheevers. She blushed prettily and bade them good morning, filled her plate, and sat next to Ninian.

Ninian stopped sending Oliver those darting glances. His attention became wholly focused on Miss Cheevers.

Oliver eyed the pair of them, and wondered how on earth he failed to notice *that* romance.

Lord Cheevers was next to enter the breakfast parlor. When he saw his daughter sitting next to Ninian, he frowned. It appeared that Primrose was right: Cheevers didn't want his daughter to marry a mere Mister.

And thus, I have to die.

Oliver hid a grimace, and demolished another egg.

Fortunately, the next person to appear was Primrose. Since Lord Cheevers had taken the seat next to Oliver, she sat alongside Miss Cheevers. "Have you seen my brother this morning?" she asked, spreading her napkin in her lap. "How is he?"

"I think he's getting worse," Oliver said, and gave her a wink.

"Such a shame," Uncle Algy said. "Poor Thayne."

"Yes," Oliver said, managing not to glare at Ninian. "Poor Thayne."

"Perhaps he needs to be cupped again?" Uncle Algy said.

"I'll suggest it, certainly." Oliver caught Primrose's eye, and stroked his nose—and then surreptitiously snapped his fingers.

Primrose understood the silent message: *Meet me in the State dressing room when you've finished eating.*

And can you please translocate to behind the screen so I can watch? She gave a tiny nod.

Satisfied, Oliver finished his breakfast. The day stretched ahead of him. Somehow, he needed to avoid private conversation with Ninian. "We must go for a walk later," he said to Miss Middleton-Murray. "Make the most of this beautiful weather. Shall we say eleven o'clock?"

Again, he saw that flash of triumph. "I'd love to, Your Grace," she said, glancing up at him through long, curling eyelashes.

Oliver pushed back his chair, and stood. Across the table, Ninian's head jerked up. An expression of consternation crossed his face. He pushed back his own chair.

Oliver was in the corridor by the time Ninian caught up with him.

"I say, Cousin," Ninian said, a little timidly. "Could we perhaps—"

"Oh, yes, that's right: you wanted a private word." Oliver made himself smile widely at him. "Let's go riding, shall we? Say in half an hour?"

Relief flooded Ninian's face. "That would be perfect. Thank you."

The sunshine made a great difference to the State dressing room. It looked opulently majestic, rather than drearily sepulchral—the red damask on the walls, the black marble fireplace, the huge red-and-black lacquered screen with its *chinoiserie* dragons.

Oliver crossed to the sofa and peeked under the Holland cloth. Gilt and red velvet. He wrinkled his nose.

Come to think of it, now that he was Duke of Westfell he probably possessed more than his fair share of gilt-and-velvet furniture.

His wife would have to help him redecorate. Better yet, he could cede that task entirely to her.

He wondered what Primrose's taste in furniture was . . . and from there, found himself pondering the same questions he'd been pondering yesterday when she'd so unexpectedly appeared from behind that screen.

Just how much did he like Primrose?

Enough to marry her?

Because if he kept kissing her, that's where they were headed.

Oliver took up his stance, leaning against the wall where he had a good view behind the lacquered screen.

Whenever he had difficult decisions to make— ones where he couldn't see the answer straight away—he liked to take them apart and tackle them step by step.

Today's decision felt like the biggest one he'd ever made in his life, bigger even than deciding to join the army. Looked at head-on, it was rather daunting. But if one came up upon it in little steps . . .

Perhaps not so daunting.

He rolled his shoulders, and asked himself his first question, which was: Did he want to marry?

And the answer to that was easy: Yes, he did.

Eventually.

The second question was: Of all the women he'd met since returning to England, whom did he like the most?

Another easy answer: Lady Primrose Garland.

Which led to a significantly more difficult question . . . Did he want to marry Primrose?

Oliver pondered this for a while. Primrose's company was stimulating. She made him laugh. He was strongly attracted to her. And most importantly, she didn't treat him like a duke; she treated him like a real person. So the answer to that question was . . .

Yes. He rather thought he *did* want to marry her.

Which brought him to the most important question of all: If he and Primrose married, would they be happy together?

But while that question was crucial, it wasn't

actually difficult to answer. It took no feat of imagination to picture them happily married. Which wasn't to say that he didn't think there'd be annoyances or disagreements, but that he thought they liked and respected each other well enough to get past those things.

See? Difficult decisions weren't really so difficult after all. If one approached them step by step they made themselves.

In fact, only one decision remained: When should he propose to Primrose?

Oliver considered this while he waited for her to appear behind the screen. He'd intended to find his feet as a duke before seeking a wife, but a woman like Primrose—brought up in a duke's household—could *help* him find his feet. He had no doubt that she knew a hell of a lot more about managing estates than he did, and a hell of a lot more about his duties in the House of Lords.

Which meant that there was no reason to wait.

However, there was one small problem . . . Primrose might not want to marry him.

How was that for irony? There were dozens of young ladies who'd leap at the chance to marry him—no, be honest: hundreds—and yet the one he wanted was quite likely to refuse his offer.

Because she believed they didn't suit one another.

Oliver frowned, and shifted his shoulders against the wall. Primrose was intelligent. Sooner or later she'd realize that they did, in fact, suit each other very well.

More kisses would probably help his cause, because the more she enjoyed his kisses, the more likely she was to—

At that moment, Primrose appeared from thin air.

Oliver didn't squeak or recoil. In fact, he barely flinched. Which pleased him.

However, there was some fun to be had here, so he gave a breathy little shriek and pretended to faint, collapsing onto the thick carpet.

He heard almost inaudible footsteps. A shadow fell over him. A toe nudged his thigh. "Duke of West*fool*," Primrose said, which only reinforced his determination to marry her.

Oliver opened his eyes and grinned. "Very good, Prim."

She rolled her eyes at him. "How's Rhodes?"

"In excellent shape," Oliver said, climbing to his feet. "He'll be fighting fit by tonight."

"Good." She looked as relieved as Ninian had done, ten minutes ago, which reminded him . . .

"Prim, can you help me out today? Ninian wants to talk privately with me, and I need to avoid it without looking as if I *am* avoiding it."

She nodded. "Of course."

"For a start, I'm going riding with him shortly. I need you to invite yourself along." The door to the State bedchamber drew his eye. What did it look like now that the sun was out? He peeked inside, and winced. Those gilded columns were really quite garish.

He walked over to the great four-poster on its dais. "Have any kings slept here?"

"One, I believe."

Oliver flung himself down on the Holland-covered bed.

"Oliver! You can't lie on that. It's a State bed."

"I'm a duke. I can lie on State beds if I wish."

Primrose shook her head at him. "What time are you riding with Ninian?"

Oliver fished out his pocket watch. "In twenty minutes."

"Twenty minutes? But I'm not dressed for riding!"

"Then you'd best hurry, hadn't you?" He snapped his fingers.

"I can't translocate to my room. My maid may be there."

"Oh. Then I guess you'd better run."

Primrose huffed a breath at him, and did just that: run from the bedchamber. A moment later, he heard the door to the reception room open and close. Oliver felt a little guilty, but mostly what he felt was an overwhelming sense of gratitude.

I can rely on her. She has my back.

Oliver went upstairs to fetch his riding gloves, hat, and crop. He dawdled in the bedchamber, because twenty minutes really wasn't long if Primrose had to change her entire outfit. Rhodes watched without comment while he pulled on his riding gloves, but his expression was eloquent enough to speak for itself: Rhodes wanted to go riding, too.

"We'll go for a long ride tomorrow," Oliver promised him.

"I bloody well hope so."

"And remember: tonight we go hunting."

"I remember," Rhodes said grimly. "Be careful."

"I'm always careful," Oliver said. He let himself out of his room, walked down the corridor, and paused at the top of the stairs.

Ninian was waiting in the vestibule below, alone. There was no sign of Primrose.

Oliver descended the stairs slowly, one second per step, thirty-six seconds in all. As he reached the bottom he heard quick footsteps behind him. He glanced back, and saw Primrose.

"Oh," she cried gaily. "Are you going riding, too? Let's all go together."

Oliver exchanged a glance with Ninian, and made a show of reluctance. "Ah . . ."

"It'll be fun!" Primrose said, arriving on the final step. She was ever so slightly out of breath.

Oliver exchanged another glance with Ninian, and obeyed the dictates of courtesy. "It would be our pleasure to ride with you, Lady Primrose."

⚬⚭⚬

Riding occupied an hour. Strolling in the gardens with Miss Middleton-Murray occupied another one. She coaxed Oliver into describing his exploits as a dragoon, encouraging him with an endless stream of compliments: How *handsome* he must have been in his uniform, how *brave*, how *gallant*, how *daring*, how *heroic*. Oliver amused himself by imagining his head swelling with each compliment. By the time they had turned back to the house and climbed the long flight of steps up to the terrace— twenty-four steps; another flight of stairs *not* to be pushed down—his head was the size of a dowager's landaulet. Fortunately, at that point, they encountered Primrose, who'd changed from her riding habit into a muslin dress.

"Where have you been?" Oliver asked.

"Down to the lake," Primrose said, and stroked her nose.

Aha! She wanted to talk with him.

Oliver smiled, to show that he understood her message, and covertly snapped his fingers.

Primrose's eyelids twitched, which showed that *she* understood *his* message.

Once inside, Oliver shed Miss Middleton-Murray as quickly as he could, and headed for the State apartments.

Primrose arrived a minute later, appearing behind the lacquered screen.

"Aargh!" Oliver shrieked, and then pretended to swoon to the floor.

"You should have been an actor, not a duke," Primrose told him dryly.

Oliver opened one eye. "I know." Then he opened the other. "Wait! Do you think I could be a duke *and* an actor?" He sat up on the floor. "That's a thought! What do you think, Prim? The Duke of Westfell as . . . Romeo!"

"The Duke of Westfell as . . . Dogberry."

"Harsh, Prim. Very harsh," Oliver said—while making a mental note to hunt down a copy of *Much Ado About Nothing* and learn some of Dogberry's lines.

Primrose ignored this comment. "I had a look at the jetty. The boathouse doesn't have any windows, but if we open the doors a crack we'll be able to see everything. It's nearly full moon, so there should be enough light."

"We?"

"Rhodes and I."

Oliver shook his head. "It's not necessary, Prim. Rhodes and I can handle it alone."

"You can't possibly think that I'm not coming."

"I do think it."

Primrose crossed her arms and looked down her nose at him. "Why? Because I'm a female?"

Oliver realized that he was at a disadvantage, sitting on the floor. He climbed to his feet. "Because there's no need."

"We want as much proof as possible, don't we? As many witnesses as possible."

"Well . . . yes."

"So, I'm coming."

Oliver took a moment to consider how much danger she could potentially be in. "Can you swim?"

"It's *you* Ninian's going to push in, not me."

Oliver grimaced at this reminder. "Even so—"

"I can swim," Primrose said. "At least, enough to get out of the lake." And then she gave a mischievous smile. "I can also wish myself ashore."

That was certainly true—but it didn't make Oliver feel any happier. He hesitated before speaking: "It might get a little ugly, Prim. If Ninian puts up a fight there'll likely be some blood, some language you'd rather not hear."

"I'm twenty-seven, Oliver. I can handle blood and swearing."

Still Oliver hesitated—and then he realized, somewhat belatedly, that he couldn't prevent Primrose from being at the boathouse tonight. If she wanted to be there she would simply wish herself there.

"All right," he said, grudgingly. "But you must promise to be careful."

"I promise."

He pointed a finger at her. "You're an observer only. You do *not* get involved."

"I promise," she said again.

"All right. You can come." But he wasn't happy about it. In fact, he was so *un*happy about it that he found himself unable to stand still. He walked to the window, looked out for a moment, then walked into the State bedroom and looked out the window there, too. Both rooms had a fine view of the rose garden. When he turned around, Primrose was standing in the doorway. "Stay behind Rhodes at all times," he told her. "Do *not* confront Ninian. Leave that to Rhodes and me."

"Yes, Oliver." She smiled, as if she found his anxiousness amusing. "I'm not an idiot, you know."

"I know." But he was still worried, damn it.

Primrose crossed to where he stood. Daylight gilded her hair, bringing out glints of silver and gold. The pendant she wore at her throat, a tiny golden acorn, gleamed as brightly as the sun. She tucked her hand into the crook of his arm in a manner that she no doubt thought was comforting. The odd thing was that it *was* comforting.

"Only a few more hours," she said.

"Yes." And that was comforting, too: knowing that this whole God-awful mess would soon be resolved. Not happily, of course—he winced at the thought of what Uncle Algy's reaction would be when he learned the truth about his son—but finished. Done with. Over.

And then he could move on with being the Duke of Westfell. Learn to manage his estates. Find his feet in the House of Lords. Take a wife.

He gave Primrose a sidelong glance. *I want you,* he thought. Although it wasn't so much a thought as a feeling, a sense of certainty.

"I'll try to stick close to you this afternoon," Primrose said. "But I think we need another signal, in case Ninian tries to arrange a tête-à-tête."

"All right," Oliver said. "What?"

Her lips tucked in enticingly as she pondered this question, and then—unfortunately—she released his arm. "How about this?" She tugged one earlobe.

"All right," Oliver said again—and then he remembered how cleverly and stealthily Ninian had taken Rhodes out of the picture. "But if you do need to interrupt a tête-à-tête, try to bring Miss Cheevers, too. Or even Miss Middleton-Murray. The more people the better. Make it look as if it's not your idea."

Primrose nodded.

Oliver returned his gaze to the rose gardens. His mood was odd. On one level, he was happy that Primrose was standing beside him right now, but on another level . . . he felt less happy than he had in years.

"Ninian will be champing at the bit by this evening," Primrose observed.

"Yes." Why did that give him no satisfaction?

Because he dreaded the upcoming confrontation with Ninian. Because he wished it wasn't necessary.

It was one thing to have strangers try to kill you in the pursuit of warfare; quite another to have one's sole surviving cousin attempt to do it.

Oliver sighed, and only realized he'd done it when Primrose tucked her hand into the crook of his arm again.

"It'll be over soon," she said.

He turned his head and smiled down at her. "Yes." And once it was over, he'd ask her to marry him.

A few kisses between now and then would be beneficial, though, because the more often he kissed her and the more often she liked it, the more likely she was to agree to marry him. Right?

He dipped his head and touched his lips to hers—and they were soft and sweet and yielding—and then he deepened the kiss, slipping his tongue into her mouth—and she drew back.

"It's luncheon in a few minutes, Oliver."

"So?"

"So, I can't go into that room looking as if I've just been kissed."

"No one will notice," he said, making another attempt on her mouth.

"Miss Middleton-Murray might."

A shiver went up his spine. "We don't want that."

"No."

"A postponement, then," he said, reaching out to touch one fingertip lightly to her lips. "Until *after* luncheon."

But after luncheon, Ninian asked to speak privately with him again. "Absolutely," Oliver said, glancing at Primrose, who sat opposite him. He tugged on his earlobe. "Shall we have a game of billiards?"

"Yes," Ninian said, with a relieved smile.

They adjourned to the billiard room, and less than a minute later Primrose, Miss Cheevers, and Miss Middleton-Murray joined them. Oliver gave Ninian an apologetic grimace, and Primrose a covert wink.

He spent the next hour instructing the ladies in the art of playing billiards, then glanced at his pocket watch and said, "Goodness, is that the time? I promised to play chess with Thayne. Excuse me, will you?"

He met his uncle in the vestibule.

"How about a walk?" Uncle Algy said. "Glorious day."

"I'd love to," Oliver said, and it was the perfect truth. "But I'm promised to Thayne right now. Perhaps later?"

He and Rhodes didn't play chess; they talked, firming up tonight's plan. Rhodes looked quite his normal self. The whites of his eyes were just that: white.

After an hour, Oliver slipped downstairs again. He found everyone in the yellow salon, drinking tea.

Ninian brightened when he saw Oliver. "I say—"

"Would you like some tea, Westfell?" Primrose asked.

"Yes, please."

Lady Cheevers did the honors, pouring him a cup.

Oliver sat on a sofa and sipped it very, very slowly, aware of Ninian hovering on the edge of his vision.

After Oliver's eighth tiny sip, Ninian made his approach. He lowered his voice. "Cousin . . ."

"Yes, we must talk." Oliver made himself smile at Ninian. "Just as soon as I've finished this tea."

Relief lit Ninian's face—and then he almost immediately sobered. "Thank you."

Oliver took his ninth tiny sip, and upended the cup on his lap. "Dash it," he said, standing quickly, brushing at the spreading dampness on his breeches. "Excuse me."

He winked at Primrose as he left the room.

It didn't take long to change a pair of breeches, but Oliver managed to draw the process out. He chatted with Rhodes, he tied a fresh neckcloth, he combed his hair, he even took a moment to buff his boots with the discarded breeches—which would have made his valet wince if he'd seen him do it.

"Be careful," Rhodes said, when Oliver finally left the bedchamber.

"I'm always careful," Oliver said.

He walked down the corridor and stood for a moment at the top of the stairs, all thirty-six of them. Thank God the Cunninghams' stairs hadn't been this numerous. He might not have survived that fall.

Oliver grimaced, and fished out his pocket watch. It was later than he'd thought. Only a few more hours of avoiding Ninian and there would be an end to this.

Although not a happy ending. Not for Ninian. And not for Uncle Algy, either.

Oliver sighed. God, he dreaded that conversation—telling Uncle Algy that his son had tried to commit murder.

He tucked the watch back into his pocket—and as he did so the hairs on the nape of his neck sprang upright.

Had someone just *breathed* behind him?

Before he could turn his head, a hand shoved him violently between the shoulder blades.

CHAPTER 21

*P*rimrose was in conversation with Miss Middleton-Murray when the door to the yellow salon opened. Miss Middleton-Murray had asked Primrose which were her favorite authors and was listening with flattering attention to her reply, but Primrose wasn't fooled; Miss Middleton-Murray had as much interest in books as Primrose had in embroidery, which was to say, none.

She's buttering me up.

The question was: Why?

Primrose was pondering this—while at the same time explaining why Pliny's letters made such fascinating reading—when the door opened and Oliver poked his head into the room. He conducted a quick scan of the occupants, saw her, rubbed his nose, and withdrew.

Primrose lost her train of thought. Oliver had looked a little odd, not quite like his usual self.

It took her a moment to pinpoint the difference: his hair had been disheveled, as if he'd been brawling with someone.

She conducted her own scan of the salon's occupants. When had Ninian Dasenby left the room? Surely he'd been there the last time she'd looked?

"Lady Primrose?"

Primrose blinked, and discovered that Miss Middleton-Murray was looking at her very intently.

"You were saying . . . ?"

What *had* she been saying? "Oh, I, uh, . . . I think Pliny's description of the eruption of Vesuvius is fascinating. An eyewitness account, you know." She glanced at the door. "Do excuse me. I think it's time I looked in on my brother."

Primrose made her way quickly to the State reception room, checked that no one was within sight, and slipped inside. The instant the door had closed, she wished herself behind the screen in the dressing room. It saved a few seconds only, but she found herself unaccountably anxious to see Oliver.

Oliver was waiting for her. He didn't screech and pretend to faint, just stood quietly—and she knew that something was very, *very* wrong.

"What is it?" she asked.

Oliver grimaced. He turned away and limped towards the bedroom.

Primrose followed, anxiously. "What, Oliver?"

Oliver didn't fling himself down on the State bed; he cautiously lowered himself.

"You're hurt," Primrose said, stating the obvious.

Oliver lay back, moving as gingerly as an old man.

"Oliver." She was afraid and impatient at the same time, wanting to shake him but not daring to. "*What's happened?*"

"Ninian pushed me down the main staircase."

Primrose stared at him, aghast. "How far did you fall?"

"All the way to the bottom."

Primrose pictured the long flight of stairs, and the hard marble floor at the bottom. "But . . . how on earth are you still alive?"

Oliver grunted a laugh. "Practice."

Primrose climbed up onto the bed and knelt beside him. "You need to see a doctor. You must have broken bones!"

"I don't need a doctor, Prim. I'm fine. Just a bit bruised, is all." He held out one hand to her.

Primrose took it in both of hers. "You're not fine. My God, there must be thirty steps at the very least!"

"Thirty-six steps," Oliver said. "But I haven't broken anything."

"But—"

"Do you know what the other fellows in my regiment used to call me?"

Primrose shook her head.

"Cropper," Oliver said. "Cropper Dasenby. Because I fell off my horse so often." He smiled crookedly at her. "'Come a cropper.' You know?"

Primrose nodded.

"So I know how broken bones feel."

"Yes, but, you really *do* need to see a doctor. Just to be certain."

"I've broken my arm before—twice—and some fingers and my collarbone, and a couple of ribs. I know how it feels, Prim."

Primrose bit her lip. She interlaced her fingers with his. "You must have fallen off your horse a lot."

Oliver's smile became a grin. "I did." He shifted on the bed, winced, and then said, "He loved to unseat me when we were on parade. I swear to God he laughed every time he did it."

"Why didn't you get a different horse?"

"Because I liked him. Only horse I've ever had with a sense of humor. And he was rock steady on the battlefield."

Primrose looked down at his hand clasped in hers, studied it, and found a faint, bloodless graze across his knuckles. She stroked it gently with her thumb. "Thirty-six steps, Oliver. That's a lot higher than a horse."

"There's a trick to falling. You've got to relax, go with it."

"And yet you broke bones when you fell off your horse."

"Not once I figured out the trick." He squeezed her fingers. "Trust me, Prim; I'm fine. I rolled down those stairs like a rag doll."

Primrose pictured the staircase again. *Thirty-six* steps. She repressed a shudder. "Did you see him? Ninian?"

Oliver shook his head. "Came up behind me as silently as a cat, pushed me, and didn't wait around to see what happened. Mind you, it took me a good minute to find my feet again. He had plenty of time to hide."

She clutched his hand a little tighter. "We'll get him tonight."

"We most definitely will," Oliver said grimly. "I'm looking forward to it." His tone seemed to promise the blood that he'd warned her of earlier . . . which was no less than Ninian deserved. In fact, if Rhodes and Oliver failed to punch Ninian, *she* would punch him herself.

Primrose discovered that her fingers were clenched rather tightly around Oliver's. She loosened her grip and rubbed her thumb across his knuckles again. "You should go upstairs, lie down until dinner."

"I'm lying on the best bed in the house," Oliver said. "Fit for a king." He slanted her a smile. "And besides . . . this bed has you on it."

Primrose felt herself blush.

"Half an hour. Then I'll go upstairs. Promise." He closed his eyes.

Primrose studied his face. He looked weary and a little rough around the edges, his hair sticking up messily, his neckcloth askew.

Oliver might not have broken any bones, but he must be black and blue beneath his clothing.

His eyelids lifted. "Lie down, Prim. It's comfy."

"Lie down?" she said, shocked. "I couldn't possibly!"

"Because it's a State bed? You're already sitting on it, you goose."

"I can't lie down because *you're* lying down. It wouldn't be at all proper!"

An emotion flickered across his face. She recognized it as disappointment. "Lady Prim-and-Proper," he said, and closed his eyes again.

Primrose huffed out a breath. The nickname stung. *Was* she being too prim and proper, too prudish?

Live each day as if it were your last, Marcus Aurelius had said, and if today were her last day, which would she regret more? Lying down beside Oliver, or *not* lying down beside him?

265

Primrose released Oliver's hand and cautiously lay down alongside him.

He turned his head and smiled at her. "See? Comfy."

Primrose couldn't think of a single thing to say.

Oliver reached out one arm and pulled her closer, tucking her against him so that her head rested on his shoulder.

Primrose's heartbeat sped up. She tried not to stiffen. "Doesn't that hurt you?"

"No." Oliver exhaled a long, sighing breath. It was hard to see his face from this angle, but she thought that his eyes were closed again.

Gradually, she relaxed. Oliver was right: it was comfortable lying like this. Extraordinarily comfortable. His body was warm, and his arm around her made her feel safe in a way that she'd never experienced before. His scent came to her faintly: sandalwood and clean linen. She heard his breathing, was aware of the rise and fall of his chest, could almost feel his heartbeat.

"I'm glad you're all right," she whispered.

"So am I. When he pushed me . . . for a moment I thought . . ."

She could finish that sentence for him: For a moment Oliver had thought he was going to die.

She felt him shiver, and then he said, "Thank God for Verdun."

"Verdun?"

"My horse."

Primrose echoed his statement: "Thank God for Verdun."

Oliver's arm tightened a little around her. They lay silently. After a moment, Primrose closed her eyes. Every fiber of her body was rejoicing in Oliver's aliveness—her skin delighting in soaking up his warmth, her ears delighting in the sound of his breathing, her nose delighting in his scent. Her heart was beating two words: *He's alive. He's alive. He's alive.*

Oliver gave a tiny, convulsive start. "Lord, I just about fell asleep. Talk to me, Prim."

Primrose opened her eyes and gazed at the State bedhangings. "What about?"

"I don't know." He yawned. "What wishes did your sisters choose?"

"Well, Violet chose to be able to fly, and—"

"Fly? Violet can *fly*?"

"Yes."

"What, does she grow wings?"

"No, of course not. It's more like levitation."

"Huh." Oliver thought about this for a moment, and then said, "What about Aster?"

"She chose invisibility."

"Invisibility?" Primrose heard surprise in his voice.

"Yes. One of my cousins chose that, too."

"Who? No—wait—let me guess. . . . Clematis?"

"Daphne."

"Daphne," he repeated, and then fell silent for several seconds. "I have to say, Prim, this is all rather . . ."

She wondered what word he'd choose. Overwhelming? Disturbing?

"My mind is boggled," he said, in typical Oliver fashion.

Primrose choked on a laugh.

"Do you think Vi would let me watch her fly?"

"Probably." She turned her head to look at him. "Is that what you'd have chosen if you had a wish? Flying?"

"I don't know," Oliver said. "Possibly. What are the other choices?"

"There are dozens. And you can make up new ones, you know. My great-great-grandmother did that. She asked Baletongue to put a wish on a charm bracelet, so that whoever wore one of the charms wouldn't get pregnant."

"What?" He turned his head and stared at her. "You're joking, right?"

"About what?"

"About the charms."

"No. My great-great-grandmother was only

twenty-three, but she already had six children. She wanted to control when she had more. *If* she had more."

"That's . . . an interesting choice."

"It's a sensible choice," Primrose said. "Women die in childbirth."

"I know." His arm tightened around her shoulders. "Your great-great-grandmother sounds like a very intelligent person."

"She was." Primrose touched the acorn pendant at her throat. "Mother and my aunts have charms from that bracelet, and so do all of us girls."

"What?" Oliver said again. "This time you *are* joking, right?"

"No."

Oliver was silent for almost a minute. "My mind is even more boggled, now," he said finally, and then: "Not that acorn you're wearing?"

"Yes."

He removed his arm from around her and rolled onto his side to face her, wincing as he did so. "May I see it?"

Primrose pushed up on her elbow and fished the pendant from her neckline. She held it out. It was small and smooth and warm in her fingers.

Oliver leaned closer and took the little golden acorn. Their faces almost touched. "A magic charm from your great-great-grandmother." His tone was bemused.

"Yes."

Oliver shook his head and laughed, then tucked the pendant back inside her neckline. "Now I'm boggled *and* discombobulated."

Primrose suddenly felt a little boggled and discombobulated, too. There had been nothing lascivious about the brief touch of his fingers against her skin—it had been friendly, if intimate, and not in the least bit seductive—but her heart began thumping hard and her skin seemed to prickle all over and part of her was disappointed that his touch *hadn't* been seductive.

Oliver gave her a small, mischievous grin. "Have you put that acorn to the test, Prim?"

"Of course not!"

His grin widened. "Didn't think so." He leaned closer and kissed her, cupping the back of her head with one hand—and then broke the kiss with a wince. "Ouch."

"Lie down, Oliver."

He gave a low, frustrated growl, and did. "Remind me to wring Ninian's neck when we catch him tonight."

Primrose sat up. "We really should send for a doctor."

"I don't need a doctor. What I need is for some-one to kiss me better."

Primrose shook her head at him.

Oliver stared back at her with wide-eyed inno-cence. "But I *do*."

Primrose bit her lip, and glanced at him through her eyelashes. "Where does it hurt?" And then she heard what she'd said, heard *how* she'd said it. Was she flirting with him? She, who had never flirted with anyone in her life?

Oliver gave another of those small, mischievous grins of his. "Here," he said, pointing to his elbow. "It hurts here."

Primrose gave him what felt like a governess look—raised eyebrows, pursed lips, more than a little skeptical.

Oliver opened his eyes even wider, exuding innocence.

Primrose huffed out a put-upon sigh. "All right, then," she said, and bent to place a kiss on the indi-cated elbow, pressing her lips to the green superfine of his tailcoat. Then she lifted her head and met Oliver's eyes.

He was watching her quite intently. He didn't look innocent any longer, or mischievous. He looked as if he was holding his breath in much the same way that she was holding hers.

"And here," he said softly, pointing to his shoulder.

Primrose obligingly leaned over him and pressed her lips to his shoulder, then she raised her head and met his gaze again. She should have felt stupid, foolish, self-conscious . . . but she didn't. Not in the slightest. Instead, she felt alive. Anticipation tingled in her blood.

"And here," he said, pointing to his ear.

She laughed. "It doesn't hurt there."

"Yes, it does."

Primrose rolled her eyes, and bent and kissed his ear. His short brown hair softly tickled her nose. She wanted to bury her face in it, an urge so strong it was almost a compulsion. With effort she forced herself to break that contact, but speech was impossible; her throat was too tight.

It seemed that Oliver had the same problem. He pointed wordlessly to the angle of his jaw.

Primrose bent her head again.

She knew what his lips tasted like, what they felt like. His jaw was quite different. Nowhere near as soft—skin over hard bone—and not as smooth, either. It felt masculine beneath her lips, faintly prickly with whiskers.

She wanted to open her mouth and taste him with her tongue and see if he *tasted* masculine, too. Wanted to bite him lightly, to sink her teeth into that thin, tantalizing layer of skin.

Primrose lifted her head abruptly. She felt a little light-headed, a little too warm.

Oliver was staring at her. His eyes looked darker than usual, as if his pupils were slightly dilated. He swallowed, and then pointed to his mouth. "Here. This is where it hurts the most."

It was patent nonsense, but she didn't challenge him on it. Instead, Primrose dipped her head and kissed him.

For a man who talked so much nonsense, Oliver had a wonderful mouth. A *perfect* mouth—yielding lips and nipping teeth and a teasing, clever tongue.

Primrose leaned over him, the better to kiss him. Oliver's arms slid around her waist. He drew her closer and sighed into her mouth.

She lost herself in the slow dance of their tongues, in the heat, the pleasure, the sheer perfection of the moment. The Prince Regent could have come into the room and she wouldn't have noticed. Her whole world was Oliver. Oliver's lips. Oliver's tongue. Oliver's arms around her. Oliver's body warm and solid beneath her . . .

Primrose came to her senses—and realized that she wasn't merely leaning *over* Oliver; she was leaning *on* him, the entire weight of her upper body resting on his chest.

She broke the kiss and lifted herself hastily off him. "I must be hurting you!"

Oliver laughed, a breathless, ragged sound. "Hurting me? That's not what I'd call it."

"But your injuries—"

"I feel a thousand times better." He caught her chin with one hand and brushed his thumb over her tingling lips. "Your kisses are magical, Primrose Garland."

Primrose felt herself blush hotly. She tried to shake her head, but Oliver didn't let her; he held her chin, his thumb pressed to her lips. Her gaze was caught in his. She couldn't have looked away if the fate of the world had depended on it.

Oliver stroked his thumb over her lips again. "We're going to have to test that acorn of yours, Prim. You know that, don't you?" His voice was a low whisper that sent a shiver up her spine.

Primrose could barely breathe, could barely speak. "Perhaps," she whispered back.

Oliver smiled at her. Not a mischievous smile; a sensual smile. A smile that *promised*. Then he released her. "But not now." He pushed up to sit with a stifled groan. "Now, I have to get ready for dinner, because tonight Ninian gets his comeuppance."

"He most certainly does."

Primrose scrambled off the bed and briskly smoothed the creases from her gown. The acorn seemed to burn on its thin, golden chain.

Oliver climbed off the bed more slowly, wincing as he did.

"What's the plan?" she asked. "When will Rhodes and I go down to the boat shed?"

"Immediately after dinner." Oliver kneaded the back of his neck. "Don't go to the drawing room at all. Make your excuses, go upstairs and change into warmer clothes, and get yourself down to the jetty." He snapped his fingers to show how she was to accomplish this. "Rhodes will already be there. He says he won't set foot on the jetty until you've arrived, so you're safe to translocate there."

Primrose nodded.

"I'll drink my port, then invite Ninian to stroll down to the lake." He craned his neck to one side, then the other, then kneaded it again. "I'll be drunk. *Very* drunk. Once we're at the jetty, I'll stand right at the end—and Ninian will push me in and watch me drown—and you and Rhodes will witness it."

"And after that?" Primrose said.

"Rhodes might punch him," Oliver admitted. "And so might I."

And so might I, she thought.

"And then we'll have a chat with him, see what he has to say for himself, ask him if he killed my uncle and cousin. And after that . . ." He blew out a breath and dragged his fingers roughly through

275

his disheveled hair. He looked grim, weary. "I don't know, Prim. We'll see how it plays out." He gave her a lopsided smile and held his hand out to her, palm up. "Ready?"

Primrose put her hand in his. "Ready," she said.

CHAPTER 22

*I*t was actually harder to pretend to be drunk than Oliver had thought it would be. He had no problem slurring his words and uttering the occasional hiccup, no problem giving a rambling and repetitive account of the six-month-long journey from India, no problem stumbling as he walked, almost losing his balance . . . but putting it all together was surprisingly difficult. He kept losing his place in the monologue—which hopefully only added to verisimilitude.

He was relieved when he and Ninian reached the lake shore. His heart gave a little kick in his chest as the jetty came into sight. *This is it.*

Oliver paused for a moment and stood swaying, looking at the silky black water, the dark hump of the island, the silvery moon and its reflection—and the boat shed, with its door discreetly ajar. "Lovely, ain' it?" he said, and then hiccuped loudly.

"Yes," Ninian said. "Cousin, I really *must* speak with you—"

"Speaking with me now, aren't you?" Oliver said cheerfully. He gave Ninian a friendly clout on the shoulder, then staggered onto the jetty.

Ninian followed. "Perhaps we oughtn't be out here," he said nervously. "You might fall off."

"Me? Fall off? Agile as a cat, I am." He gave an artistic lurch, staggered two steps sideways, and caught his balance.

Ninian clutched his sleeve. "Cousin, I don't think this is a good idea."

Oliver shook his arm free. "Nonshensh," he said loudly, and strode down the jetty, veering first to the left, and then to the right. He arrived at the very end and stood swaying, gazing up at the moon, open-mouthed. "Look at that moon. Round as a . . . as a . . . as a round thing."

He was aware of Ninian coming to stand beside him.

Oliver's heartbeat sped up. He stopped looking at the moon and pretended to be staring at its reflection in the water. The skin between his shoulder blades tightened, waiting for that familiar push. "A pumpkin," he announced. "Round as a pumpkin."

The water looked black. Cold. Bottomless. He repressed a shiver. Whose idea had this been?

"Not a pumpkin. A norange. Round as a norange. Ha!" He laughed, while the skin between his shoulder blades grew tighter. "D' you hear that, Ninian? Norange."

Ninian plucked at his sleeve. "Please, Cousin. Let's go back to the house. I really must talk with you."

Oliver repressed a sigh of frustration. *Look at all this water, you idiot. Can't you see the lake's perfect for murder?* "Norange," he said again, out loud. "Thass a new word, y' know. I made it up."

"Yes, I heard it," Ninian said. "Very clever." He took hold of Oliver's sleeve.

Oliver tensed. He was already shivering in anticipation of the shock of cold water.

But Ninian didn't push him. He clearly had something else in mind. Probably a poisoned bottle of port.

Oliver realized he was going to have to take this into his own hands.

He hiccupped and gave a lurch and stepped off the jetty—and plummeted into the water.

It was colder than he'd thought it would be. A hell of a lot colder. Cold enough to rob him of his breath for a moment. Cold enough to almost freeze his balls off.

Oliver gasped in shock, and flailed about with his

arms. One foot touched the bottom. He wanted to scramble back up onto the jetty as fast as he could. Instead, he took a deep breath and flopped over on his stomach and lay motionless, face down.

He was blind like this, quite blind. Unable to see. Unable to breathe. He imagined Ninian standing at the jetty's edge, staring down at him—

Someone jumped into the water with an almighty *splash,* grabbed one of Oliver's arms, and tried to haul him upright. "Help!" the person cried. "Someone help us!"

Oliver recognized that voice: Ninian.

He struggled free of Ninian's grasp and found his feet. "What the devil?" he said, water streaming down his face.

"It's all right, Cousin," Ninian cried, grabbing Oliver's arm again. "I've got you."

Oliver wrenched free and staggered back a step. "Why aren't you drowning me?"

Ninian gaped at him, his face ghostly white in the moonlight, his mouth a dark hole. "What?"

"Why aren't you drowning me?" Oliver demanded again.

"Why would I drown you?"

"Because you want me dead," Oliver said harshly.

"What? No, I don't."

"Then why did you push me in front of that

post-chaise?" Oliver said, even more harshly. Rage boiled in him. He stepped closer and shoved Ninian in the chest.

Ninian sat down in the water, submerged briefly, and then scrambled to his feet again. "I *didn't* push you," he protested, spluttering.

"The devil you didn't," Oliver said, his hands clenching.

"No! I didn't! I swear I never—"

"And you just happened to *fall* out of your chair yesterday," Oliver said. His voice was as icy as the water. "I'm not a fool, Ninian. I can tell when someone's trying to poison me."

"I wasn't trying to poison you," Ninian cried. "I was trying to *save* you!"

"No." Oliver shook his head.

"He *did* just jump into the lake to save your life," Rhodes said from above them.

Both Oliver and Ninian jerked around in the water. Two figures peered down at them from the edge of the jetty.

"And he called for help," Primrose observed.

"Some pretty compelling evidence right there," Rhodes said.

Oliver said nothing. His head was beginning to ache from the cold. He sloshed to the jetty and silently climbed the ladder.

Ninian followed. Neither of them spoke. The truth loomed hugely in the darkness. Oliver didn't speak. He couldn't speak. Denial thundered inside him. No. No, it wasn't true. It *couldn't* be true.

"Here," Primrose said, handing him a blanket.

Numbly, he took it and wrapped it around himself.

"And here's one for you, Ninian."

Oliver turned and walked back along the jetty, halting when he reached the shore. He didn't know what to do, what to say, didn't even know what direction to walk in. And so he stood, shivering, while the truth loomed larger and larger.

Who had given him a snuff box filled with a "special mix"?

Who had poured out five glasses of Madeira in advance, one of which was larger than the others and especially for Oliver?

Who would become the next Duke of Westfell?

No one moved. No one spoke. Oliver was aware of Rhodes standing silently beside him. A steady *drip-drip-drip* came from behind them. Ninian.

Ninian, who *hadn't* been trying to kill him.

Oliver turned towards that *drip-drip-drip* and looked at his cousin.

Ninian was little more than an amorphous shape in the moonlight—dark blanket, pale blur of a face.

"I don't understand," Oliver said. His voice didn't

sound like his own, faint and bewildered.

Ninian hunched into his blanket. He shook his head.

"I mean, I understand why *you* would want to kill me—Cheevers wants a peer for a son-in-law—but why would Uncle *Algy*—?" His voice broke on that name. He couldn't speak for a moment. The sense of disbelief, of betrayal, was too overwhelming.

Uncle Algy had been trying to kill him?

Uncle Algy, who'd visited when he'd been a boy, who'd laughed and given him guineas?

Uncle Algy, who'd dealt with all the paperwork when Oliver had inherited the dukedom, and who'd welcomed him so enthusiastically back to England?

"Why, damn it?" His voice was too loud, almost a shout, rough and hoarse, as if he was trying not to cry. "*Why?*"

"Money," Ninian said, his voice as quiet as Oliver's had been loud.

Oliver shook his head. No. It wasn't true. It couldn't be true. He wouldn't *let* it be true.

And then, as he looked at Ninian, shivering and dripping and huddling into his blanket, he realized something. This was as terrible for Ninian as it was for him. Perhaps even more terrible, because while Lord Algernon was Oliver's uncle, he was Ninian's *father.*

Oliver crossed to his cousin and hugged him. "I'm sorry, Ninian." And he *was* sorry. Sorry that he'd misjudged Ninian. Sorry at how painful this must be for Ninian. "Thank you for jumping in to save me."

Ninian shivered, and uttered a sound like a sob.

"This is why you've been trying to speak to me alone, isn't it? Your father?"

Ninian gave another convulsive shiver. "Yes. I'm sorry. I—"

"No, I'm sorry. *We're* sorry." Oliver hugged him more tightly. "We thought . . ." He couldn't say *We thought you were a murderer* to Ninian's face, so he shut his mouth instead.

"We need to talk," Rhodes said, from behind them. "All of us. But first, the pair of you need dry clothes—and a stiff drink."

CHAPTER 23

Primrose waited in her room, pacing the floor, watching the clock on the mantelpiece. When half an hour had ticked past, she hastened to Rhodes's bedchamber.

Monsieur Benoît opened the door. Rhodes stood by the fireplace, arms folded, unsmiling.

Primrose crossed to her brother. "Well?" she said, by way of greeting.

He grimaced. "Guess who I ran into outside Ollie's door?"

Her heart sank. "Not Lord Algernon?"

"None other. I bumped into him—quite literally."

"That's . . . unfortunate."

"He knows I'm up and about, now. Damn it."

A quiet knock sounded on the door. This time, it was Ninian Dasenby who stood on the threshold.

Primrose directed her warmest smile at him. "Come in, Mr. Dasenby."

Dasenby hesitated, and then did so. His manner was apprehensive, his eyes wide and a little wary.

"How do you feel?" Primrose asked, examining his face. She thought he looked extremely pale. "Here, sit in this armchair by the fire."

Dasenby hesitated again, and then crossed to the fireplace and sat. Rhodes poured brandy from a bottle Primrose hadn't noticed into a glass she hadn't noticed and gave it to Dasenby. Then he poured one for himself.

"I'll have one, too," Primrose said. "Tonight has been . . ." There were too many adjectives to describe tonight's events—dramatic and shocking were only two of them.

Rhodes didn't tell her that drinking brandy was unbecoming of a lady; he silently poured another glass.

Primrose took a sip. The taste wasn't exactly pleasant, but the heady burn of alcohol made up for it—the rush of sensation across her tongue and down her throat, followed by a soothing warmth. She looked at Dasenby, perched nervously in the armchair, clutching his glass. Perhaps it was a trick of the firelight, but he looked disconcertingly young—a boy, not a man, pale-faced and vulnerable.

He's only twenty-two, she reminded herself. Twenty-two—and dealing with the fact that his father was trying to murder his cousin.

Someone rapped on the door.

Benoît admitted Oliver, then looked at Rhodes. "Do you wish me to leave, sir?"

"No, you're part of this, too."

"As you wish." Benoît closed the door and locked it.

Dasenby stood at Oliver's entry, looking even younger and more apprehensive, but Oliver waved him back into the armchair.

"Brandy, Ollie?"

"Yes." Oliver took the glass that Rhodes held out and sat on the end of the bed, leaning against one of the posts. He sipped the brandy and turned his gaze on Dasenby. "So."

Dasenby stared back at him, clutching his glass.

"Why don't you tell us what you know, and we tell you what we know, and then we'll decide what to do next?" Oliver phrased it as a suggestion, but it sounded like a command.

Dasenby swallowed, and nodded jerkily. He took a short, shallow breath, and said, "It started the night of the Turvingtons' ball, after I said good-bye to you at the club." His voice was a little stifled, as if his throat was tight. "After I crossed Piccadilly I looked back, and I saw you. You were waiting to cross the road, and I thought . . ." He flushed faintly, and glanced down at his glass. "I thought I'd wait for you, walk with you as far as your house, and then I saw someone come up behind you and push you in front of that coach." His face blanched. "God, I thought you were dead! I ran after him—the man who pushed you—and he went down St. James's Street and into our club, and as he went in through the door I saw his face . . ."

There was a beat of silence, and then Rhodes said, "It was your father."

Dasenby nodded. He was shaking. Primrose wasn't sure whether it was from cold or distress.

"Drink your brandy," she said softly.

Dasenby obeyed, gulping a mouthful. He shuddered, and inhaled another of those short, shallow breaths, and continued: "I thought I must have been mistaken—it was dark, after all, and I'd been on the other side of the street when it happened—so I ran back to Piccadilly and you weren't there. It was as if nothing had happened."

"I was lucky," Oliver said. "Fell between the wheels."

Dasenby gave a jerky nod, and twisted the brandy glass in his hands. "I didn't know what to do. It didn't seem real. I thought I must have been mistaken, that I'd confused one person for another in the dark, that Father would never push anyone, let alone you." He looked conscience-stricken. "I'm sorry, Cousin. I should have spoken to you about it the very next day."

Oliver shook his head. "Don't be sorry. It was dark, you were on the other side of the street. You could very easily have been mistaken." He paused, and then gave a shamefaced grimace. "And I wouldn't have believed you anyway."

Dasenby flushed, and lowered his gaze to his glass again.

This time the beat of silence was uncomfortable.

"What made you change your mind?" Primrose asked quietly. "When did you realize that your father *was* trying to kill Oliver?"

Dasenby twisted the glass in his hands—once, twice—and then stilled the gesture. "It took me a while."

"What was the first clue?" she prompted gently. "Other than what happened on Piccadilly."

Dasenby looked at her. "I suppose . . . it was when he told me he'd lost the house."

"Which house?" she asked.

"Our house in Dorsetshire."

"Lost it? You mean . . . he staked it in a game?"

Dasenby nodded.

"What other assets does your father have?" Rhodes asked.

"Nothing," Dasenby said. "He ran through Mother's fortune years ago. The house was the last thing he had." He twisted the glass again, once, twice. "Father told me about it before we came into Oxfordshire. Usually when he asks me for money he makes a joke of it, but this time he was . . . he was *angry*."

Rhodes's eyebrows lifted. "Your father borrows money from you?"

Dasenby nodded. "Mother left half her fortune to me. I came into it last year."

"And your father has been hanging off your coat-tails ever since?" Oliver said, a sardonic inflection in his voice. "Nice of him."

Dasenby flushed again, and looked down at his brandy.

Primrose felt a strong pang of sympathy. The poor boy. Coming into a fortune at twenty-one, only to have his father sponge off him.

"Does he repay you?" Rhodes asked.

"He hasn't yet, but he promised he would. He said he had a scheme . . ." Dasenby's flush deepened. He clutched the glass more tightly.

They all knew what that scheme was.

"What was your next clue?" Primrose asked.

Dasenby darted her a glance, and gulped a nervous mouthful of brandy. "It was a few days ago. I'd misplaced one of my tie pins, the pearl one, and Father said he had one just like it in his jewelry box and I could borrow it if I wished, so I went to his room to fetch it." He took another, nervous mouthful of brandy. "I couldn't see the pin in the jewelry box—and then I remembered the secret drawer at the back and thought he must have put it in there, except it wasn't there, either."

"Uncle Algy has a secret drawer in his jewelry box?" Oliver asked, his eyebrows lifting.

Dasenby nodded.

"What was in there?" Primrose asked.

"A snuff box, tortoiseshell and gold, and a tiny jar labeled White Arsenic." Dasenby gave an unhappy laugh. "It scared me at first, the arsenic, because I thought Father might be planning to kill himself, and then I realized I was being silly and he was just reusing a jar that had once held arsenic, so I closed the drawer and kept looking for the tie pin. It was on the dresser." He was silent for a moment, then he lifted his gaze to Oliver's face. "And then, the next day, Father gave you that snuff box."

Rhodes and Oliver exchanged a glance.

"Go on," Oliver said. "Say it: You were right about the snuff."

"Don't need to say it, do I?"

Oliver grunted, and drank more of his brandy. He didn't look as if he enjoyed the taste any more than Primrose did.

"And the Madeira?" Rhodes asked Dasenby. "Are you certain it was poisoned?"

Dasenby hesitated, then shook his head. "But it seemed so suspicious, the way he held that glass aside especially, so I thought . . ." He shrugged with his shoulders, with his face. "I don't know."

"I do," Oliver said. "It was poisoned. And I would have drunk it—because I *trusted* him."

Primrose heard a rasp of anger in his voice. Dasenby must have heard it, too. He seemed to shrink into himself. "I'm sorry."

"You have nothing to be sorry for," Oliver said. "Nothing at all. You saved my life. Twice. I am deeply in your debt." The rasp was still in his voice.

He was angry at himself, Primrose realized. Angry at himself for trusting the wrong person, for doubting the wrong person.

"Going back to the snuff," Rhodes said. "He could have killed all three of us. Good God, you almost took a pinch and you're his son! I don't understand what the devil he was thinking."

"If I may, sir?"

They all looked at Benoît, who was standing at the door like a guard.

"I have some knowledge of arsenic," the valet said.

Rhodes put up his eyebrows. "You do?"

"Yes, sir. For a while I was in the household of

a . . . how do you call it? A man of science. I used to transcribe his notes for him."

Rhodes's eyebrows were still raised. "Go on."

"If arsenic is administered in small doses, over a period of time, it can kill a man. That is probably what Lord Algernon intended with the snuff. One pinch wouldn't kill, but ten pinches a day over several days . . ." He gave one of his expressive, Gallic shrugs.

"And the Madeira?" Rhodes asked.

"It was one glass, yes? Set aside for you?"

Oliver nodded.

"Then there were probably enough grains of arsenic dissolved in it to kill you."

There was a long moment of silence, while they all digested this statement.

"But wouldn't Oliver have *tasted* the arsenic?" Primrose asked.

The valet shook his head. "Arsenic has no taste and no smell. It is the invisible poison."

Primrose shivered.

Oliver did, too.

"You need to be careful, Your Grace," the valet said. "All of you do until this is over. Do not eat or drink anything that isn't . . ." He frowned as he sought a word. "*Communautaire.* Communal."

"I can take the arsenic from Father's room," Dasenby offered.

"No." Oliver shook his head. "We don't want to alert him; we want to *catch* him."

"With respect, Your Grace, I think the arsenic should be exchanged for something else. I am willing to do that, with Mr. Dasenby's help." The valet's dark eyes went from Oliver's face to Dasenby's, and lastly to Rhodes's.

"Do it," Rhodes said, with a curt nod. Then he looked at Oliver. "We'll repeat what we did at the jetty. Tomorrow night. Catch your uncle in the act. It worked perfectly this time. Gave us the proof we needed."

"Yes, it did." Oliver gave Dasenby a wry, apologetic smile.

Dasenby flushed again and looked down at the glass he clutched.

"All right," Rhodes said briskly. "So here's our plan. Benoît, you and Ninian exchange the arsenic tomorrow morning, just as soon as you possibly can. Be careful. We don't want Lord Algernon to know that we're on to him."

The valet nodded.

"Prim and I will make certain Ollie's not alone for a minute tomorrow. Come nightfall, we play everything exactly as we did tonight."

Primrose nodded. So did Oliver.

"Would you like to come with us tomorrow night, Dasenby?"

Dasenby tensed in the armchair.

"No," Primrose said quickly. "I don't think he should." She glanced at Oliver, trying to pass a silent message: *Don't let him see his father try to kill you.*

Oliver met her eyes. He didn't nod, but the flicker of his eyelids told her he'd understood. "I agree. Ninian shouldn't come."

"No, of course not." Rhodes looked a little crestfallen. "I beg your pardon, Dasenby. That was thoughtless of me."

Dasenby shook his head. "It's perfectly all right, sir."

But it wasn't all right. Nothing about this situation was all right. And Oliver wasn't the only victim in this room.

Primrose was struck once again by how young Dasenby was. He looked defenseless and forlorn, huddled into the armchair. And in a bedchamber crowded with people, he somehow managed to look alone. Very alone.

Her heart ached for him. She wanted to go to him and hug him. She glanced at Oliver. He was gazing at his cousin, and his expression was solemn, sympathetic.

He knows, she realized with relief. *He sees it, too.*

"Drink up your brandy, old fellow," Oliver told

his cousin. "We both need it, after that dip in the lake."

Dasenby's gaze fastened on Oliver. After a moment, he gave a tentative smile and obeyed, swallowing the last of his brandy.

Oliver drained his own glass and stood. "What you and I need most right now is a good, long sleep, Nin."

Dasenby stood, too.

"We'll talk in the morning. Just the two of us." Oliver gripped Dasenby's shoulder briefly. "We'll get through this. I promise."

For a dreadful moment, Primrose thought Dasenby was going to burst into tears. He didn't, instead making a valiant attempt to smile.

Benoît unlocked the door and opened it.

"Go to bed, Nin." There was kindness in Oliver's voice.

Dasenby swallowed and nodded and gave that unsteady smile again, and departed.

There was silence after the door had closed behind him, then Oliver sighed. "Lord, I'm tired."

He looked more than tired; he looked exhausted.

Primrose wanted to hug him, too, but she couldn't, not with her brother and Benoît standing there. "Of course you're tired," she said briskly. "You fell down thirty-six steps and then attempted to drown yourself in a lake. Anyone would be tired after that!"

Oliver gave a weary flicker of a smile.

Primrose abandoned her half-full glass of brandy. She stood on tiptoe to kiss Rhodes's cheek, did the same to Oliver, and then marched to the door.

Benoît opened it for her.

Primrose peeked into the corridor. It was empty. She turned and pointed her finger sternly at Oliver. "Bed," she told him. "Right this instant. And remember to lock your door!"

CHAPTER 24

Oliver hadn't been particularly aware of his bruises when he went to bed—he'd been too preoccupied by everything else that had happened—but he definitely felt them when he woke.

Someone knocked softly on the door.

"Who is it?"

"Monsieur Benoît."

Oliver sat up stiffly, repressing a groan. He had to repress a second groan while climbing out of bed, and a third as he staggered to the door and unlocked it.

Rhodes's valet stood there, with a steaming ewer of water. "Good morning, sir."

"Morning, Benoît."

Oliver limped across to the window and looked out, while the valet set up the washstand. Wisps of cloud trailed across a sky the color of starlings' eggs.

He cautiously stretched his arms overhead. His muscles protested, so he abandoned the movement and turned away from the window.

He found Benoît observing him astutely. "Would you take it amiss, sir, if I suggested a warm bath before breakfast?"

"No, I wouldn't take it amiss at all."

The bath helped, a lot. By the time he went down to breakfast with Rhodes, he felt human again.

The breakfast parlor had only three occupants: Mrs. Middleton-Murray, Lady Cheevers, and Uncle Algernon.

Oliver felt himself tense. He directed a general smile at the table, went to the sideboard and piled food on his plate, then sat as far away from his uncle as was politely possible. Fortunately, no one seemed to be expecting him to speak. All attention was on Rhodes and his reappearance after two days in his sick bed. Oliver concentrated on his food—eggs, sirloin, sausages—aware of Rhodes to his right and Uncle Algy at the periphery of his vision.

Finally the subject of Rhodes's recovery was exhausted. There was a lull in the conversation. Oliver didn't want to look at his uncle—but he knew he had to. It was imperative that he treat Uncle Algy exactly the same way he had yesterday. If he didn't, Uncle Algy would be suspicious.

Finally, he forced himself to raise his gaze from his plate and glance down the table.

His stomach tightened as he met his uncle's eyes.

"You've an appetite this morning," Uncle Algy said, with one of his jovial laughs.

"Yes." Oliver smiled, and looked back down at his plate, and speared a sausage.

That first glance, that first word, that first smile, were the hardest. By the time he'd eaten two more sausages, he found himself capable of meeting his uncle's eyes, conversing with him, even laughing— but it had an unfortunate effect on his appetite. Why the devil had he piled so much food on his plate? His stomach had tied itself into an uncomfortable knot, and every time he laughed at one of Uncle Algy's jokes he was afraid he might disgrace himself and throw up.

The door opened, and Primrose entered the breakfast parlor. Her gaze skipped from face to face—and halted when it reached him. She smiled.

The knot in Oliver's stomach eased slightly. He smiled back at her.

Primrose selected her food and took the empty chair to Oliver's left. She smiled at him again, and the knot eased a little more. Oliver stopped feeling like he was going to throw up. In fact, he managed to eat almost everything on his plate. He'd just laid down his knife and fork when Ninian made his appearance.

The emotions he'd felt last night came tumbling back. Shame was predominant. Shame that he'd misjudged Ninian so badly. Shame for the way he'd treated him. He might never have rebuffed Ninian overtly, but he'd labeled him a namby-pamby and a fribble, listened with only half an ear to anything he'd said, dismissed him as unimportant.

He regretted it now. Regretted that he'd never looked past Ninian's exterior to see the man who lay beneath.

Ninian chose his food, hesitated, and sat opposite Oliver. Their eyes met for a long moment.

"How are you?" Oliver asked.

Ninian ducked his head in a nod. "Very well, thank you, Cousin."

Uncle Algy pushed back his chair and stood. "I see you're finished, Oliver. Care to come riding with me?"

Oliver gave his uncle the biggest and most cheerful smile he could muster. "I'm sorry, Uncle, but I'm promised to Ninian this morning. How about this afternoon? Directly after lunch?" And he'd bring Rhodes with him, and Primrose, too, if he could manage.

Uncle Algy took this postponement with an

appearance of good grace, and departed for the stables.

Ninian watched his father go, and then stared down at his plate. He looked as if he'd lost his appetite.

"Tell me again which colors would work well at Westfell House," Oliver said. "I'm afraid I've forgotten." And it was true; he *had* forgotten—because he hadn't listened properly in the first place. And that was another source of shame.

Ninian glanced up at him. "You want to know?" He sounded a little doubtful.

"I do," Oliver said.

Ninian brightened. He dug into his breakfast and told Oliver about his vision for Westfell House, and this time Oliver listened to every word.

⬥

The State apartments were the ideal place for private conversation with Ninian, but Oliver felt possessive about those rooms—they belonged to him and Primrose—so he took Ninian down to the lake, instead. They punted across to the island and sat on the little jetty there, dangling their legs over the edge, side by side in the sunshine. It was a perfect day: blue sky, feathery tendrils of cloud, the gentlest of breezes, birdsong. The sort of day when one should be happy.

"We removed the arsenic," Ninian said. "While Father was at breakfast."

"Good. Thank you." Oliver stared out across the lake for a long moment, and then looked at his cousin. "I owe you an apology, Ninian."

Ninian shook his head.

"I do," Oliver said. "I have treated you abominably. I judged you by your clothes, not your character. I can only offer my profound apologies and hope that you will accept them."

Ninian colored faintly, and looked down at the water. After a moment, he said, "I suppose you thought me a . . . a tulip."

"No," Oliver said bitterly. "Only a fribble and a namby-pamby." He closed his eyes. "God, Ninian, I'm so sorry."

"It's all right," Ninian said.

"No, it's *not* all right. You had my back this entire time and I didn't even notice! I've been in England for five weeks, and I haven't once tried to get to know you." He shook his head, angry at himself. "I'm sorry, Ninian. I truly am."

"It's all right," Ninian said again.

It wasn't all right, but Oliver wasn't one to beat a dead horse. "Why did you have my back?" he asked.

Ninian glanced at him, then away. "Because I like you. You're nicer than Basil and Percy ever were."

Oliver was nonplussed by this answer. "I never knew them." He'd gone to Winchester and Cambridge; they'd gone to Eton and Oxford. "What were they like?"

Ninian grimaced, and watched the water lap against the jetty piles.

Oliver waited.

"They were bullies," Ninian said finally. "Both of them, although Basil was the worst. And Uncle Reginald was a bully, too. And grandfather." He looked at Oliver. "The Dukes of Westfell have always been bullies. You're the first one who isn't."

Oliver was so surprised that he found himself unable to speak.

Ninian looked out across the lake. "I'm not saying I'm glad they're dead, because I'm not. Not exactly. But I *am* glad it's you who's duke." He stole a glance at Oliver. "You're a lot nicer than they were."

It was Oliver's turn to grimace. "I'm not always nice."

Ninian shrugged with one shoulder. "Well, at least you're not a bully. That's better than nothing."

Oliver looked at him sharply, and discovered that there was a glint of amusement in Ninian's eyes. He laughed, relieved to discover that Ninian had a sense of humor. Then he sighed. "No, I'm not a bully. But I *am* a fool. I labeled you a man milliner the first time I saw you, and then cast you in the rôle of murderer. I'm sorry, Nin."

The gleam of humor disappeared. Ninian gave that one-shouldered shrug again. "You didn't know me."

"No. But I do, now." Oliver held out his hand. "Will you accept my apologies?"

"Of course."

They shook hands gravely, almost formally. "I'm glad you're my cousin," Oliver said.

"I'm glad, too." Ninian's smile was shy, and the expression in his eyes caught Oliver off guard for a moment. He remembered what Primrose had told him, days ago: *He hero-worships you.*

Oliver had scoffed then, but he realized now that she'd been right. He could see it quite clearly: the admiration shining in Ninian's eyes.

He released Ninian's hand, feeling even more ashamed of himself. He'd done nothing to deserve that admiration. He might be nicer than Basil and Percival had been, but he'd never been *nice* to Ninian; he'd only ever been polite.

He'd do better from now on. A hell of a lot better.

A fish jumped near the jetty, falling back into the water with a *plop*. Oliver watched the ripples spread outwards from that point of impact. He'd been intending to tell Ninian about Uncle Algy's other attempts at murder, but now he found himself hesitating. Did Ninian really need to know about the Cunninghams' ball or the thirty-six steps yesterday?

After a moment's reflection he decided that, no, Ninian didn't need to know; it would alter absolutely nothing and only serve to make him more miserable than he already was. But there *was* one subject they needed to discuss.

Oliver cleared his throat. "Ninian?"

Ninian looked at him.

"I hesitate to ask you this, but I must." He met Ninian's gaze squarely, took a deep breath, and said, "Do you think your father had anything to do with Uncle Reginald's death? Or Percival's?"

Ninian flinched.

"I'm sorry, Nin," Oliver said. "But I do need to know."

Ninian shook his head. His face was pale with shock, his eyes wide. "I don't know! How could I? I never thought—! I never . . ."

"Think about it now," Oliver said quietly. "Please?"

Ninian nodded jerkily and looked away. He directed his attention at one of the buttons on his tailcoat, twisting, tugging, straining the threads.

After a minute, Ninian said, "Not Percy. Father

was as shocked as the rest of us were." He glanced briefly at Oliver.

Oliver nodded, relieved. "Good."

Ninian returned his attention to the button.

Oliver watched the threads strain, watched Ninian's brow furrow, watched his lips press more tightly together. Such a beautiful day, such a grim subject. He was aware of warm sunshine on his back and the quiet *lap-lap-lap* of the water against the jetty—and Ninian's distress. It shouldn't be possible that those things could exist together, and yet they did.

"He might have killed Uncle Reginald," Ninian said finally. He looked at Oliver, and Oliver saw tears in his eyes.

"Oh, Nin," Oliver said, and he scooted sideways on the jetty and put an arm around Ninian's shoulders and hugged him fiercely. "I'm sorry."

Ninian sniffed, and inhaled a short, sharp breath. His body felt tense, brittle.

"It's all right," Oliver said, even though they both knew it wasn't.

They sat there in the sunshine, Oliver with his arm around Ninian's shoulders. Ninian didn't cry, but perhaps it would have been better if he did. Oliver could feel the misery bottled up inside him.

Gradually Ninian's tension eased. He didn't feel

quite so brittle. He gave a sigh that Oliver felt, rather than heard. "Father was different after Percy died. Distracted. Preoccupied. He would spend hours just thinking. He was on edge, that whole week before we went to Wiltshire, and once we were there he was even worse. I thought it was because Uncle Reginald was so unpleasant, but maybe it wasn't."

"Unpleasant? In what way?"

"He was angry his sons were dead. " Some of Ninian's tension returned. His shoulders hunched slightly. "I shouldn't have gone to Wiltshire. It only made him angrier. He said—right in the middle of dinner that first night—he said it was a shame I hadn't died instead."

"He *what*?" Oliver tightened his arm around Ninian's shoulders. "Jesus, Nin."

"Father didn't say anything. He just sat there and looked like he wanted to kill Uncle Reginald."

"That doesn't mean he *did* kill him," Oliver said, thinking that it was just as well their Uncle Reginald wasn't alive because he might have had to kill the man himself.

"No. But afterwards, after the fire, Father was . . . I could tell he wasn't unhappy about it. I don't mean he was cheerful or gloating. He was quiet, in fact. Quieter than I've ever seen him. But he was also . . ." It took Ninian almost half a minute to find the right adjective. "Satisfied."

Satisfied. Oliver turned the word over in his mind. Did that mean Uncle Algy had killed his brother, or merely that he was glad he'd died?

They wouldn't know until they asked him, and he doubted Uncle Algy would confess to murder—if it *had* been a murder.

"When word reached England that I wasn't dead . . . how did your father react?"

"If he was disappointed not to be duke, he hid it well. He said you being alive was the best of news—and when you came home he was happy to see you; I *know* he was." Ninian fell silent for a moment, then said, "He likes you. Everyone does."

Oliver said nothing. Whether Uncle Algy liked him or not, he was still trying to kill him.

"If it wasn't for the money, I don't think Father would have . . . you know."

"Pushed me under a post-chaise?" Oliver said dryly. "No, I don't suppose he would have."

"I'm sorry," Ninian said, in a very small voice.

"You have nothing to be sorry for. In fact, quite the opposite. You saved my life yesterday. I would have drunk that Madeira."

Ninian made no reply to this.

Oliver was struck with a sudden, unwelcome thought. "Do you think he suspects you know about the poison? That performance of yours *was* rather conspicuous."

"I don't know. I don't think so."

Oliver hoped not. He was suddenly doubly glad the arsenic had been disposed of. Another unwelcome thought struck him. "Ninian . . . If you were to die, who inherits your money?"

The brittle tension returned to Ninian's shoulders, which was an answer in itself. "Father wouldn't do that."

"Of course he wouldn't," Oliver said, trying to sound more confident than he felt. "Just . . . be careful today, won't you?"

The dissonance between the beauty of the day and the terribleness of their conversation was even worse, now. Were they really talking about the possibility of a father murdering his son, while the sun shone and the lake sparkled and wavelets lapped gently at the jetty?

"What will you do?" Ninian asked in a voice so low it was almost a whisper.

Oliver heard the words Ninian didn't utter: *After you catch my father trying to kill you tonight.*

"I don't know," he said, truthfully. "I'd like to keep it quiet, if I can. Out of the courts. But really, it depends on your father. I thought . . . I'd offer him the choice of America or Australia. Do you think he'd go?"

Some of Ninian's tension eased. Had he been

afraid his father would hang at the gallows? "Yes. I think so."

They sat for several minutes, silently, while the sun warmed their backs. Then Oliver sighed and released Ninian and climbed stiffly to his feet. He extended a hand down to his cousin. "Time to get back, Nin." And then, "You don't mind if I call you Nin, do you?"

Ninian took his hand and stood. "Of course not, Cousin."

"Oliver. Or Ollie, if you wish. Enough of the 'Cousin.'"

"All right," Ninian said, a little shyly, and Oliver caught a glimpse of that admiration again. Hero-worship, Primrose had called it—and very misplaced, it was. From Oliver's point of view, the hero this past week had been Ninian.

"Nin . . . You've had my back all this time. I want you to know that from now on I have *your* back."

Ninian flushed, and then gave him a shy, glowing smile. "Thank you, Cousin. I mean . . . Thank you, Oliver."

CHAPTER 25

*O*liver saw Ninian safely settled in the yellow salon with Miss Cheevers and her mother. Miss Middleton-Murray was there, too, wearing a gown that displayed her décolletage. She gave him a pretty, smiling glance through her eyelashes and flashed her dimples at him.

Oliver ignored her and went hunting for Rhodes and Primrose. They weren't far away—both in the library, Rhodes reading the London newspaper, Primrose perusing the shelves in the upper gallery.

They looked around at his entrance.

Oliver stroked his nose, and was delighted by the alacrity with which Rhodes thrust aside the newspaper and Primrose abandoned the bookshelves. She descended the stairs from the gallery at an unladylike pace, reaching Oliver only a few seconds behind Rhodes.

"Like magic, it is," Oliver said, beaming at them both. "All I have to do is touch my nose and the pair of you come running."

Rhodes didn't bother to respond to this comment. "Well? How did it go with your cousin?"

"I just made a joke," Oliver said. "You could at least laugh."

Rhodes crossed his arms and stared Oliver in the eyes. "How did it go?"

Oliver glanced at Primrose.

Her hands were on her hips and her expression was almost identical to her brother's: inquisitorial.

Oliver gave a doleful sigh. "I must say you're a pair of dull dogs today."

"Ollie," Rhodes said, a note of warning in his voice. "Do I have to pick you up and shake you to get you to talk some sense? Because I *will*."

Oliver knew that he would; he'd been on the receiving end of Rhodes's shakes before.

They took a long stroll through the parkland surrounding Cheevers Court. Oliver told them everything Ninian had said. "I'm worried about his safety. If Uncle Algy guesses that he knows . . ."

"It's unlikely he'll guess," Rhodes said.

"And even if he *does* guess, he wouldn't kill his own son!" Primrose said—and then, more doubtfully, "Would he?"

At that moment they heard hoofbeats. A horseman cantered down the distant avenue of yews. Oliver recognized that burly figure: Uncle Algy.

They watched horse and rider slow to a trot and disappear in the direction of the stables.

"I've promised to go riding with him this afternoon," Oliver said. "Directly after lunch. Can you both be in the stableyard then? Invite yourself to come along with us?"

"We most definitely can," Rhodes said grimly.

"And Rhodes . . . would you mind keeping an eye on Ninian? Just until luncheon? I'll stay with Primrose, I promise. We won't go out of each other's sight."

"Your wish is my command," Rhodes said, with an ironic salute. He strode in the direction of the house and climbed the long flight of steps up to the terrace.

Oliver watched him out of sight, and then looked at Primrose. Her expression was solemn.

He reached out and touched her cheek with a fingertip. "Smile, Prim."

She did, faintly. "I'll be glad when this is over."

"We all will." He took her hand and tucked it in

the crook of his arm. "Where shall we walk to next? The rose garden? The water lily pond?"

They walked to both, and then strolled back towards the house. It really was an astonishingly ugly building, a glowering gargoyle of a mansion. Oliver ran his gaze from the widow's walk at the top to the broad terrace at the bottom—and then back up again.

He remembered Uncle Algy showing him the widow's walk, their second day at Cheevers Court.

What would have happened if Rhodes hadn't tagged along?

Would Uncle Algy have pushed him off?

Oliver repressed a shiver. "Still half an hour until luncheon, Prim. Shall we visit the State apartments?"

"We can talk out here. No one can overhear us."

"Yes, but we can't kiss out here, can we? Someone might see."

They slipped into the building via a side door, trod down a silent corridor, and let themselves into the State reception room. The door snicked quietly shut behind them.

Oliver decided that he rather liked the smell of stale lavender. It made anticipation unfurl inside him, made the blood hum in his veins.

Primrose crossed to the window and glanced out. Sunlight gilded her hair. Oliver watched her, and thought of the girl she'd been when he'd sailed for India eight years ago. At nineteen, Primrose could have become any number of women. But she'd become this one. *This* Primrose. This sharp-tongued, observant, plucky Primrose who knew her own mind and was unafraid to speak it, who called him a jingle brains, who quoted Aurelius at him, who stood steadfast with him against Uncle Algy.

Thank God she hadn't become one of those other possible Primroses. Imagine if he'd come home and found that she'd turned into a shrew? Or a co-quette? Or a reclusive bluestocking, like her Aunt Lavender?

Imagine if he'd come home and she'd been *married.*

Primrose stood on tiptoe and craned her neck as she peered out the window. "I'm worried about those clouds. What if it rains tonight?"

"It won't rain," Oliver said, enjoying the glimpse of her ankles that her pose afforded him. Primrose had very nice ankles. She had a very nice waist, too, perfectly formed for a man to slide his arms around. And *very* nice breasts. And a mouth that simply begged to be kissed. In fact everything about her begged to be kissed. Her throat, her inner wrists, the nape of her neck. Those breasts. All that tender skin just waiting to be touched, tasted, explored.

A rush of warmth rolled through him as he imagined peeling off her clothes, exposing that skin, introducing her to the pleasures of the flesh.

Warmth? Call it what it was: lust. Sheer, unadulterated lust.

He wanted Primrose Garland. Wanted her clothed, wanted her naked. Wanted her under him and on top of him, wanted to make her pant and groan and laugh and cry out.

At that moment, Primrose turned to face him. Oliver's gaze skipped briefly to her lips—and then rose to her eyes. His heart seemed to beat a little faster, because as delectable as Primrose's mouth was, he liked her eyes even better. Those keen blue eyes through which that sharp brain observed the world. Those eyes that *saw* him, saw Oliver Dasenby, not the Duke of Westfell.

"What?" Primrose asked, tilting her head to one side.

He wanted to kiss her. He wanted to ask her to marry him.

One thing at a time, Oliver told himself.

He took her hand, heading for the dressing room—then paused and glanced at the door to the right of the reception room, the one he'd never ventured through before. "What's through there?"

"Another sitting room. There are two State suites. They mirror each other."

"One for the king, one for the queen?"

"Yes."

Oliver crossed to the right-hand door, tugging Primrose after him. "Let's try this side today."

Primrose had been correct; the suites mirrored one another: a sitting room, a dressing room, and a bedroom with the same ridiculous dais and gilded columns. Oliver gazed around that majestic bedchamber, and even though he quite desperately wanted to kiss Primrose, the room was just . . . wrong. "No," he said. "Not here."

He towed Primrose all the way back through the apartments—bedroom, dressing room, sitting room, reception room, sitting room, dressing room, bedroom—increasing his pace with every stride until they were running like children.

They burst into that final room and Oliver released Primrose's hand and flung himself down on his back on the bed, panting.

"Why here?" Primrose asked, breathless and laughing. "The suites are exactly the same."

"No, they're not," Oliver said, smiling up at her from the bed. "This suite has history."

Primrose blushed faintly.

"This *room* has history."

Primrose's cheeks became pinker.

Oliver wiggled his eyebrows at her. "This *bed* has history."

Primrose blushed an even brighter pink and looked away from him. "Honestly, Oliver, you are—"

Oliver didn't wait to hear what he was. He captured her hand and tugged her down to sit beside him on the bed.

"Oliver!"

Oliver lowered his eyelashes and glanced up at her through them, coyly. "Please kiss me, Lady Primrose."

Primrose gave him a stern look, but her lips tucked in at the corners in that way that meant she wanted to laugh.

Oliver fluttered his eyelashes at her, and pushed out his lower lip in an exaggerated pout. "Please, pretty Primrose." Then he heard what he'd said, and grinned. "Alliteration, Prim. That's got to be worth a kiss."

Primrose rolled her eyes at this. "Do you *never* stop playing games?" she asked, and then bent her head and lightly kissed him.

The answer to that question was, yes, he did stop playing games. Quite often, in fact. And despite what Primrose thought, he wasn't actually playing a game right now. His intentions towards her were quite serious—but that didn't mean that his *kiss* had to be serious, did it?

The kiss rapidly did become serious, though. Oliver took the nape of her neck in one hand, sliding his fingers up into her hair, pulling her closer, plundering her mouth, taking her lips and tongue hostage. No, *he* was the hostage; she the plunderer. Her kisses left him breathless, light-headed, defenseless. Whatever she wanted, she could take. He'd give her anything. Anything at all.

What Primrose wanted was his mouth, so Oliver gave it to her, over and over again. He was panting, almost winded, and it had nothing to do with running through seven rooms, and everything to do with Primrose and her eager kisses.

He didn't want it to end. He wanted to stay in the State bedroom for the rest of the day, just he and Primrose, alone together, so when Primrose broke the kiss and drew back, pushing up off his chest, he uttered an inarticulate protest.

"No, Oliver," she said, and she sounded as out of breath as he was. "We have to stop. Luncheon."

Her face was flushed, her lips plump and rosy, her blonde hair disheveled. Oliver thought he'd never seen a more irresistible sight in his life. "The devil with food," he said, reaching for her. "I have everything I need right here."

Primrose evaded his hand. "People will notice if we're not there."

She was right, damn it.

Oliver stopped trying to recapture her. He lay back on the pillow and concentrated on catching his breath. Primrose climbed off the bed. "I need a mirror."

After a moment, Oliver climbed off the bed, too, wincing as his body reminded him of the bruises he'd acquired yesterday. He found Primrose in the dressing room. She'd pulled the Holland cloth off the wide cheval mirror and was trying to tidy her hair.

Oliver looked at his own hair. It was almost as disheveled as Primrose's. He combed it with his fingers, then repaired the damage to his neckcloth. When he'd finished, he looked at Primrose. She was frowning at her reflection. "What do you think?" she asked.

Her hair was tidy again, but she still looked as if she'd been recently kissed. Those lips gave her away.

"I think we should wait a few more minutes," Oliver said, stepping behind her. He slid his arms around her waist and looked at them both in the mirror—and once he'd looked he couldn't *stop* looking.

He could see it so clearly. *Feel* it so clearly. Not just

physical lust, but connection. It was as if the years of childhood bickering and the weeks of friendly verbal sparring and the past few days of kissing had come together into something as inevitable as it was perfect.

Did Primrose feel it, too? The sense that this was how it was meant to be? That everything had led to this moment: his arms around her waist, the warmth of her body pressed against his, his gaze caught in hers in the mirror.

Perhaps she did, because she didn't pull away; instead, she lifted one hand and laid it over his.

Oliver's heart seemed to turn upside down in his chest. The sense of connection between them became even stronger. He stared at her in the mirror. Primrose. *His* Primrose. Primrose of the tart tongue and sweet mouth. Primrose, who kissed like a fallen angel. Who was gazing at him in the mirror as if he was as important to her as she was to him.

A clock struck the hour somewhere in the State apartments, breaking the moment.

Primrose looked away.

Oliver released her and stepped back. "Luncheon?" He held out his hand to her.

Primrose took it.

They walked to the reception room, hand in hand. Oliver didn't feel his bruises at all.

"How do I look?" Primrose asked, when they reached the door.

"Beautiful," Oliver said.

"No, I mean . . . do I look as if we've been kissing?"

Her lips were still slightly rosier than usual, slightly fuller. His probably were, too. But he didn't think anyone would notice. "No," Oliver said.

It was time to open the door, but he didn't want to. It felt as if they were caught in a magic spell, as if the State apartments were a place of perfect happiness and when he opened the door the enchantment would break and all the troubles of the real world would flood back in.

Oliver released Primrose's hand and reluctantly opened the door.

They stepped out into the corridor—and the real world immediately intruded, because someone was standing there.

Oliver managed not to start convulsively, but only because he'd had practice recently.

"Oh," he said. "Miss Middleton-Murray. Fancy meeting you here." He tried for a nonchalant smile. "Lady Primrose has just been showing me the State rooms."

"How kind of her," Miss Middleton-Murray said. "Did you enjoy it?"

Oliver shrugged. "Nothing but a lot of Holland

covers." He was acutely aware of his lips. Would Miss Middleton-Murray guess that he and Primrose had been kissing? He took a step forward, blocking her view of Primrose's face. "Shall we go to luncheon?"

CHAPTER 26

*L*uncheon was a lot more interesting than Primrose had anticipated. There were so many undercurrents around the table that it was difficult to keep track of them all. She could only concentrate on one person at a time. She dismissed Mrs. Middleton-Murray as unimportant, and Lord and Lady Cheevers and their daughter, ditto. She dismissed Rhodes, too, because his motivations were clear-cut.

Mr. Dasenby occupied her for a few minutes. His emotions must be in a turmoil, poor boy: the elation of being in love, the distress of his father's villainy. He hid it well, though. His manner was perfectly unexceptional. He talked and listened and ate, exactly as if everything were all right. The only things that gave him away were his glances. In the short time that she watched him, he looked at Oliver three times, and Miss Cheevers three times—and his father not at all.

Primrose next turned her gaze to Lord Algernon—and caught him looking at Oliver—and there, right *there,* was the expression that had so misled her on the island. Regret and something else that she now recognized as determination.

Implacable determination.

Implacable and *regretful* determination.

Primrose curled her lip, and attacked her luncheon. How *dare* Lord Algernon regret the need to kill Oliver? How dare he gamble away his assets and think it necessary but *regretful* to recover his fortune by killing his nephew?

It was unconscionable. Unforgivable. He should have discovered determination earlier, should have been implacable towards himself, should have stopped gambling.

Primrose chewed fiercely, and glanced at Oliver. He was watching her intently, and when he caught her gaze he leaned slightly forward over his plate and sent her an urgent look.

That urgent look was easy to read: *Be careful of Miss Middleton-Murray!* He was practically shouting it at her, signaling it with every part of him—the intent eyes, the tense shoulders, the hands gripping his cutlery.

Primrose smiled soothingly at him.

Oliver's hands clenched more tightly around the

knife and fork. His brow furrowed. His lips parted and then closed again, as if he was only just holding back words of warning.

Primrose smiled even more soothingly at him, and turned her attention to Miss Middleton-Murray.

Miss Middleton-Murray had chosen to sit next to her at the luncheon table and she was being excessively friendly. Primrose didn't think she'd had so many flattering compliments bestowed on her in such a short amount of time before. Miss Middleton-Murray was quite in *awe* of her intellect, quite *humbled* by it, in fact, and she wished *devoutly* to embark on a course of reading so that she, too, might become as *wise* and *erudite* as Primrose was.

Wise? Erudite?

Primrose almost choked on a laugh. She swallowed her ham with difficulty, and risked a glance at Oliver.

If he'd heard Miss Middleton-Murray's words, he didn't find them amusing. He sent her another of those looks that cried *Beware! Beware!*

Primrose was a little piqued. Did he really think her so oblivious—or so susceptible to flattery—that she wasn't aware of Miss Middleton-Murray's intentions?

"Do you have a favorite author?" Miss Middleton-Murray asked. "One that you recommend?"

"Marcus Aurelius," Primrose said—and then, because she wanted to make things *extremely* easy for Miss Middleton-Murray, she said, "I have a copy with me. You're welcome to borrow it. It's up in my room. I'll fetch it for you later."

Miss Middleton-Murray thanked Primrose with pretty deference—and a triumphant gleam in her eyes.

Primrose glanced across the table.

Oliver was staring at her in wide-eyed alarm.

⁂

Primrose hurried upstairs and changed into her riding habit, then she quietly let herself out of her room and tiptoed along the corridor.

Satisfied that there was no Miss Middleton-Murray in the alcove, she hurried down to the stableyard. Oliver was already there, pacing. He crossed the yard swiftly. "Prim! For God's sake." He caught hold of her upper arms, his fingers digging in painfully. "What are you *doing?*"

"Catching Miss Middleton-Murray." She tried to disengage his hands.

Oliver tightened his grip and shook her. "She's *dangerous.*"

"I know. Ouch, Oliver. That hurts."

Oliver released her hastily. "I beg your pardon."

"I'm setting a trap," Primrose told him. "It's the perfect opportunity."

"But—"

"This time we'll catch her red-handed."

"*Prim*—" His voice was anguished, and so was his expression.

"Trust me, Oliver. I know what I'm doing."

"I *do* trust you, but—"

At that moment, Rhodes emerged from the house. Behind him was Lord Algernon.

Primrose wondered what Lord Algernon was planning. Did he have a hip flask filled with poisoned whiskey? Or did he intend to lure Oliver to a secluded destination where he could kill him more crudely? Perhaps hit him over the head with a rock and claim that he fell from his horse? Shoot him and blame it on footpads?

"Ready for our ride, Oliver?" Lord Algernon said cheerfully, striding across the cobblestones.

"Yes, Uncle."

"Oh," Primrose said brightly. "My brother and I are going riding now, too. Why don't we all go together?"

"Splendid idea!" Oliver said.

Lord Algernon's jaw clenched briefly, and then he smiled. "Splendid," he echoed.

They rode for an hour, chatting and laughing, all four of them acting their parts. Primrose felt keyed up, her senses at their most alert. The mare she was riding caught her mood, sidling skittishly, trying to break into a gallop.

"Let's race," Oliver suggested, when they came to a long stretch of meadow, and Primrose gladly gave the mare her head.

It was only a light-hearted race, but it felt as if she was riding into battle. The thunder of the horses' hooves was fiercely exhilarating. Her teeth were clenched, her heart beating hard. A shout built in her throat. A berserker's wild yell. She wanted to fight. She wanted to *win.*

Primrose did win—but she didn't yell. She swallowed the sound. Fierceness still fizzed in her veins, though, and when Lord Algernon rode up alongside her he was lucky she wasn't carrying a sword, for she would have swung it and lopped off his head.

"That knock-kneed nag of yours is dashed fast, Lady Primrose," Oliver said. Then he laughed. "Did you hear that? Knock-kneed nag." He gave her a wink and she imagined his voice whispering in her ear: *Alliteration, Prim. That's worth a kiss.*

They returned to Cheevers Court at an easy trot. All was bustle and noise in the stableyard, the grooms running to take their mounts. Primrose caught her brother's eye and stroked her nose, caught Oliver's eye and stroked her nose.

"Care for a game of piquet?" Lord Algernon asked Oliver after he'd dismounted.

"I'm sorry, Uncle, but I can't," Oliver said. "Thayne and I have plans. But later, definitely."

Lord Algernon's smile was a trifle tight. He gave his nephew a nod and headed into the house.

He's getting impatient, Primrose thought.

Which boded well for tonight's trap at the jetty.

She glanced at the sky, where clouds were gathering, and hoped that it wouldn't rain.

"Let's walk in the rose garden," Oliver said.

But once they reached the rose garden, they didn't walk; they talked. "Miss Middleton-Murray has decided that Prim is a rival," Oliver told Rhodes. "She's going to try her trick with the stairs again."

Rhodes's eyebrows lifted. "Surely not? Prim's a *duke's* daughter. Miss Middleton-Murray would be mad to try such a thing!"

"She's going to," Oliver said. "I'm certain of it."

"So am I," Primrose said. "And we're going to catch her in the act."

Rhodes stared at the pair of them. "Oh, we are, are we?"

331

"Yes. There was no fresh string tied to the newel post when I came downstairs, but I'm willing to wager there's some now. Tucked out of sight."

Oliver frowned, and opened his mouth.

"I don't think she'll be waiting for me yet because she doesn't know exactly when I'll be back, but—"

"Yes, but—" Oliver said.

"But if she *is* already there, I'll let you know." Primrose snapped her fingers. "I'll translocate down to the State apartments, and then come and find you."

Oliver closed his mouth. He was still frowning.

"But I think she'll spring her trap later this afternoon—she's already laid the groundwork, asking to borrow my Aurelius."

Oliver frowned more deeply, and opened his mouth again.

Primrose rushed on: "We'll need as many witnesses as possible. Both of you, definitely, and if we can get Lord or Lady Cheevers, that would be even better."

"Agreed," Rhodes said.

"This is how I see it working," Primrose said. "I get changed. I come downstairs. The three of us sit in the yellow salon, or the blue one, wherever Miss Middleton-Murray is. She asks to borrow my copy of Aurelius. I go upstairs to fetch it. She follows me and sets her trap and hides in the alcove. *You* follow her—and we catch her. What do you think?"

"We'd need to get our timing right," Oliver said. "We have to be at the foot of those stairs at the exact moment she tries to trip you. That's not going to be easy."

Rhodes took out his pocket watch. "What time do you have, Ollie?"

Oliver fished his watch out. "Twenty-five past. You?"

The men conferred over their watches. When both timepieces were showing the same time to the second, Oliver gave his to Primrose. "Ten minutes," he said. "*Exactly* ten minutes after you leave the salon, you come out of your bedroom. Not a second earlier, not a second later."

Primrose took the watch. It was smooth and heavy and warm from his hand. "Ten minutes. Exactly."

"We'll be waiting at the foot of the stairs," Oliver said.

Rhodes nodded.

"Make sure you're quiet," she told them.

"We'll be as quiet as mice."

"Well, then . . ." She closed her hand around Oliver's watch. "Let's do this."

They walked back to the house, but Oliver hesitated at the door. "If she's already up there, waiting for you . . ."

"Why don't we look for her?" Rhodes said. "Right now, before Prim goes up to change. If she's downstairs—if she *stays* downstairs—Prim's safe, correct?"

"Correct," Oliver said.

They entered the house, walking silently along first one corridor, then another. At the door to the yellow salon, they halted. No one said a word. Rhodes opened the door, looked in, and shut the door again. He shook his head.

He looked into the blue salon next, then withdrew, closing the door quietly behind him. "She's in there," he said in a low voice.

"Then I'll go upstairs." Primrose gathered up the long skirt of her riding habit. "I'll be back as soon as I can. Don't let her follow me!"

"We won't," Oliver promised. "If there's fresh string tied to that post—"

"I'll let you know," Primrose said. "Thumbs up means there is; thumbs down means there isn't."

There was string tied around the newel post at ankle height. It was discreetly done, so discreetly done that she almost didn't see it.

Primrose crouched, and examined it: the

decorative groove, the inconspicuous piece of string looped around it. The knot was a sturdy one. There'd be no getting it off without scissors.

The rest of the string was neatly coiled up and tucked behind the post. Invisible, unless one knew to look for it. Primrose didn't need to pull it out and measure its length; she knew it must be long enough to reach the alcove.

A shiver ran along her spine, and following the shiver was a rush of anger. She clenched her jaw. Miss Middleton-Murray was *not* going to get away with this again.

She changed hastily, choosing a gown with a pocket at the waist, slipping Oliver's watch into it, then she quietly let herself out of her room and tip-toed down the corridor. The string was still tucked behind the newel post.

Primrose checked the alcove anyway. It was empty.

She hurried downstairs, in the grip of a martial emotion. This must be how soldiers felt before going into combat: hearts beating fast, resolute, focused, determined to win.

She paused outside the blue salon and took a moment to compose herself, then opened the door.

Almost the entire party was there: Lady Cheevers, Mrs. Middleton-Murray, Miss Cheevers,

Ninian Dasenby, Oliver and Rhodes, and Miss Middleton-Murray.

Oliver, Rhodes, and Miss Middleton-Murray looked up at her entrance; the others didn't. Dasenby and Miss Cheevers were engrossed in conversation, Mrs. Middleton-Murray was intent on her needlework, and Lady Cheevers was absorbed in the *Ladies' Monthly Museum.*

Primrose gave Rhodes and Oliver a discreet thumbs up and crossed the room with calm, unhurried steps. The place alongside Miss Middleton-Murray on the sofa was empty. Primrose took it, and bestowed a friendly smile upon her.

Miss Middleton-Murray smiled back, and asked how Primrose had enjoyed her ride.

The conversation lasted five minutes, and in those five minutes Miss Middleton-Murray managed to compliment Primrose on her horsemanship, her intelligence, her Christian name, her middle name, the color of her hair, her taste in clothing, her bloodline, and her scholarship. The urge to play up to it was almost overwhelming. No wonder Oliver preened and strutted as much as he did.

"I would very much like to read that book of yours," Miss Middleton-Murray said, eagerly. "Autellus, was it not?"

"Aurelius," Primrose said. "I can fetch it for you now, if you like?"

"I would be so grateful, Lady Primrose. If it's not too much trouble . . ."

"No trouble at all."

She rose and crossed to the door, opened it, and glanced back. Miss Middleton-Murray was smiling brightly at her. Primrose looked past her, to Oliver and Rhodes. She met their eyes, first one, then the other, and closed the door.

In the corridor she took out Oliver's watch and memorized the time, burning it into her memory. *Ten minutes.*

CHAPTER 27

Rhodes took his watch out and casually glanced at it, tilted the face so that Oliver could read it, too, then tucked it back into his pocket.

Oliver began counting seconds in his head. When he'd reached thirty-five, Miss Middleton-Murray rose to her feet. "How about a game of chess, old fellow?" Oliver said loudly, not watching as she slipped from the room.

"Splendid idea," Rhodes replied, equally loudly.

The door closed noiselessly. Oliver looked around. Lady Cheevers was still reading the *Ladies' Monthly Museum*. Mrs. Middleton-Murray was still plying her needle. Ninian and Miss Cheevers were still deep in discussion. It appeared that no one had noticed Miss Middleton-Murray's departure.

He met Rhodes's eyes.

Rhodes gave a nod.

Together, they stood and crossed to where Lady Cheevers sat. "Ma'am," Oliver said, very quietly. "May we please have a word with you?" He inclined his head towards the corridor.

Lady Cheevers lowered the magazine and looked up at them, a movement that set the feathers in her turban swaying. Alarm flickered across her face. "What is it about?"

Oliver laid his finger briefly across his lips and tilted his head towards the door again.

Lady Cheevers looked even more alarmed. She put the magazine aside and stood. She cast a glance at her daughter, ensconced on the window seat with Ninian, and then crossed to the door. Rhodes opened it. They stepped into the corridor one by one.

Rhodes closed the door.

Lady Cheevers turned to Oliver. "What is it, Your Grace?"

"Thayne and I need to show you something."

"What?"

"We can't tell you, ma'am," Oliver said. "You need to see it for yourself."

Lady Cheevers looked at Rhodes, wide-eyed and worried. He smiled at her reassuringly. "Trust us, ma'am."

She gave a doubtful smile of her own. "Very well."

Lady Cheevers allowed herself to be escorted along the corridor. She said nothing aloud. She didn't have to. Her face said it all: confusion, uneasiness, trepidation.

When they reached the vestibule they encountered Lord Cheevers. Oliver felt a surge of exultation. He lifted his eyes skyward. *Thank you.*

Lady Cheevers turned to her husband, relief vivid on her face. "Frederick!"

Cheevers looked at the three of them and put up his brows. "What is it, my dear?"

"Will you please come with us, sir?" Oliver said.

Cheevers's brows rose still higher. "Where to?"

"It's a great secret, Frederick," Lady Cheevers said, with a nervous laugh. "They won't tell me." She reached out a hand to him.

"It's something you need to see, sir," Rhodes said, very seriously.

Cheevers's brow twisted in bemusement. He took his wife's hand, patting it comfortingly. "What on earth—"

"Please, sir," Oliver said. "It's extremely important. We wouldn't ask otherwise."

Cheevers looked at him, and then at Rhodes, and lastly at his wife. Then he shrugged. "Very well, Your Grace."

Rhodes checked his pocket watch. "Less than six minutes left."

They climbed the thirty-six stairs Oliver had fallen down yesterday. At the top, Rhodes checked his watch again. "Five minutes."

They traversed the corridor between the North wing and the South, crossed a long gallery hung with paintings, and came to a smaller, sunnier gallery. Rhodes looked at his watch. "Three and a half minutes," he said in a whisper.

Lord Cheevers opened his mouth.

Oliver hushed him hastily.

Cheevers blinked, taken aback, and then whispered, "What is going *on*?"

"You'll see very soon," Oliver whispered back. He laid a finger warningly over his lips.

Cheevers frowned, but made no protest. He might think this a trick, some tomfoolery, but he knew he was outranked. He wasn't going to argue with a marquis and a duke.

Oliver laid his finger to his lips a second time and then crossed the gallery with exaggerated care, almost tiptoeing.

Lord and Lady Cheevers followed silently.

At the far end of the gallery, the flight of four steps rose.

A yard from the bottom of those steps, Oliver halted, in almost the exact spot that the housemaid had scrubbed away Miss Warrington's blood. He breathed shallowly.

Lord and Lady Cheevers halted alongside him, flanked by Rhodes.

Oliver narrowed his eyes and stared at the newel post. He couldn't see any string tied there. He transferred his stare to the air a few inches above the topmost step. He couldn't see any string hovering there, either.

He told himself that the string was lying flat on the floor at the moment, invisible to their eyes—and that as soon as Miss Middleton-Murray heard Primrose's door open she would pull the string taut and they would see it.

Unless she'd gone to the music room to practice on the pianoforte. In which case, they'd look like the greatest fools in England.

Oliver shoved that thought aside, turned to the Cheevers, and laid his finger over his mouth again.

Lord and Lady Cheevers stared back at him, uncomfortable, bewildered, and in the viscount's case, growing angry.

Oliver ignored those things. All he cared about was silence, and that he had—as long as the Cheevers remained intimidated by his rank.

Rhodes silently held out his pocket watch. Oliver peered at it. There was one minute left.

He put his finger to his lips one last time, then turned his attention to the topmost step and waited.

Ten seconds passed. Twenty. Thirty. Oliver could feel Lord Cheevers's growing impatience, his growing anger.

A door opened and closed in the corridor above—and as if by magic, a string appeared six inches above the topmost step.

Oliver's breath hissed in silent triumph. He turned to the Cheevers and pointed at it. *Look,* he shouted at them silently. *Look there.*

Cheevers frowned. He took a step closer and peered at the string.

Lady Cheevers's mouth opened in a silent *O* of horror.

Oliver crept closer to the stairs on tiptoe. He pointed at the string again, almost touching it with his finger, and looked back. Lord and Lady Cheevers were staring, open-mouthed and aghast. Rhodes wasn't open-mouthed. He was tight-lipped, grim.

Light, unhurried footsteps came closer. The string remained taut, hovering above the topmost step. Almost invisible. Lethal.

Oliver silently climbed the steps, arriving on the third one at the same moment that Primrose reached the top of the stairs. Their eyes met. They almost smiled at each other.

For a brief second they made a tableau—all of them frozen in place—and then a shriek of warning broke the silence. "Be *careful!*"

Oliver ignored Lady Cheevers's shrill cry. He stepped over the string and turned towards the alcove. "Hello, Miss Middleton-Murray."

CHAPTER 28

*T*here was an uproar. The biggest uproar Primrose had ever heard in her life. Rhodes bounded up the stairs, Lord Cheevers on his heels, both intent on looking into the alcove. Lady Cheevers followed more slowly, her face stark white with horror.

"What's the meaning of this?" Lord Cheevers demanded, while at the same time Lady Cheevers clutched Primrose's arm and said faintly, "Oh, my dear . . . I thought . . ." Her gaze turned to the string, lying on the floor at their feet.

"It's all right, ma'am." Primrose patted her hand.

Miss Middleton-Murray emerged from the alcove. Her face was flushed, her eyes sparkling brightly, but she didn't look cowed or repentant or even embarrassed at having been caught; she looked wrathful. She lifted her chin and stared at Primrose, and if looks could kill Primrose would have been struck dead.

For a moment Primrose was tempted to play Oliver's trick: fling out her arms and fall to the floor. The impulse was wholly inappropriate and easily mastered—but it almost would have been worth it to see the look on Miss Middleton-Murray's face.

"Explain yourself," Lord Cheevers commanded.

Miss Middleton-Murray lifted her chin. "It was merely a joke."

"A *joke?*" Rhodes's voice was loud enough to make Primrose wince.

"And was Miss Carteris's broken wrist a joke?" Oliver asked. In contrast to Rhodes and Lord Cheevers, his tone was light, almost conversational. "And Miss Warrington's nose?"

Miss Middleton-Murray tossed her head. "I don't know what you're talking about."

"No?" Primrose said. "Then perhaps you'd like to explain the scratches on the newel post. Two scratches, where two pieces of string have been cut off."

There was a long moment of silence. Lord Cheevers looked from the newel post, to the string lying on the floor, to Miss Middleton-Murray. Anger flushed his face. He seemed to swell with outrage. "You harmed my guests?" The fury in his voice made Primrose shiver.

Miss Middleton-Murray didn't shiver. Nor did

346

she weep or ask for forgiveness; she just stared coldly back at her godfather.

That was when the uproar started.

Lady Cheevers released Primrose's arm and stepped forward. The feathers in her turban bristled. "How could you do such a monstrous thing?" she cried.

"You *harmed* my guests?" Cheevers said a second time, more loudly, and then a third time, in a thunderous bellow: "You harmed *my guests?*"

Primrose exchanged a glance with Rhodes and Oliver.

Oliver nodded at the stairs.

Primrose obeyed that nod with relief, descending the four steps, Rhodes and Oliver at her heels. Behind them, the noise level rose. "A serpent!" Lady Cheevers cried. "In our bosom!"

"Out!" Lord Cheevers roared. "Out of my house!"

They hastily crossed the two galleries and stepped into the corridor beyond. The uproar was still audible.

"Despicable!" Lady Cheevers cried. "The basest, lowest behavior—"

"—gone within the hour!" Lord Cheevers shouted.

They traversed the corridor quickly, the sound fading behind them. At the top of the stairs—the thirty-six steps Oliver had been pushed down yesterday—they halted.

Oliver grimaced. "That went well."

"Yes," Primrose said, because it had gone well. It had been perfect. But it had also been deeply unsettling. She repressed a shiver.

"Did you see her face?" Rhodes said. "No remorse. None at all." He sounded baffled.

"That's because she's a harpy," Oliver said. "Metaphorically speaking."

"No, in this case I believe it's literal," Primrose said. "She truly *is* a harpy." She tried to repress another shiver, and failed.

Oliver noticed. "You all right?"

"I found it rather disturbing," Primrose confessed.

Oliver reached out and took her hand, even though Rhodes was standing there. He gave her fingers a squeeze.

"I thought she'd be mortified," Primrose said. "I would have been. But instead, she was angry." Miss Middleton-Murray's rage hadn't been hot and blustering, like Lord Cheevers's; it had been cold and silent. "She scared me a little."

Rhodes took her other hand. "You'll never see her again."

"She'll be gone from here by nightfall," Oliver said. "And you can be certain she won't dare show her face in Society after this."

"Do you think so? She has a lot of nerve."

"She was caught red-handed by a duke, a marquis, a viscount, a viscountess, *and* a duke's daughter," Oliver said. "Not even Old Nick himself would have the temerity to show his face in Society after that."

"No. I suppose not."

They descended the stairs slowly. Oliver didn't release her hand. Neither did Rhodes.

"Do you think she has no conscience?" Rhodes asked, when they were halfway down.

"I'm certain she doesn't," Oliver said.

When they reached the vestibule, they paused again. Rhodes looked back up the stairs. Primrose listened for the sound of raised voices, but heard nothing.

Rhodes released her hand. "I think I'll just drop a quiet word in Miss Middleton-Murray's ear, let her know that I'll bring her before a magistrate if she ever comes within twenty miles of you."

"Make that a hundred miles," Oliver said.

They watched Rhodes climb the stairs and disappear from sight. Oliver was still holding her hand. "I want to check on Ninian," he said. "Make sure he's safe."

Ninian was still in the blue salon with Miss Cheevers. Neither of them noticed the door open;

they were sitting on the window seat, their heads tilted towards one another, talking in low voices.

Mrs. Middleton-Murray didn't notice the door open either. She was intent on her needlework, unaware of the disaster bearing down upon her.

Primrose and Oliver retreated back into the corridor and looked at each other.

Primrose thought they were thinking the same thing, and it was confirmed when Oliver said, "The State apartments?"

A minute later, they opened the door to the State reception room and slipped inside. Oliver led her through the sitting room and the dressing room and into the bedroom, where he settled himself on the bed with a loud sigh. "Thank God that's over." He tugged her down to lie alongside him and put an arm around her, gathering her close. "How are you, Prim? You all right?"

"Yes." Primrose nestled into his warmth, resting her head on his shoulder, placing one hand on his chest. And then, as if to make a liar of herself, she shivered again.

Oliver felt it. His arm tightened around her.

"She looked *murderous*," Primrose whispered.

"She did indeed. The murderous Miss Middleton-Murray."

They were both silent for a moment, while the

alliteration echoed in their ears, then Oliver whispered, "Did you hear that, Prim?"

"I did."

"Worth a kiss?"

"Perhaps." Primrose found one of his coat buttons, and plucked at it. "Do you know what her first name is?"

"I think I heard it once." Oliver frowned. "Lucy? Lucilla? Something like that."

"Millicent. And her middle name is Mary. She told me this afternoon."

This time there was a very long moment of silence.

"Are you serious?" Oliver said finally.

"I am."

He slanted her a glance. "The murderous Miss Millicent Mary Middleton-Murray?"

Primrose bit her lip, and nodded.

Suddenly they were both giggling helplessly, and then they were laughing, laughing in great whoops, laughing until they almost cried, until they ran out of breath and lay gasping on the State four-poster bed.

Oliver released a sigh. "It's not actually funny."

"No." Primrose sighed, too, and plucked at one of his buttons again, and they were back where they had started.

She managed to repress her shiver this time. Miss

Middleton-Murray was in the past; Lord Algernon lay ahead. *That* was what they needed to think about now.

"You were right, Prim. I shouldn't have made it into a game."

"What do you mean?"

"Miss Middleton-Murray and the others. I didn't flirt with them, but I didn't discourage them, either. If I'd made it clear I wasn't looking for a wife, none of this would have happened."

Not looking for a wife.

Primrose stopped plucking at his button. She removed her hand from his chest.

"What was that quote? The Aurelius one."

"Which one?"

"The one about being yourself. Not acting a part."

It took her a moment to realize which quote he meant. "'Settle on the type of person you wish to be and stick to it, whether alone or in company.'"

"That's what I should have done," Oliver said. He stared up at the bed canopy, as if memorizing its arrangement.

"Well, yes, but . . . Oliver, that's the type of person you are. You play games all the time. So in one way you *were* being yourself."

His gaze slanted to her. "Is that what you think?"

Primrose hesitated, and then nodded.

"I play games *some* of the time," Oliver said, pushing up to sit. "Not *all* the time."

"I beg your pardon," Primrose said, also sitting up. "I didn't mean to offend you."

Oliver stared at her for a long, frowning moment.

"There's nothing's wrong with playing games," Primrose said. "As long as you don't hurt people."

Oliver looked as if she'd slapped him.

"I don't think you've hurt anyone," Primrose told him hastily.

"No?" His voice held a faint bite. "I'm fairly certain Miss Carteris's wrist is hurting right now, and Miss Warrington's nose."

"That wasn't your fault!"

Oliver looked away. "If I hadn't played my game, Miss Middleton-Murray may not have played hers."

Primrose couldn't refute this. "Yes, but *your* intention was never to hurt anyone."

"No," Oliver lay back down on the bed. He stared up at the bed canopy again. "My intention was only to amuse myself."

Primrose bit her lip and looked down at the Holland cloth. She smoothed a wrinkle with her fingertip.

"I want to be a good duke, Prim. I want to be as good a duke as your father. So . . ." Oliver took a deep breath, and released it. "No more games."

"What?" It was a horrifying thought. Oliver not playing games would be like a sunflower with all its bright petals plucked off. "Don't do that!"

His gaze slanted to her again.

"You have a natural levity, and that's a good thing, Oliver. An *enviable* thing. It will help you be a good duke."

His brows drew together. She saw his perplexity.

"You're very new at being a duke. You haven't even seen your estates yet, let alone shouldered all your responsibilities. Your secretary and your men of business and your bailiffs are still bearing the brunt of it."

Oliver's brows drew more sharply together. He opened his mouth.

Primrose held up a hand to forestall him. "That wasn't a criticism. I know you're touring the estates this summer, and by the end of the year you'll have everything in hand, but the thing is, Oliver, being a duke is a *lot* harder than it looks. It's not life and death, like in the army, but your decisions will affect hundreds of people. Perhaps even thousands."

Oliver closed his mouth.

Primrose smoothed another wrinkle in the Holland cloth, looking at it rather than Oliver's face. "It wears on Father, the responsibility of it all. Sometimes I think that if he didn't know how to laugh, he'd go mad."

Oliver said nothing.

After a moment, she glanced at him. He was watching her gravely.

"You're going to need your sense of humor," Primrose told him. "It's going to keep you *sane*. So, don't stop playing games, just . . ." She searched for the right words.

"Choose them more wisely."

"Yes." She smiled at him. "That's it exactly."

Oliver reached for her, drawing her down until she lay on his chest. "How did you get to be so long-headed, Prim?"

"I'm not long-headed," Primrose said, into the starched muslin folds of his neckcloth.

"No?" He stroked her hair. "I think you are."

Primrose's cheeks grew warm at this praise. "I read a lot."

Oliver stroked her hair again, then ran his fingers lightly and ticklingly from her temple down to her jaw. "'There are none more lazy, or more truly ignorant, than your everlasting readers.'"

"What?" Her voice was an indignant squawk. Primrose pushed up on her forearms and looked down at him.

Oliver grinned up at her. "Aurelius, Prim."

"I know it's Aurelius!"

Oliver widened his eyes. "What? An Aurelius quote you don't like?"

"It's not one of my favorites, no."

Primrose gazed down at him. Woodland eyes, green and brown and gold. She bent her head and kissed him. Their lips parted, their tongues touched briefly, and then she drew back.

"What was that for?" Oliver asked.

"Knock-kneed nag."

"I think that deserves two kisses, don't you?"

Primrose shook her head sternly. "One kiss per alliteration."

Oliver thought for a moment. "Fiddle-faddle fellow."

Primrose bent her head and kissed him again. This time it lasted longer. His tongue invaded her mouth. His hand crept up to cup the nape of her neck, holding her to him.

Primrose was breathless by the time she broke the kiss. Oliver's face was flushed and his woodland eyes were darker than they'd been before.

She watched his pupils contract slightly, and said, "Next."

Oliver's brow furrowed for a moment. "Dreadfully dull duke."

Primrose laughed and bent her head again, losing herself in Oliver's mouth, in its taste and its heat, in the wonders of his lips and tongue and teeth. She was breathless again when they stopped.

"Melancholy marquis," Oliver said. "Virtuous viscount."

"You missed out earl."

"I left it for you."

Primrose thought for a moment. "Elegant earl."

Oliver grinned up at her, and drew her head down again. His kiss was demanding yet playful, a combination that seemed uniquely him. If she were to kiss a thousand other men Primrose doubted any of them would kiss exactly as Oliver did—the mischievous nip of teeth on her lower lip, the teasing slide of his tongue against hers. Oliver might not be able to wish himself from one place to another, but he did possess magic. His kisses were magical. His mouth was magical.

The kiss deepened, became less playful, more intense. All that single-minded passion focused on her was overwhelming. Dizzying. Perfect. He was devouring her mouth now, crushing her to him, one hand buried in her hair, the other at her waist, holding her flush against his chest.

Oliver shifted on the bed, shifted *her*—and suddenly Primrose found herself with one of his legs between both of hers.

She froze and stopped kissing him. There were layers of fabric between them—gown, petticoat, chemise, breeches—but even so, his *thigh* was cradled between her legs. "Oliver?" She lifted her head so that she could see his face.

"You don't like it?"

She wasn't sure whether she liked it or not. It felt intimate and . . . and *dangerous,* as if something more than kissing might happen between them.

Oliver watched her face, waiting for her reply.

Primrose tried to find the words to articulate what she felt, but it was almost impossible to think. Her heart was beating fast and her lungs seemed to have grown smaller and she was intensely aware of the broad, solid strength of his thigh nestled between her own thighs. "It feels dangerous," she admitted.

"It's not. I promise." Oliver touched her cheek lightly, gently. "It's just something I think you might like. If you don't, we'll stop."

It was the gentleness of his touch that decided her, that feather-light caress. Oliver might play games with her, but he would never harm her.

"All right," Primrose said, and after a moment's hesitation, she dipped her head and kissed him again.

That thigh was distracting, though. It was impossible not to be aware of it—so strong, so muscular. And almost as distracting was that this position brought her pudendum level with his hipbone. Layers of clothing separated them, but that didn't alter the fact that her groin pressed against Oliver's hip, and perhaps that was why this felt so intimate and so dangerous?

Oliver tightened his arm around her waist at the same moment that his hips moved, arching slightly off the bed. Through all those layers of fabric, she rubbed against him.

Primrose gasped.

He did it again.

"Oh," Primrose said into his mouth.

"Like that?" he whispered.

"I don't know." But that wasn't completely truthful. Her brain might not know whether she liked it or not, but her body certainly knew, because when Oliver did it again, she uttered a small, unexpected moan.

Oliver laughed breathlessly and continued to kiss her, continued to move his hips, his arm strong around her waist. It was almost as if she was riding him, riding his thigh, riding his hipbone, and my God . . . that rhythmic pressure against her most private place . . .

Heavens, that felt *good*. She was melting from the inside out.

Primrose clutched his hair with one hand and his shoulder with the other and struggled to keep control of her wits, but it was futile. Her brain had

ceased to function. Oliver's hand was on her derrière now, holding her against him more firmly, and
instead of being outraged she reveled in that firm
pressure. "That's right, Prim," he whispered, and did
it again: tilting up with his hips, bearing down with
his hand.

Pleasure shivered through her.

Oliver's rhythm sped up. It became difficult to
breathe, impossible to think. She could only exist,
shamelessly pressing herself against Oliver's hipbone—she didn't want it to end—didn't want it to
end—and then it *did* end, in a cascade of bright,
unexpected ecstasy.

Oliver stopped moving. His arm was around her
waist again, holding her close and his mouth was
against her cheek, gently kissing her.

It took a while to catch her breath. Catching her
wits was even harder. What had just happened?

Oliver stroked her back, stroked her hair, chuckled softly in her ear. "I thought you'd like it."

Primrose lifted her head and looked down at
him. Her eyes took several seconds to focus. The
room seemed to swing dizzyingly around her, as
if she'd just translocated. But she hadn't; the only
magic here was Oliver. "What *was* that?"

He grinned. "My gift to you."

Gift? Primrose dragged air into her lungs and

stared at him. He looked utterly debauched—hair disheveled, neckcloth in disarray, cheeks flushed, eyes dark and glittering.

His *gift* to her?

What did that mean?

What should she say in reply?

"Thank you," she said, finally.

Oliver's grin widened. "You're welcome."

Her acorn pendant dangled between them, almost lost in the crushed folds of his neckcloth. Oliver fished it out with one hand and held it up so that he could see it. His expression changed ever so slightly, eyes fractionally narrowing, the tiniest crease between his brows, as if he weighed up a course of action.

Primrose felt a flicker of excitement. Was he going to suggest putting her acorn to the test?

Oliver's gift had made her feel more alive than she ever had before—skin tingling, blood rushing through her veins—and it had also made her feel reckless, made her want to cast propriety to the winds and do shocking things, such as touch his bare skin and let him touch hers.

Right now. On the State bed.

She held her breath, anticipating his words: *Let's put it to the test, Prim.*

Oliver released the pendant. He shifted beneath

her and grimaced. "Much as I enjoy having you on top of me, Prim, I'm going to have to ask you to get off. I need a moment to, uh, compose myself."

Her disappointment was sharp. The recklessness folded in on itself. Embarrassment took its place.

Primrose scrambled off him, and not just off him but away from him, putting a good foot of Holland-cloth-covered bed between them. What on earth had she just *done?* What on earth had she been *thinking?*

The embarrassment strengthened and began to feel a lot like mortification. She'd rubbed herself against Oliver's *hipbone.* Shamelessly and wantonly.

Alongside her, Oliver adjusted his breeches slightly. Her gaze followed his hand—and stayed there. Oliver's breeches looked fuller than they usually did. A *lot* fuller.

And then understanding rushed in.

Oh.

Primrose sat on the bed, frozen with shock. For a moment she couldn't even breathe.

She might be innocent, but she wasn't naive. Just as she knew that the place between a woman's legs was called a pudendum, she also knew that the fullness in Oliver's breeches meant that his organ was distended.

And she knew what *that* meant: He wanted to bed her.

She looked away from him, not merely embarrassed now, but confused. If Oliver wanted to bed her, why had he stopped?

This morning he'd told her he wasn't playing with her, and then this afternoon he'd said he wasn't looking for a wife. So what did that make this?

Something more than a game but less than matrimony?

A liaison?

"God damn it," Oliver said, sitting up alongside her. "Look at that, Prim. It's raining."

Primrose looked at the window. It was indeed raining.

Oliver climbed off the bed and crossed to the window, adjusting his breeches again as he walked. He peered out. "Damnation." He turned back to face her, a scowl on his brow. "I wanted to catch him tonight." His scowl faded. He tilted his head to one side and looked at her. "That's a very interesting hairstyle you're sporting."

Primrose put her hand to her hair, and discovered that it was falling down around her shoulders. "And that's a very interesting neckcloth you're wearing," she retorted.

Oliver peered down at his neckcloth. "So it is," he said, and headed for the dressing room.

After a moment, Primrose climbed off the bed

and followed him. Oliver was standing in front of the mirror, retying his neckcloth. He moved to one side, making room for her.

Primrose tidied her hair, but most of her attention was on Oliver—his deft fingers, his frown of concentration, the way his eyes narrowed and his lips pursed slightly as he tried to get the folds of his neckcloth to lie flat.

What were they doing, she and Oliver? Just how serious was it?

She opened her mouth to ask him, and then closed it again.

How serious did she *want* it to be?

Oliver met her eyes in the mirror and winked at her, and then struck a pose. "I am perfect," he declared.

And he was.

Perfectly ridiculous. Ridiculously perfect.

Ridiculously, perfectly, Oliver.

CHAPTER 29

It was raining heavily by dinnertime. Primrose wrapped a warm cashmere shawl around her shoulders—it had grown quite chilly—and marched briskly down to the drawing room. Lord Algernon was the only person there, standing by the fireplace.

"Good evening, Lady Primrose," he said. "Quite a cold snap this is, isn't it? Come and stand here by the fire."

Primrose smiled at him, and did as he bid.

"I understand you had an unpleasant experience this afternoon. Are you quite well?"

"I am, thank you."

"Such a dreadful thing. Frederick will never forgive himself! And poor Isobel is quite beside herself. She won't be joining us for dinner. I understand she's prostrate with shock."

"Oh," Primrose said, thinking of Lady Cheevers's shrill cry of warning: *Look out!*

365

"You're made of strong stuff, though, Lady Prim-rose," Lord Algernon said, in a jocular tone that she found slightly patronizing.

"I was never in any danger," she said.

At that moment, the drawing room door opened and Lord Cheevers entered. He crossed to the fire-place. "Lady Primrose," he said awkwardly. "I must apologize for what happened."

The door opened again. This time the newcomers were Rhodes and Oliver.

They didn't join them at the fireplace; instead, Rhodes caught her eye and stroked the end of his nose, then he and Oliver strolled across to one of the windows and looked out at the encroaching dusk.

"That you should almost come to harm while under my roof," Cheevers said. "Injured by my own goddaughter—"

"You weren't to blame, Lord Cheevers."

Cheevers looked at her uncertainly. She saw that his apology wasn't just for the sake of form; he was genuinely distressed by what had happened.

"You weren't to blame," Primrose repeated. "No one thinks so. I certainly don't, and I know my brother and Westfell don't either." She glanced at Lord Algernon. "You don't, do you, sir?"

"Of course not!" Lord Algernon said, clapping his

friend on the shoulder. "It's a devil of a thing, Frederick, but not your fault. Miss Middleton-Murray was a charming girl. Quite charming! No one would have thought her capable of such malice." He hesitated. "Ah . . . may I ask, Lady Primrose, how you came to suspect Miss Middleton-Murray of her, er, her dastardly deeds? As I understand it, the victims themselves were unaware there was foul play."

Lord Algernon's gaze was intent. Instinct told her that there was more to his question than mere curiosity. Was he afraid that she suspected him of *his* dastardly deeds?

"Oh, it was quite by chance," she assured him. "It was the scratches on the newel post. I noticed them in passing. I never would have guessed otherwise."

"You must have sharp eyesight."

"Tolerably sharp." Primrose glanced across at the window. "If you will excuse me? I need to speak with my brother." She nodded politely to Cheevers and Lord Algernon, left the warmth of the fire, and crossed to where Oliver and Rhodes stood. "What is it?" she asked quietly.

Rhodes glanced at her, and then back out at the rain. "Guess what Benoît found hidden in my pillows?" he said, equally quietly.

"More bishop's weed?"

Rhodes nodded.

"I wondered where Uncle Algy was this afternoon," Oliver murmured. "Now I know: picking flowers."

"Does he know you've swapped beds?" Primrose asked in a whisper.

Rhodes shook his head, his attention still on the window. "Benoît checked both rooms. The bishop's weed is only in the pillows on my old bed."

"Well, that's good, but . . . it *is* disturbing that Lord Algernon was in your old room." It was dark enough outside that she could see the drawing room reflected in the rain-flecked window panes.

Rhodes said nothing, but his reflection grimaced.

"I'm glad Benoît disposed of the arsenic," Primrose whispered. Cheevers and Lord Algernon stood at the fireplace. She watched their mouths move, heard the low murmur of their voices.

"Yes," Oliver said. He was watching his uncle in the windowpanes, too.

Her ears caught the sound of the door opening. She saw Miss Cheevers enter the room. The girl looked rather pale, or was that the fault of the dark, distorted mirror in which she was reflected? Primrose turned her head. No, the window hadn't lied; Miss Cheevers was pale. In fact, she looked quite miserable.

It wasn't difficult to guess why.

"Miss Cheevers," Primrose said, stepping away from the window. "How are you?"

Miss Cheevers hesitated, and crossed to her. "Lady Primrose, I'm so sorry that . . . that such a thing . . ."

"I'm perfectly unharmed," Primrose said. "I was much luckier than your cousins."

Miss Cheevers's eyes filled with tears at this reminder of Miss Warrington and Miss Carteris.

Primrose gave herself a mental kick. "Come," she said, abandoning Rhodes and Oliver at the window. "Sit with me on the sofa and we'll have a comfortable coze before dinner."

Miss Cheevers obediently followed her to the sofa and sat. "It's so dreadful. So shocking! To think that Milly could do something so . . . so . . ." She trailed off, and bit her lip.

Primrose eyed her. "Miss Cheevers, is this perhaps *not* a surprise for you?"

"Oh, no! It is! But . . ."

"But?"

Miss Cheevers's brow crimped faintly. She looked at Primrose uncertainly.

Primrose waited.

"Milly pushed me off the jetty once," Miss Cheevers said in a low voice. "When we were children. She said it was an accident, but it wasn't. I know it wasn't."

"The jetty?"

Miss Cheevers nodded. Her brow creased tragically. "But it was so long ago, Lady Primrose! And when Margaret tripped on the stairs, and then Emma, I never thought—not for an instant—that . . . that . . ."

Primrose took one of the girl's hands. "Of course you didn't," she said soothingly.

"I would have told my parents if I thought Milly had anything to do with it. But I *didn't* think it, and . . . and . . ." Miss Cheevers's hand trembled, and her voice trembled, and tears trembled on her eyelashes.

Primrose glanced at the fireplace to make certain that Lord Cheevers wasn't listening. She lowered her voice. "If you had told your parents, I doubt they would have believed you. In fact, they probably would have scolded you for having uncharitable thoughts."

Miss Cheevers considered this for a moment. "Probably," she said shakily.

"You would never trip anyone on the stairs, and so naturally you didn't suspect Miss Middleton-Murray of doing so. If you feel guilt, I assure you it's unwarranted. The blame rests wholly on Miss Middleton-Murray's shoulders."

After a moment, Miss Cheevers gave a watery smile. Then she hunted for her handkerchief and blotted her eyes.

Dinner was a subdued meal, the events of the afternoon hanging over them all. Even Lord Algernon seemed in low spirits. He ate quietly, without his usual good-natured jokes and jovial laughter.

Primrose's seat gave her a good view of Lord Algernon. She observed him surreptitiously while she ate. Several times she caught him looking at Oliver.

Regret and determination—those were the two emotions on his face when he looked at his nephew, but it seemed to her that his determination was stronger than it had been. The way his lips pressed together, the resolute clenching of his jaw, the set of his shoulders . . .

Lord Algernon gave all the appearance of a man hell-bent on committing an unpleasant task.

The curtains were drawn against the night, but Primrose could hear rain tapping against the windowpanes. *Stop raining,* she prayed silently. *Please stop raining so that we can finish this tonight.*

But alas, it was still raining when she and Miss Cheevers retired to the drawing room after dinner.

Primrose glanced at the girl. She looked rather woebegone.

"Why don't you go to bed?" Primrose suggested. "I'm quite happy to read by myself."

"Oh, no!" Miss Cheevers said, clearly determined to play the hostess. "I shall pour us both some tea and we shall talk. Have you seen the latest fashion plates from London?"

"I'm afraid I'm not very interested in fashion," Primrose confessed. "Although I would like to ask Mr. Dasenby's advice about my wardrobe." She looked ruefully down at the evening gown she was wearing, the silk a rather standoffish shade of blue. "He has an extraordinary eye for color, and I *don't*."

The girl's face lit up. "He does, doesn't he? Ninian always knows exactly what one should wear." Her eyes widened. "Oh! I have an idea. Wait one moment, Lady Primrose!" She ran from the room.

Primrose waited, and five minutes later Chloé Cheevers returned, flushed and breathless, clutching something to her chest. "Ninian gave me these," she said, crossing to the card table and laying down her burden.

Primrose stepped closer for a better look, and discovered that they weren't pieces of colored paper, as her eyes had first told her, but swatches of material.

"Goodness," she said, taken aback. "There are hundreds of them."

"One hundred and twenty," Miss Cheevers said, spreading out the swatches. "He helped me to pick the colors for my dresses this Season, only . . . I caught the measles from my little brothers and couldn't go to London." She glanced at Primrose and smiled. "But next year I shall."

They sorted the swatches into colors and were deep in conversation over them when the men made their appearance. Mr. Dasenby was first through the door. "Ninian!" Miss Cheevers cried. "Come over here and help us pick colors for Lady Primrose."

Dasenby obeyed this request with alacrity.

Next through the door were Oliver and Rhodes. They took one look at the card table and the swatches, and veered towards the fireplace.

Last were Lord Algernon and Lord Cheevers.

Primrose paid them little attention, for Dasenby was shuffling through the swatches and discarding a great many of them. She jumped when someone tapped her on the shoulder. It was Rhodes. "Ollie and I are going to play chess in the library."

She nodded, and glanced past him. "Where are their lordships?"

"In the cardroom."

She nodded, and lowered her voice to a whisper. "Be careful."

"Always," Rhodes said.

Primrose returned her attention to the swatches.

"You suit the softer tints," Dasenby said. "See? This pink would be perfect, and this blue and this green, but *not* these ones."

Primrose stepped closer to examine the pieces of fabric.

Half an hour later, she had eight swatches that Ninian Dasenby had chosen for her: a pink, a coral, a lavender, two greens, a yellow, and two blues. To her pleasure, one of the blues was periwinkle. "Thank you," she said. "I do appreciate this, Mr. Dasenby. I'm looking forward to ordering new gowns." And oddly, she *was* looking forward to it. She, who usually found visits to the dressmaker extremely tedious.

Dasenby gave her a smile that was both pleased and shy.

"Oh!" Miss Cheevers said. "Look at the time! I promised to look in on Mother ten minutes ago." She caught up her skirts. "Good night, Lady Primrose. Good night, Ninian." The door closed behind her.

Dasenby began gathering the discarded swatches together.

Primrose helped him. "You and Miss Cheevers have known each other a long time?"

"Since we were children," Dasenby said. He

paused in his gathering, and flushed. "You perhaps think we're too informal with one another?"

Primrose laughed. "No." What she thought was that Ninian Dasenby and Chloé Cheevers were perfect for each other. They both had the same sweetness of character, the same shyness.

Dasenby glanced around, and appeared to notice the emptiness of the drawing room for the first time. "Where's my cousin?" And then, in a note of alarm. "Where's my father?"

"Westfell and my brother are in the library together, and your father is with Lord Cheevers in the cardroom."

"Oh." Dasenby looked at the scattered pieces of fabric, and then at the door, and then back at her.

Primrose knew that Oliver was all right—he was with Rhodes, and the last thing Rhodes had told her was that they'd be careful—but Dasenby was clearly worried. "Why don't you check on them?" she suggested.

"I will, yes." He hastened to the door.

Primrose gathered up the swatches, color by color. The reds and the pinks, the oranges and the yellows. She was picking up the greens when Dasenby burst in through the door. "I can't wake them!"

She looked up. "I beg your pardon?"

"Thayne and my cousin are in the library, and I can't wake them!"

CHAPTER 30

*P*rimrose threw aside the swatches, caught up her skirts, and ran from the drawing room, along the corridor, across the vestibule—her shoes slapping on the marble flagstones—and flung open the door to the library with such force that it slammed into the wall with a sharp *crack*.

The library was a large room, but at night it seemed as vast as a cathedral, filled with shadows, the ceiling lost in darkness. The only light was by the fireplace, where two armchairs formed a cozy nook, lit by candles and firelight.

Rhodes and Oliver were seated in those armchairs, a chessboard laid out on a table between them. Neither of them reacted to the *crack*, or to her abrupt entrance.

Rhodes had slumped forward over the table, his head resting on his arms, looking for all the world like a schoolboy asleep over his arithmetic. Oliver sagged back in his chair, head lolling, eyes closed.

Primrose crossed swiftly to them, Dasenby at her heels. "Rhodes!" she cried, shaking her brother's shoulder. "Oliver!"

Neither man stirred.

Dasenby slapped Oliver's face. "Cousin! Wake up!"

Oliver didn't so much as twitch.

Primrose bent close to Rhodes. For a moment she thought he wasn't breathing, and her heart clutched in her chest, and then she heard a quiet exhalation.

"Do you think it's arsenic?" Dasenby asked in a hushed, horrified voice.

"I don't know. Fetch Benoît. Hurry!"

Dasenby ran from the room.

Primrose felt remarkably close to panicking. Her heart was beating hard and her thoughts were whirling like a flock of agitated birds. *Think!* she told herself sternly. *Keep your head!*

As well as a chessboard and a candelabrum, there were two empty punch glasses on the table. Primrose glanced around, and spied a silver punch bowl on the broad carved mantelpiece. She examined it. The punch bowl was faintly warm to the touch, still holding a glass or two of amber liquid. A ladle leaned drunkenly against the side. She picked up the ladle, stirred the punch, and sniffed.

A heady scent wafted up.

Primrose mentally sifted through the smells—rum and lemons and mingled spices—and found nothing untoward.

Arsenic has no taste and no smell, Benoît had said.

Primrose decided not to taste the punch. She replaced the ladle and went back to the armchairs. She sniffed Rhodes's glass. Sniffed Oliver's glass. They both smelled exactly the same as the punch bowl.

Dasenby had rushed so precipitously from the library that he'd failed to close the door properly. It stood a couple of inches ajar—and as Primrose looked up from sniffing the glasses, it began to open.

Her heart gave a leap of relief. Dasenby must be back with Benoît already.

She opened her mouth to tell them about the punch, but the door stopped opening. There was a long pause, as if whoever stood behind it waited and listened.

Primrose closed her mouth. Her heart gave another leap; not relief this time, but alarm. Dasenby would fling the door wide and run in. A servant would knock. There was only one person at Cheevers Court who would open the door to the library so cautiously.

Lord Algernon, coming to see whether his victims were dead or not.

Her alarm snuffed out. A fierce, vengeful emotion took its place.

Primrose dropped to a crouch behind Oliver's armchair and looked around for a better hiding place. There, up in the dark gallery, overlooking the library, where no one would see her.

She wished herself there. Even though she was crouching, dizziness caught her. She squeezed her eyes shut briefly. When she opened them, she saw Lord Algernon step into the library.

He stood motionless for a moment, his attitude alert, listening for danger—and then closed the door so quietly that she didn't even hear the faintest *click*.

He crossed on tiptoe to the fireplace.

Primrose slowly rose to her feet and watched, transfixed, forgetting even to breathe.

Lord Algernon looked down at Oliver. His face twisted. She saw his regret—and then the grimace of regret was gone, and only determination remained. He set his jaw grimly, pulled a cloth from inside his waistcoat, took the back of Oliver's head in one hand and pressed the cloth firmly over Oliver's nose and mouth with the other.

Primrose's heart seemed to stop beating. She didn't think; she just *did*—wishing herself down to stand behind Lord Algernon. As soon as her feet were planted on solid ground she cried "Stop!" even though the room was still spinning around her.

Lord Algernon recoiled so violently that he almost fell over. He jerked away from Oliver, dropped the cloth, and took several stumbling paces back, then halted, staring at her, chest heaving, eyes wide with shock, mouth open, aghast.

Oliver's head lolled to the side. He still didn't wake.

Primrose crossed hastily to him and laid one hand protectively on Oliver's head, gripping his brown hair. She met Lord Algernon's eyes. "Murderer."

Lord Algernon's nostrils flared. His jaw clenched. So did his hands.

Primrose was suddenly aware that not only was he a great deal larger and stronger than she was, he was also desperate. She felt a flicker of alarm. *He could kill me.* She gripped Oliver's hair more tightly and stared at Lord Algernon, trying not to let her fear show. "What did you put in the punch?" she demanded.

Lord Algernon shook his head. Emotions crossed his face, one after another, too quickly for her to recognize, and finally settled on one: a bleak resolve.

Primrose tensed, ready to translocate if he should attack her—but instead he turned towards the door.

"What did you put in the punch?" she demanded again.

Lord Algernon ignored her. He lengthened his stride.

Primrose released Oliver's hair and ran after him. "What did you put in it?" she cried, grabbing his arm.

Lord Algernon shook her off so violently that she lost her balance and went sprawling. He wrenched open the door and plunged out into the corridor.

Primrose scrambled to her feet and looked back at Oliver and Rhodes. Which was more important? Catching Lord Algernon, or keeping watch over them?

The punch. The punch was the most important thing—and only one person knew what was in it.

She ran into the corridor. Lord Algernon had turned away from the vestibule. Primrose gave chase, her dainty kid shoes slapping on the floor.

Ahead, Lord Algernon yanked open a door to the terrace and vanished from sight.

Primrose snatched a glance over her shoulder—the corridor was empty of witnesses—and wished herself to that door. She yanked it open, too, even as the vertigo caught her, and plunged outside—and collided with Lord Algernon.

He gave a startled cry and lashed out, striking her across the chest.

Primrose almost fell over again. She stumbled back against the closing door.

Lord Algernon turned from her and fled.

"What did you put in the punch?" she shouted after him.

He didn't answer.

Primrose pushed away from the door. It was dark out here. And wet. And cold. Lord Algernon was a burly black shape, hurrying across the terrace, almost at the long flight of steps.

Primrose wished herself to the top of those steps. She kept her eyes open despite the dizziness, and lurched to keep her balance.

Lord Algernon loomed out of the darkness, practically invisible, moving fast.

Primrose snatched for him, missing his arm, grabbing the tails of his coat. *What is in the punch?*

Lord Algernon rounded on her. He didn't try to strike her or shake her off; instead he gave a bellow of rage and picked her up and flung her down the steps.

Primrose hadn't been a cavalry officer. She didn't know how to fall without breaking her neck, but she *did* know how to translocate.

Even so, she landed on the gravel at the bottom of the steps hard enough to knock the breath from her body.

For a moment she lay there, sprawled full-length, gasping, dizzy. Footsteps smacked down the steps and then past her—Lord Algernon.

Primrose pushed up to hands and knees and found enough breath to shout, "What's in the punch?"

There was no answer. She strained to see him, but couldn't. The quick crunch of his footsteps grew fainter, lost beneath the steady patter of rain.

Primrose stayed where she was for three quick panted breaths, then wished herself back to the library. Even though she was on hands and knees, the vertigo was so strong that she nearly toppled over. She squeezed her eyes shut.

The world settled into place around her. Primrose opened her eyes and scrambled to her feet. The library was exactly as she'd left it less than a minute ago: the candles, the chessboard, the two motionless figures in the armchairs.

She crossed to Rhodes quickly and bent to listen. Was he still breathing? Was Oliver?

Yes. They both were.

For some reason, that made her want to cry. From relief? Or from fear that the next time she strained to hear those faint breaths she'd hear nothing?

Her heart was beating fast. Water dripped from her hair. Primrose wiped her face, and discovered that she had pieces of gravel stuck to her palms. She flicked them away, and bent to check Rhodes again, to check Oliver again.

Running footsteps echoed in the corridor.

Dasenby burst into the room, panting, Benoît at his heels.

"I think there may have been something in the punch," Primrose told them breathlessly. "They both drank it."

Benoît nodded, and crossed to the armchairs and crouched, listening to Rhodes's breathing. Then he felt for his pulse.

Dasenby watched anxiously.

"Your father was just in here," Primrose told him. "He tried to smother Oliver. I stopped him."

Benoît glanced up. "Smother?"

Primrose nodded, and then realized what that might mean. "They haven't been poisoned? Merely drugged?"

"Perhaps." Benoît rose. "The punch? Where is it?"

Primrose showed him.

Benoît sniffed the punch, as she'd done. "Monsieur Dasenby," he said. "Can you find one of the servants? We need to know who made this punch."

Dasenby didn't object to being given orders by a valet; he nodded, and departed hastily.

Benoît returned to the table. He opened Rhodes's mouth, leaned close, and sniffed, then he peeled back one of Rhodes's eyelids and examined the pupil.

Primrose watched, kneading her hands together,

almost wringing them. Hope and fear made a tight, sickening knot in her stomach. *Don't let them die,* she begged silently. *Please, don't let them die.*

Benoît checked Oliver next.

"What do you think it is?" Primrose asked, fighting to keep her voice steady. "Not arsenic?"

"Their breathing is very shallow," Benoît said. "And their pupils are constricted. I think . . . perhaps laudanum."

"That's good, isn't it?"

"It depends how much they have drunk." Benoît crossed to the mantelpiece and stirred the punch, then scooped some up in the silver ladle and cautiously tasted it.

Primrose watched him intently.

Benoît stood still for a long moment, his gaze abstracted, and she knew he was trying to analyze the flavors. "Well?" she asked, once he'd put the ladle back in the bowl.

"It's sweet," Benoît said. "But the aftertaste is bitter."

"Laudanum's bitter, isn't it?"

"Yes."

They both started as Dasenby burst into the library again. He was even more out of breath than he'd been before. "The punch was mixed in the cardroom, by my father. He and Lord Cheevers each took a glass, and then one of the footmen brought the rest here for Thayne and my cousin. I've spoken to the man. He says the bowl was three-quarters full."

Primrose and Benoît both looked at the punch bowl. She tried to estimate how much Rhodes and Oliver had drunk. Three glasses each? Four?

"Did Lord Cheevers drink the punch?" Benoît asked.

Dasenby nodded, gulping for breath. "Yes, and he fell asleep in the cardroom. But he woke when I shook him."

"How is he?" Primrose asked.

"Drowsy. He thought he was foxed, apologized to me for it, and went upstairs to bed."

"*Bon,*" Benoît said. "Then I think we can say it is laudanum. Lord Algernon would not poison his good friend, no?" He went back to the table and bent over Oliver.

"Should I have told Lord Cheevers there's something wrong with the punch?" Dasenby asked. He was kneading his hands together anxiously, as Primrose had done earlier. "Oliver said he wanted to keep this quiet, so I didn't, but . . . Should I have?"

Primrose glanced at Benoît.

"If he drank only one glass he should be fine. Thayne and Westfell, though . . ." The valet grimaced. "Let's get them upstairs."

"You think they're in danger of dying?" Primrose asked.

"*Non,*" the valet said. "I do not think so, but I should very much like to wake them and induce them to vomit. Monsieur Dasenby, help me get the duke to his room."

Dasenby hurried forward. Together, he and Benoît hefted Oliver to his feet. Dasenby slung one of Oliver's arms around his shoulders. Benoît did the same. Oliver sagged between them.

"Lady Primrose, stay with your brother," the valet said. "We will be back very soon."

Left in the library, Primrose had nothing to do but check Rhodes's breathing, and feel anxious. She was so anxious that it took her several minutes to notice something white lying on the floor: the cloth Lord Algernon had tried to smother Oliver with. She picked it up. It was a neckcloth, the muslin soft and unstarched and folded over many times to make a thick pad.

Primrose laid it on the table and checked Rhodes's breathing again. Was it shallower than it had been before?

She removed Rhodes's neckcloth, crisp with starch, and placed it alongside Lord Algernon's one.

"You're going to be fine," she whispered, kneeling beside Rhodes, stroking his hair. "Just keep breathing." And even though Benoît believed there was no danger, grief welled in her chest. If Rhodes died . . . If Oliver died . . .

She leapt to her feet in relief when Benoît and Dasenby returned, then hovered, feeling useless, while they hauled Rhodes from his chair, slung his arms over their shoulders, and staggered towards the door. Primrose grabbed up the two neckcloths and followed. "Which room are you putting him in?" she asked, when they reached the vestibule and the men paused to catch their breath.

"Same as Westfell," Benoît said. "Easier to look after them together."

Primrose nodded and ran up the stairs. She hurried along the corridor, knocked once on Oliver's door, sharply, and opened it without waiting for an invitation to enter.

Oliver lay on the four-poster bed, out cold. His valet, Grimshaw, was struggling to strip him of his tailcoat.

Primrose cast aside the neckcloths and hurried to the bed. "Let me help."

"Lady Primrose, you shouldn't—"

"Now isn't the time for propriety!"

The valet didn't disagree. Together they wrestled

Oliver out of his tailcoat. He was heavy, limp, un-wieldy, and the tailcoat was very well tailored across his shoulders. The seams strained and the valet grunted with effort before the coat relinquished its grip.

Primrose left the valet unbuttoning Oliver's waistcoat, ran back to the door, and peered down the corridor.

Benoît and Dasenby staggered into view.

She held the door wide for them.

Both men were panting heavily as they deposited Rhodes on the bed beside Oliver. Benoît began immediately to remove Rhodes's tailcoat. Primrose sprang to help him.

When Oliver and Rhodes had been stripped down to shirtsleeves and breeches, Benoît turned to Primrose. "I am going to try to wake them now, and make them vomit. You do not need to see this, Lady Primrose."

"Oh, but—"

"Give us half an hour, please. Monsieur Dasenby, it would be best if you went with her ladyship. Do not let her be alone."

His words made Primrose blink—and then understanding flooded in.

She was the only witness to Lord Algernon's attempt to smother Oliver.

The valet bent over Rhodes, then glanced at her again. "The punch. Please make sure none of the servants drink what is left."

"The servants?" Dasenby said. "Why would they do that?"

"Because that is what servants generally do," Benoît said. He turned back to Rhodes, and lifted an eyelid to examine the pupil.

Dasenby and Primrose exchanged a glance. Benoît was a servant himself. He probably knew what he was talking about.

They left the bedroom and made their way down the stairs silently.

The library was as they had left it: chessboard laid out, candles burning, punch bowl on the mantelpiece.

Dasenby picked up the bowl, hesitated for a moment, as if uncertain what to do with it, then tipped the punch on the fire.

There was a loud *hissss,* a few spits and crackles, and then an unpleasant smell of burning sugar.

Dasenby put the punch bowl on the table, alongside the chessboard. "Now what?"

"Let's check the cardroom."

They found two glasses of punch in the cardroom. One was empty, the other full. Dasenby carried the full glass to the fireplace, and upended it. There was another *hisss,* and the same unpleasant smell.

Dasenby placed the glass on the mantelpiece and looked at Primrose. His expression was sober.

The door opened, and they both started as a footman entered. The footman started, too. "I beg your pardon. I didn't realize anyone was in here." He began to back out the door.

"Oh, no, we've finished," Primrose said.

They retreated to the corridor, leaving the footman to pick up the glasses and snuff the candles.

Primrose exchanged a glance with Dasenby. Was he wondering whether the footman would have drunk that glass of punch? She certainly was.

A chilly draft curled around her ankles. She shivered, and realized that her hair was wet, and her gown was, too. She wondered where on earth she'd left her shawl.

It was in the drawing room, along with the one hundred and twenty swatches of fabric. A maid was in there, too, tidying cushions and snuffing candles.

Primrose gathered up the eight colors Dasenby had chosen for her. They went back out to the corridor again. Primrose huddled into her shawl, aware of how large the house was, how silent.

Where was Lord Algernon? What was he planning next?

"Lady Primrose . . . I hope you don't think it presumptuous of me, but I think you ought to have your maid sleep in your room with you tonight."

Primrose glanced at Dasenby.

"My father," he said, and then halted.

"He ran outside."

"Even so." Dasenby swallowed, and looked at her with diffident entreaty. "Lady Primrose, I do think it would be for the best."

Primrose thought of all the ways inside the house—dozens of doors, hundreds of windows. She thought of the empty wing in which she slept—the Carterises gone, the Warringtons gone, the Middleton-Murrays gone. "Perhaps you're right."

They asked a footman to set up a truckle bed in her room. Dasenby accompanied her upstairs to oversee its placement.

"Has half an hour passed yet?" Primrose asked Dasenby, when the footman had finished struggling with the truckle bed.

He checked his watch. "Yes."

They hastened back to Oliver's room and rapped on the door.

"Who is it?" a voice asked. Three words only, but unmistakably Monsieur Benoît.

"It's us," Primrose said.

A key scraped in the lock and the door opened. Benoît stood back to let them enter, then relocked the door.

Rhodes and Oliver lay side by side in the bed, fast asleep, the covers drawn up to their chins.

"Weren't you able to wake them?" Primrose asked, feeling a chill of foreboding that had nothing to do with her damp gown.

"We woke them," Benoît said. "Both of them." He looked rather disheveled. He'd shed his coat, and rolled up his shirtsleeves. "It was not easy."

"Did they vomit?" She crossed to the bed and bent to stroke Rhodes's hair back from his face.

"They did."

Now that she noticed it, the room did have an unpleasant odor, but she didn't care about smells; she cared about Rhodes and Oliver. "They'll be all right?" she asked, laying her hand on Rhodes's brow. His skin was neither too cool nor too warm, but precisely as it should be.

"I believe so, yes."

Relief brought stinging tears to her eyes. She blinked them back and went around to the other side of the bed and bent over Oliver, stroked his hair, too, and felt the same teary relief.

"Monsieur Grimshaw and I will take turns watching over them tonight."

Primrose looked around for Oliver's valet. He wasn't in the room.

"He is taking away *le vomi*," Benoît said. "He will be back soon."

Primrose nodded, and stroked Oliver's hair again.

Oliver's eyelids drowsily lifted. He blinked several times, and focused on her face. "Prim." He fumbled one hand free of the covers and held it out to her.

Primrose took it, wrapping both of her hands around it. "How do you feel?" She looked into his eyes, examining his pupils. They were small and tight, almost lost in those green and brown and gold irises.

Oliver didn't answer her question, he merely smiled at her, slowly and sleepily.

That smile affected her more than any smile she'd ever received in her life. Her throat tightened and her heart squeezed and more tears stung her eyes, not relief this time but another emotion, something strong and painful.

Oliver's eyelids drooped shut. His hand was large and warm and relaxed in hers. He'd drifted off to sleep again.

Primrose had to swallow several times to find her voice. "Did you explain to him what had happened?" she asked the valet. "Did he understand?"

"Yes. But whether he will remember in the morning . . ." Benoît gave one of his Gallic shrugs.

Primrose became aware that Mr. Dasenby was hovering anxiously behind her. She yielded her place to him and watched him bend over Oliver. He blinked half a dozen times and swallowed twice. A muscle worked in his cheek. Primrose felt a strong pang of sympathy for him. Poor Dasenby. How dreadful this situation was for him.

She turned to the valet. "Thank you for your help tonight, Monsieur Benoît. We are truly grateful."

"It was my pleasure, Lady Primrose."

Primrose would have liked to have kept watch over Rhodes and Oliver, but she trusted Benoît. The valet was young and strong and clever. Moreover, this was Oliver's bedroom and she shouldn't be in it at all. So, reluctantly, after another five minutes of watching the men sleep, she left.

Dasenby escorted her to her bedroom in the South wing. He waited until she'd opened her door, then said, "Good night, Lady Primrose," and turned away.

Primrose touched his arm, halting him.

He glanced back at her.

"Don't look for your father tonight, Mr. Dasenby. Please. Wait until Oliver and Rhodes are on their feet again."

Dasenby hesitated, and then nodded.

"And lock your door."

He hesitated for longer, and then nodded a second time.

"Good night, Mr. Dasenby."

She watched him walk down the corridor. The

candles in the sconces flickered as he passed them, sending shadows skittering. *Poor boy.* His life was falling down around his ears.

Primrose sighed, and stepped into her bedchamber, where her maid, Fitchett, waited, and locked the door.

CHAPTER 31

$\mathcal{P}$rimrose woke to the sound of Fitchett opening the curtains. Sunshine streamed into the room. Her thoughts slowly shook themselves awake—and then she remembered the events of last night. She sat up suddenly. "What's the time?"

"Eight o'clock, ma'am."

Primrose flung back the bedclothes and scrambled out of bed. She attended to her morning ablutions hastily and dressed as swiftly as she could. The only sign that Lord Algernon had tossed her down the terrace steps was a small bruise on her hip.

She fastened the acorn pendant around her throat, snatched up a shawl, and hurried from the room, along the corridor, down the four steps, through the short gallery, through the long gallery, along another corridor, and arrived out of breath at the door to Oliver's bedchamber.

She rapped on the wooden panels. After a moment, Monsieur Benoît opened it.

"How are they?" she asked anxiously.

"Awake and in perfect health," the valet replied. "But it is not *convenable* for you to see them, I am afraid, Lady Primrose. They are still dressing."

"Oh," Primrose said. "Well. In that case . . ." She bit her lip, hesitated, and said, "Have you seen anything of Lord Algernon?"

"Non." Benoît shook his head. "But Monsieur Dasenby looked in ten minutes ago. I believe he has gone down to breakfast."

"Oh," she said again. "Well . . . Will you please tell my brother I'll see him in the breakfast parlor?"

"Naturellement," the valet said, with a courteous bow. He closed the door.

Primrose went downstairs, eager to speak with Mr. Dasenby, but he wasn't the only occupant of the breakfast parlor. Lord and Lady Cheevers were there, too, and their daughter.

They exchanged morning greetings. Primrose chose food at random and sat alongside Mr. Dasenby. "How are you?" she asked politely. "I trust you slept well?"

"I did, ma'am," Dasenby answered, equally politely. "And you?"

"Yes." Primrose was telling the truth, but she

didn't think Dasenby was. His eyes were shadowed with tiredness.

There was so much she wanted to speak with him about, but the Cheevers were present, so she confined herself to an innocuous, "Have you seen your father this morning?"

Dasenby glanced at her. "No." Then he looked down at her plate. "You have an appetite this morning, Lady Primrose."

Primrose looked down at her plate, too, and blinked in astonishment. Had she really chosen three sausages *and* kedgeree *and* eggs? What had she been thinking?

She ate slowly, hoping the Cheevers would leave and she could speak to Dasenby alone. She was just finishing the kedgeree when the door to the breakfast parlor opened. She looked up eagerly.

It was a footman, bringing a fresh pot of tea.

Primrose ate even more slowly, while both Lord and Lady Cheevers refilled their teacups. Lady Cheevers's turban was in the Moorish style this morning.

Primrose had eaten both eggs and was embarking on her first sausage when the door opened again. This time, it was her brother, with Oliver behind him.

She laid down her knife and fork. "Good morning," she said. "How are you?" But she could see for herself. Both men were clear-eyed and alert, looking as fit and healthy as she'd ever seen them.

"In excellent form, thank you," Oliver said. "Slept like a baby." He gave her a wink and turned to the sideboard and the array of dishes.

Primrose pushed aside her plate thankfully. Sausages were all very well at breakfast, but not three of them, and not after she'd eaten eggs *and* kedgeree. She reached for her teacup while Rhodes and Oliver piled their plates high and took places opposite her and Dasenby.

Primrose was pleased to observe that both men had healthy appetites. The laudanum had clearly done them no harm. She sipped her tea while they ate, and directed her thoughts at the Cheevers. *Leave. Leave.* It didn't work. The Cheevers sipped their tea, too, showing no inclination to depart the sunny parlor.

The butler entered the room, his expression grave. He crossed to Lord Cheevers and bent to whisper in the viscount's ear.

Cheevers's face paled. He put down his teacup, almost missing the saucer, causing a loud clatter.

Primrose tensed. Something was wrong.

Lady Cheevers sensed it, too. "Frederick?" she said, a note of apprehension in her voice. "What is it?"

Cheevers opened his mouth, and then closed it again. He seemed speechless with shock. He didn't look at his wife; he looked at Dasenby.

Primrose realized with alarm that the butler was looking at Dasenby, too.

"What is it?" Lady Cheevers said, more sharply.

Lord Cheevers swallowed, and then said, in a hoarse voice, "The gardeners have found someone drowned in the lake."

Lady Cheevers gasped, and placed her hand at her throat.

Oh, God, Primrose thought. *It must be—*

"It's Algernon," Cheevers said.

The color drained abruptly from Dasenby's face. He put his teacup down with a clatter similar to the one Lord Cheevers had made.

Cheevers's face creased with distress and sympathy. "My dear boy, I'm so sorry."

Oliver put down his knife and fork hastily, pushed back his chair, and came around the table. He gripped Dasenby's shoulders and spoke to Cheevers. "Where's the body?"

Cheevers shook his head and glanced at the butler.

"On the jetty, Your Grace," the butler said.

Primrose saw Oliver's fingers flex comfortingly on Dasenby's shoulders. "Come on, Nin," he said quietly. "Let's go see him."

Dasenby stood. So did Lord Cheevers.

Oliver took Dasenby by the arm, and steered him towards the door. No one spoke as the four men filed from the room: Cheevers, the butler, Dasenby, Oliver. Oliver looked back at the last moment—a flicker of a glance at her, a flicker of a glance at Rhodes, and then he was gone.

The door closed.

Primrose realized that she was frozen in the same position she'd been in when the butler had entered: teacup half raised to her mouth. She put it down in its saucer, quietly, and met Rhodes's eyes across the table.

"Oh, dear," Lady Cheevers said, fumbling for her handkerchief. "How terrible this is!"

Yes, it was terrible, but it was also . . .

Fitting. Just.

The murderer was dead.

CHAPTER 32

Oliver had seen more than his fair share of corpses. Uncle Algernon was one of the easier ones to look at; his body wasn't mutilated, his face wasn't twisted into a rictus of agony or despair. He looked sodden and bedraggled, but peaceful.

Lord Cheevers probably hadn't seen many corpses. He turned his face away, as if the sight was too much for him.

Ninian didn't look away.

Oliver gazed down at the body, remembering Uncle Algy's laugh, remembering how he'd slipped him guineas all those years ago—remembering that he'd tried to kill him last night.

Uncle Algy looked smaller dead than he had alive. He also looked vacant, his big personality extinguished. The only clue to the man he'd been was the deep laughter lines around his eyes.

Oliver released his breath in a slow sigh. "I'm so sorry, Nin."

"It's not your fault," Ninian said, tears in his voice.

Those four words were acknowledgment of something they both knew and Lord Cheevers didn't: Uncle Algy hadn't drowned by accident. He had chosen this—the lake—in preference to the alternative.

Oliver stared somberly down at the body. If Uncle Algy had known that banishment was to be his fate, not the gallows, would he still have chosen to drown himself?

There was no way of knowing now.

He sighed again, and put his arm around Ninian's shoulders and hugged him. "Come on, Nin. We need to talk. Lord Cheevers will take care of everything here, won't you, my lord?"

"Yes," Cheevers said, wiping his eyes with a handkerchief.

❧

They walked for several minutes, he and Ninian, the grass damp beneath their boots. Neither of them spoke. At last they came to a little bower overgrown with roses. The wooden bench beneath was dry.

"Here, Nin," Oliver said.

They sat. Ninian put his elbows on his knees and bent his head and stared down at his clasped hands. There was misery in every line of his body, and even though he was sitting next to Oliver, he seemed lonely and forlorn. Oliver felt a surge of protectiveness. He put his arm around Ninian's shoulders again, and hugged him.

"How could he do it?" Ninian whispered.

Oliver didn't ask Ninian to clarify what he meant by "it." He imagined that Ninian meant all of it: the attempts at murder, the taking of his own life.

"We'll never know," he said. "But I'm guessing . . . he went down a path that he hadn't meant to go down, and once he'd started he found that he couldn't turn back, or even stop, and all he could do was follow the path to its end." And instead of a dukedom, that end had been death.

They were both orphaned now, he and Ninian.

Oliver tilted his head to the side, until his temple touched Ninian's. "You're not alone," he told him. "I've got your back."

"I know," Ninian said, in a wobbly voice.

Oliver tightened his arm around Ninian's shoulders. "We're not the last of the Dasenbys, Nin; we're the beginning of them again. It starts with us. You and me."

Ninian inhaled a shaky breath. He gave a little nod.

"I know that on paper we're only cousins, but . . . in my eyes we're brothers."

There was a moment's silence, and then, "Brothers?"

"Yes," Oliver said firmly. "You're my brother and I'm yours. If that's all right with you?"

Ninian gave an unsteady laugh, and blotted his eyes with his cuff. "It is."

They sat in the rose-covered bower for half an hour, and then Oliver took Ninian back to the house. Lady Cheevers embraced Ninian and fussed over him like a mother hen with a chick, and Miss Cheevers sat alongside him on the sofa and clasped his hand when she thought no one was looking. Lady Cheevers rang for a pot of tea. Oliver declined a cup; instead, he went looking for Primrose and Rhodes. He found them in the library. "We need to talk."

"We do, rather," Rhodes said. "Come upstairs, where we won't be interrupted."

They held their conference in Rhodes's old bedchamber. Primrose took the armchair, Oliver rested his hips against the windowsill, and Rhodes leaned against one of the carved bedposts. They both listened intently while Primrose related the events of the previous night. "He held a cloth over my mouth and nose?" Oliver repeated, when she reached that point in her narrative. "And I didn't wake up?"

"That's right."

"Good God," he said. "That's . . ." Disturbing, was what it was. "Thank you, Prim. If you hadn't been there . . ."

"You should thank your cousin. I was only there because of him. He was worried about you; I wasn't. I thought the pair of you were safe together."

Oliver exchanged a glance with Rhodes. "So did we."

"Keep going, Prim," Rhodes said. "Did Lord Algernon say anything to you?"

"No."

Oliver listened with his mouth open as Primrose described how she'd given chase.

"He threw you *off* the terrace? Down all those steps?" Rhodes's voice slid up half an octave.

"I translocated," Primrose said.

"Yes, but . . ." Rhodes seemed almost incapable of speech. Oliver knew exactly how that felt, because he was almost incapable of speech right now, too.

A shiver originated deep in his chest. Primrose had almost *died.*

"But . . . but if you hadn't been able to translocate . . ." Rhodes said. "If you hadn't . . ."

"But I can translocate," Primrose said, matter-of-factly. Then her brow creased. "However, I think it would be best if we don't mention that part to Mother and Father."

"Agreed," Rhodes said.

"Were you hurt?" Oliver asked.

"The merest bruise. That's all." Her tone dismissed it as unimportant. She changed the subject: "I suggest we leave after the funeral. Go to Gloucestershire. Do you agree?"

Oliver didn't respond to this question. His attention was still fixed on Primrose and Uncle Algy and the terrace.

Rhodes's attention must have been fixed on it, too, because he said, "Bruise?"

The door opened. Benoît stepped into the room. He halted when he saw them. "I beg your pardon," he said, with an apologetic bow, and began to retreat.

Oliver held up his hand. "Please wait a moment, Benoît. Close the door."

The valet did. "What is it, Your Grace?"

"If the opportunity arises . . . if you should happen to speak with my uncle's valet, I would like to have a better understanding of my uncle's last hours."

"I have already taken the liberty of doing that,"

Benoît said. "Lord Algernon's man waited up until one in the morning, but his lordship never came. The bed wasn't slept in. It appears that his lordship didn't return to his room at all. The footmen are saying that he died wearing the same clothes he wore to dinner."

Oliver frowned, and tried to remember what Uncle Algy had worn last night, and what his corpse had been wearing on the jetty this morning. He realized the footmen were correct: they were the same clothes.

"He can't have returned to the house after I confronted him," Primrose said.

"Probably thought you'd raise a hue and cry," Rhodes said, rubbing his eyes.

"Was that all, Your Grace?"

"Yes," Oliver said. "Thank you." When the valet had gone, he said to Rhodes, "That man of yours is dashed clever. If you ever let him go, I'll take—"

"He's mine," Rhodes said, rubbing his eyes again. "No poaching."

"Wasn't going to poach," Oliver said indignantly. "I said *if*—"

"We need to leave this room," Primrose said, rising from the chair. "Now."

Oliver blinked. "We do?"

"That's the second time Rhodes has rubbed his

eyes, and Lord Algernon *did* put bishop's weed in the bedhangings." She pointed to the door. "Out. Now."

"Dash it," Rhodes said, pushing away from the bedpost. "I forgot. Thanks, Prim."

They went outside and strolled in the gardens for a while, not saying much, and then Rhodes turned back to the house. "I want to write to the children. Let them know I'll be in Gloucestershire soon."

Oliver watched him out of sight, then turned to Primrose. "Told you I'd get Rhodes to Gloucestershire."

Primrose didn't try to puncture his smugness. All she said was, "So you did."

Oliver thought back over the past five days, and then shook his head and gave a wry laugh. "Poor Lord and Lady Cheevers. What a disaster this house party has been. A broken wrist, a broken nose, *and* a death. I doubt they'll ever host another one again."

"Oh, I think that if you offered for Miss Cheevers they would consider this house party extremely successful."

"Very funny," Oliver said. He took her hand, tucked it into the crook of his arm, and headed for the house.

"Where are we going?"

"The State apartments."

CHAPTER 33

They met no one on their way to the State rooms. Oliver opened the door and Primrose slipped inside. She knew why Oliver had suggested coming here: he wanted to kiss her again.

She didn't object to kissing him, in fact, she rather wanted to, but what she *most* wanted to do was talk. Not about Lord Algernon or Ninian Dasenby, not about Rhodes or his children. She wanted to talk about herself and Oliver. Specifically, she wanted to know what this—kisses stolen in the State apartments—meant to him.

The second rule is to look things in the face and know them for what they are. Well, she had looked this in the face last night, when she'd thought Oliver was dying, and she knew it for what it was.

She was in love with him.

How had that happened? How had the person

who had annoyed her throughout her entire childhood suddenly become so important to her as an adult?

Or perhaps it hadn't been sudden? Perhaps the seeds had been sown years ago and been lying dormant all this time?

The *how* and *why* of it were irrelevant. What mattered was that it had happened—and she needed to do something about it. Specifically, she needed to tell Oliver how she felt and ask whether he returned her feelings.

If he didn't love her—if he never *could* love her—it was better to find that out now.

Primrose led the way through the State sitting room and the State dressing room, into the State bedchamber with its ridiculous dais and even more ridiculous gilded pillars.

Oliver didn't fling himself down on the bed, as he so often had; instead, he crossed to the window and looked out.

Primrose watched him. Oliver had revealed his true colors this past week. Not a fribble, not a fool, but a man who was decisive, intelligent, compassionate, and fair-minded. Even when things had been at their toughest, he'd still managed to laugh—not the foolish merriment of a man too dull-witted to see danger bearing down on him, but the laughter of a man who saw the danger and decided to laugh anyway, because life was better when he did.

She liked that in him. She liked it a lot. His laughter brightened her world.

Oliver turned away from the window. He was backlit by sunshine, his face in shadow, his expression difficult to discern. "Prim," he said, and then hesitated.

Primrose hesitated, too, wondering how to broach her subject. It was absurdly daunting, but delaying would only serve to make it *more* daunting, so she took hold of her courage and inhaled a deep, bracing breath.

"Prim . . . will you please marry me?"

Her heart gave an enormous leap—and then plunged back down. This wasn't the first time Oliver had asked her to marry him. It wasn't even the second or third time.

It's another one of his jokes, she told herself, but hope was flowering in her breast.

"Why?" Fear of his answer made her voice sharper than she'd meant it to be. "To save you from Miss Cheevers?"

"She wouldn't have me even if I asked," Oliver said. "And I wouldn't ask her because I don't want to marry her." He took a step away from the window. She still couldn't see his expression clearly, backlit as he was, but she could see enough to tell that he was staring at her. "The person I want to marry . . . the person I very *much* want to marry . . . is you, Prim."

The hope began to flower more wildly. Primrose gripped her hands together. "Why?"

"Why?" Oliver laughed. "Because . . ." His voice trailed off. He stood silently for several seconds, and then said, "Because I love you."

Primrose opened her mouth to ask why again, but Oliver beat her to it.

"I love the way your mind works," he said. "I love the things you say." He took a step towards her. "I love that I'm not a duke to you; I'm just Oliver. Because that's all I am: just Oliver." He took another step closer. She could see his face clearly now, that intent gaze. "And I love you because you're beautiful and brave and funny and clever and wise, and you read too many books and have a dashed tart tongue and you kiss like a debauched angel and there's no one else in England like you."

Primrose found herself incapable of speech. She could only stare at him.

"So, Primrose Garland . . . will you marry me?"

She nodded, and found enough of her voice to whisper, "Yes."

Relief lit Oliver's face. He gave a laugh, and

caught her up in an embrace that was so exuberant that it squeezed all the air from her lungs.

"Did you doubt it?" she asked, breathlessly.

"Of course I doubted it." Oliver set her carefully on her feet. "I have it on good authority that I'm a jingle brains, and not everyone wants to marry a jingle brains, even if he *is* a duke."

He smiled down at her, and then bent his head and kissed her.

Primrose kissed him back enthusiastically.

It was several minutes before they drew apart, by which time they were both rather flushed and short of breath. Oliver scooped her up and laid her on the Holland-covered bed, then lay down beside her and gave a beatific sigh. Primrose let her eyes feast on him: the rumpled brown hair, the tanned skin, the woodland-colored eyes, the laughter lines, the smiling mouth.

Her Oliver.

Happiness shone from him, she could see it in every part of him—not just his mouth and eyes, but his chin, his eyebrows, his nose. Even his ears looked happy. But that was what Oliver was best at: being happy. He excelled at it.

And his happiness made those around him happy.

Her gaze drifted to his mouth, and fastened there. In addition to looking happy, Oliver's mouth looked . . . There was really only one word for it, and that was *kissed*. His mouth looked kissed. Very kissed.

Oliver reached out and touched her cheek, touched her jaw and throat, a deliciously light and tickling caress that made her shiver. His fingertips trailed down to her collarbone. He found the thin golden chain and the little acorn that was suspended from it.

He held the acorn between thumb and finger for a moment, and then released it and stroked his way back up her throat.

"Would you like to . . . you know?" Primrose asked.

His eyebrows quirked. "That's very cryptic, Prim."

"Put the acorn to the test," Primrose said, and felt herself blush.

Oliver studied her for several seconds, and then said, "Is that what you'd like?"

"Maybe." Her blush became hotter. "What would you like?"

"I don't mind. We can wait. We can do it now. Whatever you prefer."

Primrose tried to decipher his expression, because despite his diplomatic words Oliver undoubtedly *did* have an opinion. It wasn't obvious on his face, though.

"Your choice, Prim."

Do every act of your life as if it were your last.

"I want to try it now."

Oliver considered her answer for a moment, and then grinned. "All right."

He didn't kiss her, though; he climbed off the bed, crossed to the door, closed it, and wedged a Holland-covered chair beneath the door handle.

Then he turned back to the bed. "You're sure about this, Prim?"

"I am."

Oliver stepped up onto the dais and shrugged out of his tailcoat.

Primrose's throat became a little dry. She sat up on the bed. Should she take off her clothes?

Oliver removed his boots, with not a little effort.

Primrose removed her shoes. Her heart was thumping fast.

Oliver stripped off his neckcloth and tossed it aside.

Primrose didn't do anything. She was beginning to feel rather nervous.

Oliver stood in waistcoat, shirt, and breeches on the dais, looked at her sitting on the bed, rubbed his hands briskly together, and said, "Right," in a very businesslike tone. "Let's get started. Should only take a minute."

"A minute?" Primrose said, both startled and disappointed. "It that all it takes?"

Oliver winked. "Only joking, Prim." He climbed up onto the bed on hands and knees. "We'll be half an hour at the very least." And then he paused, met her eyes, and said, "Are you *certain* about this?"

"Yes," Primrose said, even though, at this moment, she was more nervous than she'd ever been before in her life.

Perhaps Oliver saw her nervousness, because he made a game of undressing. There were two rules. Firstly, that they had to undress one garment at a time, turn and turn about. Secondly, that they each had to act as valet or maid for the other.

Oliver unbuttoned her dress; she unbuttoned his waistcoat.

He removed her petticoat; she removed his shirt. His upper right arm was heavily bruised.

"The stairs?"

"The stairs."

Oliver's chest had hair on it. Not a lot, but a very distinct line of it that ran down into his breeches. His nipples were brown, the areolae larger than her own. Muscles flexed beneath his skin as he moved. Primrose stared, transfixed.

Oliver cleared his throat. "Focus, Prim."

She jerked her gaze up to his face.

"Stockings," he told her.

He peeled off her stockings; she peeled off his.

Oliver's calves were hairier than his chest, and quite muscular. Her legs looked very smooth and slender in comparison.

He undid her stays; she undid his breeches, blushing hotly. Now she was wearing only her chemise and he only his drawers.

Oliver's thighs were less hairy than his calves, but just as muscular. There was a bruise on one knee and another on his thigh.

Primrose lifted her gaze to his drawers and forgot all about bruises. She found herself suddenly a little breathless. Oliver's drawers were distorted in an extremely interesting fashion. She wanted to see what his organ looked like.

Primrose reached for the waistband of his drawers, but Oliver evaded her hand. "Time for a different game."

"But I want to play this one."

"We'll come back to it later. Lie down."

After a moment, Primrose did, wrestling with her disappointment.

Oliver leaned over her. "I'm going to touch you," he said. "And then you have to touch me in *exactly* the same way I touch you. You get it wrong, you lose your turn."

"Oh." Her disappointment fled. Anticipation took its place.

He laid his fingers lightly on her inner wrist, over her pulse, and then slowly drew them all the way up her arm to her shoulder, a tickling, gossamer caress that made heat rise in her body, that made her belly clench and her nipples stand taut against the thin linen chemise. Primrose stared up at him, unable to look away from his intent gaze, her breath as shallow and fluttery as her pulse.

Oliver did it twice for each arm, then said, "Your turn."

Primrose sat up.

"I hope you paid attention," he said, as he lay down.

She had paid attention, although the sight of Oliver stretched out on the bed, wearing only his drawers, was extremely distracting.

Primrose knelt alongside him, bit her lip, and mimicked what he'd done—her fingertips on his pulse, then gliding up his arm. The texture of his skin and the way his muscles quivered beneath her touch were fascinating. She trailed her fingers up his arm once, twice, a third time—

"No," Oliver said, sitting up.

"What?"

"Twice," he said, wagging his finger at her. "I only did it twice."

"But—"

"Rules are rules, Prim. You lose the rest of your turn."

Chagrined, Primrose lay back down. How could she have made such an elementary mistake?

"Don't move," he told her. "That's another rule: no moving while I touch you."

"I won't." She scowled up at the bedhangings, cross with herself, waiting for Oliver's fingers on her wrist again . . . and felt them below her inner right anklebone.

Primrose lost her scowl. She tensed in delicious anticipation. Was he going to . . . ?

Yes, he was.

Oliver's fingers ghosted slowly across her skin, over her ankle, up her calf, under her chemise, past her knee. Primrose inhaled a sharp breath. His fingers tickled, and in their wake came a rush of heat. She'd never before realized how sensitive her inner thighs were. It took effort not to squirm. She began to feel rather breathless.

Oliver halted halfway up her thigh, and removed his hand.

Primrose dragged air into her lungs and braced herself for his exploration of her left leg. She barely survived it; the muscles in her stomach were clenched tight from the effort of not squirming, her hands were clenched tight on the Holland cloth, and her lungs were clenched tight, too, each inhalation so shallow that she might as well not be breathing. Her wits weren't clenched tight; they were unraveling.

Oliver lay down and smiled angelically at her. "Your turn."

Primrose let out a shuddering breath, and tried to gather her unraveled wits. She felt hot, flustered, and incapable of coherent thought. She released her grip on the Holland cloth, and sat up shakily.

Concentrate, she told herself. *Don't make any mistakes this time.*

She inhaled a deep breath, and a second one. Anticipation was gathering in her belly. What would it be like to touch Oliver the way he'd just touched her?

Oliver put his hands behind his head and gazed up at the bedhangings, looking extremely relaxed. Nonchalant, even. Except for whatever was inside his drawers. *That* wasn't relaxed.

Primrose inhaled deeply again, and placed her fingertips carefully on his bare ankle. Slowly—very slowly—and very, *very* lightly, she drew her fingers up his leg, teasing him as he'd teased her, drawing it out. Up the curve of his calf. Past his knee. Up his inner thigh.

Oliver's skin twitched and quivered. His pose was still nonchalant but the muscles in his stomach were tight. His jaw was clenched with the effort of holding still.

Was he even breathing?

Primrose rested her fingertips high on his thigh, at the hem of his drawers, and watched his chest for several seconds—those tempting nipples that were so like and yet so *un*like her own—and reassured herself that Oliver was indeed breathing.

She removed her fingers and began again, on his left ankle. Obedient to Oliver's directive she climbed no higher up his leg than he had hers, but she wanted to. Wanted to very much. She didn't want to stop exploring him. She wanted to slide her hand higher and discover the secrets his drawers hid.

What did his organ look like?

It would be hairy, that much she had already guessed. She had hair on her pudendum, so it stood to reason that Oliver had hair on his organ. But how much hair? Would it be like fur?

"Finished, Prim?" Oliver asked.

"Yes." Primrose removed her hand from his thigh and lay down again, eager for the game to continue.

Oliver leaned over her. "All right. Pay attention."

She caught her breath, anticipating his touch,

but this time Oliver didn't use his hands; he used his mouth.

He kissed the corner of her jaw, then licked his way down her throat and feathered light kisses along her collarbone, above the neckline of her chemise. A delicious shiver ran through her. Her wits began to unravel again.

Oliver lifted his head. "Think you can remember that?"

Jaw, throat, collarbone. "Yes."

"Good." He bent his head again and then, to her shocked delight, pressed his mouth to one of her breasts, dampening the thin linen with his tongue, taking the nipple lightly between his teeth. The chemise might as well not have been there. She felt the softness of his lips, the warmth of his tongue, the sharpness of his teeth.

He nipped lightly.

Primrose gasped.

Oliver gave a chuckle. "You like that?"

"Yes."

He did it again, making her gasp, making her want to squirm, and turned his attention to her other nipple . . . and then it was her turn.

Primrose sat up. Oliver wasn't wearing a shirt—there'd be no fabric between her mouth and his skin—and she *wanted* that, wanted to taste him, so why was she nervous?

She gazed down at Oliver, lying on the bed. He was watching her, his eyes intent on her face.

Primrose moistened her lips. *Jaw, throat, collarbones, nipples,* she told herself. She inhaled a shaky breath and bent to kiss the very edge of his jaw.

The nervousness evaporated, leaving only eagerness.

Primrose did exactly what Oliver had done, licking down his throat. The taste of him blossomed on her tongue, subtle and salty. His scent filled her nose: sandalwood, and something else. Something as subtle and masculine as his flavor.

His collarbone next, placing kisses softly, his skin smooth beneath her lips, and then . . .

Primrose paused, while anticipation coiled tightly in her belly. She looked at those tempting nipples with their broad areolae, then bent her head. She felt bold and daring. Here she was, Lady Primrose Garland, about to touch her mouth to a man's naked chest.

She licked that taut, upthrusting nipple, then took it between her teeth and nipped lightly. Oliver's whole body twitched. Encouraged, Primrose nipped harder. Harder than Oliver had nipped her.

"Rules, Prim," he said, breathlessly. "Rules."

"Your rules are silly," she told him, and then, to see what he would do, she took his nipple between her teeth and tugged.

Oliver's whole body twitched again. He uttered a sound between a gasp and a groan.

Primrose released his nipple. "I propose some changes to your game."

"Oh, you do, do you?"

"Yes. For a start, I think you should remove these." She slid her hand down over Oliver's belly to the waistband of his drawers.

He became very still. His muscles clenched beneath her fingers.

She looked at his face. He seemed not to be breathing again. "Nothing to say?"

Oliver swallowed, then said, "We can do that. If you wish."

CHAPTER 34

"*I* do wish," Primrose said. She undid the two buttons. Her heartbeat accelerated as the drawers fell open.

Oliver's organ wasn't hairy. That was her first surprise. It was surrounded by a thick thatch of dark hair, but the thing itself was quite smooth. Strong, sturdy, sleek, blunt-headed.

The second surprise was its color. It wasn't the color of his skin, or the color of his nipples. It was . . . She searched for a word. Rubicund? Rubescent?

Oliver lifted his haunches to help her peel the drawers off, exposing another terrible bruise on his hip, and then he was naked. Absolutely naked.

Primrose feasted her eyes on his body—and on his groin in particular—and then lifted her gaze to his face.

He was watching her again, waiting for her reaction.

"Classical statues are very misleading," Primrose said.

Oliver laughed—and then sobered abruptly. "Disappointed?"

"Oh, no," Primrose said. "Not at all." She reached out to touch that fascinating organ, and caught herself, curling her fingers into her palm. She knew nothing about male organs. Could one touch them? *Should* one touch them? She glanced at Oliver's face again. "What's it called?"

Oliver regarded his organ as if he'd never seen it before. "We can call it George, if you like?"

Primrose laughed before she could stop herself, and then smacked his arm. "No, you great idiot. I mean, what is it called? Like arm, or leg, or elbow . . ."

Oliver grinned at her. "I call it a cock."

Cock. What an odd name. Primrose wrinkled her brow. "You mean, like a rooster?"

"*Not* like a rooster." He shook his head with a laugh. "Honestly, Prim, you do know how to puncture a man's vanity."

If he was vain, he had every right to be. Despite the bruises, he was beautiful. Magnificent. The sheer perfection of him, naked and grinning, took her breath away.

"Your turn," Oliver said. "Off with that chemise."

It was suddenly impossible to breathe. Her heart began to beat tremendously fast.

Oliver knelt and gently lifted the chemise over her head—and he was *naked*, right next to her—and *she* was naked, too, and it was all . . . exciting and scary and almost overwhelming.

Oliver tossed the chemise away and surveyed her body, an appraisal that took in her breasts, her waist, and the triangle of fair hair at her groin. She saw satisfaction in his expression. And hunger.

His gaze wandered all the way down to her toes and then back up, pausing at the faint bruise on her hip. "The terrace steps?"

"Yes."

His eyes lifted and met hers. "I'm glad you're all right."

"I'm glad *you're* all right."

Oliver's gaze fastened on the little golden acorn dangling on its chain. "Lie down," he whispered.

"What?"

Oliver tutted. "We're halfway through a game, Prim. Focus."

It didn't feel like halfway. It felt much further than halfway.

Primrose lay back on the Holland cloth, tense with self-consciousness and anticipation. Her skin prickled with awareness of her nakedness.

Oliver laid his hand on her right ankle. He slid his fingers up over her calf and then gently hooked his hand under her knee and lifted it up and to the side, exposing her more fully to him. Primrose instinctively stiffened.

Oliver met her eyes. "Trust me, Prim."

She *did* trust him, utterly and absolutely, so despite the acute embarrassment of it, she allowed him do the same to her left leg. She was hot, flustered, torn between acute embarrassment and an even more acute sense of anticipation. She wanted to cover herself. But even more, she wanted to know what Oliver would do next.

What Oliver did next was run his hand slowly up her inner thigh *all the way to the top*. And once he'd gained that vantage point, he allowed his fingers to wander.

Primrose discovered that she was holding her breath. She was also gripping the Holland cloth tightly.

Oliver explored slowly, his expression intent as he acquainted himself with that most private part of her, fingering his way intimately through her folds.

Primrose tried to remember to breathe. Her entire being was focused on what Oliver was doing. Heart, lungs, belly, brain, all were focused on him.

His thumb found a spot that sent a pulse of pleasure through her.

Oliver glanced at her, and grinned. "Do you like that, Prim?"

Speech was beyond her, but she managed to nod.

He stroked her with his thumb, and Primrose realized that not only did Oliver have a magical mouth, he had magical hands. Her eyes squeezed shut as sensation built inside her.

Oliver's thumb stilled.

Primrose opened her eyes.

Oliver was watching her.

She should have felt embarrassed, spread out like this on the bed, naked, but she didn't feel embarrassed at all. She felt amazing. Incredible.

Oliver held her gaze, and slipped a finger inside her.

"Oh!" Primrose said.

Oliver flexed his finger, and Primrose found herself incapable of speech again.

He did it a second time. "Do you like that, Prim?"

She couldn't speak, couldn't even nod.

Oliver grinned. "I'll take that as a yes."

He slid another finger inside her, and then his thumb did that magical thing again. Pleasure rippled through her. Primrose made a sound similar to the one he'd made before, both gasp *and* groan. She was melting from the inside out. Her body moved of its own accord, back arching slightly, quivering on the brink of a cascade of pleasure . . .

Oliver withdrew his fingers. "Your turn."

Primrose opened her eyes. He wasn't stopping *now,* was he?

Oliver gave her a jaunty grin. "Your turn," he said again, and stretched out on the bed, his hands behind his head, waiting.

Primrose sat up with difficulty. Her body hummed with unreleased tension. He was teasing her, damn him. Well, two could play *that* game.

She looked at him, naked and grinning, beautiful and aggravating. Her gaze fastened on his cock. That strange, fascinating organ that she had yet to touch. And then she realized that she had a problem. "I can't do to you what you did to me. We're shaped differently."

"I explored," he said. "You can explore, too."

Explore. The word sent a shiver of anticipation through her.

She reached for his cock, eager to know what it felt like—and then remembered the rules of this game. She'd miss her turn if she skipped straight to that part.

Primrose meticulously arranged Oliver's legs, spreading his knees apart. He looked quite lewd, on display like that. His cock thrust up from its nest of hair, and below it dangled two plump, egg-shaped objects. "What are those?" she asked.

"My balls."

As names went, it made more sense than "cock"; they *were* rather round.

Explore, Oliver had said.

Primrose moistened her lips, and then repeated what Oliver had done to her, skimming her hand up his inner thigh. His skin was surprisingly smooth, and as sensitive as her own, judging from the way he shivered. She let her fingers delve into that thicket of hair, warm, and rougher than her own.

"One caveat," Oliver said, his voice a little breathless. "George's baubles are rather sensitive, so don't squeeze them."

"Baubles? You mean these? I thought you said they were balls." She reached out and stroked one with a fingertip, and observed his answering full-body shiver with satisfaction.

"Balls, baubles . . . means the same thing." Oliver's eyes were dark, his cheeks flushed, his lips parted.

Primrose stared at him for a long moment—God, he was beautiful—then tore her gaze away and bent her attention to playing the game he'd devised. He'd wanted exploration; he'd get it.

She spent minutes acquainting herself with his balls, mindful of his caveat, fondling them carefully, watching the way his body twitched and shivered, and then moved on to the thing she most wanted to touch: that intriguing cock.

It was quite different from his balls, harder and hotter and smoother. It seemed to pulse with vigor beneath her fingertips.

"George is made of sturdy stuff." Oliver's voice was tight, breathless. "You can be fairly rough with him before it hurts."

She looked at his cock dubiously. The skin looked rather delicate.

"Go on. You won't hurt me."

Primrose wrapped her hand around that strong shaft, trying to measure its girth. She couldn't quite get her fingers around it. *You can be fairly rough,* Oliver had said, so she tightened her grip cautiously, hesitantly, and when he didn't flinch she took hold of him even more firmly, but still her fingers and thumb didn't quite meet.

His cock seemed to thrum in her hand. How *alive* it felt. How exciting. How different. She'd never touched anything like it before.

Primrose released her grip and ran her fingers up its length, learning the texture: hot, hard, sleek. She trailed her fingertips over the smooth, blunt head, and then around the rim, over that flange of skin. Oliver gave another of his whole-body shivers and his cock moved eagerly, flexing. Oh, yes, he liked that.

She did it again and glanced at him. His eyes were squeezed shut, his face set in a grimace. Every muscle in his body appeared to be clenched: jaw, shoulders, stomach, thighs.

Primrose rubbed her thumb over that ridge of skin a third time, lightly and teasingly, and watched the muscles in Oliver's belly clench even tighter, watched the tendons in his throat stand out.

If Oliver's cock had its own unique texture, it also seemed to have its own unique scent: masculine and musky and arousing. She was tempted to lean closer and fill her lungs with the smell. Tempted to see what that hot, sleek skin tasted like.

Suddenly, Oliver sat up. He took hold of her wrist and removed her hand from his cock.

Primrose stared at him, alarmed. Had she hurt him?

His eyes were extremely dark, his cheeks quite flushed, and he was panting, but he didn't appear to be in pain.

"What's wrong?" she asked.

"Your turn's over."

But she hadn't brought him almost to the brink. Primrose opened her mouth to protest—and then realized that she *had* brought him there and that was why he was having such difficulty breathing.

Oliver released her hand. "Prim . . . George asks me to inform you that we can either continue with this game *or* put the acorn to the test, but not both. Not today."

"Oh."

Oliver looked a little shamefaced. "George doesn't have sufficient self-control for both. Regrettably. He's a little out of practice, but he wants you to know that his self-control will improve if he's regularly exercised."

Primrose bit the inside of her cheek to keep from laughing. Did all men talk about their cocks in the third person? "If we keep playing the game, what happens next?"

Oliver smiled at her. "We use our mouths."

She felt a rush of heat and nervousness and eager anticipation. What would it be like to kiss his cock? To taste that hot, taut skin?

"Your choice, Prim. What would you like most?"

She wanted both. But there was always tomorrow, and the next day, and the one after that. Dozens of days, hundreds of them, thousands.

Primrose weighed the two options. "The acorn."

CHAPTER 35

The acorn stopped her conceiving, but it couldn't stop it hurting the first time. Even though Oliver warned her, and even though she was expecting it, that first thrust was more painful than she'd anticipated. Primrose inhaled sharply and tensed.

Oliver halted, his body braced over hers. "Prim?" He began to withdraw.

She gripped his biceps, digging her fingers in. "Don't you dare stop."

"Ow," Oliver said, and then he bent his head and nipped her earlobe. "Bossy."

"An absolute shrew," Primrose agreed, aware of the enormous and painful size of his organ inside her. It *hurt,* dash it.

"That's not alliteration."

"What?"

"An absolute . . . what? Give me some alliteration, Prim."

437

Primrose struggled to think. "An absolute . . ." God, her mind wasn't working. "An absolute . . . Autocrat! I am an absolute autocrat."

"Alliterative *and* accurate," Oliver said, and then he grinned. "That was alliteration, too. I'm a genius."

"You're a jingle brains," she told him.

"A jingle-brained genius?" His face brightened comically. "More alliteration!"

Primrose laughed, and realized that the burning pain had faded. Oliver's organ was still as large as it had been, but it no longer felt like a painful invader. In fact, it felt as if it fitted rather nicely inside her. Very nicely, in fact.

Her hips moved instinctively, arching slightly, trying to gather him a little closer.

Oliver lost his grin. His expression became intent. "Prim?"

"It doesn't hurt anymore."

"Well, in that case . . ." He bent his head, kissed her, and moved his own hips, giving her body what it craved: more of him.

Primrose gasped against his mouth and clutched his biceps.

Oliver slid into her again, and again and again, a delicious rhythm that she responded to instinctively. He picked up his pace, their bodies straining together. Primrose reached the brink and fell over it, and Oliver fell with her. She felt his fall—great spasms that racked his body. And Oliver being Oliver, he laughed as he fell, breathlessly, and Primrose found herself laughing, too.

The falling stopped. Oliver's body was heavy on hers, and then he pushed up on one arm and rolled off her and lay panting, and then he laughed again, and flung an arm around her shoulders and hauled her close.

They lay together, chests heaving, legs tangled.

It felt very good, this hot, sweaty, panting aftermath. Primrose pressed her nose against Oliver's shoulder and inhaled his scent, breathing it deeply into her lungs. She loved how he smelled.

Her body slowly cooled. She became grateful for Oliver's warmth. They were breathing in time with one another, again. She didn't need to feel for his pulse to know that their hearts were beating in time, too.

The relaxed, perfect intimacy between them felt almost unreal. She'd long ago decided that the things she'd wanted in a marriage—passion and love and a meeting of minds—were unattainable, and yet she'd found them all in Oliver Dasenby. Annoying, absurd, ridiculously wonderful Oliver Dasenby.

"You know, Prim, I've become rather fond of this

room. I think I may have to have gilded columns in my own bedroom. Not four, though—paltry number. I want a full dozen."

"Gilded columns are only for royalty," Primrose told him firmly.

They lay in silence for another warm, perfect minute, and then a question sprang into her mind. "Oliver? Do you really call your cock George?"

"As of today, yes."

Idiot, she wanted to say, but she didn't, because Oliver wasn't an idiot, or a jingle brains. He was just . . . Oliver. Uniquely Oliver. There was no one else like him in the world, and she was never going to call him an idiot again.

"George asks me to tell you that you may call him George, too. Or Mr. George, if you wish to be very polite."

Primrose huffed a faint laugh. "You *are* an idiot, Oliver." And then she felt immediately contrite. "I beg your pardon. You're not an idiot. I won't ever call you that again."

"What? No. Don't say that! Dash it, Prim, your tongue's the only reason I'm marrying you."

Primrose smiled against his shoulder. "It is?"

"You're the only woman in England who would dare to call the Duke of Westfell a jingle brains," Oliver informed her. "So don't start being polite to me or I shall have to withdraw my offer."

He really, truly does love me. Her throat tightened. "All right," she whispered.

Oliver shifted slightly, not a large movement, and she sensed a corresponding shift in his mood, towards something more serious. "I'm going to run a lot of decisions past you, Prim, and I need you to be honest with me. If you ever think I'm making a mistake, for God's sake *tell* me."

"What sort of decisions?"

"Dukely decisions."

She didn't tell him dukely wasn't a word; he already knew that. "Your men of business will advise you."

"They will, and I know I can ask advice of your father and Rhodes, too, but I'd like to be able to talk things through with you first."

"Of course. If that's what you wish."

"It is. I value your opinion, Prim."

Primrose felt herself blush. It didn't just heat her cheeks; it seemed to heat her chest as well, as if her heart blushed, too.

Oliver stroked her shoulder with his thumb. "You're a better judge of people than I am. You had Ninian's measure long before I did."

"But I was wrong about your uncle." Primrose remembered the expression on Lord Algernon's face when he'd tried to smother Oliver—regret and determination—and shivered. "And you recognized Miss Middleton-Murray as a harpy before I did."

"Perhaps, but two heads are wiser than one. You see things from a different perspective than I do. I think we can do a better job of being the Duke of Westfell together than I could alone."

Primrose considered this for a moment, and then nodded. "Yes. We could."

His thumb moved lightly across her shoulder again, an idle caress. "So . . . the first decision I need to discuss with you concerns Ninian."

"In what way?"

"I'd like to give him one of my estates—and I know my men of business will advise me against it, but I want to, Prim. It feels *right*."

She understood what he meant. It did feel right. Profoundly right. "How many estates do you have?"

"Nine. Six unentailed."

"Then absolutely, give him one."

"Truly?" Oliver shifted, so that he could see her face. "You mean that?"

"Of course. He saved your life. Three times. Four, if you count him jumping off the jetty when he thought you were drowning."

"You don't think I'm being careless with my property? Profligate? Dooming my heirs to hardship and poverty?"

"If you had six cousins and you wanted to give each of them an estate, then I might try to dissuade you. But one estate to Ninian? No. I think it's an excellent idea."

"Good." Oliver laid his head back down on the rather wrinkled Holland cloth. "That was our first decision as Westfell. I think it went well, don't you?"

"Yes."

"Are you ready for the next one?"

"Of course."

"Which estate shall I give him?"

"Whichever one is his favorite."

Oliver laughed. "Why didn't I think of that? See, I knew there was a reason I was marrying you. Which brings me to my next decision—*our* next decision . . . When shall we marry?"

"When would you like to marry?"

"As soon as possible," Oliver said. "I'd ride to London today for a special license, if I could, but . . ."

"Your uncle's funeral."

"Yes." He sighed. "Tell me, Prim, how soon after the funeral can we marry without it being deemed unseemly?"

Primrose considered this question carefully. "We really should wait a few months, but . . . we could probably get away with marrying next month if we don't make a celebration of it. If we keep it small and quiet and unexceptional. Immediate family only."

Oliver groaned. "Next month? How will George and I survive?" He removed his arm from around her shoulder and rolled to face her. "Just as well we've got this," he said, taking the acorn pendant in his hand.

Primrose blushed.

Oliver laughed and kissed her, still holding the acorn, and then he sobered. "You don't regret it, Prim?"

She knew what he meant by "it": the lovemaking. "Certainly not. 'Live each day as if it were your last.'"

Oliver released the acorn and grinned. "Do you have an Aurelius quote for every occasion?"

"No." Primrose hesitated, and then verbalized a thought that had been slowly forming over the past few days: "I think Marcus Aurelius might have been rather like you."

"Me?" Oliver looked astonished. "I doubt it."

"'Very little is needed to make a happy life; it is all within yourself, in your way of thinking.' That's you, Oliver."

"Well, yes, but—"

"'Death smiles at us all; all a man can do is smile back.' That's you, too. Except you don't just smile back; you laugh."

Oliver looked at her oddly. "You're quite uncanny, Prim."

"Why?"

"Because that's one of my favorite quotes, and I always change 'smile' to 'laugh.'"

They stared at each other. Primrose didn't know what to say. It *was* a little uncanny.

Oliver grinned, and lightly flicked the tip of her nose. "We're meant for each other, Prim." Then he sat up. "We'd better get dressed. They'll be sending out search parties if we don't show our faces soon."

Primrose sat up, too, and scrambled off the bed. How long had they been here? It felt like hours. "What's the time?"

Oliver found his waistcoat and looked at his pocket watch. "Nearly twelve. Still an hour 'til luncheon."

"Thank heavens."

They helped each other to dress, then went through to the State dressing room for the finishing touches. Oliver spent several minutes in front of the mirror, retying his neckcloth; Primrose tried to tidy her hair, and then gave up. She needed a hairbrush, and there wasn't one down here.

When he'd finished with the neckcloth, Oliver met her eyes in the mirror. "About our betrothal . . . I'd rather not tell Ninian until after the funeral. Let him cope with one thing at a time."

"I agree."

"But we can tell Rhodes today. I can't wait to see the expression on his face!" Oliver's grin faltered. "It won't send him into the doldrums again, will it? Us getting married when Evelyn is dead?"

"It might a little bit, but I know he'll be happy for us, too."

Oliver gave a nod, and examined his neckcloth again. He tweaked it carefully.

Primrose watched him in the mirror—that tiny, intent frown on his brow—and realized that she'd not yet told Oliver that she loved him.

"I love you," she blurted.

Oliver stopped fiddling with his neckcloth. His frown vanished. Their eyes met in the mirror again. He smiled at her. "I know."

"How?"

"Because you wouldn't have done any of that if it wasn't serious for you." He gestured to the State bedroom.

He was right, of course. "Would you have done it if it wasn't serious for you?"

"With you?" Oliver smiled at her. "No. This was never a game for me, Prim." And then he cocked his head to one side and studied her reflection. "I hate to tell you this, but your hair is rather disreputable."

"So is your neckcloth."

"No, it isn't. I'm setting a new fashion. Dukes are allowed to do that." Oliver puffed out his chest, and preened in the mirror.

All Primrose could do was laugh.

CHAPTER 36

Oliver went in search of Lord Cheevers while Primrose went upstairs to fix her hair. He found the viscount in his study. "May I have a word with you, sir?"

They discussed the details of the funeral. Cheevers was taking Algernon's death hard. He had to dab a handkerchief to his eyes several times.

"Thayne, Lady Primrose, and I will leave the day after the funeral," Oliver told him. "Ninian is welcome to come with us, but he may wish to stay here."

"He can stay as long as he likes. All summer if he wishes. Now that his father is gone . . ." Emotion trembled in Cheevers's voice. To him, Lord Algernon wasn't a villain, but a beloved friend. "Algernon's son will always be welcome here. Always."

Oliver wondered whether Cheevers valued

Ninian for himself, or only because of who his father was. And then he grimaced inwardly. That was the only reason he'd tolerated Ninian initially: because of Uncle Algy.

Well, he was going to rectify that. And he'd do his best to make certain that Lord Cheevers saw Ninian's worth, too.

To which end . . .

"I haven't told Ninian yet, but . . . I'm going to sign one of my estates over to him."

Cheevers lowered his handkerchief and looked at him, startled. "That's extremely generous, Westfell."

"Ninian saved my life," Oliver said bluntly. "I can't tell you the particulars, because it involves someone else, but I *can* tell you that I wouldn't be here today if not for him."

Cheevers looked even more startled.

"Ninian has more integrity and personal courage than most men. Your daughter will be extremely lucky if he offers for her."

Lord Cheevers stopped looking startled and looked uncomfortable instead—and Oliver could guess why: Cheevers wanted a duke for a son-in-law.

"Lady Primrose and I will be making an announcement in a few days," he said. "You understand, of course, why we can't make it now. It would be . . . inappropriate."

"Oh," Cheevers said, taken aback. He kneaded the handkerchief between his fingers. "I quite understand. Of course. Yes. Absolutely." He gave a weak smile. "Congratulations."

"Thank you," Oliver said.

He left Cheevers in the study and went in search of Primrose—and found her coming down the main staircase. He met her on the third step from the bottom. "You look lovely."

She blushed a very fetching shade of pink. "Thank you."

Oliver took her hand, squeezed it gently and discreetly, then released it. "Your brother?"

"My brother."

They found Rhodes in the library, writing letters.

Oliver closed the door, and took Primrose's hand again. They crossed to the great library desk, with its cabriole legs and tooled leather top, and waited for Rhodes to notice them. Oliver held his breath, anticipating Rhodes's surprise when he saw them holding hands, the stupefied expression on his face.

Rhodes looked up. His gaze flicked to their faces, flicked to their clasped hands. "About time."

"About time?" Oliver said. "What do you mean 'about time'?"

Rhodes laid down his quill. "I mean that I saw this coming years ago."

"The devil you did!"

Rhodes smiled smugly and leaned back in his chair. "I told Father you'd make a match of it one day. Told him the summer after our first year at Cambridge. How long ago was that?" He wrinkled his brow and pretended to think. "Ten years?"

"You did not," Oliver said.

"Did, too."

"But how could you know when *we* didn't?" Primrose said.

Rhodes smirked. "Well, I am very intelligent."

Oliver rolled his eyes. He was fairly certain that Primrose did, too. "He's humbugging us," he told her. "He had no idea at all."

"Scoff all you like, but I have proof. Look . . ." Rhodes picked up one of his finished letters. "To Mother and Father," he said, as he unfolded it. "Listen: 'I think Oliver and Primrose are finally going to make a match of it. They've been smelling of April and May all this past week. I anticipate a wedding before the end of summer.'" Rhodes turned the letter around and pointed to a paragraph.

Oliver read the lines, and discovered that he was telling the truth.

Rhodes smiled even more smugly. "Told you so."

Oliver looked at Primrose. "He's very irritating when he says that, isn't he?"

"Extremely."

Oliver bent and gave her a loud, smacking kiss.

"Oi," Rhodes said. "Not in front of me, you barbarian."

"Did he just call me a barbarian?" Oliver asked Primrose.

"He did, yes."

Oliver kissed her again, even more loudly.

Rhodes covered his eyes, like a prude at the opera when the dancers came on stage. "Go away."

"Aren't you going to wish us well?" Oliver asked.

Rhodes lowered his hands. "I don't need to. The pair of you will deal extremely well together." His gaze dropped to Oliver's neckcloth. "For God's sake, Ollie, fix your neckcloth. Anyone would think you've been tumbling my sister."

"Well, actually—"

Rhodes winced, and covered his ears. "Don't tell me. I don't want to know."

Oliver laughed, and tugged Primrose towards the door. His heart was light with relief. Rhodes had taken their news even better than he'd hoped.

"You are a degenerate," Primrose told him, once they were in the corridor. "Kissing me like that in front of my brother!"

"A degenerate duke," Oliver agreed, and then heard what he'd said. "That's alliteration." He cocked an eyebrow at her.

"Honestly, Oliver, you're dreadful."

"A dreadfully degenerate duke," he said, and then grinned at her. "Come on, Prim. Surely *that's* worth a kiss?" He bent his head and pointed helpfully to his lips.

Primrose's mouth tucked in at the corners as she tried to suppress a smile. "Heaven only knows why I agreed to marry you."

"Because you love me," Oliver told her. He picked her up, his hands at her waist, and swung her around. "And I love you." He swung her around a second time, lifting her higher, making her laugh and clutch at his shoulders. "And we are going to be *very* happy together."

AFTERWARDS

Ninian Dasenby laid his father to rest and then, the following month, attended his cousin's wedding in Gloucestershire. After that, he accompanied the duke and duchess on their tour of the Westfell estates.

At the end of the tour, the duke said, "Nine estates. It's too much for one man to bear. I shall go into a decline under the strain of it all." And then he gifted one of the estates to Ninian, and not just any estate, but Ninian's favorite, a fifteenth-century manor house nestled in one of Shropshire's gentle valleys.

Ninian spent a very happy month selecting colors for his new home.

In November, he went to London with the duke and duchess, so that the duke could attend the House of Lords and Ninian could choose the colors for the Westfell residence on Berkeley Square. He and the duchess were discussing the color scheme for the drawing room when the duke returned from his very first parliamentary session.

"How was it?" the duchess asked.

"An ordeal that I barely survived," the duke said, advancing into the room. "I was crushed by the tedium of it."

"Were you?" the duchess said mildly.

"Crushed," the duke repeated. "*Crushed.*" And then he toppled back onto the floor and lay with his eyes closed and his arms outstretched.

Ninian was used to his cousin's theatrics by now. He bit his lip and glanced at the duchess.

The duchess rolled her eyes. "About this red," she said, as if her husband lying on the floor was nothing out of the ordinary. Which, to tell the truth, it wasn't.

After a moment, the duke opened his eyes. "Brandy," he said plaintively.

The duchess stood and went to the decanters and poured her husband a glass of brandy, then she crossed to where he lay on the floor and handed it to him. "Idiot," she said, with great affection.

The duke pushed up on one elbow to accept the brandy. "Yes, but I'm *your* idiot."

They exchanged the sort of smiling, intimate

look that always made Ninian blush, and then the duchess returned to the sofa and the discussion of colors.

The duke survived his first parliamentary sessions, and Ninian and the duchess agreed on the colors, and come spring the redecoration of the residence on Berkeley Square was complete. It was a profoundly different house from the one it had been under the previous dukes' occupations. As soon as one set foot inside, one knew it was a happy house. A house where people laughed.

Early in the Season, the Duke and Duchess of Westfell hosted a dress ball, which proved another ordeal for the duke. Planning a ball, he declared, was even harder than planning a military campaign. In fact, it was so difficult that he succumbed to a dramatic attack of the vapors two days prior to the event. The duke's performance made his audience—Ninian, the duchess, and one extremely fortunate footman—laugh so hard that they cried.

Despite the duke's vapors—or perhaps because of them—the ball was a great success. Ninian danced with Chloé Cheevers. Twice. He danced with her many times that Season, and on the last day of May he gathered his courage and requested Lord Cheevers's permission to pay his addresses to her.

Not long after that, Ninian went down on one knee and asked Chloé Cheevers to marry him.

She said yes.

$\mathcal{A}$UTHOR'S $\mathcal{N}$OTE

Arsenic trioxide, or white arsenic, was widely available in Regency times and was very inexpensive. It was used by dye makers and glass blowers, candle makers and taxidermists, and anyone who had a vermin problem. It was also prescribed in small doses as a medicine and was used in beauty treatments, both internally and externally.

Because arsenic was so ubiquitous, it ended up in a lot of things by accident. It was mistaken for flour, sugar, and plaster of Paris (which confectioners used), with deadly consequences.

Not all deaths were accidental, but the symptoms of arsenic poisoning were similar to food poisoning and other common ailments, so many deliberate poisonings went undetected. It wasn't until 1836 that a reliable test for arsenic poisoning was perfected.

Thank You

Thanks for reading *Primrose and the Dreadful Duke*. I hope you enjoyed it!

If you'd like to be notified whenever I release a new book, please join my Readers' Group, which you can find at www.emilylarkin.com/newsletter.

I welcome all honest reviews. Reviews and word of mouth help other readers to find books, so please consider taking a few moments to leave a review on Goodreads or elsewhere.

Primrose and the Dreadful Duke is part of the Baleful Godmother series. I'm currently giving free digital copies of the series prequel, *The Fey Quartet*, and the first novel in the original series, *Unmasking Miss Appleby*, to anyone who joins my Readers' Group. Here's the link: www.emilylarkin. com/starter-library.

The Garland Cousins series runs concurrently with the Pryor Cousins series. The first Pryor novel,

461

Octavius and the Perfect Governess, features a governess in jeopardy and the marquis's son who goes undercover as a housemaid to protect her.

If you'd like to read the first chapter of *Octavius and the Perfect Governess*, please turn the page . . .

OCTAVIUS
and the
Perfect Governess

CHAPTER ONE

Octavius Pryor should have won the race. It wasn't difficult. The empty ballroom at his grandfather-the-duke's house was eighty yards long, he'd lined one hundred and twenty chairs up in a row across the polished wooden floorboards, and making his way from one side of the room to the other without touching the floor was easy. His cousin Nonus Pryor—Ned—also had one hundred and twenty chairs to scramble over, but Ned was as clumsy as an ox and Octavius knew he could make it across the ballroom first, which was exactly what he was doing—until his foot went right through the seat of one of the delicate giltwood chairs. He was going too fast to catch his balance. Both he and the chair crashed to the floor. And that was him out of the race.

His cousin Dex—Decimus Pryor—hooted loudly.

Octavius ignored the hooting and sat up. The good news was that he didn't appear to have broken anything except the chair. The bad news was that Ned, who'd been at least twenty chairs behind him, was now almost guaranteed to win.

Ned slowed to a swagger—as best as a man could swagger while clambering along a row of giltwood chairs.

Octavius gritted his teeth and watched his cousin navigate the last few dozen chairs. Ned glanced back at Octavius, smirked, and then slowly reached out and touched the wall with one fingertip.

Dex hooted again.

Octavius bent his attention to extracting his leg from the chair. Fortunately, he hadn't ruined his stockings. He climbed to his feet and watched warily as Ned stepped down from the final chair and sauntered towards him.

"Well?" Dex said. "What's Otto's forfeit to be?"

Ned's smirk widened. "His forfeit is that he goes to Vauxhall Gardens tomorrow night . . . as a woman."

There was a moment's silence. The game they had

of creating embarrassing forfeits for each other was long-established, but this forfeit was unprecedented.

Dex gave a loud whoop. "Excellent!" he said, his face alight with glee. "I can't *wait* to see this."

When Ned said that Octavius was going to Vauxhall Gardens as a woman, he meant it quite literally. Not as a man dressed in woman's clothing, but as a woman dressed in woman's clothing. Because Octavius could change his shape. That was the gift he'd chosen when his Faerie godmother had visited him on his twenty-fifth birthday.

Ned had chosen invisibility when it was his turn, which was the stupidest use of a wish that Octavius could think of. Ned was the loudest, clumsiest brute in all England. He walked with the stealth of a rampaging elephant. He was terrible at being invisible. So terrible, in fact, that their grandfather-the-duke had placed strict conditions on Ned's use of his gift.

Ned had grumbled, but he'd obeyed. He might be a blockhead, but he wasn't such a blockhead as to risk revealing the family secret. No one wanted to find out what would happen if it became common knowledge that one of England's most aristocratic families actually had a Faerie godmother.

Octavius, who could walk stealthily when he wanted to, hadn't chosen invisibility; he'd chosen metamorphosis, which meant that he could become any creature he wished. In the two years he'd had this ability, he'd been pretty much every animal he could think of. He'd even taken the shape of another person a few times. Once, he'd pretended to be his cousin, Dex. There he'd sat, drinking brandy and discussing horseflesh with his brother and his cousins, all of them thinking he was Dex—and then Dex had walked into the room. The expressions on everyone's faces had been priceless. Lord, the expression on *Dex*'s face . . .

Octavius had laughed so hard that he'd cried.

But one shape he'd never been tempted to try was that of a woman.

Why would he want to?

He was a man. And not just any man, but a good-looking, wealthy, and extremely well-born man. Why, when he had all those advantages, would he want to see what it was like to be a woman?

But that was the forfeit Ned had chosen and so here Octavius was, in his bedchamber, eyeing a pile of women's clothing, while far too many people clustered around him—not just Ned and Dex, but his own brother, Quintus, and Ned's brother, Sextus.

Quintus and Sextus usually held themselves

distant from high jinks and tomfoolery, Quintus because he was an earl and he took his responsibilities extremely seriously and Sextus because he was an aloof sort of fellow—and yet here they both were in Octavius's bedchamber.

Octavius didn't mind making a fool of himself in front of a muttonhead like Ned and a rattle like Dex, but in front of his oh-so-sober brother and his stand-offish older cousin? He felt more self-conscious than he had in years, even a little embarrassed.

"Whose clothes are they?" he asked.

"Lydia's," Ned said.

Octavius tried to look as if it didn't bother him that he was going to be wearing Ned's mistress's clothes, but it did. Lydia was extremely buxom, which meant that *he* was going to have to be extremely buxom or the gown would fall right off him.

He almost balked, but he'd never backed down from a forfeit before, so he gritted his teeth and unwound his neckcloth.

Octavius stripped to his drawers, made them all turn their backs, then removed the drawers, too. He pictured what he wanted to look like: Lydia's figure, but not Lydia's face—brown ringlets instead of blonde, and brown eyes, too—and with a silent *God damn it*, he changed shape. Magic tickled across his skin and itched inside his bones. He gave an involuntary shiver—and then it was done. He was a woman.

Octavius didn't examine his new body. He hastily dragged on the chemise, keeping his gaze averted from the mirror. "All right," he said, in a voice that was light and feminine and sounded utterly wrong coming from his mouth. "You can turn around."

His brother and cousins turned around and stared at him. It was oddly unsettling to be standing in front of them in the shape of a woman, wearing only a thin chemise. In fact, it was almost intimidating. Octavius crossed his arms defensively over his ample bosom, then uncrossed them and put his hands on his hips, another defensive stance, made himself stop doing that, too, and gestured at the pile of women's clothing on the bed. "Well, who's going to help me with the stays?"

No one volunteered. No one cracked any jokes, either. It appeared that he wasn't the only one who was unsettled. His brother, Quintus, had a particularly stuffed expression on his face, Sextus looked faintly pained, and Ned and Dex, both of whom he expected to be smirking, weren't.

"The stays," Octavius said again. "Come on, you clods. Help me to dress." And then, because he was damned if he was going to let them see how uncomfortable he felt, he fluttered his eyelashes coquettishly.

Quintus winced, and turned his back. "Curse it, Otto, don't do that."

Octavius laughed. The feeling of being almost intimidated disappeared. In its place was the realization that if he played this right, he could make them all so uncomfortable that none of them would ever repeat this forfeit. He picked up the stays and dangled the garment in front of Ned. "You chose this forfeit; *you* help me dress."

⌘

It took quite a while to dress, because Ned was the world's worst lady's maid. He wrestled with the stays for almost a quarter of an hour, then put the petticoat on back to front. The gown consisted of a long sarcenet slip with a shorter lace robe on top of that. Ned flatly refused to arrange the decorative ribbons at Octavius's bosom or to help him fasten the silk stockings above his knees. Octavius hid his amusement. Oh, yes, Ned was *never* going to repeat this forfeit.

Lydia had provided several pretty ribbons, but after Ned had failed three times to thread them through Octavius's ringlets, Dex stepped forward. His attempt at styling hair wasn't sophisticated, but it was passable.

Finally, Octavius was fully dressed—and the oddest thing was that he actually felt *un*dressed. His throat was bare. He had no high shirt-points, no snug, starched neckcloth. His upper chest was bare, too, as were his upper arms. But worst of all, he was wearing no drawers, and that made him feel uncomfortably naked. True, most women didn't wear drawers and he was a woman tonight, but if his own drawers had fitted him he would have insisted on wearing them.

Octavius smoothed the gloves over his wrists and stared at himself in the mirror. He didn't like what he saw. It didn't just feel a little bit wrong, it felt a *lot* wrong. He wasn't a woman. This wasn't him. He didn't have those soft, pouting lips or those rounded hips and that slender waist, and he most definitely did *not* have those full, ripe breasts.

Octavius smoothed the gloves again, trying not to let the others see how uncomfortable he was.

Ned nudged his older brother, Sextus. "He's even prettier than you, Narcissus."

Everybody laughed, and Sextus gave that reserved, coolly amused smile that he always gave when his brother called him Narcissus.

Octavius looked at them in the mirror, himself and Sextus, and it *was* true: he was prettier than Sextus.

Funny, Sextus's smile no longer looked coolly amused. In fact, his expression, seen in the mirror, was the exact opposite of amused.

"Here." Dex draped a silk shawl around Octavius's shoulders. "And a fan. Ready?"

Octavius looked at himself in the mirror and felt the wrongness of the shape he was inhabiting. He took a deep breath and said, "Yes."

They went to Vauxhall by carriage rather than crossing the Thames in a scull, to Octavius's relief. He wasn't sure he would have been able to get into and out of a boat wearing a gown. As it was, even climbing into the carriage was a challenge. He nearly tripped on his hem.

The drive across town, over Westminster Bridge and down Kennington Lane, gave him ample time to torment his brother and cousins. If there was one lesson he wanted them to learn tonight—even Quintus and Sextus, who rarely played the forfeit game—it was to never choose this forfeit for him again.

Although, to tell the truth, he was rather enjoying himself now. It was wonderful to watch Ned squirm whenever Octavius fluttered his eyelashes and flirted at him with the pretty brisé fan. Even more wonderful was that when he uttered a coquettish laugh and said, "Oh, Nonny, you are so *droll*," Ned didn't thump him, as he ordinarily would have done, but instead went red and glowered at him.

It had been years since Octavius had dared to call Nonus anything other than Ned, so he basked in the triumph of the moment and resolved to call his cousin "Nonny" as many times as he possibly could that evening.

Next, he turned his attention to his brother, simpering and saying, "Quinnie, darling, you look so *handsome* tonight."

It wasn't often one saw an earl cringe.

Dex, prick that he was, didn't squirm or cringe or go red when Octavius tried the same trick on him; he just cackled with laughter.

Octavius gave up on Dex for the time being and turned his attention to Sextus. He wasn't squirming or cringing, but neither was he cackling. He lounged in the far corner of the carriage, an expression of mild amusement on his face. When Octavius fluttered the fan at him and cooed, "You look so *delicious*, darling. I could swoon from just looking at you," Sextus merely raised his eyebrows fractionally and gave Octavius a look that told him he knew exactly what Octavius was trying to do.

But Sextus had always been the smartest of them all.

They reached Vauxhall, and Octavius managed to descend from the carriage without tripping over his dress. "Who's going to pay my three shillings and sixpence?" he asked, with a flutter of both the fan and his eyelashes. His heart was beating rather fast now that they'd arrived and his hands were sweating inside the evening gloves. It was one thing to play this game with his brother and cousins, another thing entirely to act the lady in public. Especially when he wasn't wearing drawers.

But he wouldn't let them see his nervousness. He turned to his brother and simpered up at him. "Quinnie, darling, you'll pay for li'l old me, won't you?"

Quintus cringed with his whole body again. "God damn it, Otto, *stop* that," he hissed under his breath.

"No?" Octavius pouted, and turned his gaze to Ned. "Say you'll be my beau tonight, Nonny."

Ned looked daggers at him for that "Nonny" so Octavius blew him a kiss—then nearly laughed aloud at Ned's expression of appalled revulsion.

Dex did laugh out loud. "Your idea, Ned; you pay," he said, grinning.

Ned paid for them all, and they entered the famous pleasure gardens. Octavius took Dex's arm once they were through the gate, because Dex was enjoying this far too much and if Octavius couldn't find a way to make his cousin squirm then he might find himself repeating this forfeit in the future—and heaven forbid that *that* should ever happen.

Octavius had been to Vauxhall Gardens more times than he could remember. Nothing had changed—the pavilion, the musicians, the supper boxes, the groves of trees and the walkways—and yet it *had* changed, because visiting Vauxhall Gardens as a woman was a vastly different experience from visiting Vauxhall Gardens as a man. The gown undoubtedly had something to do with it. It was no demure débutante's gown; Lydia was a courtesan—a very expensive courtesan—and the gown was cut to display her charms to best advantage. Octavius was uncomfortably aware of men ogling him—looking at his mouth, his breasts, his hips, and imagining him naked in their beds. That was bad enough, but what made it worse was that he knew some of those men. They were his friends—and now they were undressing him with their eyes.

Octavius simpered and fluttered his fan and tried to hide his discomfit, while Ned went to see about procuring a box and supper. Quintus paused to speak with a friend, and two minutes later so did Sextus. Dex and Octavius were alone—or rather, as alone as one could be in such a public setting as Vauxhall.

Octavius nudged Dex away from the busy walkway, towards a quieter path. Vauxhall Gardens sprawled over several acres, and for every wide and well-lit path there was a shadowy one with windings and turnings and secluded nooks.

A trio of drunken young bucks swaggered past, clearly on the prowl for amatory adventures. One of them gave a low whistle of appreciation and pinched Octavius on his derrière.

Octavius swiped at him with the fan.

The man laughed. So did his companions. So did Dex.

"He *pinched* me," Octavius said, indignantly.

Dex, son of a bitch that he was, laughed again and made no move to reprimand the buck; he merely kept strolling.

Octavius, perforce, kept strolling, too. Outrage seethed in his bosom. "You wouldn't laugh if someone pinched Phoebe," he said tartly. "You'd knock him down."

"You're not my sister," Dex said. "And besides, if you're going to wear a gown like that one, you should expect to be pinched."

Octavius almost hit Dex with the fan. He gritted his teeth and resolved to make his cousin *regret* making that comment before the night was over. He racked his brain as they turned down an even more shadowy path, the lamps casting golden pools of light in the gloom. When was the last time he'd seen Dex embarrassed? Not faintly embarrassed, but truly, deeply embarrassed.

A memory stirred in the recesses of his brain and he remembered, with a little jolt of recollection, that Dex had a middle name—Stallyon—and he also remembered what had happened when the other boys at school had found out.

Dex Stallyon had become . . . Sex Stallion.

It had taken Dex a week to shut that nickname down—Pryors were built large and they never lost a schoolyard battle—but what Octavius most remembered about that week wasn't the fighting, it was Dex's red-faced mortification and fuming rage.

Of course, Dex *was* a sex stallion now, so maybe the nickname wouldn't bother him?

They turned onto a slightly more populated path. Octavius waited for a suitable audience to approach, which it soon did: Misters Feltham and Wardell, both of whom had been to school with Dex.

"You're my favorite of all my beaus," Octavius confided loudly as they passed. "Dex Stallyon, my *sex stallion*. You let me ride you all night long." He uttered a beatific sigh, and watched with satisfaction as Dex flushed bright red.

Feltham and Wardell laughed. Dex laughed, too, uncomfortably, and hustled Octavius away, and then pinched him hard on his plump, dimpled arm.

"Ouch," Octavius said, rubbing his arm. "That hurt."

"Serves you bloody right," Dex hissed. "I can't believe you said I let you ride me!"

Now that was interesting: it was the reference to being ridden that Dex objected to, not the nickname.

Octavius resolved to make good use of that little fact.

He talked loudly about riding Dex when they passed Lord Belchamber and his cronies, and again when they encountered the Hogarth brothers.

Both times, Dex dished out more of those sharp, admonitory pinches, but Octavius was undeterred; he was enjoying himself again. It was fun ribbing Dex within earshot of men they both knew and watching his cousin go red at the gills.

He held his silence as two courting couples strolled past, and then swallowed a grin when he spied a trio of fellows sauntering towards them. All three of them were members of the same gentleman's club that Dex frequented.

Dex spied them, too, and changed direction abruptly, hauling Octavius into a dimly lit walkway to avoid them.

Octavius tried to turn his laugh into a cough, and failed.

"You're a damned swine," Dex said. It sounded as if he was gritting his teeth.

"I think you mean bitch," Octavius said.

Dex made a noise remarkably like a growl. He set off at a fast pace, his hand clamped around Octavius's wrist.

Ordinarily, Octavius would have had no difficulty keeping up with Dex—he *was* an inch taller than his cousin—but right now he was a whole foot shorter, plus he was hampered by his dress. He couldn't stride unless he hiked the wretched thing up to his knees, which he wasn't going to do; he was already showing far too much of his person. "Slow down," he said. "I've got short legs."

Dex made the growling sound again, but he did slow down and ease his grip on Octavius's wrist.

Along came a gentleman whom Octavius didn't recognize, one of the nouveau riche judging from his brashly expensive garb. The man ogled Octavius overtly and even went so far as to blow him a kiss. Instead of ignoring that overture, Octavius fluttered his eyelashes and gave a little giggle. "Another time, dear sir. I have my favorite beau with me tonight." He patted Dex's arm. "I call him my sex stallion because he lets me ride him all night long."

Dex pinched him again, hard, and dragged him away from the admiring gentleman so fast that Octavius almost tripped over his hem.

"*Stop* telling everyone that you ride me!" Dex said, once they were out of earshot.

"Don't you like it?" Octavius asked ingenuously. "Why not? Does it not sound virile enough?"

Dex ignored those questions. He made the growling sound again. "I swear to God, Otto, if you say that one more time, I'm abandoning you."

Which meant that Octavius had won. He opened the brisé fan and hid a triumphant smile behind it.

Dex released his wrist. Octavius refrained from rubbing it; he didn't want to give Dex the satisfaction of knowing that it hurt. Instead, he walked in demure silence alongside his cousin, savoring his victory . . . and then lo, who should he see coming towards them but that old lecher, Baron Rumpole.

"I warn you, Otto," Dex said, as Rumpole approached. "Don't you *dare*."

Rumpole all but stripped Octavius with his gaze, and then he had the vulgarity to say aloud to Dex, "I see someone's getting lucky tonight."

The opening was too perfect to resist. Warning or not, Octavius didn't hesitate. "That would be *me* getting lucky," he said, with a coy giggle. "He's my favorite beau because he lets me ride—"

"You want her? She's yours." Dex shoved Octavius at the baron and strode off.

Octavius almost laughed out loud—it wasn't often that he managed to get the better of Dex—but then Rumpole stepped towards him and the urge to laugh snuffed out.

He took a step back, away from the baron, but Rumpole crowded closer. He might be in his late fifties, but he was a bull-like man, thickset and bulky—and considerably larger and stronger than Octavius currently was.

Octavius tried to go around him to the left, but Rumpole blocked him.

He tried to go around him to the right. Rumpole blocked him again.

Dex was long gone, swallowed up by the shadows.

"Let me past," Octavius demanded.

"I will, for a kiss."

Octavius didn't deign to reply to this. He picked up his skirts and tried to push past Rumpole, but the man's hand shot out, catching his upper arm, and if he'd thought Dex's grip was punishingly tight, then the baron's was twice as bad. Octavius uttered a grunt of pain and tried to jerk free.

Rumpole's fingers dug in, almost to the bone. "No, you don't. I want my kiss first." He hauled Octavius towards him and bent his head.

Octavius punched him.

If he'd been in his own shape, the punch would have laid Rumpole out on the ground. As it was, the baron rocked slightly on his feet and released Octavius's arm.

Octavius shoved the man aside. He marched down the path, his steps fast and angry. How *dare* Rumpole try to force a kiss on him!

Behind him, Rumpole uttered an oath. Footsteps crunched in the gravel. The baron was giving chase.

Octavius was tempted to stand his ground and fight, but common sense asserted itself. If he were a man right now he'd *crush* Rumpole, but he wasn't a man and Rumpole outweighed him by at least a hundred pounds. Retreat was called for.

Octavius picked up his skirts and ran, even though what he really wanted to do was pummel the baron to the ground. Fury gave his feet wings. He rounded a bend in the path. The shadows drew back and he saw a glowing lamp and two people.

The baron stopped running. Octavius didn't, not until he reached the lamp casting its safe, golden luminescence.

He'd lost his fan somewhere. He was panting. And while rage was his predominant emotion, underneath the rage was a prickle of uneasiness—and that made him even angrier. Was he, Octavius Pryor, *afraid* of Baron Rumpole?

"The devil I am," he muttered under his breath.

He glanced over his shoulder. Rumpole had halted a dozen yards back, glowering. He looked even more bull-like, head lowered and nostrils flaring.

The prickle of unease became a little stronger. *Discretion is the better part of valor*, Octavius reminded himself. He picked up his skirts again and strode towards the people he'd spied, whose dark shapes resolved into two young sprigs with the nipped-in waists, padded shoulders, and high shirt-points of dandies. "Could you escort me to the pavilion, kind sirs? I'm afraid I've lost my way."

The sprigs looked him up and down, their gazes lingering on the lush expanse of his breasts.

Octavius gritted his teeth and smiled at them. "Please? I'm all alone and this darkness makes me a little nervous."

"Of course, darling," one of the sprigs said, and then he had the audacity to put his arm around Octavius's waist and give him a squeeze.

Octavius managed not to utter an indignant squawk. He ground his teeth together and submitted to that squeeze, because a squeeze from a sprig was a thousand times better than a kiss from Baron Rumpole. "The pavilion," he said again. "Please?"

The man released his waist. "Impatient little

thing, aren't you?" he said with a laugh. He offered Octavius his arm and began walking in the direction of the pavilion. The second sprig stepped close on Octavius's other side, too close, but Octavius set his jaw and endured it. The pavilion was only five minutes' walk. He could suffer these men for five minutes. They were, after all, rescuing him.

Except that the first sprig was now turning left, drawing Octavius down one of the darker paths . . .

Octavius balked, but the second sprig had an arm around his waist and was urging him along that shadowy path. "I don't like the dark," Octavius protested.

Both men laughed. "We'll be with you, my dear," one of them said, and now, in addition to an arm around Octavius's waist, there was a sly hand sidling towards his breasts.

Octavius wrenched himself free. Outrage heated his face. His hands were clenched into fists. He wanted nothing more than to mill both men down, but he was outweighed and outnumbered and the chances of him winning this fight were slim. "I shall walk by myself," he declared haughtily, turning his back on the sprigs and heading for the lamplight.

Behind him, he heard the sprigs laughing.

Octavius gritted his teeth. A plague on all men!

He reached the slightly wider walkway, with its

lamp, and glanced around. Fortunately, he didn't see Baron Rumpole. Unfortunately, he couldn't see *any*one. He wished he'd not steered Dex towards these out-of-the-way paths, wished they'd kept to the busier promenades, wished there were people around. He picked up his skirts and headed briskly for the pavilion, but the path didn't feel as safe as it once had. The lamplight didn't extend far and soon he was in shadows again. He heard the distant sound of music, and closer, the soft crunch of footsteps.

They weren't his footsteps.

He glanced around. Baron Rumpole was following him.

Octavius began to walk more rapidly.

The footsteps crunched faster behind him.

Octavius abandoned any pretense of walking and began to run, but his skirts restricted his strides and the baron caught him within half a dozen paces, grabbing his arm and hauling him into the dark mouth of yet another pathway.

"Let go of me!" Octavius punched and kicked, but he was only five foot two and the blows had little effect.

"Think too highly of yourself, don't you?" Rumpole said, dragging Octavius deeper into the dark shrubbery. Rough fingers groped his breasts. There was a ripping sound as his bodice gave way. Octavius opened his mouth to shout, but the baron clapped a hand over it.

Octavius bit that hand, punched Rumpole on the nose as hard as he could, and tried to knee the man in the groin. He was only partly successful, but Rumpole gave a grunt and released him.

Octavius ran back the way he'd come. There were wings on his feet again, but this time he wasn't fueled solely by rage, there was a sting of fear in the mix, and damn it, he *refused* to be afraid of Rumpole.

The path was still too dark—but it wasn't empty anymore. There, in the distance, was Sextus.

Sextus was frowning and looking about, as if searching for someone, then his head turned and he saw Octavius and came striding towards him.

Octavius headed for him, clutching the ripped bodice with one hand, holding up his skirts with the other. He heard fast, angry footsteps behind him and knew it was Rumpole.

The baron reached him first. He grabbed Octavius's arm and tried to pull him towards a dark and shadowy nook.

Octavius dug his heels in. "No."

"Stupid bitch," Rumpole snarled, but Octavius was no longer paying him any attention. He was watching Sextus approach.

His cousin's stride slowed to an arrogant,

aristocratic stroll. His expression, as he covered the last few yards, was one that Sextus had perfected years ago: haughty, aloof, looking down his nose at the world. "Rumpole," he drawled.

The baron swung to face him, his grip tight on Octavius's arm. "Pryor."

Sextus glanced at Octavius. He saw the torn bodice, but his expression didn't alter by so much as a flicker of a muscle. "I must ask you to unhand the lady."

Rumpole snorted. "She's no lady. She's a piece of mutton."

"Always so crass, Rumpole. You never disappoint." There was no heat in Sextus's voice, just boredom. His tone, his words, were so perfectly insulting that Octavius almost crowed with laughter.

Beneath that instinctive laughter was an equally instinctive sense of shock. Had Sextus actually said *that* to a baron?

Rumpole flushed brick red. "She's mine."

"No," Sextus corrected him coolly. "The lady is a guest of my brother tonight."

"Lady?" The baron gave an ugly laugh. "This thing? She has no breeding at all."

"Neither, it appears, do you." Again, Sextus's tone was perfect: the boredom, the hint of dismissive disdain.

Octavius's admiration for his cousin rose. Damn, but Sextus had balls.

Rumpole's flush deepened. He released Octavius. His hands clenched into fists.

"I believe that's Miss Smith's shawl you're holding," Sextus said, and indeed, Octavius's shawl was dangling from one meaty fist, trailing in the dirt.

Rumpole cast the shawl aside, a violent movement, and took a step towards Sextus.

Sextus was the shortest of the Pryors, but that didn't mean he was short. He stood six feet tall, eye to eye with Rumpole, but whereas the baron was beefy, Sextus was lean. He looked slender compared to Rumpole.

Octavius found himself holding his breath, but Sextus gave no hint of fear. He returned the baron's stare with all the slightly bored arrogance of a duke's grandson.

For a moment the threat of violence hung in the air, then the baron muttered something under his breath that sounded like "Fucking Pryor," turned on his heel, and stalked off.

Sextus picked up the shawl, shook it out, and put it around Octavius's shoulders. "You all right, Otto?"

Octavius wrapped the shawl more tightly around himself, hiding the ripped bodice. "You were just like grandfather, then. All you needed was a quizzing glass to wither him through."

Sextus ignored this comment. "Did he hurt you?"

Octavius shook his head, even though his arm ached as if a horse had kicked it. Damn Rumpole and his giant-like hands. "It's a shame you're not the heir. You'd make a damned good duke."

"Heaven forbid," Sextus said, which was exactly how Octavius felt about his own ducal prospects: heaven forbid that *he* should ever become a duke. It was little wonder Quintus was so stuffy, with that multitude of responsibilities hanging over him.

"Come on," Sextus said. "Let's get you home." He took Octavius by the elbow, matching his stride to Octavius's shorter legs.

They were almost at the Kennington gate when someone called out: "Sextus!" It was Dex. He reached them, out of breath. "You found him! He all right?"

"Rumpole practically ripped his dress off," Sextus told him. "What the devil were you doing, leaving him like that?"

Dex looked shamefaced. "Sorry, I didn't think."

"That is patently clear," Sextus said, a bite in his voice. "Tell the others I'm taking him home."

Dex obeyed without argument, heading back towards the pavilion.

"It was my fault," Octavius confessed, once they were through the gate and out in Kennington Lane. "I pushed Dex too far."

Sextus glanced at him, but said nothing. He still looked angry, or rather, as angry as Sextus ever looked. He was damned good at hiding his emotions.

Several hackneys waited in the lane. Sextus handed Octavius up into one and gave the jarvey instructions.

"It *was* my fault," Octavius said again, settling onto the squab seat.

"What? It's your fault that Rumpole almost raped you?" A shaft of lamplight entered the carriage, illuminating Sextus's face for an instant. Octavius was surprised by the anger he saw there.

"He didn't almost rape me," he said, as the carriage turned out of Kennington Lane and headed towards Westminster Bridge. "And honestly, it *was* as much my fault as Dex's. Neither of us thought Rumpole was dangerous. I didn't realize until too late just how puny I am." He remembered the baron forcing him into the dark shrubbery and gave an involuntary shiver. And then he remembered Sextus facing Rumpole down. "I can't believe you spoke to him like that. He'd have been within his rights to call you out."

Sextus just shrugged.

The carriage rattled over Westminster Bridge. When they reached the other side, Octavius said, "When I was fourteen, Father and Grandfather had a talk with me about sex. Did your father . . . ?"

"We all had that lecture," Sextus said.

Octavius was silent for several minutes, remembering that long-ago conversation. He'd given his word of honor to never force any woman into bestowing sexual favors, regardless of her station in life. "I'd wager Rumpole didn't have a talk like that with his father."

"No wager there," Sextus said dryly.

They sat in silence while the carriage trundled through the streets. Octavius had given his word all those years ago—and kept it. He'd never forced women into his bed, but he had ogled the ladybirds, snatched kisses, playfully pinched a time or two. It had seemed harmless, flirtatious fun.

Harmless to *him*. But perhaps those women had disliked it as much as he'd disliked it tonight?

Octavius chewed on that thought while the carriage rattled its way towards Mayfair.

Like to read the rest?
Octavius and the Perfect Governess is available now.

$\mathscr{A}$CKNOWLEDGMENTS

A number of people helped to make this book what it is. Foremost among them is my developmental editor, Laura Cifelli Stibich, but I also owe many thanks to my copyeditor, Maria Fairchild, and proofreader, Martin O'Hearn.

The series logo was designed by Kim Killion, of the Killion Group. The cover and the print formatting are the work of Jane D. Smith. Thank you, Jane!

And last—but definitely not least—my thanks go to my parents, without whose support this book would not have been published.

Emily Larkin grew up in a house full of books. Her mother was a librarian and her father a novelist, so perhaps it's not surprising that she became a writer.

Emily has studied a number of subjects, including geology and geophysics, canine behavior, and ancient Greek. Her varied career includes stints as a field assistant in Antarctica and a waitress on the Isle of Skye, as well as five vintages in New Zealand's wine industry.

She loves to travel and has lived in Sweden, backpacked in Europe and North America, and traveled overland in the Middle East, China, and North Africa.

She enjoys climbing hills, reading, and watching reruns of *Buffy the Vampire Slayer* and *Firefly*.

Emily writes historical romances as Emily Larkin and fantasy novels as Emily Gee. Her websites are www.emilylarkin.com and www.emilygee.com.

Never miss a new Emily Larkin book. Join her Readers' Group at www.emilylarkin.com/newsletter and receive free digital copies of *The Fey Quartet* and *Unmasking Miss Appleby*.

OTHER WORKS

THE BALEFUL GODMOTHER SERIES

Prequel
The Fey Quartet novella collection:
Maythorn's Wish
Hazel's Promise
Ivy's Choice
Larkspur's Quest

Original Series
Unmasking Miss Appleby
Resisting Miss Merryweather
Trusting Miss Trentham
Claiming Mister Kemp
Ruining Miss Wrotham
Discovering Miss Dalrymple

Garland Cousins
Primrose and the Dreadful Duke
Violet and the Bow Street Runner

Pryor Cousins
Octavius and the Perfect Governess

OTHER HISTORICAL ROMANCES

The Earl's Dilemma
My Lady Thief
Lady Isabella's Ogre
Lieutenant Mayhew's Catastrophes

The Midnight Quill Trio
The Countess's Groom
The Spinster's Secret
The Baronet's Bride

FANTASY NOVELS
(Written as Emily Gee)

Thief With No Shadow
The Laurentine Spy

The Cursed Kingdoms Trilogy
The Sentinel Mage
The Fire Prince
The Blood Curse